CERVANTES STREET

by Jaime Manrique

Published by Akashic Books
©2012 by Jaime Manrique

Hardcover ISBN-13: 978-1-61775-107-3
Paperback ISBN-13: 978-1-61775-126-4
Library of Congress Control Number: 2012939261

Akashic Books
PO Box 1456
New York, NY 10009
info@akashicbooks.com
www.akashicbooks.com

I do not want to be who I am. Petty luck
Has offered me the seventeenth century,
The dust and constitution of Castile,
The things that come and come again, the morning
That, promising today, gives us the evening . . .
—from "I Am Not Even Dust" by Jorge Luis Borges
(translated by Eric McHenry)

Glory is perhaps the worst incomprehension.
—from "Pierre Menard, Author of *Don Quixote*" by
Jorge Luis Borges

In memoriam

Bill Sullivan, painter,
partner of thirty-three years,
to whom this book owes so much,
with love forever.

Note to the Reader

What follows is a work of fiction about Alonso Fernández de Avellaneda's appropriation of Cervantes's *Don Quixote Part I*. In that spirit, my own novel appropriates four passages from *Don Quixote*, two scenes from the play *The Bagnios of Algiers* and one from the short play *The Judge of Divorces*, and paraphrases from the prologue of *The Exemplary Novels*. The readers of *Don Quixote de la Mancha* and the other works will be able to identify these passages without any difficulty; if I have succeeded in my attempt, the rest of the hypothetical readers of my novel will not be able to distinguish them from my own writing. My "borrowings" were chosen to emphasize different autobiographical aspects of Cervantes's *Don Quixote*. There are also nods to the great poets of Spain's Golden Age, and an homage to Shakespeare.

BOOK ONE

CHAPTER 1
THE FUGITIVE
1569

Sheltered by the moonless sky, I rode on a narrow little-trodden path of La Mancha with the stars as my only guide. As I galloped on the dark plain, anguish raged in my chest like a sail flapping in a storm. I clapped spurs to the horse and whipped its flanks. My mount snorted; the pounding of its hooves on the pebbly ground pierced the quiet of the Manchegan countryside and echoed with painful intensity in my head. Crying "*ale, ale,*" I incited my stallion to exert greater speed, hoping to outrun the bailiff and his men.

The night before, I had been playing a game of cards in the Andalusian's Tavern. Antonio de Sigura, an engineer who had arrived in Madrid to build roads for the court, lost a large sum of money quickly. I was feeling the effects of too much wine and not enough food in my stomach and decided to quit playing while I was still ahead. The engineer insisted that I keep playing. When I refused, he said, "Why is it I'm not surprised, Miguel Cervantes? I wouldn't expect honorable conduct from those who come from dishonorable stock."

The men nearby snickered. I got up from my chair, kicked one leg of the table, and demanded an explanation.

Antonio de Sigura shouted, "I mean that your father is a stinking Jew and an ex-convict and your sister a whore!"

I grabbed a carafe, smashed it on de Sigura's head, and overturned the table. When I saw the engineer's face awash in wine and blood I felt I was going to evacuate my bowels down the legs of my pants. I stood in front of him, shaking, waiting for de Sigura to make his next move. He wiped the liquid from his eyes with a handkerchief and then pulled out his pistol. Because I was a commoner, I was not allowed to carry a sword. My friend Luis Lara drew his sword in a flash and offered it to me. As de Sigura aimed at me, I jumped toward him and plunged the tip of Luis's sword into the engineer's right shoulder. He dropped to his knees, with the tip of the sword still jutting out from his back shoulder dripping scarlet. He opened his mouth in the shape of a huge O. As he pitched forward, I pulled out the sword and flung it on the floor. The swiftness of the violence left me stunned. Next, I heard commotion in the room as many customers scrambled out of the tavern yelling, "Run, run, before the bailiff arrives!"

In the confusion, the wine racing in my brain, I quit the tavern and bolted down Madrid's shadowy streets as if a pack of hungry hounds trailed after me. I realized that the rash act had irrevocably changed my life forever: my dream of becoming Court Poet had become a chimera.

The following morning, in the friend's house where I was hiding, the news reached me of the sentence meted out by the authorities: I would lose my right hand and be banished from the kingdom for ten years. Both forms of punishment were unacceptable to me. But if I stayed in Madrid, it was just a matter of time before I was denounced, arrested, and then crippled forever. I sent word to my best friend, Luis Lara, about my predicament and asked for a loan so I could escape from Spain. Later that afternoon, his personal servant delivered a hefty leather pouch. "My master says this is a gift, Don Miguel," the servant told me, as I counted sixty gold escudos. "He says you should leave Spain and not come back for a long time."

So later that night, I slipped out of Madrid by a back way. Fleeing in disgrace, the worst punishment of all was that I would not see my beloved Mercedes for a long time. It was unimaginable I would recover from this cruel parting with my first love. I was sure love would never again be as pure, as idealistic, and that I would mourn the loss of Mercedes for the rest of my life. I was certain that no matter how far from home I wandered, or how long I lived, I would not find another woman like Mercedes who united beauty, modesty, and intelligence in one body. The next time I saw her—if there were a next time—I was sure she would be a married woman.

My plan was to join Maese Pedro's troupe of actors and magicians in the outskirts of Tembleque, in La Mancha, and ride south with them to Sevilla, where I would hide until I could board a ship bound for foreign lands. From abroad, I would appeal the sentence and wait in safety until I was pardoned, or the incident forgotten. I had met Maese Pedro when I was seven and living in Córdoba. Every year in late spring, his troupe would arrive and set up camp outside the city walls.

From the time I was a boy I had longed to go abroad, but this precipitous flight was not the way I had envisioned the start of my travels. Yet the thought of losing my right hand to the sharp-edged blade of the law—the same hand that I used to write my verses, the hand with which I wielded a sword and caressed Mercedes's face—was insupportable. One-handed, forced to beg, I saw myself as an exile dying on foreign soil—like the old, skeletal slaves who roamed the roads of Spain, the ones who were granted their freedom when they could no longer do hard work. This thought made me desperate to quit Spanish soil. I'd *rather cut my throat than live as a useless man*, I said to myself as I fled Madrid.

I had been on the road practically all my life. My father's poor head for business had forced our family to forever be on the move, dragging our pathetic possessions, running from his creditors and the imminent threat of his incarceration. Early on, I had learned that it was only a matter of time before I had to say goodbye to my favorite teachers, my new friends, the streets and plazas I grew accustomed to, the houses I called home, all too briefly. The mule-drawn cart on which we Cervanteses traveled from splendid cities to dismal towns was my most permanent home. We had lived in so many places I could barely remember their names: Alcalá de Henares, my birthplace; Valladolid, which we left when I was six; the next ten years in Córdoba; then a few glorious years in Sevilla, which my family left in disgrace to return to Castile, to Madrid.

That first night as a fugitive, I remembered my mother grumbling, in those moments when she could no longer contain her frustration at father's peripatetic ways, "We are no better than those bands of Gypsies traveling the roads of Spain. My children are being educated like thieves and loose women. Your father will only stop chasing rainbows when his bones are dust in the ground."

I consoled myself by thinking that to be a poet in Spain often meant to be an outlaw. I had turned out similar to so many Spanish poets: an exile, like my beloved Garcilaso de la Vega. Looking back, I wonder if my fate would have resembled that of Gutiérre de Cetina—who had died violently in Mexico; or maybe I would be like Fray Luis de León, who languished in jail for many years in Valladolid. Or would I follow in the footsteps of Francisco de Aldana, who died in Africa fighting for the Portuguese king Don Sebastian? Perhaps in another, less unjust country, in a place where a poor but talented young man had real chances of advancing himself, things might be different for me. Away from Spain's rigid society, and hollow, pompous, and hypocritical conventions, I might amount to something. I believed there was greatness in me. And this belief was something that nobody—not even Spain's almighty king— could kill.

If I wanted to be master of my own destiny, and choose my path to manhood, my only two options were fame as a poet or glory as a soldier. To become the most famous poet and warrior of my time—now that was a worthy goal. Another cherished dream was to become a celebrated playwright like Lope de Rueda. First, though, I had to make sure I left Spain with my right hand still attached to my arm, so that I could return covered in riches and honor— because a glorious destiny awaited me, I was sure.

I rode into Tembleque at dawn where Maese Pedro's troupe, gathered in the town's main square, was getting ready to start their journey south.

"I throw myself at your mercy, Maese Pedro," I said, when I was taken to him. Then I explained to my old friend why I was in danger of losing my right hand unless I fled Castile.

"Say no more, Miguel," he responded. "You're almost a member of our family." He paused, looked me up and down, and added, "But you cannot travel with us like this. We must find a disguise for you."

So it was that dressed in women's clothes and wearing a wig, I rode in the same wagon with my thespian friend and his wife, Doña Matilde, pretending to be their daughter Nicolasa.

That first day on the road, I kept looking over my shoulder to make sure the bailiff and his men were not running after my scared behind. But as the hours passed, and I began to think that I might be able to evade the law, I fell into reminiscing about the first time I saw Maese Pedro's troupe in the Plaza del Potro. I was on my way home from the Colegio de Córdoba, the Jesuit school where I learned the little Latin I know. The actors were performing a show about doomed lovers who died dancing and singing and looking beautiful. After the show was over, the colorfully dressed thespians, pretending to be great and low personages of the world (the men dressed as women), came from behind the makeshift stage and mingled with the audience to announce the theatrical production of the night. I became mesmerized. Who were these people? How did they achieve this kind of magical metamorphosis?

I ran all the way home and entered the kitchen where my mother and sister Andreita were making a cocido, and screamed, "Mamá, mamá, can I go see the play the actors are putting on tonight?"

My mother gave me a scolding look. "So that's where you've been, instead of coming home after school to do your homework?"

"Oh Mother," I continued, still breathless. "It's a play about a Moorish princess who converts and elopes with her Christian lover. I have to see it."

"Enough of that, Miguel. Where would I find a maravedí to send you to see actors? Go and do your homework." She went back to chopping vegetables.

"Mother," I pleaded.

"Basta, Miguel." She stabbed the green head of cabbage destined for the soup. "Go study your lessons."

In the windowless cubicle in which I slept with Rodrigo, I crouched in the darkest corner against the damp walls. Andrea found me there, biting my fingernails, shaking with anger. She sat next to me, roped an arm around my shoulders, and said, "I've saved a few reales"—she earned them knitting and embroidering—"and I, too, would love to see this play. We'll go together tonight. Now, Miguelucho, make Mother happy and study your lessons."

My despondent mood changed to happiness. I kissed her face and hands. "Thank you, Andreita. Thank you, sister."

That night, when I saw the actors on the stage in their outlandish costumes, their faces painted with loud colors, speaking in a Spanish more eloquent and persuasive and loaded with more double meanings than I'd ever heard before, and becoming people other than themselves, I felt as if, for the first time, I could breathe freely. I wanted to be around these characters constantly. Perhaps if I spent time with them, I told myself, I would learn their art and someday I, too, could act in plays and say those beautiful speeches, and play princes and princesses, kings and queens, Christians and Moors, scholars and fools, thieves and knights.

The next morning back in school, my teacher and classmates seemed dull, colorless, and made of coarse materials. That spring, every day after school, I went to visit the actors. In exchange for helping to clean the horses' dung and feeding them, and fetching water from the fountain inside the city walls, I was tolerated with good humor and allowed to see the performances for free.

I made friends with Candela, who was twice my age. She helped in the kitchen and took care of her small siblings. Candela's eyes were as green as the new leaves in the orange trees in early spring; her hair was as black as the blackest piece of coal; and she was not bashful like all the other girls I knew. As she did her chores, she sang romances and danced barefoot. The men could have eaten her with their eyes. Candela had never set foot in a school, and her clothes were ragged and dirty. When I mentioned this to Andreita, she sent with me a package of clothes that my sisters had outgrown. I was happiest when I was around Candela, who treated me with the tenderness older sisters reserve for their little brothers.

"Look at the lovebirds," the actors would tease us, making me blush. "But she could be his mother." Or, "Candela, you've bewitched this boy. Why don't you make love instead to a real man?" And, "Look at the smoke coming out of Miguelín's ears. You'd better drag him to the river, Candela, and douse his head in the water before his brains stew."

Candela laughed and kissed me on the cheek. To the men she yelled, "Go pick the fleas that breed in your posteriors!" She was the first girl I kissed, not counting my sisters.

My mother was so taxed making sure that we had enough to eat, and clean garments to wear, that she did not notice I had fallen under the magical spell of the world of the theater until one day when a neighbor asked her at the market if I was training to become an actor, since I was always visiting Maese Pedro's troupe. That night, before I went to bed, Mother took me to the kitchen to be alone and sat me on her knees. "Please, Miguel," she entreated me, her voice and her eyes filled with disappointment, "stay away from those disreputable actors who live such miserable lives. Please don't become a useless dreamer, like your father. One in the family is enough. God gave you a good brain, so use it to learn a profitable trade."

I put my arms around my mother's waist and promised, "I will study hard, Mamacita, and enter an honorable profession. Don't worry anymore." I refrained from promising I would stop visiting my friends.

When the troupe got ready to leave Córdoba in early June, I considered running away with them. I mentioned what I was thinking to Candela.

"My father won't allow it," she said. "Already the authorities suspect us of stealing children. Our lives are hard, Miguelín. People come to see our plays, and love to be entertained, but to them we are all dishonest pagans, and as bad as the Gypsies." She took my face in her hands. The tips of our noses almost touched; I could breathe in her lemony breath. My eyes reflected in the liquid green mirrors of hers. "Just wait a few years. When you grow up, then you can join us, if you like."

I shook my face free. "It'll be years before I grow up."

"Go, go, feed the horses," she ordered me and walked away, calling her siblings, "Martita, Julio. Come here this instant."

The rest of that year, and for a few years afterward, from June to April, I dreamed about the return of the actors. Each June, as the troupe began to pack, Maese Pedro would say to me, "Next year, Miguel, if your parents give you permission, you can come with us."

By the time I turned twelve, Candela had married an actor in the troupe, she had her own children, and, though friendly, she treated me as if our old intimacy had never been.

Later that day, when our caravan had left La Mancha behind us, what I had been dreading happened: the bailiff and his men caught up with us and stopped us for a search. As the troopers approached the wagon in which I was riding, I started to tremble. I began to choke with fear, as if I had swallowed a pork bone. We were commanded to come down off our wagon. *It might be better if I take off my wig and give myself up to the authorities before they discover my deception,*

I told myself. Just as I was about to turn myself in, and ask for their clemency, Maese Pedro pulled me by the elbow, slapped me so hard I tasted blood, and shouted, "Where are you going, you shameless wench? Stop making eyes at the troopers! Why did God curse me with a whore for a daughter?"

The troopers laughed, and ogled me. A dribble of urine snaked down my legs.

Doña Matilde started yelling, "Pedro, may God forgive you! You're much too cruel to the poor girl. If she's bad, it's because you're bad. Come here, hija mia." She enveloped me in her arms and shoved my nose between her gelatinous and sweaty breasts. "With a father so cruel it's a wonder she hasn't run away from us," she said to the troopers. Doña Matilde patted my wig. "There, there, Nicolasita."

The snickering troopers moved on to search the wagon behind ours. It wasn't until we were given the sign to continue on our way that I dared hope I might reach Sevilla undetected after all.

The following day, and the next day after that one, my spirits sank and soared, plunged to Hades and spiraled to the heavens. But as we traveled away from autumn, as we entered the lush and dense gardens and forests of Andalusia, so bursting with green that I imagined the jungles of the New World must be like this, I felt hopeful and revived.

My heart beat faster the more ground our caravan covered on that verdant world, that land of towns and cities planted with palm trees and flaming pomegranate bushes and orange trees, always in fruit; that land whose forests and meadows were filled with the music made by the endless variety of songbirds of that region of mirth and sunlight. As a boy, I had loved the first days of March on Andalusian soil when the hot breezes gusting from the Sahara, cooling as they sweep the surface of the Mediterranean, arrive on Spanish soil, breathing life into dormant trees and brown grasses, awakening the seeds and bulbs in the ground, spurring the growth of buds in the fruit orchards, painting the hills and hillocks a light olive with the first leafing of the trees. By early April, the song of the returning nightingales, serenading the oncoming evening, promised a trove of sensual pleasures that the hours of darkness would uncover. As the sun set, its silken light draped first the tops of the mountains, then the valleys, and released, as it fell, the scent of honeysuckle, intoxicating you by the luxurious promises hidden in the approaching darkness. The whole of Andalusia was a beckoning land that mesmerized you, like the seductive thrusts of the hips, the eyes, hands, and feet of the dancers in the teahouses of Córdoba, with bells rasping around their ankles and wrists as they shed veil after veil and wrapped the heads of gawking men with supple, translucent fabrics.

My heart filled with delight when, in the distance, I spotted the vast wheat fields to the east of Córdoba. If the wheat was in full ripeness, one could believe they were fields of gold. Delight turned to pure happiness when the hills of the Sierra Morena to the west of the city spread before my eyes with the soft shapes of a curvaceous odalisque lying naked on a carpet in a seraglio.

But my heart grew sad when I remembered the year before Andalusia's Moorish people had started the rebellion of the Alpujarras to protest the treatment they received in Spain. Now they were fighting ferociously in the mountains near Cádiz and Málaga. If my childhood friend Abu were still alive, surely he would be fighting with the rebels. And his sister Leyla, on whom I had a boyhood crush, must be a married woman and a mother.

This time, however, Maese Pedro's troupe was bypassing Córdoba as my best chance to escape the law was to get to Sevilla as soon as possible and hide myself among the throngs of the city. So it was with a heavy heart that I left behind the city of ancient palaces and great mosques, the court of the Umayyads; the city where I saw large numbers of Moors for the first time.

Two days later, we camped on the outskirts of Sevilla. Four years had passed since my family and I had left the city in disgrace. Now I was returning to Sevilla as a fugitive.

Sadness and joy, dread and hope, all commingled in my chest as we set up our camp that first night. Could the bailiff have gotten to Sevilla ahead of me? I wallowed in despair contemplating the wreckage of my future. Without my right hand, there was no point in going to the Indies; without my right hand, I had no chance of climbing the highest mountains of the Andes to find the treasure of El Dorado that would make me the richest man in Christendom. Without my right hand, I might as well be flogged to death or burned at the stake. How I wished there was some kind of magic that could transform me into a new person, the way actors metamorphosed themselves into characters. Then I would have chosen to become, once again, a young man with an unblemished past, and I would have stayed in Sevilla.

My turbulent state of mind was relieved somewhat when I reminded myself that this was no dream, that I was once more in Sevilla, city of wonders. While I felt in danger of being discovered, I was happy to have returned to the city where my literary vocation was born. Although I had seen Maese Pedro's troupe perform in Córdoba, the actors on the stage in Sevilla were marvelous, and the pasos and plays they produced were things of beauty, written by our great writers. I fell under the spell of the artistry of these fabulous performers—I did not care that actors were held as low in esteem as the Gypsies, that to most people the theater was to be enjoyed but also to be mistrusted, because it was believed to incite depraved behavior. My favorite playwright was Lope de Rueda, whose fictional creations—gossipy barbers, wanton priests, miserly hidalgos, dissolute students, rogues, lewd whores—were more vivid and interesting than their counterparts in real life. There was nothing higher to aspire to, I told myself, than to create people like these. I could only imagine how powerful Lope de Rueda must have felt creating characters out of his observations of humanity. I wanted the fame and financial rewards of the successful writers of comedies, who were greeted at street corners by Sevillanos with cries of "Victor! Victor!"

Years later, I poked fun at Sevilla and its citizens through the snouts of two talking canines, Cipión and Berganza, in my *Exemplary Novel, The Colloquium of the Dogs*. "Sevilla," says Berganza, "shelters the destitute and gives refuge to the worthless. In its magnificence, it has ample room for all sorts of scoundrels, but no use for virtuous men."

That first night camping outside the city gates, the uncertainty of my situation kept me awake, staring at the starry sky and remembering how when I was young in Sevilla, the scent of orange trees in permanent bloom attenuated the sweet reek of bodies buried under rose beds, or at the foot of trees. Sevillanos believed that the loveliest and most fragrant roses and sweetest oranges were those fertilized by the flesh of Nubian slaves. This tang of human decay and fruit trees in bloom was the first thing a visitor noticed upon nearing the city.

The Guadalquivir was barely more than a sandy stream as it ran past Córdoba; but as it got close to Sevilla, it swelled into a wide olive-colored river. At dawn, the river bustled with barges, swift sloops, feluccas, shallops, tartans, and piraguas. The smaller vessels carried merchandise destined for the bellies of big ships that sailed to the West Indies and beyond.

The river fed my wanderlust, making me hunger for the world beyond the confines of the Iberian Peninsula. The river was the road that led to the Mediterranean and the West, to the Atlantic Ocean and the Canary Islands, halfway to the wondrous New World. Young Sevillanos who became sailors—often for the rest of their lives—were referred to as those who had been "swallowed by the sea."

There was no more thrilling sight than the fleets of cargo ships, accompanied by powerful galleons to protect them from English corsairs and privateers, sailing off twice a year for the world Columbus had discovered. The ships sailed away with the hopes of the Sevillanos, who would send off their men with festive songs of farewell. When fortune smiled on these adventurers, they returned from the Indies laden with gold and glory.

As a boy, my imagination was set afire, my eyes bulged, as I watched the ox-drawn carts on their way to the royal chambers, carrying open trunks that brimmed with glowing emeralds, shining pearls, and stacks of blinding bars of silver and gold. Other carts transported bales of tobacco, furs of animals unknown in Europe, spices, coconuts, cocoa, sugar, indigo, and cochineal. For weeks after the arrival of the ships, I remained intoxicated by these sights. A great desire awakened in me to visit New Spain and Peru.

In the heart of the city, buildings faced each other so closely that I could run down the cobblestone passageways with arms outspread to touch the walls on either side. These were the streets that schooled me in the customs and costumes, religions and superstitions, foods, smells, and sounds of other nations. Merchants arrived in Sevilla with white, black, and brown slaves from Africa. The names of the countries they came from—Mozambique, Dominica, Niger—were as exotic as their looks. I would get dizzy from hearing so many languages that I didn't understand, whose origins I couldn't pinpoint. What stories did they tell? What was I missing? Would I ever get the chance to learn a few of them and visit the places where they were spoken?

During those years, I felt as though I were living in the future, in a city that had nothing to do with the rest of Spain. Pícaros from every corner of the world—false clerics, false scholars, impostors of every imaginable and unimaginable kind, pickpockets, swindlers, counterfeiters, sword swallowers, gamblers, assassins for hire, soldiers of fortune, murderers of every sort, whores, Don Juans (whose profession was to ruin the most beautiful and chaste maidens), Gypsies, fortune-tellers, fire-eaters, forgers, puppeteers, ruffians, bon vivants, and snake charmers—came to Sevilla and made the city their stage. Life there was dangerous and thrilling, as festive and bloody as a bullfight. Successful gamblers were as admired as the bullfighters or famous military heroes. It was common to hear a child say that when he grew up he wanted to be a gambler like Manolo Amor, who on one occasion had gambled away an entire fleet of galleons that was not his.

Sevilla was the place where I belonged. It was created for me and I wanted to be its historian. Sevilla was mine and it owned me.

Most Sevillanos stayed inside during the hottest hours, and went out only at night, when the evening breezes, sweeping up the Guadalquivir from the Mediterranean, cooled the city by a few degrees. Then it was as if a curtain rose, and the proscenium that was Sevilla became a magical stage for the theater of life. Lying there on my blanket in the outskirts of the city, I imagined I heard in the recesses of my brain the clacking sounds of castanets, coming from every street and plaza. The clacking was a reminder to strut with the arrogant elegance of a peacock displaying all its colors. People rushed out of their homes to sing on the plazas and dance the salacious zarabandas, which were forbidden by the church. In the plazas, illuminated by torches, beautiful and lascivious women dancers (young and old alike) wiggled their behinds with impudence and rapped their castanets with fury, turning the instruments into weapons that could seduce and then snuff the life out of you.

The dancers' looks were an invitation to dream about the countless pleasures of the body; and the movements of their hands spoke intricate languages and summoned the spectators with seductive signs to caress the dancers' amber-flushed cheeks. It was thrilling to see the male dancers leap high in the air, spinning in circles, as though to exorcize demons that were eating them from the inside out. Midair, these men seemed half-human, half-bird. From midnight until dawn, the loveliest señoritas were serenaded by their inflamed wooers. Brawls often broke out during these serenatas, and the corpses of unfortunate lovers were found in the mornings, beneath the balconies of their inamoratas, glued to puddles of coagulated blood.

Sevilla was a city of witches and enchanters. You had to be careful not to cross a woman, because any female, aristocratic or peasant, married or unmarried, old or young, beautiful or ugly, Christian or Moor, slave or free, could have satanic powers. Witches made red roses bloom in their homes in December. They could make or break marriages, could make grooms hang themselves or evaporate on the eve of the wedding, could make pregnant women give birth to litters of puppies.

Unlucky men who crossed the enchantresses were turned into donkeys. As husbands and lovers disappeared, new donkeys materialized and the women who owned these donkeys took delight in making them carry heavy loads. It was common to see a woman whose husband had vanished go around the city addressing every donkey she saw by her husband's name. When an ass brayed in response, the woman would drop on her knees, cross herself, and give thanks to God that she had found her husband. If she wanted her man back, she had to buy the donkey from its owner. Then she would go back home, happy to have found her spouse, and spend the rest of her life trying to undo the enchantment. Or she might be just as happy to keep her husband in donkey form. It was said that some of the happiest marriages in Sevilla were between a woman and her ass.

The Holy Office whipped many women in public plazas for the extraordinary pleasures they boasted of receiving from their equine lovers. Debauched cries and crescendos of lust traveled to remote villages in the mountains where herds of wild asses brayed with envy. Gypsies took to bringing donkeys that brayed anytime a desperate woman addressed them. If a donkey became erect and tried to mount a young wife who called him by her husband's name, or a donkey tried to kick an old, withered harpy who claimed him as her husband, or scurried away when an ugly one threw her arms around his neck, that, too, was considered proof of having found her husband. When a Sevillano allowed inflated notions to swell his head, he was told, "Remember, today you are a man, but tomorrow you may well be a donkey."

During Holy Week people did penance for all the sins they indulged the rest of the year. Then alone would Sevillanos fast and drag themselves on their knees to the cathedral. But Sevilla's cathedral was not oppressive. Instead, it was filled with light, color, ostentatious displays of gold and jewels, illuminated as much by its oil lamps and its candles as by the iridescent light that poured in through stained-glass windows. It was a place where we went to experience the splendors of the world, not a glum building where we expiated our sins. It seemed to me, as a young man, that God had to be more receptive to our prayers in a place like this, where everybody knew that hope, joy, and beauty were part of His covenant with us. I used to walk out of Sevilla's cathedral content, as if I had just eaten a mariscada and washed it down with wine.

Often, in those days, I escorted my mother on her visits to the cathedral. Our enjoyment of the place was a secret between the two of us that excluded the rest of the family and gave us respite from our dingy house, with its worn-out, secondhand furnishings and leaks in the ceiling of every room. The cathedral's sumptuous altars seemed to relieve Mother, momentarily, of the pain caused by Father's impecuniousness. She loved music above all things. It's true Father played the vihuela at home, but nothing he did gratified her. Only in the cathedral could she listen to music. Her face glowed, her eyes gleamed as the sounds of the clavichord or spinet swelled. Singing made Mother happy. Her untrained voice was clear, and it could hit many of the high notes. I'd only heard it when she sang romances in the kitchen, as she went about her chores, on those occasions when my father left to visit relatives in Córdoba. In the cathedral she would let her voice spill out and rise, with the same abandon and ecstasy I heard in the lament of the singers in Andalusia.

After church, she would hook my arm in hers, and we would stroll along the banks of the Guadalquivir and stop to gaze at the foreign ships and glorious armada galleons.

One evening, grabbing my hand by the wrist, she implored me, "Don't stay in Spain, Miguel. Go far away from here to someplace where you can a make a fortune for yourself. In the Indies you will have a brilliant future awaiting you, my son."

She did not mention my father's name, yet I sensed she was pushing me to look for a life completely different from his. Because I was a dreamer, like my father, she feared that, like him, I would become a ne'er-do-well. She had begun to see me as another unrealistic Cervantes male: I would live surrounded by criminals, constantly borrowing reales from my friends and relatives, incapable of understanding how to put food on the table. But if I let my imagination flow, the wide waters of the Guadalquivir would eventually lead me to the Indies in the West, or to Italy in the East, or to burning Africa in the South, or to the Orient, beyond Constantinople, to the splendors and mysteries of Arabia, and perhaps even to the fabled court of the emperor of China.

Those dreams of my youth had been pulverized by my immediate reality. The next day, Maese Pedro returned from Sevilla with the news that the bailiff was looking for me and there was a reward for my capture. I said goodbye to my dream of going to the New World. "Miguel," he said, "I think your best chance of escaping lies with asking the help of my friend Ricardo, El Cuchillo. He is the chief of a caravan of Gypsies leaving for the Carpathians tomorrow; every year they pass through Italy on their way home. Get ready and I'll take you to him as soon as it gets dark. And remember, don't haggle over the price he charges you and you'll get to Italy safely."

The Gypsies had set up an encampment in the woods west of Sevilla, on the bank of a stream. Maese Pedro pointed at a man sitting by a bonfire who wore a hat that resembled a crow spreading huge wings over his head. Children surrounded him, listening raptly to what he was saying. We dismounted and walked toward him.

When he recognized his visitor, El Cuchillo clapped loudly, and the children scampered squealing into the darkness. The men embraced with the affection of old friends. Maese Pedro spoke first: "Ricardo, I've never asked a favor from you before today. I've known Miguel," he said, throwing an arm around my shoulders, "since he was a boy." He proceeded to explain the gravity of my circumstances.

El Cuchillo listened, pulling gently at his pointy beard with bony, weathered fingers. His fingernails bulged with dirt. The wrinkles on his face were pronounced, as if his face had been sliced horizontally with a blade, leaving it runneled and channeled—hence his nickname. The Gypsy removed his hat, shook his head to let down a thicket of silvery hair, and replied, "I want to be paid the full amount in advance. But I warn you, Don Miguel, if you do anything foolish, I'm not risking my balls for your culo. Is that understood?"

So in Gypsy rags, with a black kerchief tied around my forehead, and golden hoops dangling from my ears, I left Spain. The City of the Caesars was my final destination. Relieved as I was to leave *la madre patria* before my right hand was lopped off, I was anxious about traveling with people who dwelled in caves and wild forests and who most Christians regarded as sorcerers and cannibals. When Gypsies camped near a town, parents would keep their children indoors and sleep in the same bed with them at night. Gypsies were infamous for kidnapping children and selling them in Berber lands to the Moors. It was also said that they fattened stolen infants, roasted them during their festivities, cut them up, and tossed the tender pieces of flesh into their pucheros, a soup made with dry horse-meat, chickpeas, mushrooms, and purslane.

The Gypsy women who practiced palmistry were feared and despised even more than the men. Their powers were said to be as formidable as the devil's. If a Gypsy palm reader approached you, her eyes shining with seduction, and you refused to hear your fortune told, she would—without forewarning—turn into a frightful Fury, spitting out bone-chilling curses.

As a boy in Sevilla, I saw a man refuse to have his palm read. The tumorous-faced harpy started screaming: "You son of a whoring bitch! May the devil's curse fall on you for turning a deaf ear on an old woman in need!" When the man walked away, a big, smoking black rock plunged from the sky and thumped his head with such force that it was severed and rolled—wailing—down the street, as the body stumbled around looking for it. From that moment on, I made a point of never crossing a Gypsy woman. It was because of their devilish powers that even the forces of the king left them alone as much as possible.

From the moment we were on the road, I kept hearing the words Maese Pedro had whispered to me as we said our goodbyes: "Miguel, always keep an eye on your purse. Make sure the Gypsies don't leave you the way you came into the world. After you shake hands with a Gypsy, re-member to count your fingers. Roma people, as you know, are the biggest thieves and rascals in the world. Other than that, they are no worse than the rest of humanity."

CHAPTER 2
THE STAIN

⁓LUIS⁓

Knowing it would be hard for Miguel's parents to obtain funds overnight, I decided to help my friend finance his flight. I lived on the generous allowance my father gave me to attend the university in Alcalá de Henares, so I could not go to him to ask for a large sum of money. Like any good Castilian, he was thrifty. My grandfather, Carlos Lara, was my only hope; Papá Carlos always indulged me. Appreciative of his generosity, I never imposed on him.

He was not in his bedroom. I looked for him in the library, and he wasn't there either. Next I looked for him in the family chapel, where he went twice a day for his devotions. Through the keyhole, I saw him on his knees, hands clasped, head bowed, lost in prayer. While I waited outside the door, I feared that one of my parents would find me standing by the chapel's entrance and I would have to explain the situation. I shifted from one foot to the other to make time fly faster. As Papá Carlos exited the chapel, serene after the absorption of his morning prayers, I accosted him without any preamble. "Papá Carlos, I need money to help a friend in grave danger."

"Is it for Miguel Cervantes?" he asked, without the slightest surprise.

I nodded. From the start, Papá Carlos had frowned upon my growing intimacy with Miguel.

"I knew the boy's grandfather well when our monarchs held court in Valladolid," Papá Carlos said. "Mark my words: like grandfather, like grandson. Juan Cervantes was a spendthrift—slaves, horses, and clothes fit for a nobleman. He was a clothmaker, a commoner with pretensions, who looked down on his Jewish brethren and sought to befriend the rich, the powerful, the Christian nobility." He shook his head and narrowed his eyes. "It's true he ended his life respected and prosperous. One hates to think how he achieved a high station in life." My grandfather emphasized every word, the way he did when he wanted to teach me a lesson. "He was a true member of his nationless, Semitic race. Luis, it behooves us Christians not to get too close to people with the stain." He rested a hand on my shoulder, and looked me directly in the eye. "Never forget this: even when a Jew swears to be a devout Christian—centuries after their so-called conversion—at heart he always remains a Jew."

I had nothing against the Jews who had converted. What's more, the conversos' secretive life held a fascination for me. Besides, from the very beginning, Miguel and I had shared so many joyous moments that I would have disobeyed my parents—whom I otherwise respected and heeded, as was my duty—if they had forbidden our friendship.

Yet, in spite of his disapproval, there was not even a look of reproach from my grandfather. "Come with me," he said.

I followed Papá Carlos into his sleeping chamber, where he opened a wooden box inlaid with Moorish designs carved in ivory, the kind made by the artisans of Toledo. He removed a handful of coins, and counted out sixty gold escudos which he placed in a leather pouch. Not another word was said, then or later. I understood his extraordinary generosity was due to his unspoken wish that Miguel would use the money to travel far, far away from me and from Spain, so that I could escape his influence. It was certainly enough money to pay for Miguel's passage to the New World, a place he dreamed of reaching one day.

I had met Miguel at the Estudio de la Villa, the municipal school in Madrid where students prepared for entrance to the university. For two years Miguel had been the brother I didn't have. For two years, during that period of youth when we dream our purest dreams, and no dream seems too improbable to attain, we had shared the hope of becoming poets and soldiers, like many of the great warrior poets of Spain, like our beloved Garcilaso de la Vega. Those two years before I turned twenty, Miguel and I had enjoyed the communion of twin souls. Everyone referred to us as "the two friends." Our friendship seemed to me the perfect embodiment of the ethical union of souls that Aristotle describes in his *Nicomachean Ethics*. That ancient ideal of friendship was one of the goals I pursued in life.

Madrid was a small village during the reign of Philip II. Soon after Miguel's family arrived from Sevilla, rumors spread that his father, Don Rodrigo Cervantes, had been jailed many times for his inability to honor his debts. Another rumor, even more shameful, preceded the family.

At Estudio de la Villa, my teachers and classmates held me in the highest esteem. Studying came easily to me. Knowledge was prized in my family; it was expected that after I left la Villa I would attend the Universidad Cisneriana in Alcalá, where many of the sons of the best families in Castile studied theology, medicine, literature, and other appropriate professions for an hidalgo, before taking their place in the world.

Miguel enrolled at la Villa during my last year there.

His father must have used an important connection to get him accepted. Miguel hadn't been brought up to be a caballero like the rest of my classmates. Among the finest youth of Castile, of the world, he stood out like a wild colt in a stable of thoroughbreds. I hadn't met anyone like him before. His boisterousness, unrefined charm, and extroverted nature earned him the nickname of El Andaluz.

Like an Andalusian, Miguel spoke Castilian as if he could not quite grasp the language: he chopped off the last syllable of every word, and his enunciation was harsh—the way Arabic sounded to my ears. Miguel had that swagger, brio, and spontaneity of the people from the south, who cannot be called true Iberians since they have a mixture of Spanish and Moorish blood. He behaved as if he didn't know whether to act like a Gypsy or a nobleman. In both roles, he was an impersonator. He would exhibit the confidence of a noble; while at the same time displaying the wild spirit and manner of the Gypsies, who would arrive in Madrid each spring along hosts of chirruping swallows, then flee to the warmer climates of Andalusia and the Mediterranean as soon as the first dusting of gold painted the leaves of the madroños.

Miguel made a memorable impression on me when I heard him declaim in class Garcilaso's "Sonnet V." It was a poem I recited to myself as I ambled along the streets of Madrid, or wandered by myself in the woods, or lay in my bed at night, after I said my prayers but before I went to sleep. I recited those verses thinking of my cousin Mercedes, the woman I had been in love with since childhood. Until I heard Miguel reciting the sonnet in class, I thought I was the only person alive who understood the full import of Garcilaso's words.

The instant he began, "*Your face is engraved on my soul,*" I was rapt. He wasn't merely saying the words, the way my other classmates did when we were asked to recite poems we had to memorize. With Miguel, it was as if he had experienced the feelings Garcilaso described. He felt each word deeply, the way only a true poet could. With mounting passion he recited the next thirteen lines:

when my verses invoke you
you alone deserve credit for them: they are
inspired by your perfection.

This is how it is now and shall be forever.
I am unworthy of your grace,
and of comprehending your splendors—
a divine gift to a mere mortal like me.

I was born only to love you;
your face is the object of my adoration;
the sole purpose of my soul is to mirror yours.

Everything I am belongs to you.
I was born in you, you gave me life,
I shall die for you—for you, I'm dying.

When Miguel finished his recitation, his pupils shining as if he were consumed by fever, his lips quivering, his hands trembling as if they had a life apart from him, his forehead dewed with perspiration, his shoulders curving inward to nestle all the words and sounds of the poem in his chest, retaining the emotion they awakened in him, it was as if a sword had pierced his heart and he were dying of unrequited love. I knew right away that, even though we came from different worlds, worlds that in the Spain of our youth were nearly irreconcilable, I had to become Miguel's friend. The way he made Garcilaso's verses pulsate with fervor told me that here was someone who loved poetry, and Garcilaso, as much as I did.

This recitation surprised all of us who, until that point, had seen him as just another rustic Andalusian. A few of my classmates whooped and applauded his heartfelt display. I saw Miguel rise instantly in the esteem of Professor López de Hoyos, famed for his knowledge of the classics. Overnight, he became the professor's protégé—even though Miguel was an indifferent student in all other subjects. He seemed to live for poetry, which I found to be an admirable trait—since poetry was for me the highest of all the arts.

Not long afterward, I overheard Professor López de Hoyos talking to another of our instructors and referring to Miguel as "my treasured and beloved disciple." A twinge of jealousy gripped me, as I realized that from this moment on I would take second place in the professor's affections. *I will be a true caballero*, I said to myself, *and rise above petty jealousies*. I offered my friendship to Miguel with an open heart.

That day, we left school together and went for a walk. As soon as we were far enough from school, Miguel put a pipe between his lips, with no tobacco in it. (When I knew him better, I came to see how important it always was for him to create an affect.) He insisted we go to a tavern to talk about poetry over a mug of wine. I resisted the invitation because my parents expected me at home every day at the same hour, and I couldn't come back smelling of alcohol and tobacco. Instead, quoting Garcilaso's verses, we walked the streets and plazas of Madrid until nightfall. That night my friendship with Miguel was founded on our love of Garcilaso de la Vega—the great bard of Toledo, the prince of Spanish poetry. Not one of my other classmates shared with me this passion. Garcilaso's freshness of language, sincerity of sentiment, and stylistic innovations—incorporating Italian lyricism into Spain's stagnant poetic tradition—plus the fact that he had been a soldier, contributed to making him our hero. That night, as we rhapsodized about the noble Toledano, Miguel remarked, "He died still young, before he was corrupted by the world." I wondered then whether that, too, was Miguel's ambition.

At that time, only young bards and poetry lovers knew Garcilaso's work. On that first walk, we pledged we would be like Garcilaso and Boscán (Garcilaso's best friend, a great translator and poet). We were both sick of the sentimental poetry filled with stilted conventions that was then in vogue, and swore—with vehemence—to dethrone the official poets, whose surnames were so detested we would not soil our lips by mentioning them. We shared the same aspiration: to write only about love that arose from a living, breathing woman, a tangible reality—not the vaporous, affected love of the poets that preceded Garcilaso.

"We will cultivate the lyric," I said. "Our poems will be a questioning of our minds and hearts. Not the tearful rubbish that's so popular today."

"Yes, yes," Miguel concurred. "We are manly poets. Poet warriors like Garcilaso, like Jorge Manrique. Not like the weeping poetasters of today."

The torches were beginning to be lit on street corners. I started heading for my house, but Miguel continued to walk alongside me. When we reached the front door of my home in the neighborhood of the Royal Alcázar, he made no comment, yet I could see he was in awe of the imposing front door, and the antiquity of the bronze family shield emblazoned on it. I invited him to come in.

"I appreciate your kind invitation," he said, "but I should be heading back home. Next time."

* * *

We became inseparable, to the exclusion of all the other students. Almost every day, we took long walks in El Prado Park. Miguel kept an eye on the ground for chestnuts, which he picked up and put in his school satchel. To me, they were merely food to fatten pigs. To Miguel, they were a delicacy. I soon discovered that despite his sensitive soul, and his complete devotion to poetry, there were vast gaps in his literary education. He knew Garcilaso's poetry, and very little else. His ignorance of the classics, of Virgil and Horace, for example, was inconceivable in someone with ambitions of becoming not just a poet, but Court Poet. Garcilaso had held this post in the court of Carlos V and I knew how hard it would be for Miguel to achieve this, if his family, as was rumored, as my grandfather had confirmed, were converted Jews. The nobility in the court of Philip II would not have accepted this. Long gone were the days of the Catholic kings, when Isabella's court had been a haven for Jewish scientists, doctors, and scholars—before she expelled all Jews from Spain, pressured by the Vatican. We lived closer to the days when Jews were routinely burned at the stake in Madrid and all over Spain.

My Lara ancestors hailed from Toledo. As far back as the times of the Holy Roman Empire, my relatives had lived in houses and castles with library shelves containing, in Castilian, Greek, Latin, Italian, and Arabic, all the books considered essential for a gentleman's education.

Among my ancestors I count warriors, illustrious writers, and noble adventurers who gave their lives defending our faith on the battlefields of Europe and in the conquest of Mexico. My father was twice a marquis. My grandfather made his name in the Battle of Pavia in which our Emperor Charles V defeated François I of France. In 1522, my grandfather also participated in an expedition against the Turks on the island of Malta. It was there he had gained the friendship of Juan Boscán and Garcilaso, soldiers in that campaign. So I grew up hearing about these great poets not as distant figures, but as men of flesh and bone, people that I myself might have known.

My mother was a countess; her family, the Mendinuetas, was every bit as ancient and noble as Father's. Mother liked to remind me, "For generations, both sides of our families have ridden in carriages pulled by two mules. That's the kind of people we come from."

Notwithstanding Miguel's gregarious nature, he was reticent when it came to talking about his family, pecheros with meager financial resources. Even having ink, paper, and quills to do his homework was a luxury for Miguel. I invited him to visit our library to read. It became his second home. When he entered our house for the first time, it was obvious to me that he felt he didn't belong there. Around the members of my family he became tongue-tied.

Books were like a treasure to Miguel. To be sure, he had read Jorge de Montemayor's pastoral romance *La Diana*, and was acquainted with a few of the Spanish classics, but in our library he held for the first time an edition of Petrarch's sonnets, Erasmus's *Colloquia* and *Copia*, and Boscán's translation of Castiglione's *The Book of the Courtier*. We spent hours reading aloud Ariosto's *Orlando Furioso*. When I showed Miguel the first edition of Garcilaso's poetry, which had been published in the same volume with Boscán's poems in 1543, Miguel could not control his tears as he caressed the cover. Then he fell silent for the rest of the evening.

Miguel stroked the old editions of the classics as if they were not just precious objects, but frail living forms. His index finger would trace the lines on the pages, grazing over them the way one does the skin of one's beloved for the first time. His appetite for literature was voracious. He could read a book in a matter of hours, as if that were the last time he would ever have access to it. He had the thirst for knowledge that a camel has for water after completing a long trek in the desert. He would read by the light of the candelabrum, until the wicks burned out.

Although my mother extended Miguel invitations to stay for supper, he always claimed his parents were expecting him. At first, it was unclear to me where he lived. When I showed interest in his domicile, he waved in the direction of the center of town, away from the towers of the Alcázar—our lofty neighbors. Going in and out of our house, it was an everyday occurrence to see carriages accompanied by corteges, transporting the royal family and other important personages as they made their way to and from the Alcázar. Notable Madrileños, carried by their slaves on the finest palanquins, went by our door as frequently as peddlers hawking their wares in the poorer neighborhoods.

Months after we had become close, Miguel finally invited me to visit his home. His family lived in a crumbling two-story house near the Puerta del Sol, on a gloomy street reeking of cabbage soup, urine, and excrement. These were dwellings without cisterns, whose inhabitants collected their water from the public fountains. The shuttered windows kept a wood strip open to peek out on the street life. This was a part of Madrid hardly frequented by hidalgos and duennas; instead, it was home to beggars, to mutilated, suppurating, shoeless people, and grown men and children who walked about practically naked, fighting with the street dogs and rats for a bone without flesh.

Miguel had mentioned that his father was a surgeon. But on my first visit to the Cervantes home, I discovered Don Rodrigo Cervantes was not a university-educated doctor, but one of those barber/doctors who bled penniless ill people. Don Rodrigo's barbershop and clinic were housed in one large, dark, pestilent room on the first floor of their home. When we came in, Don Rodrigo was busy with a patient. Miguel said, "Good afternoon, Papá," and his father nodded in our direction without acknowledging me, as if he were so distracted he hadn't seen me.

We walked across the airless room—where you could practically breathe in sickness—housing people asleep or moaning in makeshift beds that were no more than wooden planks covered with dirty straw. Then we ascended the broken wooden steps that led to the family's living quarters on the second floor. One smoky oil lamp burned in the parlor, shedding its weak light on a threadbare carpet with a few worn-out cushions on it, a table made of crude wood, and a wooden crucifix hanging above the entrance. Everything in the room was impregnated with the acrid smell of the cabbage used as the main ingredient in poor man's soup.

Miguel led me to his bedroom, a windowless area off the main chamber, with a curtain of rough cloth full of holes in place of a proper door. I had to bend my knees and lower my head to enter it. Miguel shared the one cot with his brother Rodrigo, the youngest of the family.

When we returned to the parlor, we found seated on a cushion, with a crying baby in her arms, a young woman who Miguel introduced as Andrea, his older sister. He mentioned that Magdalena, the other sister, was in Córdoba visiting relatives. Miguel was finishing the introductions when his mother, Doña Leonor, came out of the kitchen. My presence took her by surprise, I could tell, from which I deduced that the family was not used to visitors coming upstairs. Miguel's mother was tall and thin, with the haggard look of an ascetic. In her youth, she must have been good-looking, but now her face resembled a frieze of tiny mosaics broken and reassembled, to expose a landscape of crushed hopes.

When Miguel mentioned my full name, she became slightly awkward. "Don Luis Lara," she said, pronouncing each syllable slowly as if to make sure she had heard right. "Welcome to our humble home. Your visit honors us." Despite her disheveled state and modest garments, Doña Leonor had the good manners of a woman of some education and refinement. I learned later, she came from landed gentry of old stock. She turned to Miguel, "You could have mentioned you were bringing Don Luis to visit. I would have at least prepared a refreshment for him."

"It's my fault, Doña Leonor," I interjected. "Miguel didn't know I was coming. I insisted on stopping by to pick up a schoolbook. Forgive me for my rudeness."

At that moment a boy came running up the stairs yelling, "Miguel, Miguel, Father needs you downstairs!"

"Rodrigo, what happened to your manners?" Doña Leonor reprimanded him. "Don't you see we have a visitor? Don Luis must think we scream in this house all the time."

"This is my little brother. I'll be back soon," Miguel said to me as he left with his brother.

Doña Leonor insisted that I stay for a refreshment. Before returning to the kitchen, she addressed Andrea: "Let me take the young one to her crib. Keep Don Luis company while I prepare him a cup of chocolate."

Andrea handed the now quiet baby to her mother. We were left alone in the parlor, sitting on cushions across from each other. She was the first one to break the silence. "Don Luis should know that the baby girl my mother took to her crib is Constanza, my own daughter, though my parents tell everyone that the baby is theirs." Her astonishing revelation came out of her lips with a bluntness that was almost savage.

Andrea's hair hung down to her waist like a black silk mantilla. She was dressed plainly in a gray dress, and wore no adornments. Her features were classically perfect and the skin of her face unblemished. Her eyes shot the same steely shafts of defiance that the women who prowled the seamy alleys of Madrid hurled at men, demanding that you engage their services. Andrea had a dimple on her chin that was like a well where men's desires went in and didn't come out again.

"It's not my fault, Don Luis, that God, if I am to believe what people say of me, made me beautiful. For a girl of humble parentage, beauty is her only dowry." She paused and grimaced. Because she whispered her words, I had to lean in her direction until I was so close I could feel her breath brushing back my eyelashes. Her proximity was perturbing. She was indeed exceptionally beautiful. But hers was a beauty etched in acid. Smoothing the hair around her face with both hands, she took a deep, sorrowful breath. With an exaggerated lisp, penciling the air with the pink tip of her tongue, she went on: "I met a lad in Sevilla who delighted my eye and whom my heart chose as the object of its adoration. Yessid was his name. His intentions toward me were honorable. My love for him was as true love is: undivided and unconstrained. He was a carpenter, but what made him unacceptable as my husband in my father's eyes was that he was of Moorish descent. This, despite the fact that Yessid's family had converted to our religion, and he was a true Christian. Nonetheless, my family forbade me to see him. *That's all we need*, my father said to me when I informed him that Yessid wished to ask for my hand in marriage. *After many generations, we still haven't been able to establish our own purity of blood. If you marry a Moor, our family will never be free of the stain. I'd rather see you dead. I forbid you to see Yessid alone again. And that young man had bet-*

ter not show his face around here anymore." She paused, pained
by her confession. Then Andrea took another drawn-out
breath before she continued, "Don Luis is young, but I'm
sure you're already acquainted with the enslaving tyranny
of love. Yessid was broken-hearted, and he returned to the
mountains near Granada to live with his parents. Later, I
heard the news that he had taken his own life by hanging."

"I'm sorry," I whispered.

Andrea didn't seem to have heard me. She studied her
hands, caressing her shapely fingers for a moment. She had
more to say. "From the time I was old enough to help my
father with his patients," she went on, raising her face and
holding my gaze, "I've worked with him taking care of ill
people. If I had had a dowry, I would have joined a religious order and gone to the Indies to succor the ill and to
spread our faith among the natives. In his infinite wisdom,
God had something else in store for me. That's how I met
my evil seducer, a rich Florentine merchant by the name of
Giovanni Francesco Locadelo, the father of my daughter.
He had been wounded at sea near our coast by Turkish corsairs, and was taken to Sevilla where he required a nurse
by his side all the time. I took the work, happy to have
an opportunity to help my parents, and to distract myself
from my loss.

"I nursed the Florentine through his long convalescence, staying up many nights cooling his forehead with
wet rags to bring down his fever. When his health improved, he was grateful to me. At first, he said that I was
like a daughter to him. I didn't know this was his first step
in his malevolent plan to seduce me and rob me of my virginity, the only prize I owned."

I wanted to look away, to stare at the smoky ceiling,
but Andrea's eyes were glued to mine.

"One day he told me he had grown to love me and

asked me if I would consent to marry him. I said no without giving him explanations. I had vowed secretly to remain Yessid's widow for the rest of my life.

"However, as the Italian's entreaties continued over a period of months, to punish my father, I let him seduce me. Weeks later, when I told Don Giovanni I was gravid with his child, he announced he was well enough to return to Florence where he had been recalled on urgent business."

I began to perspire, and she noticed.

"Forgive me, Don Luis, for making you uncomfortable with my woeful tale. But I've never told this story to anyone, and I feel I cannot go on another day without unburdening myself." She looked in the direction of the kitchen to make sure her mother was not in the room. Then she continued with urgency, "So, before he left Sevilla, to assuage his conscience—though to everyone else he explained he was doing it out of gratitude and because I helped him to regain his health—he presented me with a jacket made of silver cloth, and one of crimson gold; a Flemish desk; a table made of walnut wood; sets of the finest bed linen; silk sheets; pillows made in Holland; embroidered tablecloths; silver fountains; gold candelabra; Turkish carpets; braziers; one convex mirror, framed in gold leaf; paintings by Flemish masters; a harp; two thousand gold escudos; and many, many other gifts. In other words, he gave me a rich woman's dowry to attract unscrupulous men who would not mind that I was not virginal anymore. This was enough to appease my father. He was more content to see me a dishonored wealthy woman than a happy one married to an honest lad of Moorish ancestry.

"*Where are all these riches?* you are probably asking yourself," she said, with a sweep of her hand, to call my attention to the pitiful furnishings of the room. "Not for the first time, Don Luis, my father accrued major debts from gambling, and was in danger of being sent to jail until he was an old man. He sold with what he could of the spoils of my disgrace, and pawned the rest. That's how he was able to pay his creditors and still have enough money leftover to move the family to Madrid.

"As you know, Don Luis, honor and virtue are the only true ornaments a woman has. Without them, a beautiful woman becomes hideous. To save my honor—by which they meant to save the honor of the family—before we left Sevilla my parents tried to convince me to give away my daughter as a foundling. I swore I'd kill her, and then kill myself, if they did that. Everyone in Sevilla knows what happens to those pitiful babies left at the door of a convent in the cover of night: the wild pigs and dogs that roam the streets before dawn are likely to eat the infants before the nuns find them in the morning. Usually, all that's left of those unfortunate angels are the dark bloodstains on the ground, and sometimes little chips of bone and tiny pink pieces of flesh."

I felt faint. I wanted to run away from that room and her awful confession. But Andrea would not stop. "You know how it is, if a girl loses her virginity outside of marriage: she's labeled a hideous fiend, a basilisk. I offered to take my daughter with me and go to the mountains near Granada and become a shepherdess. That way, my parents would not have to be shamed by my disgrace. Thank God and His Holy Mother, my parents relented in their plan to give away my daughter, and so we left Sevilla together. In Madrid, no one knows us. My parents invented the absurd story that I am the widow of a man named Nicolás de Ovando who died in Sevilla of a violent fever. That's why you find me here, Don Luis, buried alive, my heart turned to wood. I tell you, if I didn't have my daughter, I would have—God forgive me!—killed myself long ago."

When she had finished her dreadful tale, Andrea rose from her cushion. Her beautiful face was as livid as the head on a marble statue—perfect, but lifeless. Without saying another word, she vanished down the dark corridor that led to the back of the living quarters, where her child was crying once again. Sitting there alone by the lamp's weak light, I felt that in that room I had been introduced to some unspeakable darkness of the world. I shook my head, trying to expel the evils to which I had been exposed. Why had Andrea confided her awful secret? How did she know I would not use this shameful story to ruin her family's honor? All that occurred to me was that she seemed to blame her father for her tragedy.

I decided not to mention what had transpired to Miguel, or to anyone else. By confiding in me, my friend's sister had entrusted me with an unwanted burden; worse yet, her monstrous secret had made me her prisoner.

Almost thirty years later, reading Miguel's *Don Quixote Part I*, I recognized Andrea as the original of Marcella, the beautiful shepherdess who is blamed for the death of a man madly in love with her. I wondered whether Andrea ever read her brother's novel, and how much it must have stung to have her sibling reveal to the world her disgraceful past. There you have the main difference between Miguel and me as writers. Miguel de Cervantes (he had added the *de* by then) lacked imagination; he was just a borrower from life, whereas I came to develop the conviction that true literature is not an excuse for poorly disguised autobiography. In the degenerate times in which I had been condemned to live, that was not apparent to anyone. But in the future, I was convinced, the truly great writers would be those who wrote anew—and not just rewrote—stories that needed to be perfected. In the future, all long, tedious novels—including Miguel's *Don Quixote*—would be whittled down to their essence, so that the whole story could be told in a handful of pages.

The next time I visited Miguel's home, many of the objects Andrea had mentioned as part of her "dowry" were on display. The shabby main room had been transformed into an elegant, colorful chamber. Miguel's father must have had a windfall at the gambling tables, for he had reclaimed the articles he had pawned.

I learned what true domestic unhappiness was after I set foot in Miguel's home. Doña Leonor constantly displayed her contempt toward her impractical, spendthrift husband. He was an avid reader, and prided himself on his knowledge of Latin. Don Rodrigo (as people called him, though he had no right to that honorific title) made more money writing sonnets commissioned by young men to woo their ladies than as a doctor. He entertained the young lovers who engaged his services, as well as his neighbors, by reciting poetry and playing the vihuela. His consulting room and barbershop, he reminded everyone, served as a cultural gathering place for superior minds. It was something to hear him sing the couplets he composed, which he would do without much prodding, to the friends and customers who dropped by to drink and talk.

"Don Luis, people heal quicker when there's music and poetry around," he explained to me. "Gaiety is the best cure for all illnesses." To put his philosophy in practice, while he bled his patients, he would sing romances to them, accompanied by the vihuela. No wonder more people trusted him with their beards than with their health. The wounded men who came to have their gashes sewn up looked like dangerous criminals who could not go to a hospital. The fascination Miguel had all his life with low-life characters began with the people who patronized Don Rodrigo's barbershop. I was repelled and yet also attracted by this rabble, whom I had always seen from afar, and whom, without knowing Miguel, I would never have come in contact.

"Don Luis," Don Rodrigo said to me once, after he had gotten to know me better, "this is what I have to do to keep body and soul together. But I'm really a poet at heart. I know you can see that."

During holidays, and after school every day, Miguel was supposed to help his father bleed patients, kill flies, and wash the chamber pots and blood-splattered floor. He was deeply ashamed of these tasks and had no interest in learning his father's skills. "Why should I learn about leeches and hair?" he confided in me once, bitterly. "When I am Court Poet, I will not have to bleed people to relieve them of their bad humors. The beauty of my verses will cure them of all their illnesses."

Miguel inherited his love of poetry from his father. But he was determined to make something of himself, not to be a failure like his progenitor. "You don't know how many times I've had to take soup to my father in jail," Miguel told me one night in a tavern after he had had too much wine. "Sometimes my mother and my little brothers and sisters went hungry so he could keep his big belly full." I felt sorry for my friend that his life had been so harsh.

Though Doña Leonor prized an education, and was proud that nuns had taught her to read and write, she begrudged Miguel the cost of the paper to write his compositions. Buying paper for his classes meant there were other things the household would have to do without. Doña Leonor lost no chance to remind everyone within earshot that it was her dwindling inheritance that supported the family. She had inherited a vineyard in Arganda, which provided a small income to feed and clothe the Cervantes children.

Years later, when I was ready to begin my *Don Quixote*, I modeled some of its most important characters after Miguel's parents. Here I would like to stress the difference between autobiography (cannibalizing one's own life) and biography (which relies on the writer's powers of observation). It was from the figure of the father that I began to hatch the idea of a dreamer who ruined his family. Don Rodrigo was the model for the mad Don Quixote, and Miguel's mother would be transformed into the realistic housekeeper and the practical niece. I repeat, it was I who conceived of turning these people into fictional characters. The grave mistake I made was that one night when we were out drinking, and I had imbibed a little too much wine, I mentioned my brainchild to Miguel (keeping to myself that my characters were based on his parents). He then went ahead and stole the idea from me, publishing the rambling and inartistic first part of his *Don Quixote* before I had a chance to complete mine.

Yet despite all our differences, the fire of poetry strengthened my friendship with Miguel. Two friends united forever in literary history, that's how I saw us. Whenever we pondered what the future might bring us, we recited the opening verses of one of Garcilaso's most famous sonnets, which expressed to perfection the uncertainty of our young lives:

When I pause to contemplate my life
and study the steps that have led me to this place . . .

In October 1568, the third wife of King Philip II, the French princess Isabel de Valois, died after miscarrying a five-month-old fetus. Not yet twenty-three years old, Isabel had been known as the "Princess of Peace" because her betrothal to our king sealed the peace between France and

Spain in 1559, and gave our kingdom domination over Italy. Like all Spaniards, I adored her.

Isabel was still playing with dolls when she arrived in Spain. The king had to wait two years, until Isabel menstruated for the first time, to consummate their marriage. The newlywed couple did not speak a language in common (our king did not speak Latin). He was twice her age, and was having an affair with a lady-in-waiting for his sister Princess Joan. Isabel was heartbroken because her own father had had a mistress, Diane de Poitiers, who had made Isabel's mother miserable. Isabel pretended to be ignorant of the king's infidelity. But the queen endeared herself to the Spanish people by learning Castilian to perfection. She became a patroness of the arts—especially of painters— and wrote musical compositions. During her all too brief reign, Isabel turned Philip's court into one of the most refined in Europe.

Isabel's subjects prayed for the birth of an infante. Her first attempt at childbirth resulted in miscarrying twins. She fell gravely ill, and all of Spain feared for her life. During those agonizing weeks, Spaniards of all social classes crowded cathedrals and churches to light candles and pray for their queen. Prayer meetings attended by large crowds were held in Madrid's plazas and squares. Thousands of candles were lit near the gates of the Royal Alcázar where the young queen's life was an extinguishing flame. In our chapel, we said Masses twice a day, praying to the Almighty to save her. The prayers of the people in the plazas and churches were so fervent that they rose toward heaven in a sonorous cloud and echoed throughout the city all night long. The devotion that humble Madrileños felt for Isabel moved me deeply.

An Italian surgeon visiting the court saved her life. After she recuperated from her near-death experience, the king, the court, and all Spaniards lived for the day she would become gravid again. When she remained infertile, the archbishop of Toledo recommended that the uncorrupted remains of Saint Eugene be brought from France to Madrid, so that Isabel could pray to him in person to cure her infertility. Such was her desire to give an heir to the Spanish throne, and such was her pure devotion to God's saint, that Isabel slept naked in bed with the corpse of Saint Eugene until she became pregnant again. The Spanish people rejoiced in the birth of two princesses. It was a matter of time, everyone believed, before she gave birth to a male heir.

Instead, Isabel suffered a disfiguring illness. A rumor spread that she had contracted syphilis from the licentious king. Her doctors diagnosed chicken pox and, to prevent her disfiguration, they recommended she be kept in a tub filled with she-donkey's milk, her face covered with a paste made of pigeon stool and butter. When Isabel recovered, and her skin was unblemished, the people believed that, because of her suffering and her miraculous recoveries, the spiritual queen might be one of God's saints on earth. After a long convalescence, Isabel became pregnant again, and it was the miscarriage resulting from this pregnancy that killed her. The grief we all felt was worse than if we had been reconquered by the Moors or had lost our armada. The entire nation went into mourning. No music was heard in Madrid for thirty days; the theaters were closed, bullfights forbidden, birthday celebrations canceled, and marriages postponed for six months. The women in my family wore black, and covered their faces with veils of gold cloth for three months. I wrapped a mourning band around my right arm. My grief was more personal than most: I had met the princess at a court function. My aunt, the countess of La Laguna, had introduced me to her saying I was one of the future glories of Spanish poetry. Her Royal Highness invited me to send her, via my aunt, some of my poems. The princess sealed her invitation with a smile. I never found out what she thought of my verses; but it made me happy just to know that she might have read my words.

King Philip announced a literary competition to reward the best sonnet written to commemorate the beloved late queen. Winning a literary tourney was one of the few ways open to an ambitious young man to gain fame and prestige; and it could lead to the patronage of a vain and wealthy nobleman, or, in some cases, to an appointment as Court Poet.

I wrote a sonnet about Isabel, but did not submit it to the competition. Like Horace, I believed a poem should be nurtured and burnished for nine years before being sent out into the world for publication. Besides, I was not hungry for fame, nor did I need the monetary reward.

I hope I don't sound arrogant when I state that my elegy for the queen was crafted with more rigor, rhymed with more delicacy and refinement, and infused with loftier sentiments than Miguel's crude versifying in the sonnet he wrote for the occasion. I knew how important it was for my friend to win this competition. His future might depend on it. The least I could do for him was not to become an obstacle in his hunt to achieve a piece of literary glory.

We were in the habit of showing our poems to each other. I read Miguel's middling sonnet to Isabel. When he asked for my opinion, I said, "I think you will win the competition." That made him happy. He was too self-assured to ask for any suggestions; still, I tried to improve his lusterless choice of words and to furnish his lines with a mellifluous and classic rhyme scheme. Next, Miguel sought the help of Professor López de Hoyos, whose devotion he had secured with unceasing flattery.

Then the sole judge of the literary tourney, in a drunken state, fell from his horse and cracked his skull on the cobblestone street where he lived. Professor López de Hoyos was appointed as his replacement. It did not surprise me that he awarded Miguel first prize, as all literary competitions, to begin with, are held: 1) to reward the friends of the judges; and 2) to punish their enemies. I will quote the first quatrain, just to give you an idea of the quality of Miguel's winning sonnet:

When our Motherland had finally
bid adieu to war, in a chariot
of fire headed for the sky, earth's
loveliest flower departed from us.

The sonnet was nothing but a feeble imitation of Garcilaso, the laughable effluvium of an ambitious young poet desperate for recognition.

Miguel's little literary success brought out his true personality: he acted as if he believed he was the brightest bard in the kingdom, and he boasted to everyone who would listen: "I am the true successor of Garcilaso de la Vega." The day after the winner was announced, many of Miguel's remarks were prefaced with, "When I become Court Poet . . ." This kind of bragging was ridiculous, but since I am not a cruel person, I did not point out that Jews were, de facto, excluded from such a post. In those days, blinded by Miguel's charm, I forgave him everything; the things that united us were stronger than those that eventually opened a chasm between us.

After I concluded my preparatory studies at the Estudio de la Villa, I had no desire to linger in Madrid, fighting for crumbs of literary glory. I was ready to commence my studies in classic literature at the Universidad Cisneriana in Alcalá de Henares. I chose it over the more famous university in Salamanca because it was the most select of our institutions of higher learning, and I wanted to remain close to Toledo and Madrid. In spite of my growing misgivings about Miguel's lack of modesty, I was sorry to see him remain behind in Madrid. Poor families could, at great sacrifice, send their sons to study at a university. The parents of the wealthy students, on the other hand, rented them houses, furnished with servants and horses, while they completed their studies. The less-privileged students paid for their education by working for the scions of Castile. When I hinted to Miguel that this was a possibility, he snapped, "I'd rather remain an ignoramus than be one of those starving students begging for a hunk of bread; or one who has to depend on cast-off clothing to be warm in winter."

"May I remind you that you'll be living in my house, Miguel, where you'll be treated as a brother, not as a servant."

"I know that. And I'm not ungrateful to you for your generous offer. But the other students would know about the situation and treat me as an inferior."

I did not press the issue, hoping that in time he would see the advantages of my proposition. Without an education, Miguel's prospects—despite the ephemeral fame that had befallen him as a poet—would be few. I suspected that he did not accept my offer because there was pressure from his parents to start earning money and contribute to the expenses of the Cervantes household. I did cajole Miguel into accompanying me to visit the grounds of the university and to help me search for a suitable house. "Wouldn't you like to see the town where you were born?" Miguel had left Alcalá de Henares when he was a boy, but he often spoke of it with fondness and nostalgia. "On the way back," I added, "we can stop in Toledo to visit Garcilaso's tomb." I knew Miguel was eager to see the city where Garcilaso de la Vega was born, and to visit his tomb at the cathedral. "We'll stay at my grandparents' home and you'll meet my cousin Mercedes, who lives with them. I am eager for Mercedes and you to meet." I wanted to bring together the woman I adored and the best friend I had ever had. Such was my innocence of heart, and my·affection for Miguel, that I added, "I mentioned our friendship to Mercedes, and she wrote back saying she looks forward to meeting you. I want the two of you to be as close as brother and sister."

When Miguel and I stood in front of the white marble façade of the Universidad Cisneriana, I hoped he would change his mind and accept my invitation to live together during my university years. But when the offspring of the great families arrived to attend the day's lectures wearing dark velvet cloaks and hats adorned with fancy feathers, armed with daggers and swords, mounted on fine horses, and accompanied by their pages, valets, and footmen, who set up camp in the plaza to wait while their masters attended classes, I knew that Miguel must have compared himself to them and felt inferior, knowing he could not aspire to such displays of wealth.

The scions of Spain's nobility stood in marked contrast to the other students milling about, the ones known as the *capigorristas*, who wore capes made of humble material and cloth caps that could barely protect their heads in the cold weather.

We spent a few pleasant hours visiting the august buildings. Miguel admired in particular the Great Hall's golden wooden ceilings carved with Moorish motifs; its stained-glass Gothic windows; the imposing chapel; the patios with Romanesque arches and columns flanked by tall cypresses; and the various flower gardens among the buildings. Birds stopped to drink, splash, and sing in their marble fountains.

Later that day, I inspected a few houses that were available as residences. Afterward, I insisted we go visit the house where Miguel was born, which he told me was a short distance from the grounds of the university. I had heard Don Rodrigo Cervantes talk about the family's former days of glory, before bad fortune befell them, when they lived in a fine residence in Alcalá. The two-story building, with a garden big enough for a few rosebushes, was situated on the corner that separated the Moorish from the Jewish neighborhood, and was adjacent to the hospital, where the sick, the dying, and the mad coexisted, as was the case with such places all over Spain. I pitied Miguel, who had to grow up listening to insane people raving day and night; the moaning of lepers; and the lamentations of patients dying in pain. The pestilential fumes emanating from the hospital made me nauseous. It was inconceivable to me how anyone could have pleasant memories of that place.

We walked to the schoolhouse where Miguel learned to read and write. It was a tiny abandoned medieval building. Through a broken window, I peered into a room with a low ceiling whose walls were covered with broken Moorish tiles. That visit to Alcalá gave me a new understanding of Miguel, made me feel compassion for the way he grew up, and made it easier for me to overlook his grating ambition. We spent the night in an inn near the university where students went to drink. Miguel consumed carafes of wine in desperation. Twice, I had to intervene to prevent him from starting fights. His volatile temperament, I knew, would get him in trouble, sooner or later.

* * *

My love for my cousin Mercedes was a well-guarded secret. Although she and I had never discussed our attachment to each other, I didn't need any proof that my feelings for her were returned. From the time of our childhood it was understood by my parents, our grandparents, and everyone else in our family that we would eventually be united in marriage after I finished my studies.

Mercedes had come to live with my maternal grandparents in Toledo while still an infant. Her mother, Aunt Carmen, had died in childbirth. My cousin's father, Don Isidro Flores, was so overcome with grief at the death of my aunt that he left Mercedes in my grandparents' care and went to the New World, where he was killed during a skirmish against the savages in an inhospitable jungle.

It was midmorning when we arrived at my grandparents' home. I was impatient to see Mercedes. A servant led Miguel to a guest chamber to wash off the dust from the road. I wiped my face with a wet rag, combed my hair, dusted off the sleeves of my jacket, brushed the dirt from my boots, and went to Mercedes's chambers. She knew of my arrival and was expecting me. Leonela, her lifelong maid, opened the door. My cousin rose from her drawing desk and rushed toward me. We held each other in a tender embrace. When Leonela left us alone, I kissed Mercedes's smooth rosy cheeks, which smelled of jasmine.

She led me by the hand to the cushions by the window overlooking the orchard. Her blond hair was covered with a scarf, but little threads escaped along her temples, gleaming like flecks of gold. "Did you find a house in Alcalá? I heard you went there to look for one." Her exquisiteness was so enthralling, I hardly heard what she was saying. A fleeting cloud of melancholy swept over her face. "I hope you don't find me too immodest, when I say that I wish I could be a student at the university myself." Before I could comment, she asked, "How long can you stay with us?"

I took her soft hand and studied her delicate fingers. "I promised Miguel's parents we'd be back in Madrid by tomorrow. And I have to return to school right away. But I'll come back soon and I promise to stay a few days." She closed her eyes and then smiled.

Grandmother Azucena had ordered a fine dinner in my honor, which included many of my favorite dishes: pottage of chickpeas and partridge, roast leg of baby lamb, serrano ham, trout stuffed with mushrooms, a salad of fruits, almonds, quail eggs, and a spread of olives, cheeses, and turrones. We washed all this down with vintage wines from the family's vineyards near Toledo. Throughout the meal, Mercedes was the picture of reserve, purity, and refinement. She kept her gaze lowered and only looked at me and at my grandparents.

Despite my grandparents' warm welcome, Miguel said little during the delicious meal and only spoke when he was addressed. I had never seen him so quiet around others, but I attributed it to his lack of social sophistication. He favored the serrano ham and was served an extra portion, which he ate heartily. Was this his way of showing my family that he was not a Jew?

When the meal was over, we retired to our chambers for a siesta and agreed to reconvene at four to stop by the cathedral to visit Garcilaso's tomb.

We rode in my grandparents' coach, with Leonela as the fourth member of our party. As soon as we were inside the coach Mercedes removed her veil. Her beauty illumined the inside of the carriage.

She asked Miguel how he had liked the Estudio de la Villa. His mood changed immediately: he started to mimic some of our eccentric teachers' demeanor in the classroom, and told off-color jokes about their appearance. His bawdy sense of humor was uproarious, though perhaps inappropriate in a lady's company. But Mercedes seemed to enjoy his antics.

She asked, "Do you sing, Señor Cervantes?"

As Miguel demurred, I said, "Yes, he has a very fine voice. You should hear him singing Andalusian ballads."

Miguel started to protest, but Mercedes interrupted him. "Then you must sing for us. You wouldn't refuse a lady's request, would you?"

Miguel's face turned scarlet. He cleared his throat and began to accompany himself by clapping his hands as he started singing a love ballad. The thought crossed my mind that Miguel's coyness was a form of seduction; it was almost as if he had set out to make an impression on Mercedes. Though nothing in my cousin's behavior gave me pause for suspicion, I felt a twinge of jealousy. When Miguel finished singing, we all cheered and clapped; then silence reigned inside the coach for the rest of the ride. Mercedes stared out the window, all the way to the cathedral.

After we said our prayers in front of the main altar, we went to see Garcilaso's tomb. I was eager to show it to Miguel. He dropped to his knees in front of the marble sarcophagus and kissed the cold stone. I, too, had been overcome with emotion the first time I visited Garcilaso's resting place. Leonela gave Mercedes a small bouquet of roses she had been carrying and my cousin laid it at the base of the poet's sepulcher. Miguel offered to recite a sonnet he had written in honor of the great Toledano. The less I say about that sonnet, the better. But Mercedes seemed to approve of it.

I was relieved when we left Toledo together. On the ride back to Madrid, Miguel raved about Mercedes and proceeded to ask me questions of a personal nature. I was careful not to reveal too much.

"She's so beautiful, and intelligent, and vivacious," Miguel said.

I nodded but said nothing.

He went on, "Her spontaneity is so captivating."

Before he had a chance to continue talking about her, I said: "My parents and grandparents have always expected us to get married." Miguel's face could not hide the disappointment my news caused him. He had little to say on the remainder of our trip back to Madrid.

I started classes at the university and was kept busy, delighted with my studies and my new acquaintances. One day a letter from Mercedes came in the mail giving me the usual news about my grandparents' health and full of questions about university life. In a postscript, as an apparent afterthought, she added that Miguel had stopped by to visit them. At first I thought nothing of it. However, I wrote to Miguel without mentioning the visit; he didn't answer back. A week passed, then two. His silence preoccupied me. Then the poison of jealousy began to well up in my heart. Immediately, I repudiated the thought that my best friend would try to make love to my intended. As for Mercedes, I knew she was too noble and pure to be capable of betrayal. I had my doubts about Miguel, though. Jealousy began to consume me to the point that I became increasingly distracted and could not study, could not sleep, could not eat. I took residence in the student taverns of Alcalá, where I drank by myself in a corner, until I fell into a stupor. My servants would carry me home before I was robbed and stabbed. I could not continue in that state. I owed an obligation to my family's name to behave always like the caballero I was. One dawn, after an interminable sleepless night, I got dressed and, on an impulse, woke up the man in charge of the stable and asked him to saddle my fastest horse. I left for Madrid determined to . . . what was it I hoped to find out? I prayed that my suspicions were unfounded.

I rode directly to Miguel's house and found Don Rodrigo changing smelly bandages on a patient. "Don Luis," he exclaimed, "to what do we owe the honor of your visit?"

I was too impatient for his usual foolishness, so I said, "Good morning to you, Don Rodrigo. Is Miguel at home?"

My abruptness seemed to startle him. He continued changing the bandages as he spoke. "Come to think of it, I haven't seen Miguel since . . . yesterday? I thought he had gone to Alcalá to visit you. Is there anything wrong?"

I shook my head.

"My wife is at the market, Don Luis, but why don't you go upstairs and ask Andrea? She might know where Miguel is. He should be here this morning, helping me. That's where he should be."

I found Andrea breast-feeding her baby. "Please don't get up," I said. "I need to find Miguel. It's urgent."

"Miguel left for Toledo yesterday," Andrea responded, hoisting the baby to cover her exposed breast. "He's been much distracted lately."

"Excuse my bad manners, but I'm in a hurry." I bowed to Andrea and ran down the stairs, past Don Rodrigo, and into the street. I was choking for lack of breath.

Insane with jealousy and murderous rage, I left for Toledo later that morning. I had to find out the truth once and for all. I entered my grandparents' home, our ancestral home, as a burglar: I jumped over the wall in the back of the orchard and then climbed to the balcony of Mercedes's chambers. The door was open and the room was empty. As if I were a criminal, I hid behind a wall tapestry in her bedchamber and decided to wait for her. I had lost my mind, but I couldn't help myself. I didn't have long to wait.

Mercedes and Leonela entered the room followed by Miguel. I almost gasped. Leonela soon left the room and closed the door behind her. Miguel tried to grab Mercedes's hand. My first impulse was to draw my sword and drive it through his heart, but I had been taught to value restraint.

"I am promised to another man," she said emphatically. "Now please leave this room and never come to visit me again. You are not welcome in this house anymore. Leonela!" she called.

Her maid entered immediately, as if she had been standing guard just outside the door.

Mercedes said, "Miguel is leaving now."

Standing at the door's threshold, the wretch asked if there was any hope for him.

"No," Mercedes said firmly. "None whatsoever."

He persisted: "I will never give you up. I will wait for you the rest of my life, if necessary."

Mercedes approached him, placed her palm on his chest, and pushed him, until he was on the other side of the door. Then she closed it in his face. Her admirable behavior appeased me. I felt ashamed of ever having doubted her. I didn't have to stay hidden behind the tapestry—I had seen all I needed to see. Mercedes need not ever know what I had witnessed. She threw herself on the bed and started sobbing, burying her face in a cushion. I tiptoed to the balcony and climbed down to the garden below, then I rode back to Alcalá with a mortally wounded heart: I would never again believe in friendship.

Later, in *Don Quixote Part I*, Miguel gave a version of his betrayal in the novella *The Curiosity of the Impertinent Man*, one of those tedious stories he inserted without the least regard for artistry within the main novel. In that narrative he tried to absolve himself of his guilt by implying that I, like Anselmo, had encouraged him to woo Mercedes to test her purity.

As the days passed, my rage swelled and became a living entity that festered in my heart. I had to retaliate in some way, so my life would belong to me once more. I would punish Miguel Cervantes for his impudence and his unforgivable betrayal.

I left Alcalá and went to Madrid. My parents were surprised to see me. I said I had a school project that required my presence in Madrid for a few days. I wrote an anonymous sonnet exposing Andrea's secret, made a dozen copies, and asked my personal servant to post them on the doors of churches and other important public buildings of Madrid. Then I went to see Aurelio, the man in charge of the stables and pigpen. "I want you to cut off the head of our biggest pig," I said, "and deposit it in front of a house." I gave him Miguel's address. "Do it at dawn. Make sure that nobody sees you." This was something that was commonly done when you wanted to expose publicly a family of conversos.

It would just be a matter of time before someone insulted Miguel by calling him a Jew, or the brother of a whore, and he would have to fight a duel to defend his honor.

A few days later, I sent word to Miguel with a servant, asking him to meet me at a tavern where poets and other rough types met. When Miguel arrived at the tavern that night, he was in a sullen mood and looked genuinely troubled. We started a game of cards. A man named Antonio de Sigura asked if he could join us. I had seen de Sigura around; he was an engineer who had arrived in Madrid to work for the court, building new roads. De Sigura lost a considerable amount of money quickly, then Miguel refused to keep playing. The inevitable insult came, Miguel wounded de Sigura, and he became a fugitive. My plan had worked! The way he was living his life, it would not be long before Miguel was a dead man.

I left for Toledo at dawn the day after Miguel escaped from Madrid; tumultuous emotions raging inside me. As the golden rays of the rising sun began to warm me up, I felt myself slowly returning to my own life. Sunlight intensified the starkness of the rocky soil of Castile, which spread endlessly toward the south. It made me think of the corrugated skin of a monstrous dragon left out to dry in the open. Flocks of partridges flew above the woods in thick brown clouds, then disappeared in the thicket of low encinas. An intoxicating smell infused the air, as if the earth released it to awaken all the creatures of La Mancha. It was the same smell of rosemary and sweet marjoram from my grandmother's herb garden in Toledo.

Though now I hated Miguel, my most fervent wish was not that he would get caught, but that he would manage to escape to the Indies, that he would settle in a foreign land, far away from Castile, and from Mercedes. It would be even better if he died on the other side of the world.

As Toledo appeared in the distance, I held back the reins and sat still atop my horse. The pale morning light spilling upon the hills and fields of La Mancha painted them terra-cotta. It was a sight that only a painter could capture. It wouldn't be until many years later, when El Greco settled among us, that an artist existed who could do justice to those skies.

The windmills in the distance, crowning the hills of reddish soil and limestone, resembled giants awakening, rotating their arms to shake off the morning stiffness, preparing to guard La Mancha for the rest of the day, ready to hold back any invading hordes from the wild, unchristian world that lay to the south—where Miguel was heading, and where he truly belonged, because in Castile he would always be an interloper, never one of us.

By providing Miguel with ample funds for his escape, I had done the honorable thing—even though he didn't deserve it. Fray Luis de León's verses, which I had read in a copy of a manuscript that circulated in Madrid among poetry lovers, echoed in my mind:

> I want to live by myself
> to enjoy alone, without witnesses,
> the blessings heaven bestows on me
> free from false love, from jealousy
> from hatred, suspicion, and illusive hopes . . .

Realizing my happiness with Mercedes would forever be in jeopardy as long as Miguel was around, I made a promise to myself: *If Miguel de Cervantes ever again returns to Castile, I swear to destroy him.*

CHAPTER 3
LEPANTO
1571

O nce we had crossed the Pyrenees, where they taper off at the shoreline of the Mediterranean, I felt optimistic that I could make it to Italy. I put all my hopes on an invitation Cardinal Giulio Acquaviva had extended to me to visit him in Rome. Perhaps he would help me out of respect for his friendship with my professor. It had been a defining stroke of luck to become the protégé of Professor López de Hoyos, a man of personal integrity who seemed to have read all the great books. His belief in my talent gave wings to my ambition. "Reach for the highest stars in the literary firmament, Miguel. Aim for no less!" he had said to me on a number of occasions.

At the recommendation of my professor, Cardinal Acquaviva had asked to see some of my poems. He was only a few years older than me, but his tall, aristocratic presence; his aura of power; his worldly manners; the precision and elegance of his speech; his white, soft hands and elongated musician's fingers garnished with impressive blood-red stones that matched the hue of the princely vestments he wore—it all made me feel like a mere boy in his presence. I memorized his compliments about my poetry: "Professor López de Hoyos speaks of you as one of the future glories of Spanish letters," he said to me one evening at dinner. "He raves about the elegance of your verses, the originality of your conceits, and your persuasive flourishes. I dabble a little in poetry myself. Will you show me some of your verses?"

At the professor's house I left for the cardinal a selection of my poems rolled up and tied with a ribbon. When I saw him next, Acquaviva said, "Cervantes, you must come to Rome to learn the language and study Italian poetry. You will always have a job waiting for you in my household." I took his invitation to mean that he liked my poems. I clung to that casual offer as the only bright spot in my dire circumstances, the one beacon of light on my shadowy horizon.

That autumn, as I traveled with the Gypsies through the leafy valleys of southern France, the weather was mild, the foliage afire, and the languid afternoons were filled with buzzing, inebriated golden-gloved bees. We camped in idyllic chestnut and cork tree forests that reminded me of the settings in pastoral novels. The French countryside teemed with rabbits, hedgehogs, deer, pigeons, partridges, pheasants, quail, and wild boars. By day the women and children rummaged in the wooded areas for berries, pine nuts, eggs, snails, mushrooms, wild herbs, and truffles. The older women stayed in the camp minding the smallest children and tatting lace, looping multicolored threads of cotton and linen to make the tablecloths that were highly esteemed as decorations for the dining rooms of the prosperous homes in Spain.

We camped on the banks of cold, burbling streams or narrow but fast-flowing rivers, thick with fat trout that we caught from the mossy banks with our bare hands. At night we bivouacked around a bonfire. New mothers squatted on the ground breast-feeding their babies; they displayed their bursting teats in front of the men without any shame. This custom added to the reputation the Roma had of being immoral. As the night wore on, the clapping of hands and the ringing notes of the tambourines charged the air of the camp; caskets of red wine were uncorked; pipes with aromatic hash were smoked. The dancing and singing went on until everyone—the very young and the old included—collapsed on the ground exhausted and intoxicated.

I never let out of my sight the few gold escudos I had left after I paid El Cuchillo. Before I went to sleep, I hid the leather pouch between my scrotum and my undergarment. Perhaps I need not have been so vigilant. Maese Pedro had introduced me to the Gypsies as a criminal poet wanted for numerous murders. Once my murderous identity was established, I was always called "Brother Miguel" or "Poet." The children could not hide the awe my reputation inspired in them.

My lifelong fascination with Gypsies was cemented by that trip. Their love of drinking, dancing, making love, and fighting, and their ferocious attachment to their customs and their people, were qualities I held dearly. They spoke Castilian—and a little bit of many European languages—but they communicated among themselves in Calo. I passed many of my waking hours talking to the children, trying to learn the rudiments of their language. I was speaking from direct experience when I wrote in *The Gypsy Girl*, "It seems that Gypsies, both male and female, are born into the world to be thieves: their parents are thieves, they grow up among thieves, study to become thieves, and graduate with honors in the arts of thievery. The desire to steal and the act of stealing are inseparable traits that only death can part."

I said goodbye to my Roma friends in Italy, as they continued on their way to their ancestral land in the Carpathians. I rode to Rome as fast as my horse would take me, afraid to run out of money before I reached my destination. Six days later, my exhausted horse rode under the arch of the Porta del Popolo. I dismounted and, with tears clouding my vision, I kissed one of the columns that marked the entrance to the city of the Caesars.

Without delay, I headed for the residence of Cardinal Acquaviva, near Vatican City. I didn't care that I was dirty and close to collapsing when I came knocking on the door of the cardinal's grand residence and was brought into his presence. Acquaviva received me with an open smile that dissipated my worst fears.

"I was afraid Your Excellency would have forgotten me," I mumbled, as a way of apologizing for my unannounced visit.

"Of course I remember you, Cervantes," he said. "I don't ever forget a promising young poet. How good of you to remember me. Welcome to Rome and to my, and your, house."

I kissed the white-gloved hand he offered me. No questions about my precipitous arrival in the city were asked, to my great relief. I was wondering if he had heard anything about the incident in Madrid, when he put me at ease, saying, "I have a pressing need of a secretary who can answer my correspondence in Spanish. How is your calligraphy?"

"I speak the truth when I say to Your Excellency that my handwriting, though small, is clear, and has been praised by my teachers." I was flabbergasted by his offer. "And I hope not to embarrass you with my spelling."

He motioned to his aide de chamber. "Take Signor Miguel's bags to the visitor's apartment on this floor." Addressing me, Cardinal Acquaviva added, "Cervantes, I can put you to work immediately. In the meantime you'll have your meals here. How does five florins a month sound to you?"

Besides his love of poetry, the cardinal was interested in

painting, music, philosophy, history, and both local and world politics. He liked stimulating conversation, especially when accompanied by good food and the finest red wines. Talk of religion seemed to bore him, making him distracted and impatient. Even though at that point I had written little and published less, he treated me with the respect due a serious poet.

Those first months in Rome, I took every free moment I had from my duties to explore the magnificent, immortal city. As a new pilgrim, I vowed to love Rome with tender affection, humble devotion, and an open heart, and soon surrendered to her bewitchment. The streets and sun-filled piazzas on which I walked, bedazzled, had been soaked with the blood of Christian martyrs and were sacrosanct ground to me. The footsteps of Michelangelo still echoed in the parks, avenues, and narrow streets. His frescoes on the ceiling and altar of the Sistine Chapel seemed more the work of a deity than a single artist. Admiring their vastness, their beauty, and their perfection for hours, I began to comprehend what it meant to create a work of art that, like Dante's *Comedy*, was a summa of all that could be said about the human spirit.

There was no part of Rome—no gigantic marble column or broken arch, no ancient tomb, no mysterious alley, no ancient wall, no venerable cemetery, no crumbling church, no fading fresco, no vandalized palace, no penumbrous forest of cypresses, no romantic piazza where lovers met at night—that was not an example of the endless bounty of marvels that God had bequeathed men.

Memories of my troubled past in Spain receded, as well as nostalgia for the life I had left behind. Visiting Rome's churches, chapels, shrines, and basilicas, studying the statues and the paintings adorning their walls, the frescoes gracing their ceilings, the intricate gold-work of their altars and domes, I felt a perpetual intoxication. Determined to succeed at something at least once in my life, I worked assiduously for the cardinal. My parents had sacrificed themselves to send me to the Estudio de la Villa, and I had failed them. In my letters home, I talked at length about the duties I performed in the house of the great man (magnifying their importance) as well as the important people who visited the cardinal's palazzo. I wrote to my parents that Pope Pius V had blessed me. I did not mention he had blessed—at the same time—thousands of other believers from his balcony. I hoped this would lighten the burden of shame I had caused my parents and make them proud.

Yet, I was restless. Rome was the political capital of the world. The fat-assed prelates, who seemed to love their young acolytes as much as they loved the luxurious life they led, talked more about political intrigue in the ranks of the church than about God. I realized I did not fit in that society of spies and intrigue; I did not have the subservient spirit required to reside in the palaces of people who hungered for power, even if they were so-called men of God. The world of the Vatican was not where I wanted to make a career. There was grave danger of becoming a lying and pompous poet if I let that sybaritic life seduce me.

Pope Pius V wielded more power and commanded more fear than many mighty kings and emperors. Concerned that Selim II, son and murderer of Sultan Suleyman the Magnificent, emboldened by recent Ottoman conquests in the Mediterranean, was gathering massive forces in nearby Greece, the pope created a Holy League to embark on a new crusade against the Turks. The talk in Rome was that the invincible Turkish navy was preparing an assault on Italy, to extirpate Christianity and enslave Christians. Once the Ottomans had conquered Italy, it was believed they intended to retake Andalusia, if not the whole of Spain, in the name of Islam.

Selim II was the son of Suleyman the Magnificent with the ex-slave Roxelana, his favorite wife. He was called The Sot because he lived in a permanent state of debauched drunkenness. He cared nothing about the affairs of state and demanded enormous revenues from his navy so that he could live in grand splendor and unrestricted decadence. To this end, he had given license to Algerian corsairs to terrorize and plunder the peoples of the Mediterranean. But his grand vizier, the Serbian renegade Mehmed Sokollu, was obsessed with expanding the frontiers of the Ottoman Empire. He sought to gain control of all the Mediterranean nations and, afterward, all of Europe. Sokollu had become emboldened by the Turks' conquest of Yemen, Hejaz, and—the jewel of all—Cyprus.

The thought of Selim II and his grand vizier subjugating the Christian nations, stocking the Ottoman harems with our women and selling our children to the Turkish sodomites, was unbearable to me. I was ready to give my life to defeat such a monster. And the decision of Philip II to name Don John of Austria as commander of the Spanish armada was all the encouragement I needed. The young prince and I had been born the same year, and I was not alone in revering him. Though he was an illegitimate son of Charles V, the Spanish people preferred him to King Philip, who was more comfortable in court, with his mistresses, than on the battlefield. Don John's campaign in Andalusia squashing the Moorish revolt had made him famous as a soldier and leader. He gained further renown as a naval tactician by attacking and capturing the Algerian ships that sailed our waters and raided our coastal villages in search of slaves. His bravery made him a hero in the eyes of Spain's youth. I dreamed of becoming a soldier in his army.

Don John was the prince Spain was in desperate need of, if we were going to recapture our leadership among the nations of the world. For me, it was a clear-cut choice: the noble prince—a true knight and righter of the world's injustices, and a warrior against evil—versus the cruel, degenerate, and despotic Selim II. Depending on which side emerged victorious, the Mediterranean nations would be either Christian or Muslim.

I rejoiced when Spanish forces joined the Catholic states of Genoa, Naples, and Venice to fight back the imminent assault by the Turks. Their forces began to gather off the coast of Italy, near the port of Messina. The imminence of the approaching war saturated the air we breathed; it dominated our conversations, our thoughts, and our dreams. It made all the young men in Rome walk about with their chests puffed out. I had never been so thrilled to be alive.

When Cardinal Acquaviva did not require my services, I was drawn to visiting the Colosseum. I would find myself alone, late at night, sitting high up, looking down at the empty arena until I could imagine it drenched in blood that blazed in the moonlight. Then I could hear the roaring echo of the bloodthirsty Romans. If I closed my eyes I saw the angry populace making signs of life and death with their thumbs; signs that screamed silently, *Life, death, life, death*. Life.

I would kill Turks the way I imagined myself killing lions and slaying gladiators in the Colosseum. My head was filled with patriotic fervor for the Spanish land and our Christian faith. One night, alone, with the shadows of the monument and the stars in the firmament as my only witnesses, I pledged to give my life, if necessary, to defeat the Turks. If I lived, the battlefield, I was convinced, would provide me with experience, and a great subject to write a magnificent poem, something that would rival *The Iliad* or *El Cid*. And if I never became a great poet, I would at least be an active participant in a decisive moment in history.

That was my state of mind when my brother Rodrigo arrived in Rome as a soldier in a Spanish regiment commanded by Don Miguel de Moncada. We drank in the taverns, visited whorehouses, and talked incessantly about the glorious future that awaited us in the service of our king.

All that remained was for me to inform Cardinal Acquaviva of my decision. There was no displeasure in his voice when he said, "Miguel, I will miss you. If my circumstances were different, I, too, would become a soldier. I will pray for your safety. Remember that there will always be a place in my home for you."

The last days of that humid August of 1571, the Christian fleets began to gather in the harbor of Messina. I was feverish with my zeal to serve under the command of our noble and magnificent prince, who had promised to bring Spain into another Golden Age. On the days leading to the great battle, Rodrigo and I waited aboard *La Marquesa*, hearing the Masses said by the priests who went from galley to galley reminding us that to die in the defense of the only true God was a worthy enterprise. Along with thousands of other Christian youths we waited for orders from our commanders to ready for battle, hearing changing reports of the strategic movements of the Turkish navy.

That September, which seemed to be the longest thirty days of my young life, we whiled away the time cleaning and oiling our weapons, rehearsing different attack scenarios, and praying under our breath to kill multitudes of Turks in order to preserve our faith and the Christian world.

At last the moment came, that glorious day of October

6, when, hearts inflamed with dreams of immortality, we sailed forth in two hundred galleys—thirty thousand men under the command of Don John with orders to destroy the fearsome Ottoman navy.

We sailed under clear skies until night fell. A moonless sky favored us. In complete darkness we slipped through the narrow and heavily fortified entrance to the Gulf of Corinth. The Turkish navy awaited us at the eastern end of the gulf.

On October 7 I woke up feverish and vomiting, and was ordered to stay below deck during the battle. "Your Grace," I said to Captain Murena, "I joined the king's forces to do my duty, and I would rather die for God and Spain than survive the battle without fighting."

The captain frowned and said: "As you wish, Cervantes. But you will be stationed by the skiff and not move from there." He added, "You must be a great fool. Most men in your condition would be happy to be exempted from fighting. God favors fools and madmen. May He be with you."

On the southeast side of the gulf, where the Peloponnesian Mountains rose, witnesses to many epochal ancient wars, I imagined I saw and heard the great Greek heroes of antiquity cheering us on from the wooded hills. The currents of the gulf steered our fleet toward the Turkish ships, which were stationed in a line across the bay. Dawn revealed the triangular red flags of the enemy decorated with the moon star; they seemed like an airborne wave of brilliant color. In the center of their formation Ali Pasha's immense galleon stood out; on its mast was hoisted a colossal green flag on which, it was said, Allah's name was woven in gold twenty-nine thousand times. The Turks' fearsome chants, and the spectacle of their glowing sails, lent majesty to the occasion. Their battle cries sounded as if they'd erupted from a giant common throat, one that belonged to a dragon whose red eyes stared at us from the clouds.

For hours both navies were frozen on the surface of the sea. The noon sun was blazing above us when the orders came to prepare for battle. Don John's strategy became evident as the fast currents in the greenish waters thrust us in the direction of the enemy: we would not meet the Ottoman navy head-on. Our armada parted to form two flanks, while leaving behind in the middle a line of ships with our most powerful cannons facing the Turks. Both columns of ships traveled close to the shores of the bay. Rodrigo and I were both in the northern formation, but on different ships. I no longer felt sick.

The Turks fired first, producing a rushing wall of flame, which was followed by a thundering sound, as if the sky had crashed down to earth. I felt my heart stop, until the cannons of our galleons blazed back, aiming at Ali Pasha's ship. This was the sign for our two columns to aim our prows at the Turkish vessels. We prepared to ram their fleet as our artillery fired. Of all their weapons, we feared most the Greek fire the Turks used. Once it hit a ship, it was impossible to put out: no amount of water or sand could quench its burning, steady fury.

As the two fleets got within striking distance of each other, and the harquebuses and cannons fired salvos on both sides, a hot mass of smoke swallowed up Christians and Turks alike. A force I did not understand seized me: I was no longer myself, no longer just one body, but part of something prodigiously large—a nation, a religion, a way of life, a soldier in the army of the true God. I became thousands of men, invulnerable, as tall and fearsome as a cyclops.

Orders came to board the Ottoman ships, and to engage the enemy in hand-to-hand combat. Battle-axes were wielded. For the next few hours severed fingers, hands, arms, feet, and heads pelted me, and I was drenched by mutilated and headless bodies shooting streams of blood.

Once the fighting started, my fear evaporated. When one man died, he was replaced by another; when that other man fell wounded, a healthy one emerged from behind him, creating an endless reserve of soldiers always venturing forward, a bloodthirsty horde shouting slogans, insults, prayers, curses, in Spanish, in Italian, in Turkish, in Arabic.

I had slain many Turks when a gunshot tore my left hand to pieces, leaving the bones exposed and protruding. At first I felt no pain and kept fighting, striking and killing with my healthy arm until a thump on my chest sent me reeling back: a harquebus blast had dug a hole in my torso. I was trying to block the flow of blood by pressing my fist against the orifice, when another deafening charge hit inches from my fist. My chest was heavy with the gunpowder and iron embedded in my flesh, and I staggered around as if drunk, smelling my charred flesh, trying to hold onto anything to keep my balance, to keep myself from collapsing on the deck of the ship where I knew I would be trampled to death.

As men were wounded and killed all around me, as ships caught fire and sank with loud groans, as choking black smoke enveloped us, I continued to swing my sword at anything that moved, intending—despite my weakened state—to vanquish every heretic in my path until I died.

Where was my brother? I prayed that he had been spared; prayed that if he was mortally wounded, and in excruciating pain, a compassionate soul would put an end to his suffering. I prayed that our parents would not lose both sons in one day.

* * *

I thought I must have been dreaming when I began to hear, in Spanish and Italian, cries of "Victory! Victory!" The fate of the battle had been sealed when the oarsmen of the Turks—Christian and Greek slaves who were unshackled so they could maneuver better during battle—jumped off the ships and swam toward the shores of the bay, disappearing into the thick forests that covered the hills. By sundown it was clear that we had slaughtered a great number of Turks; that our losses had been smaller; that we were the victors; that we had defeated the hitherto invincible Ottoman navy. Our men cheered when what was left of the enemy fleet was spotted fleeing the Gulf of Corinth, carrying their commander.

For what seemed hours, I lay on my back in a corner of *La Marquesa*, semihidden by empty barrels and dead men. My burning desire not to die so far from Spain kept me alive. The orders not to pursue the Turks reached my ears. Our men took a rest from the killing; the world hushed. The glorious battle of Lepanto had ended—I was a part of history.

Our ship, however, caught on fire and started sinking fast. With the last of my strength I crawled on the blood-crusted deck and hoisted myself overboard. The sea was so thick with corpses that soldiers walked over them—as if they were on land—to move from ship to ship. The soldiers who had been hit by Greek fire bobbed in the water like human torches, illuminating the bay. I floated next to a raft heaped with men—Muslim and Christian—dead and dying. In death all of them looked like pitifully broken marionettes made of the same material. With my good hand I grabbed onto a corner of the raft. When a hand aflame emerged from the sea as if to grab me by my throat and pull me to the underworld, I screamed and my entire body shook in the water.

The sea was scarlet with flames that spread in waves over the roiling waters. The stench of burning wood, gunpowder, and above all, of roasting and charred flesh, was the work not of God but of the devil, I told myself. The world around me lost all its edges; everything became a blur. *Heavenly Father, forgive my sins*, I prayed. *Forgive me for the many times I offended You. Have mercy on my soul.* I closed my eyes, certain I would open them again only in the afterlife.

Weeks later, when I regained consciousness, Rodrigo sat by my side. His eyes filled with tears. "You are in a hospital in Messina. The Blessed Virgin saved you," he said. The pain in my chest, and in my useless hand, was excruciating. I howled. The Sisters fed me drops of water, but breathing itself was painful, as if the insides of my chest were ablaze. After a few drops of laudanum subdued my agony and I was calmer, my brother explained that he had found me on the beach the night after the battle, buried under a heap of dead soldiers.

For the next two years I languished in Italian hospitals, on bug-infested straw cots, in wards full of the ill, the wounded, the mutilated, the pus-ridden, the insane, the dying, of men who were rotting while still alive. Many nights I woke up screaming, panicked that the Greek fire had turned me into a burning torch, or that I was the only survivor after a gory battle, roaming in a desolate land, a landscape of severed limbs and decomposing corpses that was more frightening than any vision of hell I could ever have imagined.

Rodrigo left the army and found employment so that I could have the proper medications, and eat something besides the watery broth patients were fed in the hospital. When finally I was strong enough to go out into the world, with my scarred, patched-up chest and my limp arm, I was half the man I once had been. And I felt twice my age.

Three long years crawled by after the glorious days of the Battle of Lepanto, and I was desperate to return to Spain to see my family. I did not want to die on foreign soil. Over five years had passed since I fled Madrid. I was weary of the never-ending bloodshed, weary of being always on the move, engaged in endless campaigns against the Turks; weary, too, of the pestilential hospitals where my fellow soldiers rotted on their cots, eaten alive by maggots.

When I announced to Rodrigo that I was ready to walk back to Spain if necessary, he said to me, "Brother, I'm ready to return home with you. I have satisfied my curiosity about war and heroism. I want to go back home, find work, and help our parents. I would like to get married and have children."

With the belated, pitiful payment of the wages owed us for our service as soldiers, we booked passage from Naples on the galley El Sol, bound for Barcelona. The irony of my return did not escape me: I had fled Spain to save my right hand and I was returning with my left hand hanging by my side like a dead appendage, ending at the wrist in a knobby, swollen stump, a ball of skin filled with blood, ready to burst if scratched. It was the hand of a monster.

Traveling on a lone ship back to Spain would make us easy prey to the corsairs. But the alternative was to wait for weeks to join a fleet of vessels, and our funds were dangerously low. At Lepanto, the Christian navy had made the costly mistake of not finishing off the slaughter of the Ottomans when they were at our mercy. Barely a year later, the Turks had regrouped, rearmed, and regained control of the Mediterranean, where once more they reigned supreme and were the bane of seafarers and people living in coastal towns. I had left some of my flesh and bone at Lepanto for nothing more than a taste of glory; it was as if the battle had been fought for naught. Mediterranean people quickly came to see Lepanto as a defeat; any mention of it was met with scorn.

Considering the circumstances, I wondered whether it was too late to receive from the Spanish crown compensation for my injuries. All my hopes rested in two letters I carried, one signed by Don John of Austria; the other, by the Duke of Sessa. The letters recommended me to his Catholic Majesty for a pension to reward my heroism in battle. Don John's letter further pleaded with King Philip to grant me a recompense for additional service to the crown in the campaigns of Corfu and Modon, and a full pardon for the wounding of Antonio de Sigura.

But I knew the sluggish wheels of Spanish justice meant it could be years before my case was heard in court, and additional years before a pension was awarded to me. How would I survive until then? I could not hope to live on the charity of my impoverished family. With my lame arm, I could not be of much help to my father with his patients. What trade did not require the use of both hands? Could the experience I had acquired in Rome, as Cardinal Acquaviva's Spanish secretary, help me to get work copying documents? I had failed to acquire riches as a soldier, but perhaps it was not too late to make my mark as a poet. My heart harbored a nugget of optimism; I clung to the belief that through poetry I might yet make my family proud. The naïve young man who arrived in Italy with the Gypsies would barely recognize himself in the man who was returning to Spain poor and crippled. But one thing had not changed: my belief that I was meant to achieve greatness.

The first night at sea, as *El Sol* sailed toward the Spanish mainland, after the passengers retired to their berths, the weather was so gentle, the sky so clear and alive with the light of the stars, that I decided to sleep on deck. Lying on the floor of El Sol, smoking a pipe, my head resting on a heap of coiled ropes, I wondered about the course my life would have taken if I had sailed to the Indies back then. The closer El Sol sailed to the coast of Catalonia, the more I thought of Mercedes. Would I see her again? I had written many letters to her over the years, but never received a reply. It was true that my love for her was tempered by the passage of time, but I still treasured her memory as an oasis in my past, before my life became a chain of misfortunes.

Four days and three nights later, we caught glimpses of the snowy peaks of the Sierra Nevada de Granada; it began to feel as if we might reach Spanish soil without incident. After a day of sailing turbulent waters the moon rose over a serene sea, and the African breezes were favorable. Captain Arana gave orders to lash the oars and let the winds blow us homeward. The moon's brightness illuminated the sea in all directions. The passengers aboard El Sol were enjoying the balmy breezes and the shimmering stars as the sailors played cards on deck. Rodrigo amused himself and the female passengers by singing Spanish songs accompanied by the vihuela. But adverse luck is never readier to strike than when the world seems affable and inviting.

Suddenly, as if emerging from the bowels of Poseidon's realm, three large ships approached us at such speed that, before our oarsmen could take their positions, or the remainder of our crew man El Sol's guns, or the captain order the sails raised, the helm of the largest of the ominous ships came so near our vessel that we could hear the questions men shouted at us in a strange language, which I recognized as the lingua franca spoken in North Africa.

Captain Arana yelled, "They are Algerian corsairs! Ignore their questions!"

These were the infamous buccaneers in the service of Hassan Pasha, ruler of Algiers, who hunted for human chattel in the Mediterranean. Even the bravest among us were fearful. Captain Arana shouted from his post: "All the women and children must go immediately to their cabins and bolt their doors! And, for the love of God," he continued, "I implore you to keep them locked! Do not open the doors until our fate is decided and you receive orders from our men."

The women grabbed their children and rushed to their compartments in a flurry of rustling dresses and cries of, "Protect us, saintly Mother of God! Holy Virgin Mary, do not abandon us!"

We drew our pistols, prepared the muskets, wielded daggers, and unsheathed our swords to defend ourselves and our women and children. I turned to Rodrigo. "If we have a fight, let's stay together," I told him. The prospect of combat excited, rather than frightened, my brother: he was born to be a soldier. His pupils sparkled with the fire I had seen in the eyes of soldiers during battle. The Cervantes were all hot-blooded, impulsive, and easily excitable, but Rodrigo was the most fearless of us all. The prospect of death in battle did not frighten him. He was young, healthy, and strong, and could defend himself better than I could, yet I felt protective. *Even with my lame arm, I will fight the corsairs to the death*, I told myself.

Below deck, the boatswains shouted at our oarsmen to row faster and faster to put some water between us and the Algerians, and we began to outdistance them. Just when it looked as if we would evade being captured, the corsairs discharged two roaring cannon blasts: the first missed our ship; the second broke the ship's mast in half. A swell of ocher smoke choked everyone, yet we managed to chant, "For Christ! For the only true religion! For the honor of the king! For Spain!" The bodies of two of our men lay crushed under the severed mast. They looked glued to the floor in a pool of bright blood—their entrails floating next to their bodies. Images of Lepanto flashed in front of my eyes.

The Algerians lowered to the sea a flotilla of boats, filled with hundreds of men who rowed furiously in our direction. The fifty men manning *El Sol* did not stand a chance against the swarm of corsairs approaching us. We were going to be slaughtered.

Captain Arana's resonant voice rose over the din of our men: "Do not resist. They will kill all of us if we fight them. We are outnumbered. Listen to me, men, do not resist."

There were cries of, "Rather dead than a slave!"

Captain Arana implored, "For the sake of the women and children, do not resist. For the sake of the innocents, we must surrender. Pray to our Lord Jesus for His great mercy. That's our only chance."

Without encountering any resistance, the corsairs came aboard *El Sol*, yelling: "Death to the Christians! You will be our slaves!" Then they cursed Christianity and King Philip. As our men were herded in a circle, a renegade who spoke Spanish barked, "If you want to live, throw down your weapons! This ship is now under the command of Arnaut Mamí. From now on, you are his property."

Mamí was an Albanian notorious throughout the Mediterranean for his barbarous cruelty. It was easy to spot him among the corsairs: he was a head taller than most of his men, bulky, with long blond hair and large blue eyes that seemed made of ice. His lips were drawn into a smirk. Growling insults in imperfect Spanish, he pulled out of our group two young members of the crew, unsheathed his scimitar, and drove its point through the throat of one of them. As the sailor fell on the deck, blood gushing from his neck, Arnaut Mamí drew his weapon back and, with one fulminant stroke, beheaded the man. The other sailor—so stunned he had not moved—met the same fate. Arnaut Mamí kicked their heads into the sea, then ordered his men: "Bring out all the trunks in the cabins. Blow open the doors if need be."

Buccaneers carrying large coarse bags demanded all the coins, jewels, and valuables we carried on our bodies. We obeyed in silence. I kept the precious letters from Don John of Austria and the Duke of Sessa in a leather pouch under my shirt. My fate hung on those letters. We were asked to undress. Surreptitiously, I took the letters out of their pouch and balled them in my hand. I was about to place them between my buttocks when a corsair struck me in the head with the handle of his dagger, and shouted, "Give me that or I'll kill you like a dog!"

The commotion attracted the attention of Arnaut Mamí who asked for the letters and inspected the wrinkled documents. Apparently Mamí could butcher our language but was unable to read it. He said, "Yussif, what's in these letters?" A corsair, who looked like a Spanish man who might have been captured long ago and then converted to Islam, revealed the contents. As someone who was used to assessing the monetary value of people, Mamí immediately noticed my lame arm. "Show me your other one," he commanded. I extended my right arm. Mamí's bejeweled index finger ran vertically over my palm. "You have the hand of a lady," he sneered, his eyes appraising me up and down with curiosity. "You must be an important person, or a high-ranking nobleman. The letters prove it." Then he said to his men in Spanish: "If any one of you harms this man," he held up his right hand, making a V with two long-nailed fingers, "I will pluck out your eyes. Is that understood?"

Corsairs were returning to the deck with heavy trunks. They waited for Mamí's orders. Wielding a heavy ax he shattered one of the locks, then rifled through the contents of the trunk, chortling with revolting delight at his splendid booty. He selected some coins and rings, which he threw at his men, who fought over them like starving vultures over carrion. He handed the ax to another corsair and made a motion to crush the locks of the rest of the trunks.

We were commanded to remain absolutely quiet, or else our heads would be lopped off. We watched as the loot was inventoried and transferred to Mamí's ship. Next we were separated into three groups: The women and children were removed to Mamí's ship. The men who looked like laborers, and therefore did not have prosperous families who could pay to ransom them, were transferred to another ship. These unfortunates would be put to work as oarsmen, which was the same as receiving a death sentence. The rest of the captives—those who were dressed as clergymen or as gentlemen or who had the manners of such—were reassigned to the third boat.

I was greatly relieved when Mamí determined that Rodrigo, as my brother, was valuable too, and included him with me in the third cluster. Once our transfer was finished, the corsairs stripped El Sol of everything of value. The last man to abandon it poured tar on the deck and set it on fire. As El Sol went down in flames and smoke, my hopes sank as well. Even when it went under, the Greek fire kept burning on the deck, illuminating El Sol's descent to the bottom of the Mediterranean.

We were stuffed into a small crawl space below deck, forward of the midsection where the oarsmen rowed. On each side of the vessel they sat on wooden planks, four rowers to an oar, attached at the wrists and ankles by iron chains that ran through hooks connected to the sides of the galleon. The oarsmen spoke Spanish and other European languages. They were naked except for a swatch of fabric they wore around their midwaist. The backs of many of the men were verdigris and purple slabs of raw flesh, crawling with green maggots. Swarms of flies feasted on the pus that suppurated from their wounds. We learned not to breathe too hard, or to open our mouths unnecessarily, for fear of swallowing the buzzing shiny flies, which fought to enter our bodies as if to devour us from the inside out.

For days and nights, the low ceiling above our heads forced us to remain on our buttocks, pressed against each other like salted fish in a sealed barrel. Rodrigo found a space near me. Being so close to each other was a great consolation. Forward from the front of the crawl space was a globular window through which I caught glimpses of the sea and sky. There was also a hole in the floor, which we used to relieve ourselves. But it was hard to move around: often it was easier to urinate and defecate in place. In this extreme confinement all the class differences were soon erased. After a while aristocrats, prelates, and hidalgos all acted like beasts fighting for a chance at survival.

Fleas, chiggers, and lice feasted on our blood; fat black roaches crawled on the walls, and angry rats scurried between our legs. Now and then a bucket of fresh water with a cup was brought to the front of the crawl space, and each man was allowed to fill half the cup and pass it around until everyone had drunk. If the bucket was emptied before each had his ration, the unlucky thirsty men would have to wait until the bucket was brought again later. When our thirst was extreme we began to drink each other's urine. The soggy biscuits that were handed to us now and then were fat with worms. We resorted to eating the fleas, and the lice that infested our heads. We began catching the roaches and the rats and mice, pounding them to death with our feet and fists, then tearing them to pieces and devouring their flesh and entrails.

Grown men cried inconsolably over the lack of news about their wives and children. The married men were tormented that their wives and daughters would end up in Turkish harems, and the fathers of male children could not hide their horror that their sons would be sold to Turkish sodomites. One of our men had managed to hide a Rosary and we found solace in saying the Lord's Prayer and reciting Hail Marys in a whisper. Only through prayer could I escape a voyage that seemed bound for hell. The gentlemen in our midst knew that their families would pay their ransoms promptly; but the rest wondered what the future held for us. My parents would never be able to raise the money to buy the freedom of my brother and me, perhaps not even one of us. What kind of future awaited me with a lame arm? Would I become a servant in Mamí's house? I refused to accept that either Rodrigo or I would remain in Algiers the rest of our lives. Despite my pitiful state, I developed an unshakable conviction that by whatever means at my reach I would try to escape at the first opportunity to the Spanish town of Oran to the west of Algiers. From there, I would make the crossing on a floating log, if necessary.

Some nights, I would wake up from a nightmare, and it would be so dark and the air so putrid that for a moment I would think I was still on the beach in Greece, that night after the Battle of Lepanto, buried under a heap of dead soldiers, and the little air that reached my nostrils would bring with it the sickening smell of roasting human flesh.

Despair is more contagious than hope. Yet as ephemeral as my hope to survive this ordeal was, I could not give it up—it was all I had. One day, a Spanish hidalgo, who now looked like one of those sick, starving beggars in Spanish cities, asked, "Cervantes, is it true you are a poet?" When I said I was, he said, "Why don't you recite us one of your poems to relieve our boredom?"

I was not the type of poet who memorized his poetry. In my despondent state, I could barely remember a few scattered verses of my beloved Garcilaso de la Vega, whose poetry in former days I had been able to recite in my sleep.

One of our men caught a virulent fever, and he urinated and defecated blood. I remembered Father saying: "Song and play will chase sorrows away." To make his last hours more pleasing, Rodrigo and I chanted patriotic songs we had sung before going to battle against the Turks. The man had been moaning in agony, but as we sang to him he became quiet and listened attentively, and the grimace of pain on his face became a faint smile. Our singing was not enough to snatch him from the claws of death, but for a moment made him forget he was dying.

Our captors made no effort to remove the rotting man. His belly kept distending, until one night his stomach burst, making a deafening explosion, and those close to the corpse were covered with decomposing organs. Then the body caught aflame. The great commotion awoke the oarsmen who started to scream and rattle their chains. By the time the pirates came down, the man's body resembled a twisted branch that had burned until it turned to coal.

In the aftermath, many of us woke up from nightmares screaming and shaking; some men began to choke their neighbors, mistaking them for pirates; others started to talk like children and called out to their mothers. Another man screamed that we were in hell paying for our sins. Another one cried, "Strike me dead, Lord! If You have any compassion for this sinner, kill me now! Don't let me live another day!"

Rodrigo proposed: "Why don't we write a song? Just think of some words and I'll compose the melody." Though the buccaneers had confiscated his vihuela, we passed hours composing it. One night, as our ship was tossed in a tempest so violent that we began thinking in anguish that we would sink in chains to the bottom of the Mediterranean, Rodrigo and I began to sing our song:

In the middle of the sea
the hungry, water-heavy sea
with the eyes of desire
we captives gaze
in the direction of Spain.
The waves rock
the ship's human cargo.
We cry as we sing:
How dear you are, sweet Spain.
Luck has abandoned us;
our bodies are in chains;
our souls are in grave danger.
Cascades of tears fall from the sky
As we are taken to a land
of warlocks and black magic.
How dear you are, sweet Spain.

A few men requested an encore. By the third time, some had memorized the words and we sang together forgetting about the angry sea. Singing our song whose words we had strung together as if to prove we were alive, I felt a taste of freedom.

It was dawn. Behind a veil of fog there emerged a shape resembling a gigantic beehive rising from the base of a verdant mountain. White buildings amassed atop each other—

it could only be the port of Algiers. Remaining quiet, in case it was a dream, I shook my head and rubbed my eyes as the image of that city rose like the Tower of Babel, and then disappeared behind the fog. But the snoring, farting men, and the excrement we were covered in, were real enough. As the minutes passed, and the sky lightened, I saw clearly the breakwater that had been built as a barrier to make Algiers impregnable.

I nudged Rodrigo and said, "We're here." One of the men heard me, and soon all of them were awake, feverish with excitement and dread. Some of the men wept, sensing that our arrival there signaled merely the continuation of their torment. But I knew my chances of survival would be greater on land than in that hellish crawl space.

It was morning by the time the infamous port of Algiers loomed before us. The closer we got to land, the louder I heard droning drums punctuated by jubilant trumpets. The galleons carrying us entered the harbor, firing volleys at the sea behind them; in response, a deafening rumble sounded from within the walls of the city.

Once the ships had been secured, we were herded to the deck where silence settled over our group. I had been crouching for so long that I walked with bent knees throbbing as if I had nails hammered into my kneecaps. On the other hand, the fresh air and the scorching African sun on my damp, moldy flesh felt invigorating.

Our women and children had already disembarked and were waiting on the quay. Their husbands and fathers breathed with relief to see them, accompanied by their chambermaids and duennas. The women stood in a tight circle clutching their Rosaries, praying, looking with silent longing at their husbands and then at heaven imploringly. The mothers embraced their children and cradled their infants. Young women seemed to have grown wrinkles in captivity; the hair of other women had turned white. They would be put to work as maids and companions of rich Turkish and Moorish women. We all knew that if the ruler of Algiers, or any important Algerian, took a fancy to one of them, she would become part of his harem. How many of them had been defiled by the corsairs, as was the custom?

Arnaut Mamí's men busied themselves unloading the ships' loot, pulling down the sails, and rolling them up lengthwise. The oars were brought to the deck and then transported to a storage building nearby, along with the ballast. Eager to set foot on land and enter their city, the boatswains cracked their whips to make the men work faster. Yet all this activity could not distract me from the fact that we were now captives in the slave capital of North Africa.

We were ordered to remove our putrid clothes and crouch together on the deck. My rags adhered to me like a leprous skin. The corsairs hauled buckets of water from the sea and doused us, throwing squares of black soap at us, so that we could begin to wash off the grime which clung to our bodies like a dry, tough hide. Our scabby skin gave off a foul odor. When we were deemed sufficiently clean, we were instructed to soap and rub our faces and heads until they were lathered. Wielding sharp, gleaming blades, the corsairs shaved our heads and facial hair. Again we were drenched with buckets of water until we had washed away all vestiges of foam. I barely recognized the hairless and naked young man next to me as Rodrigo. By the time the corsairs put iron rings around my ankles, I already felt like a slave.

Buckets of drinking water and cups were distributed to us for the first time in days, as well as pieces of puffy and dry Algerian bread. We put our teeth to work, chewing without dignity, fighting for crumbs. Water and bread had never tasted better. It felt good to be clean and with a full stomach. Rodrigo and I sat next to each other in silence. As long as he was in my proximity, I was hopeful. I had to be strong and brave, to provide him a good example.

We were left in the sun for what seemed like hours. Our bodies dried, and our faces took on color—we no longer looked as if we were made of yellow wax. The sun's rays returned us to a human state.

"Now that we look presentable, they're ready to auction us off," a man near me commented.

"My children, remember we belong to God and not to any man," Father Gabriel, a young priest in our group, reminded us. Then one by one we approached him and kneeled at his feet. "Go with God, my child," he said to each of us as he made the sign of the cross on our foreheads.

The men hugged each other in farewell, whispering words of encouragement, as we waited for the ordeal to begin. It had already been my experience that when fortune turned her back on me, it would be awhile before she smiled again.

We were ordered off the ship, walked down a long wooden plank, and assembled on the quay. Algerian corsairs pointing long, sharp lances stood between us and the women and children.

Suddenly we were startled by a din that sounded like hundreds of iron hammers tapping the street. The viceroy of Algiers, Hassan Pasha, a Sardinian renegade sent by the Grand Turk to rule that den of thieves and murderers, was arriving with his attendants to have first choice of the new crop of captives.

A squadron of showily attired warriors entered first through the doors of the city. They were the infamous Albanian Janissaries I'd seen portrayed in paintings and picturebooks. Just the mention of the word *Janissary* struck terror in the hearts of Europeans. It was well known that they were paid according to the number of Christian scalps they presented to their captains after battle. When they killed scores of the enemy, ears or tongues were taken as proof. If the slaughter had been greater, index fingers would be accepted instead.

As the Janissaries entered, I felt as if a noose had tightened around my neck. Even our captors looked at them in awe. Their blue eyes resembled smooth, dull pieces of glass that had been in the ocean for a long time and then washed ashore. Their eyes caught no light, as if they belonged to soulless creatures. A chill shot down my spine.

The Janissaries carried harquebuses and wore long daggers. A horn shape, wrapped in shiny green cloth, extended from one side of their white turbans. From the tips of the horns drooped white and black ostrich plumes, which nodded as they marched in. The Janissaries' red leather shoes ended in a curled tip.

Behind the Janissaries marched Hassan Pasha's infantry, wearing long-sleeved blue robes that fell all the way to their ankles, and over them red vests open at the chest. These men projected the strength of monumental beasts. Their arrogant strut, which created an infernal metallic clatter with the heels of their shoes, was mesmerizing. For the rest of my captivity in Algiers, I feared that sound more than any other. Once a captive heard it, it was time to run, hide, cower, jump over a wall, try to become inconspicuous, wish you could disappear with a puff.

A pageant of gold-haired boys, dressed in rich Turkish costumes, marched behind the soldiers. They played drums, trumpets, flutes, and cymbals. Their music was funereal, as if meant to put dread in people's hearts, and their faces expressionless.

Behind the boys entered the cavalry, riding graceful white and black Arabian horses with bushy, perfectly groomed tails and bearing headdresses made of colorful plumes that fanned out in the manner of a peacock. Finally, there came Berber warriors on camels wearing dark-blue robes and headscarves that covered their faces, except for their midnight-colored eyes, which were rimmed by thick black lashes. These were the descendants of the Berber tribes that had invaded and conquered Andalusia centuries ago.

Neither the pope's processions that I had seen in the Vatican, nor those of the king of Spain when he paraded through the streets of Madrid on special occasions, could match such a vision of luxury, color, and might.

Hassan Pasha, beylerbey of the Grand Turk, viceroy of the province of Algiers, made his entrance seated on red cushions, on a platform that was carried by giant, barefoot Nubian slaves dressed in loincloths that barely covered their private parts. Their smooth skin was so lustrous they did not need ornaments to make them beautiful. Hassan Pasha's huge turban of crimson and deep blue was shaped like a full moon; from the middle of it projected a blue conical cap. He was draped in a cherry-colored robe that gleamed in the burning North African sun; a short animal wrap—copper-russet like the fur of a red fox—covered his shoulders. His full-length beard matched the color of the fur. He was massive, as if made of granite. His arched eyebrows and long, beaked nose gave him the look of a hawk ready to strike—and crack open—the skull of his prey.

With the help of a Nubian page he stood up and stepped off the platform, exuding immense power combined with unfathomable corruption and cruelty. The corsairs dropped to their knees, and placed their hands and foreheads on the ground. Arnaut Mamí was the first to raise his head. With a barely detectable nod, the beylerbey beckoned him to approach. Mamí advanced, taking small steps and bowing low. As he kneeled in front of Hassan Pasha, he took the hem of the beylerbey's robe, kissed it, and cried, "Praise be to Mohammed!"

The beylerbey inspected the boys first, but showed no interest in the crop offered to him. From the cadre that accompanied his regiment, I deduced that he was already well stocked with European lads. Quickly he moved to the women, and reserved for himself the most beautiful and distinguished-looking señoritas and their duennas.

As the auction of the men began, Mamí said to Hassan Pasha, pointing at me, "The cripple is mine, Your Highness." When the pasha saw my deformed hand, he flicked his own hand as if to make me vanish. I was pushed to one side of my group of compatriots and ordered to stand as close as I could to the women and children while still remaining chained to the other men. I felt then a pain more acute than that of the wounds I had received at Lepanto. Fear, disgust, and boiling anger overtook me. I swore I would do my best to someday hurt that walking incarnation of the devil.

The almighty pasha took more time choosing the men. First he singled out the strongest looking. Fortunately Rodrigo was of slender build—like all the Cervantes men. Then he engaged Arnaut Mamí in conversation, asking him to list the qualities and skills of the rest of the captives. Hassan Pasha claimed the two surgeons who were traveling aboard *El Sol*, as well as the carpenters, blacksmiths, and cooks. It was heartbreaking to see the desolation on the faces of these men, who knew that the pitiless ruler would value their skills so much they would die as slaves.

When Pasha finished his selection, he spoke in Spanish to the men who were now his property: "Listen well, Christians: as of this moment you're part of my army. From now on, if you work hard and don't try to escape, I will reward you. And if you convert to Islam," he paused so that the importance of his words would register on all present, "I swear by the name of Allah, I will give you your freedom."

The rest of the men the viceroy had discarded were ordered to stand aside. They would be auctioned last, to rich people who needed house servants, gardeners, and teachers.

The beylerbey returned to his cushion, sheltered from the sun under a parasol of white ostrich plumes held by an African colossus. The auction of the remaining captives began. Hassan Pasha presided over the scene with a stony expression and sleepy eyes.

The Spanish and Italian children traveling with their parents, and the cabin boys, were sold first. A handful of men clothed in luxurious garments approached the innocents. We had all heard about the Turkish sodomites, who were the greatest fear of all parents in Christendom. These merchants of innocence looked inside the boys' mouths and proceeded to count their teeth. Next, they pulled down the boys' pants. "This will have to be removed right away," said one buyer, yanking the foreskin of a trembling boy. It was the custom of the Turks to circumcise the boys as a first step in their conversion to Islam. There was no Christian unfamiliar with the story of a North African ruler who tied Christian boys to a column, then had them lashed until they embraced the Muslim faith. Those who refused to convert were beaten until their bodies were drained of blood.

A couple of sodomites started to haggle over two blond brothers. "I've fallen in love with these puppies!" a man shouted. "Arnaut Mamí, I must have them. I plan to adopt them as my own children when they become Muslims."

The mother of the boys convulsed as she shrieked and then fainted. There was a commotion among the women who came to her succor and tried to revive her.

Arnaut Mamí made a face of disgust at the women. He said to the merchant, "I can sell the youngest for a hundred and thirty gold escudos, he's just seven years old. At that age they never offer any resistance. You'll be able to mold him to your own liking, without too much trouble. As for the oldest"—he took the boy by the hand and paraded him like a dog of the finest breed—"even Ganymede's beauty would pale in comparison. You may not be able to afford him. This is the most perfect example of earthly beauty you'll ever see." Mamí ran his fingers through the boy's hair.

The boy's father tried to break away from our group. We restrained him, but he managed to yell, "Take your revolting hands off my boy, you monster!"

Mamí turned toward the man. "If I hear another sound from you, I will behead you and your woman." And to the buyer, "You'll never find a fairer catamite than this one. He will fetch easily five hundred gold escudos in any port on the Barbary Coast—and more in Turkey. Cadi, I'll sell you the oldest if you buy the runt too."

"By Mohammed, stop your haggling, Mamí," the man named Cadi replied, becoming extremely agitated. "If that's how it is, I'll take both of them. Just name your price. I must have this boy"—he pointed again at the eldest. "I've fallen for his beauty, his gentle manner." He addressed the trembling unfortunate: "What's your name?

"Felipe, sir."

"Listen to that honeyed voice," Cadi said in a swoon to those around him. "And he has the grace of a gazelle." To Felipe he cooed, "From now on, you will be my son and your name will be Harum."

The man embraced Felipe tightly. The boy tried to wrestle himself free, and Cadi motioned to two of his slaves to grab the brother. The smaller boy wailed and kicked violently.

Felipe started yelling, "Father, where are they taking us?"

The boys' father sobbed inconsolably as he shook his head. His mother had been revived and, feebly, she begged the buyer, "Please, please, sir. Let me embrace and kiss my boys for one last brief moment, since I'll have to live forever with the pain of losing them."

I feared for her life.

"Hurry up, woman," Cadi grumbled. "These boys are no longer your children: they belong to me."

Our women and men wept, some loudly.

Through her sobs, Felipe's mother said to her sons, "My children, never forget that you're Christians. Never deny our Lord Jesus Christ, our true Savior. Pray every day to His Holy Mother, who is the only one who can sever the chains that enslave you and who will give you back your freedom someday. Felipe, Jorge, never waver in your faith. Pray to Mary every day. Do not forget your parents, because we will never forget you. You will be in our thoughts and our prayers always."

She dropped to her knees and pounded the floor with her closed fists, and the boys were led away.

The auction of the women soon began. They held each other and cried as they prayed. The protests of our men rose in volume, and we pulled and rattled our shackles. The beylerbey gestured to his giants to lash us until we quieted down.

Later I learned that many of these buyers were Moriscos expelled from Andalusia; that they bought Spanish slaves as a way of humiliating the crown and as an act of nostalgia for the land from which they had been expelled, and which they still considered theirs.

The auction of the rest of the captives commenced. The orifices and limbs of our men were inspected, and poked, as if they were beasts of burden. Rodrigo was put on the auction block. The face of my beautiful brother had turned the color of snow, and his hands trembled slightly, but he did not show fear, and behaved with the dignity of a true hidalgo. I felt miserable and worthless, fearing that I would never see Rodrigo again. Once more I had failed my family. I thought of the pain of my parents when they found out what had happened to their sons.

"He's the cripple's brother." Mamí pointed at me. "The cripple will fetch a good ransom because he's a war hero and a protégé of Don John. So this one should fetch a good ransom too. I am not selling him cheap."

There were many bids for my brother, who was a fine and handsome example of the best of Spanish manhood. When Mamí advertised that Rodrigo played the vihuela, and had a beautiful singing voice, a merchant dressed in rich vestments offered two hundred gold escudos. The transaction completed, I overheard the man say to Rodrigo, "I'm buying you to teach music and singing to my children. You look like you will be a good tutor. If you teach my children well, one day you'll be free."

I knew that as a tutor in the house of a wealthy man, Rodrigo would be spared harsh labor and the lash, and he thus would have good chance of surviving in captivity. All was not lost.

The auction over, the beylerbey and merchants gone, those of us who stayed behind—about twenty men—were the property of Arnaut Mamí. He had kept the priests from *El Sol*, as well as the handful of gentlemen whose rich families would pay their ransom. The rest of the men would be put to hard labor, or become oarsmen on his ships.

We were handed our new slave clothing: two pieces of fabric—one to wrap around our waists, the other a coarse blanket to keep us warm—and we were informed the Bagnio Beylic was our destination. In single file, dragging our chains, we were led through the city gates. A throng of people—who had been waiting for the end of the auction—met us with taunts and jeers. Thus I entered the city known as the refuge of every depraved specimen of humanity that Noah had rejected from his ark. We began to climb the steps of Algiers's ancient casbah, and dragged our shackled feet over steep and ever narrowing streets. Children followed us screaming, "Christian dogs, you will eat desert sand here!" "Your Don John is not coming to rescue you! You will die in Algiers!" The demonic urchins hit us with rotten oranges and balls of still-steaming donkey dung. I would gladly have shoved the dung down the urchins' throats.

The casbah was a winding labyrinth, penumbrous, cool. Many of the houses looked as if they'd been built in Roman times, or even earlier, when Phoenicians had occupied Algiers. As we shuffled up the hill, the stone steps seemed to multiply. Near the summit of the city the streets were so narrow only one man at a time could traverse them. Sturdy burros carried weighty loads up adjacent alleys. From the roofs of the dwellings men cackled and insulted us as we struggled with the slippery steps. Unveiled, but demure, Moorish women peered at us from the oval-shaped windows of their homes. Christians were considered so lowly, I later learned, that Algerian women did not have to cover their faces in our presence.

It was late afternoon when we arrived at a plaza at the top of the casbah. A rectangular white fort rose before us; its tall corner towers were patrolled by armed guards. We had arrived at Bagnio Beylic, infamous throughout the Mediterranean for its harshness. It had been built almost a hundred years earlier by the brutal Barbarosa brothers as a detention camp for those they had captured at sea and were holding for ransom. We were herded inside, where the long chain linking was removed; but our ankles remained shackled. The prison's interior walls, lined with rooms on two levels, faced a cobblestone courtyard where hundreds of men milled about.

Despite my exhaustion, I wended my way through the crowd. My ears recognized many languages being spoken. The captives, it seemed, were gathered by nationality: Englishmen, Frenchmen, Greeks, Italians, Portuguese, and Albanians. Others spoke in languages I did not recognize.

A large number of Spaniards squatted on the floor, gambling. My fellow captives began to mingle timidly with our compatriots. I watched the scene, unsure of what to do next. If there were any gentlemen among my captive countrymen, slavery had transformed them into untrustworthy types. As soon as possible, I would have to grow eyes in the back of my head.

A captive playing dice shouted from the circle huddled on the floor, "You standing there! What's your name? Where were you captured?"

When I satisfied the man's curiosity, the gamblers went back to their game. My aching legs and blistered feet prompted me to sit down on the cold floor. I threw around my shoulders the blanket we had been given at the quay and drew up my knees to rest my head against them before closing my eyes. I was in that position when a voice addressed me.

"Are you the son of Don Rodrigo Cervantes?"

A short man, with an extended belly and stubby legs,

stood before me, his bare feet caked with dirt. He smiled, and instantly his face took on a picaresque air, that of a survivor.

"I knew you when you were a youth," he said. "My name is Sancho Panza, a son of the noble town of Esquivias, somewhere deep in La Mancha, famous for its fat tasty lentils and the best, most medicinal wine. Which, in case you don't know, is the only wine our magnificent king drinks." He crouched across from me.

This was all too incredible, yet the mention of my father cheered me up. "How do you know my father, Señor Sancho?"

"Don Rodrigo treated me when I had no money. After my master, His Worship the late Count of Ordóñez, died, his unnatural children threw me out on the street, even though I had served their father since long before they were born." Sancho sighed. "What's past is past," he said, then rubbed his eyes, as if to make sure I was still there. "You were a student at the Estudio de la Villa at that time; a mere lad. You've changed a lot. I would not have recognized you from those days. But when I heard you say your name, I knew you had to be Don Rodrigo's son. You look like you were made from the same mold."

Despite my exhaustion, this odd man amused me. Perhaps he could, for a brief moment, make me think of happier times.

"Your father was so proud of you," he went on. "Did you know he recited your poems to his patients? That sonnet, the one that got the award, I must have heard it a hundred times. After Don Rodrigo finished his recitation he would say, *My friends, Ars longa, vita brevis*. One day, a patient with a gangrenous leg, who wasn't getting any better despite all the leechings your father subjected him to, asked what those words meant.

"*Those are the words of the great Virgil*, Don Rodrigo said.

"*Was Virgil a doctor?* the man wanted to know.

"*My friend,* your father explained, as if to a child, puzzled there was *anybody* who didn't know who Virgil was—I knew a Virgil in Esquivias, Don Miguel, but I don't think your honorable father meant him, as the Esquivian Virgil was a butcher—*those are the only words we ever need to remember: Art is forever, life is short. Virgil was a poet—a doctor of souls.*

"The patient shouted: *And this is what you, as a doctor, believe, Don Rodrigo—that life is short? No wonder my leg keeps rotting here!* He barely finished speaking when the man rolled over on his cot to the floor and practically crawled out of your father's infirmary."

Sancho patted his mountainous stomach to stop his fit of laughter. I laughed too. It had been awhile since I'd heard the sound of my own laughter.

His reminiscing finished, Sancho said, "I don't mean to pry, my young squire, but what happened to your arm? And pray tell your story including its periods and commas. I like well-rounded tales."

Not wanting to relive painful moments of the past, I gave him an abbreviated account of how I was wounded at Lepanto.

But Sancho was determined not to leave me alone. "What do you know about the bagnio?"

"Is there anything I should know?"

"You do know this is not a bathhouse, don't you? Though most men here need to take a bath urgently. This is not a jail like the ones in Spain. The Turkish dogs let us come and go as we please, as long as we are back behind the walls by the first evening call to prayer, when they close the doors. We are allowed to go out, not because they are good-hearted, but because we have to earn the money to feed and clothe ourselves. We are the lucky ones. These asses think we all have families that will pay our ransom. That's why our backs won't be broken repairing roads, pushing huge pieces of marble, making pagan monuments, building mosques or tombs for Moors with deep coffers, or, the worst of all possible punishments, becoming oarsmen in their death ships. They think your family has money. Has Don Rodrigo become prosperous since I last saw him? His Worship used to talk about his rich relations."

I told him about Don John of Austria's letter.

"What bad luck that a letter from our great prince would bring so much misfortune. As for me, my illustrious friend, I'm as poor as the day I came bawling out of my sainted mother's belly. But I was damned if I was going to work as an oarsman or a laborer, so I told them I was a member of a rich Galician family. Thank God during my years of service to His Excellency the Count of Ordóñez, all I did was wash the chamber pots of my master and serve his meals. I have the hands of a prince." He extended them in front of me for my approval. Indeed, despite his general uncouth aspect, his hands looked immaculate. "These are hands that have worn gloves for many years. When the dim-witted Turk asked to inspect them, that son of an infidel whore remarked they were as smooth as polished ivory. Since the Turk was still not convinced, I said: *Adversus solem. Amantes sunt. Donecut est in lectus consequat consequat. Vivamus a tellus.*" Sancho burst in laughter. "An educated hidalgo such as you will know that I was speaking nonsense. These were all words I'd heard my master say over the years." Again he patted his belly with quick taps to collect himself.

I laughed out loud. Sorrow had been my companion for so long that I hadn't had a good laugh since before Lepanto.

"Now listen to me, my young and esteemed squire. Try to stay healthy, for he who has health has hope; and he who has hope has everything. Even though some days free-

dom seems farther than earth from heaven, I pray to God
to send with speed Don John's forces to Algiers to liberate
us. I will die an optimist. Yes, sir."

Who was this philosopher? I wondered.

"Young Miguel, thank your lucky stars you've met me.
For your own sake, be so good as to favor me with your
complete attention. The least I can do to show my gratitude
to your noble-hearted father is to teach you everything you
need to know to survive in this viper pit. I've been here
four years, and I've seen many men who arrived with me
die in this land of pagans and idolaters. I'm sure I don't
need to remind you that the early sparrow gets the worm.
Tomorrow, as soon as the doors of the bagnio open with
the first call to prayer from the mosque—you'll recognize
the call because it sounds like a man who's been trying to
relieve himself for a month and still can't do it—we'll go
down to the port to meet the fishermen who return with
the rising sun. All the fish they don't want, they toss to the
dogs or throw back to the sea. If they don't have any fish to
throw away, there are always plenty of sea urchins." Sancho made a face. "I would not have eaten such repulsive
creatures back in Spain, where I never lacked for a crust
of bread, a slice of cheese, or an onion. But when there's
no horses, we saddle dogs." He paused, then added, "It's
going to be hard for you to survive here with a lame arm."
Sancho held his head between his hands and then smiled.
"Do you still write poetry? I hope so. Algiers is the best
place in the world for a poet. These cruel Moors only respect two kinds of people: madmen and poets. According
to their crazy religion, poets and locos are God's blessed
people and must be respected because they are in constant
contact with Him."

I wondered what other pieces of wisdom the fat man
had in store for me.

Sancho got up. "The warden's men are collecting the fee to sleep in the rooms. If you don't have enough money for a place in a room, you have to sleep out here with heaven as your blanket. Unfortunately, I have barely enough to pay for my own place tonight. Many are the nights when I've had to stay out here."

All I possessed were the iron chains around my ankles—which didn't belong to me—and the clothing hanging on my emaciated body.

"You wait here while I go inside to find you an extra blanket. The nights get chilly this time of year."

Notwithstanding Sancho's ample frame, he sprang to his feet with the agility of a dancer and hurried away, zig-zagging among the crowd.

The Algerian sky shimmered with the light of the moon. I closed my sleepy eyes. I was beginning to drift off when I heard, accompanied by a flute, an eerie wail, a lamentation that was not meant for humankind, but for the heavens: it was a late-night call to prayer coming from the mosque. The plaintive voice, like an invisible kite, ascended from the tip of the minaret toward the grape-black African sky powdered by stars. An absolute exhaustion overtook me, a weariness at what I was beginning to accept as the curse of my sad fate. I saw my soul leave my body and fly over a glassy, doleful sea, a sea without any shoreline. The first day of my life as a captive in Algiers had come to an end.

CHAPTER 4
MY MORTAL ENEMY
1576

~*Luis*~

All things change and we change with them. It was hard to believe that the tender affection I felt for Miguel during our school days in Madrid had turned to animosity. Our Redeemer's message is to forgive those who injure us, but my heart blackened and seethed with hatred and I couldn't stop its petrifaction. I did not recognize myself anymore. If I examined my features in a mirror, I looked exactly the same, but my soul was no longer that of the gentleman and Christian I professed to be. There was no light in my eyes. My best friend's betrayal revealed to me that hatred, like love, is an uncontrollable emotion, one that lived and grew in me like a heaving, insatiable incubus I could not exorcise. Hatred, I discovered, could outlast love.

I was relieved when Miguel wrote me from Rome. I had won. What the eyes cannot see, the heart cannot feel. There was truth to that. He was far enough away not to represent an immediate threat to my happiness with Mercedes. The epistles he sent me during the time he worked for the cardinal went unanswered. They were full of anecdotes about the colorful—and important—people he met in Rome, his excited comments about the Italian poets he read in Dante's language, his swooning descriptions of the great works of art in the churches, basilicas, and private homes. Yet after a while there was a lull in his letter writing. Perhaps he came to realize I was not going to answer him.

Two years went by. Then, one evening at my grandparents' home after dinner, Mercedes and I went for a stroll in the flowering orchard. We meandered in silence until Mercedes sat down on a stone bench in an arbor. I sat next to her. It was April, the air was redolent of fragrant blossoms. The birds that hid in the thickets during the hot hours of the day had begun to emerge in search of insects and had commenced their evening twitters. Mercedes seemed enraptured by the sweetness of the moment. I said, "I've been thinking, my love, why wait three more years for the start of our happiness?"

Mercedes looked away, her gaze lost in a shadowy corner of the orchard. Though physically she remained by my side, her mind was somewhere else. After graduation I hoped my family would intercede to find me work in His Majesty's court. My dream was to settle with Mercedes in Madrid, to raise a family, and to devote my free hours to poetry. I had been taught that modesty is a quality every true gentleman must have. So I had no grand dreams; big dreams were for adventurers and soldiers of fortune. My aspirations were those of most men of my station.

"Why the sudden change in plans?" She looked puzzled. "Why not wait until you graduate, as we discussed? Marriage could distract you from your studies, Luis."

I was not one of those men who thought that a woman was by nature a defective creature. Despite my obfuscated state I could see that her objection was perfectly legitimate. Mercedes was discreet, the embodiment of immaculate virtue, of purity itself. Her reputation was above all suspicion and blemish. I was sure there was no other woman in Spain as chaste as she was. However, this was the first time she had said no to me, and the beast of jealousy roared inside me. What reason could she have for delaying my wedding proposal, other than secretly loving Miguel and hoping he would return?

"I've consulted with my parents and our grandparents, and they have raised no objection. Besides," I added, knowing she loved living in Toledo with our grandparents, "if you like, you can live here until I finish school. I will come visit at every possible opportunity."

"I cannot give you an answer today, Luis." Mercedes sighed, then took my hands in hers and held them against her cheek. The warmth of her hands made me want to kiss her on the lips and ravish her. When her long hair and her eyelashes brushed my skin, I had to still the trembling I felt overcoming me. She spoke, remaining in the same position, and her breath stroked the skin of my hands. "This is a complete surprise. I need more time to think about it before I agree to the change in our plans."

At that moment I regretted not having punctured Miguel's heart with my sword the day I found him in Mercedes's chamber. I pulled my hands away from hers, got up, and walked back to the house alone.

The joyous news came to Alcalá that our forces had defeated the Turks at Lepanto. As was the case after major battles fought in foreign lands, it took months before the names of the survivors were printed on the broadsheets that were glued on the walls of the government buildings. The day I heard from a visitor to my house that the broadsheets were posted, I rushed out to read with rapt attention the names of the survivors. Rodrigo Cervantes's name appeared as a survivor, but there was no mention of Miguel. The Turks had taken no prisoners. Could it be that he was dead?

A few days later in Toledo, my grandmother, who went

to early Mass every day, asked during supper, "Luis, is Rodrigo Cervantes a relative of your friend Miguel?" It was the first time since Miguel had fled Madrid that his name had been mentioned in my presence. "I read his name on a broadsheet outside the church this morning."

"I read the list of survivors that was published in Alcalá," I acknowledged. "Miguel's name was not on it." I kept my head low, staring at the roast leg of lamb in front of me. The meat on my plate suddenly nauseated me. I dared not look in the direction of Mercedes. I took the silence around the table to mean that I was expected to say more. "Abuela, I've been very sad, as you can imagine. He was my dearest friend in the years before I went to Alcalá. I'd never had a friend like that before." I should have ended it there. Instead, I heard myself saying, "I wanted to spare all of you. But I might as well tell you that one of my classmates ran into Miguel's father in Madrid. Don Rodrigo informed him that Miguel's body has not been found. The last time he was seen during the battle, he was fatally wounded. Don Rodrigo fears that Miguel's corpse sank to the bottom of the Bay of Corinth." It was the biggest lie I had ever told, a lie so grievous I wondered whether it was a mortal sin to wish the death of someone I knew—anyone's death, for that matter. It was too late now. I could not go back in time to erase my words.

"I'm sorry to hear it," my grandfather responded. "I know he was like a brother to you. May God keep him in His Glory." He crossed himself.

My grandmother also crossed herself. "I will have a Mass said for his soul," she said.

I looked in Mercedes's direction: her eyes were closed, and a gleaming tear slid down her cheek.

A few months after the scene in the garden, I heard from

Miguel. The wretch was still alive. This time his letters were filled with a woeful tale of the wounds he received fighting the Turks, making it sound as if his heroics alone were responsible for crushing the Ottoman navy. When he was not boasting, Miguel complained about his slow recovery in the Italian hospitals, and the loss of the use of his left hand. I felt a burst of joy when I heard he was crippled. In the same breath, I hated myself for rejoicing in the misery of another human being, especially someone I had once loved without reservation. I knew it was a sin and unchristian to feel that way, even about my enemy, but my hatred was stronger than my faith.

In his letter, Miguel pleaded with me to intercede in the king's courts with high officials I knew through my family, to expedite the back payment of his wages and to grant him the pension due to invalid soldiers. I burned his letters.

Praemonitus pramunitus, my father used to say. Why leave it to chance? As unlikely as it seemed, what if Miguel somehow managed to return to Spain? I was aware that the wheel of Fortune took unpredictable turns. Was my fear justified or irrational? I would never let Miguel take Mercedes away from me. Still, I had to take decisive action.

Mercedes married me in a private ceremony in Toledo attended only by our family. That day, which should have been one of the happiest of my life, was marred by the circumstances under which Mercedes had changed her mind. Had she been hoping that Miguel would return to Spain?

My jealousy notwithstanding, I couldn't have asked for a more beautiful or considerate or gentle wife. Our harmonious domesticity seemed to indicate that we would be as happy in our marriage as my parents were in theirs. As for Miguel, Mercedes was now my wife. Even if he managed to return to Castile, he could never take her away from me.

Mercedes remained with our grandparents until I finished my studies at Alcalá. Not long after our wedding, she became gravid with child. The news filled me with the greatest joy I've ever known. If it pleased God, I hoped there would be many more children to come. Though her health had always been good, from the very beginning her pregnancy was fraught with complications. Diego was born in the seventh month, and Mercedes bled so much during the birth that the doctors feared for her life for the first forty-eight hours afterward.

The joy of fatherhood was diminished by Diego's sickly constitution. He would often refuse the teats of the wet nurses we brought to the house, and Mercedes's breasts produced but a few opaque drops of milk. My son's growth was almost imperceptible. A year after his birth, Diego was so skinny and frail I feared crushing one of his ribs when I lifted him in my arms. He was as pale as a white lily, as if no blood ran in his veins. Without an apparent reason, he would cry for hours, sometimes for days, not with the anger of infants, but as if he mourned an inconsolable loss. No matter where I was in the house, or how far I tried to get away from his wailing, I could still hear him. Even when I was leagues away in my residence in Alcalá, after I said my prayers at night and snuffed the candle, I could hear him crying in the darkness, as clearly as if his cradle were next to my bed.

Diego's frailty was our greatest worry, and Mercedes became his shadow. Her precautions bordered on the unhealthy: she insisted on first tasting everything he ate; she made sure that he never stepped on the floor barefoot; that he was not exposed to the sun during the hottest hours of the day; that he was not ever caught in the rain; that he avoided the evening's dew; that he was never in the proximity of anyone with a cold, or a cough, or recovering from a fever or any kind of illness; that he was swaddled in heavy fur wraps at night; that after his baths, he sat by a fire, sipping a hot cup of chocolate, until his entire body was dry.

Diego seemed to accept all the excessive concern with forbearance. Mercedes's devotion to our son was so complete that she began neglecting her appearance. Yet despite her lack of vanity, motherhood had endowed her with a ripeness and softness that made her lovelier than ever. My desire for her grew. She would never again be as beautiful as she was after the birth of Diego. But I became invisible to her, an acquaintance living in the same house. She forgot her wifely duties to me, and slept on a cot by Diego's bedside.

Was God punishing me for my unfounded jealousy about Mercedes? For my hatred of Miguel? Hatred was, I knew, a slap to God's face. Obviously I was not a good Christian. In my youth, as a student in Madrid, poetry had been my religion. Yes, I was a dutiful Catholic: I fasted when I was supposed to fast; I went to Mass on Sundays; I confessed and received Holy Communion every week; I observed the religious holidays. I did everything that was expected of me, but I did not *live* for God: I wanted the earthly rewards. I worked harder to attain those than to earn my place in heaven, which I believed was virtually guaranteed me by the apposite life I led. I began to go to Mass at dawn daily; when that proved insufficient to quell the disquiet in my soul, I started to pray for a few hours every day, like Grandfather Lara did. I prayed for the health of my son; that he would grow stronger and become a man; above all, that the sins of the father would not be visited on the son.

As a graduation present, my parents gave us a large

and handsome house near our ancestral home. I hoped the move to Madrid would signal a new start for our marriage, and that Madrid's distractions would bring some gaiety into our lives. Perhaps furnishing the house would provide a pleasant diversion for Mercedes. As befitted our station, our home was one of Madrid's elegant residences. Momentarily, the old spark in Mercedes's eyes came back. But as the months passed, and we settled into our new life, she became once more solely concerned with Diego's well-being. Leonela had come to live with us as Mercedes's maid-in-waiting. She supervised the servants, arranged the furniture, hung the portraits of our ancestors, oversaw the work of the gardener, planned our meals with the cook.

Through my family's influence, I was secured a position as an officer in the Department of Collections of the Guardas of Castile. My office was in charge of collecting everywhere in the kingdom the taxes that financed the king's army, navy, and public works. My work required that I travel throughout Spain to supervise the books kept by our auditors. I enjoyed seeing all of Spain and visiting its remotest corners. Yet I always looked forward to returning home, where Diego would receive me with his sweet smile, kisses, and hugs. My son hadn't stopped crying, but now he wept silently, and only while he slept. Some nights I would sit by his bed and watch his fitful crying, tears falling out of his eyes so copiously that his pillow would be wet by morning. The most eminent doctors in Madrid came to visit Diego and proclaimed him small for his age; otherwise, he was in good health. One day, when he was old enough to understand, I asked him, "Tell me, my son, are you in pain at night? Show me where it hurts."

"It doesn't hurt, Papá, but it's sad here," he answered sweetly, as he placed his little hand on his chest, on top of his heart.

I kept this conversation to myself. I became convinced my son's crying was a sign from God. Could Diego be one of His saints? Had he come into the world to shed tears for the sins of humanity? For my sins?

Mercedes and I had no choice but to accept Diego's chronic crying as no more than an idiosyncrasy. It was in our interest not to allow the situation to be known all over Madrid. If the Holy Office found out about it, how would they interpret my son's crying? How would they react? Would he have to appear in front of them?

Mercedes became more distant, yet there was little discord between us. It was apparent to me, and perhaps even to my parents, that I loved her more than she loved me. The intimacy of our youth was gone, and this saddened me. It was hard to pinpoint at what exact moment we had begun to live separate lives. Was it after Diego's birth? Had my unvoiced suspicions created a distance between us? She spent most of her time with Diego and Leonela. I tried to reignite the old bond: I brought Mercedes lavish presents from my trips; I inquired about her life when I was not around. Her usual reply was a litany: "Diego's health requires my constant attention, Luis. He's not like other children. I have no other life. I want no other life. If my son is not well, I am not well."

There was so much corruption among the officials in government that I wanted to do my work with exemplary probity. My assiduousness caught the eye of my superiors and, before long, His Catholic Majesty rewarded my vigilance with an important position in the Guardas. I would be based in Madrid, in a building that belonged to Las Cortes.

It could not be good for Diego to spend all his time surrounded by women. Despite the doctors' pronouncements, no friends were allowed to visit him, for fear of the illnesses of childhood. Diego was bright, full of questions, and loved to hear stories read to him. My dreams of becoming a poet had been derailed by the path fortune had laid out for me. I had little time to read and savor poetry, let alone write it. But when I noticed Diego's interest in stories, I began to hope he would grow up to become the poet I knew I'd never be. My work and the education of my son became the center of my life.

Mercedes's remoteness was now a permanent state. I thought that if she became less anxious about Diego's health, she might return to being the Mercedes I had known all my life.

Then word reached Madrid that the passengers on the vessel *El Sol*, including Miguel and his brother Rodrigo, had been captured on their way to Spain by Algerian corsairs. Why had I been cursed with Miguel's shadow? What would I have to do to never hear about him again?

One night soon after I heard the news, I was dining in my chamber alone, as had become my habit since we moved to Madrid, when there was a knock on my door. My attendant opened it and Mercedes came in, apparently upset. Something important must have happened: it had been awhile since she had visited my chambers. "I'll ring for you when I've finished my supper," I said to my servant and waved my hand in the direction of the door. Mercedes sat at the table across from me. I moved my dinner plate aside and took a sip of wine. By the light of the candle, she looked spectral, as if she hadn't slept in a long time. The gleam in her eyes perturbed me. "Has anything happen to Diego?" I asked.

"No, Diego is well, thank God. He's already asleep." She went on, "Leonela came home with the news about Miguel de Cervantes and his brother. Why did you lie to me, Luis? Why did you tell me he had died at Lepanto?"

That she could be interested in Miguel after so many years hurt me, and it made me want to hurt her back. So I had not been imagining things—there was a basis for my suspicions. I said, "I didn't think you'd care whether he lived or died. As I got to know him better, I realized he was no friend of mine, but someone who wanted to harm me. I didn't want to hear his name mentioned again in my home. As far as I'm concerned, he's dead."

"From the time we were children, Luis," she began, her voice quivering with anger, "I admired your rectitude, your sense of what's right and what's wrong. Unlike me, unlike most people, I thought you were incapable of lying. You represented the best of Spanish manhood; I was sure I would never meet a better man than you. That's why I grew up loving you, not the way one loves a cousin, but the way a husband is loved; that's why I accepted the idea that one day we would get married. I didn't know what romantic love was—except for the way it was talked about in the novels of chivalry—so I confused the admiration you inspired in me for love."

I should have asked her to say no more and leave my chamber. Better, I should have left it myself. I knew that the longer she went on, the more irreparable would be the damage done to our marriage. Instead, I hung my head and kept silent, though I wanted to scream, *If I became a liar, Mercedes, it was because Miguel de Cervantes forced me to do so. Unlike him, I was not born an impostor!*

Mercedes's features became distorted; her pallor intensified. She got up from her chair and paced in front of me, with her fists clenched against her breasts.

"While my feelings for you were genuine and pure," she continued, "I knew I didn't love you the way a wife is supposed to love her husband. I thought that because of your wonderful qualities, and with the passage of time, I would come to love you the way I ought to. But from the moment I saw Miguel de Cervantes, something that had lain dormant in my heart was stirred." Her eyes teared, and her open hands, which she rested on her cheeks, trembled in tiny spasms. Mercedes seemed incapable of measuring her words, or of comprehending the effect they had on me. "Miguel brought laughter into my secluded world. He awakened my fantasy; he made me dream. He represented the world from which I had been sheltered. How often I had thought of those unfortunate women who dressed as men to go out in the world—to see all the things that are impossible to examine with your own eyes when you are a woman forced to spend most of your life behind the walls of your familial home. When Miguel came through our front door it was as if the world—that part of the world that I could only intuit—had been brought to me. He represented a knowledge of things I didn't know and for which I was hungry."

The reasons for her betrayal were untenable. If she had confided in me how much she longed to see the outside world, I would have shown her what lay beyond the walls of our grandparents' home. Yet, despite the jabbing pain I felt in my heart, a part of me was relieved. My suspicions were not unfounded after all: I had not maligned Mercedes; I did not have to ask her forgiveness; she was not the pure example of womanhood I had taken her for. It was as if in an instant my life, everything I had loved and believed in, had been sullied. At that moment I wanted to die. I would have run out of that room and killed myself, if I didn't know that suicide is the worst offense to God. I will live for Diego. I will live for my son. And then I thought, I will not rest until Miguel de Cervantes is dead.

Mercedes had more to say: "Believe me when I tell you

that I fought my feelings for him." She shook her head with violence and let out a sharp sob of a wounded beast that made me shudder. "But my passion was stronger than me. I have loved Miguel all these years, and always will." There was hatred in her gaze; I felt faint when I realized that it was aimed at me. "I agreed to marry you, Luis, because I believed you when you told us at the dinner table that Miguel had died in battle." She paused. There was absolute silence in my chamber, but a chorus of voices clamored in my head. The volume of her voice reached a crescendo. "Why did you lie to me? If you hadn't, perhaps in time I might have forgotten Miguel and come to love you as my husband. Now I can never forgive you for your lie, Luis. Never. Never."

"I did it because I loved you," I blurted out pathetically, not wanting to believe that *my* Mercedes was bent upon humiliating me. "I did it because I didn't want to lose you. I didn't want to see you dishonored by a man unworthy of you."

The horrible words she said next have festered in my brain and heart from that night: "Do you remember that scene in my bedchamber, when Miguel professed his love for me and I turned him away? We staged that, so you would not suspect us anymore and we could continue seeing each other. It was hard for me not to laugh knowing you were behind the curtain. But I didn't want to harm you; I just couldn't live without Miguel's caresses."

The way she said "we" made me feel as if she had sliced me into hundreds of pieces and then sprinkled them with salt. "Basta!" I screamed, rising from my chair and rushing out of my chamber before I strangled her to death. From that moment on, the tranquility in which I had spent most of my days vanished, never to return.

For a true Castilian, honor is everything. My honor, my

surname, and my blood were one. Mercedes's dishonorable behavior dishonored my family and me. And a man despoiled of his honor was better off dead. If her reputation was stained in my eyes, my whole life was a fraud. Still, I wanted to find something good in my wife. How was it possible that I had been so mistaken about her? If the woman I thought I had known from the time I was a child was a complete stranger to me, if I had been mistaken about Mercedes, what could I believe in? If I had been so obtuse about her true nature, what kind of oblivious life had I led? If I could not tell the truth from a lie, who was I? Had I played any role in her dishonesty? If she was a villainess, perhaps I was not blameless. If she had been corrupted by her proximity to Miguel, was I not just as guilty for having brought him into her life?

My wife, the only woman I had loved, the woman I had continued to love despite the joylessness of our marriage, the woman who had been my paradise on earth, the mother of my only son, in an instant had become my torturer. And I, who thought of myself as one of the luckiest men, because unlike so many others I had heard of, I would never have to place my wife in a house guarded by iron rails to safeguard her chastity, I now knew that I could never again trust Mercedes. Without trust there could be no true love. And I, who had dreamed that our marriage would be the perfect union of two souls, two different people becoming one flesh, one blood, now saw my wife cast in a lewd light. I had been cruelly deceived. Was the Mercedes who had appeared to me in the guise of one of God's angels really Satan in female guise?

Anyone who met Mercedes was immediately struck by her exquisite diamondlike perfection. But that diamond had cracked, and an excremental vein had ruptured its crystalline pool of light, rendering it worthless. That day, and for many days afterward, I wanted to strangle Mercedes and watch life ebb out of her as her eyes went dark.

Over the past several years, my loathing of Miguel had, if anything, abated. But after Mercedes's confession I wanted desperately to do violence not just to her, but above all to him. From that night on, the tenacious weed of hatred found in my soul fertile ground and shot out roots that choked everything alive inside me. The very ground I stood on felt barren and scorched, as if it had been razed by hell's flames. The measures I had taken to prevent Miguel from returning to Spain were not enough. My fantasies of the ways in which he would die grew more elaborate: I would have him poisoned; I would send a paid murderer to Algiers to kill him; but first, I would have his brother's head hacked off, while Miguel watched, before he himself was decapitated.

I no longer had anything that deserved to be called a life. My dreams reenacted Miguel's and Mercedes's betrayal, and I could not control the nightmares of fire-breathing, winged gargoyles that howled demonic tirades into my ears. I would wake up covered in sweat, feverish, gasping for breath, my head throbbing, my fists clenched, my jaws locked, my limbs aching, as if the ceiling of my bedchamber had crumbled on top of me. I dreaded going to sleep. Often I would stay awake all night, praying. I had the sensation I went through life sleepwalking.

My feelings were unchristian, I knew. I despised who I had become; my self-loathing was unbearable. I was convinced that God would punish me horribly if I continued to stew in hatred. My own shadow frightened me. My own reflection made me shudder: the flames of hell flickered in my eyes.

"Say the Rosary every night, or as many times as you

need, until the voices in your head quiet down," my confessor, Father Timoteo, advised. "Only the Holy Mother of Christ can restore you to your former humanity. Pray to her, my son, dedicate your life to her, and to Jesus Christ, because only they can deliver you from Satan's clutches. Don't act on your wrath," he added, "and the door to God will remain open to you, Luis. You must purify yourself, my son; you must wash your sinful thoughts with holy water. Only your total devotion to the divine mercy of Jesus will save you."

I found a measure of relief from the burning hatred for Miguel and for Mercedes only when I said the Holy Rosary. All my life I had heard it prayed in churches and in my own house, daily. I always was a good Catholic, but not a particularly pious one. Occasionally, I had joined my family and said it too. I said it respectfully, dutifully, but without the fervor of my elders, or of most of the parishioners I saw in Spain's churches. I needed to pray to the Virgin Mary with all my heart. I would pray until, convinced of my sincere remorse, she would reveal to me the face of Christ when I touched the depths of His immense love for us sinners.

"If you believe with purity of heart," Father Timoteo promised me, "you will be showered with Graces that the Mother of Christ herself will place in the palms of your hands."

Of the three Mysteries of the Rosary, it was the contemplation of the Mystery of Joy that brought me the fullest consolation. Christ's mystery, I realized, was the joy He spread, the happiness He brought us and which delivered the world from darkness each day. I would not know Our Redeemer's love until His loving joy washed away my sins and I felt cleansed. That would be the sign that He had forgiven me. Only then would my soul be reborn by the

Holy Spirit. Holding the Rosary in my hands, counting the beads, pausing to reflect on the Mysteries, I was aware of the sweet chain that bound me to God. But I needed a constant heart to get close to Him. Unless I let Christ's loving joy into my heart, I would live in torment for the rest of my days. If Christ had become a servant of man, and forgave those who had wronged him, I had to devote my life not to hatred, but to forgiveness and to helping others, in order to follow His example. Only then would I become worthy of understanding the Mystery of Mary's immaculate conception. It was her complete purity and goodness that had made her worthy to be the mother of the Son of God. I had to practice goodness in all my acts, if I was going to be rewarded with the precious vision that would deliver me: to see the Virgin dressed by the sun, standing on a full moon, and wearing a crown of twelve stars. Only then would I know that Christ had forgiven me for my pride, my arrogance, the lovelessness that dwelled in my barren heart.

Most nights, on my knees, alone in my chamber, I recited the Holy Rosary until dawn. Then I lashed myself ten times and wore a hair shirt to go to sleep for a few hours. My back was always swollen and painful, and sweated blood as if I bore the stigmata. Only my faithful servant Juan, who helped me bathe, who helped me dress, who washed out the blood from my garments, and ironed them, and who applied ointments to my tortured flesh, knew of it.

My love of Christ would be shown through my good deeds. Under the guidance of Father Timoteo, I began to give alms to the poor—to feed the hungry who knocked on our door, to clothe the naked and shoeless who lived in Madrid's filthy alleys and who died from exposure in the cold months. I opened my coffers to the city orphanages. I gave generously to the Dominican missionaries who traveled to the Indies to convert the heathens. Through these actions I was blessed with grains of peace.

Time passed. I was named a magistrate of the king's Royal Council, a position of high rank. Diego was still small for his age and prone to childhood illnesses, but his gentle nature provided me with the warmth and affection that otherwise remained absent from my life. Mercedes and I attended family functions together, but we were really strangers dwelling under the same house made of ice. My former love for her had withered. I hadn't quite forgiven her, but I felt no hatred for her, either. I thanked God for the precious joys in my life, for His blessings and His Grace. I couldn't say I was happy, but I found a measure of solace in beginning to accept my grievous fate.

One day, an envelope made of expensive paper arrived on my desk. There was no forwarding address. It was not the usual kind of official mail I received at work. I tarried before opening it. Then, curiosity tempted me. I broke the seal and pulled out a sheet of scented rose paper that read:

Your Excellency,

My name is Andrea Cervantes, the younger sister of Miguel. I wouldn't be surprised if you don't remember me. It has been many years since the last time I saw you at my parents' home. It is my most fervent wish that this letter finds you and your loved ones enjoying good health and God's blessings.

After much hesitation, knowing how busy you must be and the important affairs you must attend to, God gave me enough courage to ask, on my knees, for an audience with Your Excellency. You must have heard, Don Luis, about the dire circumstances under which my brothers are held in Algiers . . .

Although my memories of Andrea filled me with revulsion, later that day—after much debating with myself—I made up my mind to pay her a visit. Miguel's sister's home was located in the respectable vicinity of the Convent of the Descalzas Reales, on a street too narrow for coaches. I alighted and told my carriers not to wait for me. The bells of the churches had just tolled four times, and my plan was to make my visit brief, so that I could walk home while there was still daylight.

Unhealthy curiosity was always one of my gravest defects. I knew it was better to let sleeping dogs lie; that poison-filled, angry scorpions crawled out from under stones when you began digging in the remains of the past. And yet, I wanted to hear from the lips of Andrea Cervantes about the miserable life Miguel was living as a slave in Algiers. I was standing before her door, the iron knocker in my hand, when suddenly it opened and Andrea Cervantes herself greeted me with, "Don Luis, please excuse my appearance, I wasn't expecting to see you so soon." She was breathless and rushed her words. "I happened to be looking out the window," she pointed to the second floor of her home, "when I saw you arrive. Thank you so much for coming to visit me so promptly, Your Grace. God has listened to my prayers. Please come in." She stepped aside.

She was wearing a black housedress that left her throat and arms exposed. With nervous hands she brushed back her midnight-black hair. Andrea had aged since the last time I saw her, but she had grown in allure. The sparkling onyx of her eyes reminded me of Miguel—she had the smiling Andalusian eyes of the Cervantes brood.

Andrea led me up the stairs to a sitting room in the Moorish style. She pointed to a low divan and offered me a glass of sherry. "No, thank you. I'm afraid I cannot stay very long," I said. "My wife is expecting me."

Andrea nodded to indicate she understood. She sat

across from me on a large scarlet cushion. She wore black satin slippers, embroidered in red. Her feet were very small, the size of my hand. From the patio floated the laughter of a girl and the voice of an older woman.

Andrea explained, "It's my daughter, playing with the maid in the garden. The last time Don Luis saw her she was still an infant."

A warm flush spread all over my face. I squirmed on my divan.

"I will get straight to the point, Don Luis," she said, noticing my discomfort. "My poor mother's suffering breaks my heart. We don't have the means to pay for the ransom of my brothers. The Trinitarian friars who negotiate the liberation of captives in that port of Moors and idol worshippers have informed us that they do not have sufficient funds to rescue both of my brothers, even though Rodrigo's ransom is much lower than Miguel's. You may have heard Miguel lost the use of his left hand fighting the Turks. To leave him in Algiers indefinitely amounts to a death sentence. You were Miguel's best friend." Tears moistened her eyes.

I didn't know what to say. Andrea continued, "As you know, the king has established a fund to loan money to needy widows of good families. Don Luis may not be aware that my mother comes from landed gentry. She can put a vineyard her parents left her as a guarantee that she will repay the debt and the interests. She would like to borrow enough money to acquire a license to export Spanish goods to Algiers. If everything goes well, she should be able to save enough money to pay the debt within two years."

Doña Leonor's widowhood was news to me. "I'm very sorry to hear about your father's passing, Señora Andrea. I didn't know."

She crossed herself. "Thank heavens, my father is still

alive, Don Luis. But we know people who can, for a fee, produce the necessary documents to make it look as if my father were deceased. I pray the good Lord will forgive us for this deception because our motives are pure: to free our brothers from that land of infidels, where their Christian souls are in grave danger."

"I'm afraid I don't understand," I said. "How can I help you in this matter?"

"You see, Don Luis, my father would go to Andalusia to stay with our relatives up in the mountains, and hide for as long as it's necessary. We would tell people he had died while he was away visiting relatives. Later, when he reappears, we'll say we were misinformed."

Clearly, she had been hatching this deception for a while. The luscious temptress was asking me to be complicit in breaking the law. "I'm afraid you forget I am an officer of the king," I said. "I could never knowingly do something that would jeopardize my honesty or my family's honor, even for the noble cause of helping a friend."

"I understand, Don Luis. But you are our last hope." She covered her face with her hands and started sobbing.

Being in Andrea's proximity felt as dangerous as playing with an asp. Once more, my unhealthy curiosity won the best of me. I remained glued to the divan.

She stopped sobbing with a series of short hiccups, then dabbed her cheeks with a handkerchief she pulled from a pocket in her dress. "Don Luis, my husband, Don Diego Obando, had to leave for New Spain on urgent business to claim the title to a property a relative of his left him in his will. He's been gone longer than we had anticipated. If he were here, my family would have no need of my desperate rescue plan."

(The next day, I learned that the man she called her husband was a married man who had abandoned her and left for the New World. As reparations to her honor, Don Diego gave her the handsome house with all its furnishings.)

"If you can help us, I don't know how I can ever repay you for your goodness of heart. But you will certainly have my eternal gratitude and you will constantly be in my prayers. You can always count on me as your most loyal servant." She was talking now in the breathy voice I remembered from our first meeting, when Miguel and I were students at Estudio de la Villa in Madrid and she had told me the bizarre story of her child and the child's father. Every word she uttered was draped in gossamer. A breeze that wafted in from the garden cooled the sitting room, yet perspiration dewed the swale between her breasts.

My hands were sweating; I felt light-headed, disoriented. I hadn't been with a woman in a long time; I could no longer go to Mercedes to satisfy my manly desires, but I was not the kind of man who would engage with prostitutes. Was Andrea insinuating something indecent? Was it the devil making me see something that was not there? Or was this further proof—as if I needed any more—that the Cervanteses were immoral people?

I could have denounced Andrea to the authorities for trying to bribe an officer of the court. If I helped her, I became her accomplice. Then an insidious thought crossed my mind. I could help Andrea to obtain the loan and then denounce the living Don Rodrigo to the authorities. I didn't care about his punishment, and knew that hers and her mother's would be severe. After all, Miguel had destroyed my marriage. He had soiled what I held most pure and sacred. I would repay him in kind, making sure he spent the rest of his days as a slave along the Barbary Coast. *Aeternum vale, Miguel,* I thought. *I'll never see you again. You'll never get another chance to come near my family and harm me.*

* * *

After I left Andrea's house, I felt impure. I needed to go to the cathedral to pray, to confess my grave sin. But as I knelt in our family pew, my face sunk in the palms of my hands, I realized I could not confess to Father Timoteo what I was about to do to Miguel and his family. He would dissuade me from it. He would never again see me as a good Christian. The clarity with which my hatred made me see myself was excruciating.

The murmurs of the devout praying in the cathedral reverberated in my head like a swarm of furious bees. Were they praying for me? The din rose, and I wanted to get out of the cathedral and then run, run until I disappeared into the oncoming night. The prayers became more ominous-sounding—like a flock of garrulous blackbirds clustered together in a pine tree to protect themselves from the winter cold. Were the birds chattering in Latin? I looked around me, and the flickering lights of the votive candles made me think of the searing flames of hell. No priest could help me now. No human being, even if he was God's most devoted servant, could deliver me from my poisoned heart. I would beg to our Celestial Father directly for His forgiveness and then, as penance, devote my life unequivocally to Him. I would become a monk, leave my family, and spend the rest of my life fasting and praying. Better yet, I would become a hermit, and live in a remote cave where only wild beasts could find me. But I knew my flesh, was too weak to withstand such rigors. I didn't know what it was to be hungry or cold, or to sleep on the bare ground, or to spend my nights in darkness. Was God speaking to me? Was this heresy? Who was I to deserve such a miracle? I, who was so far from being Christlike. *As long as I keep this revelation to myself, I'll be saved. God wants me to stay in Madrid and do His work in this city of sinners and apostates. He's calling me to be a soldier in His army of Divine Light.*

At that moment I was at peace. God's Grace had touched me, and I knew happiness.

CHAPTER 5
THE CASBAH
1575-1580

No one entered or left Algiers without being reminded of death. Before it is too late to deter once and for all time future historians from picking up their quills and dipping them in the mendacious ink used by those abject scribblers of words to dress up their rachitic tales, I will relate myself what happened— at a time when I was still young and bold and despised cowardice—in that city with a scarcity of mercy and a surfeit of cruelty, in that purgatory of life, that hell on earth, that port of pirates and sodomites called Algiers, and I swear upon the salvation of my eternal soul that the events I'm about to describe are the truth, without any embellishments.

The first ones to leave the Bagnio Beylic in the morning were the captives who worked in the giardini of the rich; they returned at the end of the day, to be counted and to rest for the night. The most unfortunate ones had to walk for hours before they could reach the orchards where they tended the fruit trees, the vegetable and flower gardens, and the irrigation channels. These pitiable men lived in constant terror of the nomad and pagan tribes of the south, who conducted raids in the orchards, capturing and enslaving the workers whether they were Christians, Moors, or Turks.

Ransomable captives like Sancho and me were exempted from hard labor. But we were expected to feed ourselves. Without Sancho I would have starved; nourishment reached my belly thanks to his ingenuity. When he smelled food, Sancho had wheels in his feet, the eyes of a falcon, the nose of a wolf, and the ferocity of a Barbary lion. As soon as the guards opened the doors of the bagnio, we rushed down the deserted casbah. At that hour, the streets teemed with nocturnal criminals who didn't bother with slave beggars. Sancho and I raced to be the first ones at the shoreline to meet the returning fishermen and scavenge the discards they tossed on the beach. Even when the rough winds prevented the fishermen from going out to sea the night before, there was always a plentiful supply of sea urchins for the taking along the rocky shore. I would slurp their mushy bits of sweet orangey caviar until I appeased my vocal stomach.

At the foot of the casbah, a small gate opened to the strip of beach where fishermen moored their boats and unloaded their daily catch. On both sides of the gate were impaled the men who had incurred Hassan Pasha's wrath by attempting to cross the Mediterranean in barques and balancelles made of big pumpkins strung together with twine. These desperate escapees would stand in the middle of the floating pumpkins holding in their stretched-out arms a robe, a rag, any large piece of clothing—hoping the wind would make a sail out of it. The lucky ones drowned. The survivors were tortured and left for the African vultures, which plucked out the men's eyes while they were still alive. After a while, the stench of rotten flesh was just another unpleasant city smell, indistinguishable from the stink of the latrines in the casbah, which expelled revolting fumes. The stench lifted only when strong winds blew in from the Sahara.

As the fishermen approached the shoreline, I would stand for a brief moment gazing at the dark sea; the pain of my incarceration was accentuated by the reminder that such a beautiful body of water—the Mediterranean of the Greek mythic heroes—lay between my freedom and me; between my family in Spain and the lair of criminals where I was trapped, which I was determined to escape from no matter what.

When the boats beached, Sancho and I ran in their direction like hungry hounds to snatch the discarded fish from the air before the belligerent seagulls flew away with them. The fishermen greeted us with taunts of, "Run, Christian dogs, run if you want to eat!" The fear of hunger overruled my shame. Their unwanted catch, seasoned with their insults, was preferable to a strict diet of sea urchins. These meager scraps were sometimes our only meal of the day.

Chewing fast, and spitting out the prickly bones, Sancho would say, "Quick, Miguel, eat the worms before they fill their bellies."

After we sated ourselves, we searched for mollusks and crustaceans, edible to Christians. Later we would sell them in the souk. Sancho excelled at killing the highly prized crabs with the throw of a stone. He bundled our catch in rags he reserved for that purpose, and we set out for the market.

The souk was the heart of the casbah. I was fascinated by the fabulous bazaar where people admired, purchased, and sold goods from all over the world: pipes of Spanish and Italian wines, butter, wheat, semolina, curried rice, flour, lard, chickpeas, olive oil, fresh and dry salted fish, eggs in many sizes and colors (ivory ostrich eggs the size of a man's head; speckled quail eggs the size of a fingernail), vegetables, fresh figs and figs preserved in syrup, smoky African honey, almonds, oranges, grapes, and sugared dates. Earthenware, perfumes, incense of many kinds, wool, precious stones, elephant tusks, lion and leopard skins were also displayed, as well as stunningly colored fabrics that shimmered in the hot sunlight.

When luck smiled on us, we sold our bits of fish and made the twenty aspers charged to sleep in the bagnio on the floor of a room crammed with men, the only protection from the chilly and unhealthy night winds that arrived in the autumn.

On my first tours of the labyrinths of the casbah, Sancho served as my Virgil. "Look, Miguel," he said, pointing toward the roofs of the houses, "I swear these people must be half cats. See how they hang their laundry on the roofs? That's because the poor houses have no patios. See how the women travel from roof to roof? That's how they visit each other because their husbands don't want the Turks and Moors to lay eyes on them."

I learned how to glimpse the inside of the dwellings with their ancient tiled floors of intricate design and beautiful colors. The interiors of the houses were immaculate, in stark contrast to the mounds of filth on the streets. Algerian women went about barefoot, swathed in billowing fabrics, their gleaming black hair uncovered, as they sailed through the shaded interiors and vanished behind drapes. The gold bracelets around their arms and ankles, and the necklaces of long strands of lustrous pearls, glistened fleetingly inside the homes as the women darted about. Now and then a woman would stand still for a second to stare bracingly at Christian men, her alluring eyes gleaming golden like those of wild cats.

Neither courtly Madrid, nor Córdoba with its rich ancient history, nor magnificent Sevilla where the great treasures and marvels of the world were displayed, and not even immortal and mythic Rome with its glorious ruins and its ghosts of the great still wondering about, could compete with Algiers, where Moors, Jews, Turks—and over twenty thousand Christian captives—made their home. I learned to identify the Algerians right away: their skin was the same shade of color as the desert dunes at sunset, which separated Algeria from dark Africa.

Jews were easily recognizable by the white cloaks they wore, and the black caps that covered their heads. Their white cloaks made them stand apart in the dark of the night. Under their garments they were compelled to wear black. I was grateful that my family had converted to Christianity so long ago that I could not be recognized as a Jew. Christian slaves were lucky compared to the way Jews were treated. Even street cats were held in higher esteem than the Jews. If they felt like it, Algerians spat in their faces when they passed Jews on the street. The slaves of the Moors and Turks ranked higher than them. At the fountains, Jews had to wait until everyone else filled their jars before they could collect water themselves.

Algiers was more Turkish than Arab. The Turkish men were robust and imposing. They wore loose-fitting pants under their short-sleeved jackets: a piece of cloth that hugged their ankles and which they tied with a band around their bellybutton. Their outsized turbans resembled cupolas. Scimitars, daggers, and pistols bulged under the sashes around their waists. Everyone in Algiers deferred to them. One of the first things Sancho told me was: "Rule número uno, never argue with those toads! Run away from them as you would from an elephant's fart."

I had no trouble learning to spot the Christian renegades from every known corner of the world. The ones who wore the turban adopted the look and the customs of their Moorish and Turkish masters. They spoke in Spanish among themselves, but not to Christian captives. These renegades were the most unsavory inhabitants of Algiers, for there was no greater criminal in my eyes than a man who abandoned his faith and then turned against the people of his own blood. To prove their allegiance to their new masters, and to be rewarded with riches and privileges, renegades invented lies and accused the captives, who had formerly been their brothers in faith, of unspeakable crimes.

I was spellbound by the Azuaga people, the Berbers, who were as white as the snowy peaks of the mountains where they came from. Tattooed crosses were carved on the palms of their hands. Their women had their entire bodies covered with tattoos, including their faces and their tongues. The women made a living weaving and knitting, or working as domestics in the palaces and houses of rich Moors.

Other foreigners came from as far away as Russia, Portugal, England, Scotland, and Ireland to the north; Syria, Egypt, and India to the south and east; and Brazil to the west. Many of these foreigners were adopted as sons of the Turks if they were circumcised, converted to Islam, and practiced sodomy like their masters.

I heard Spanish spoken everywhere in the souk, not only by my compatriot inmates of the bagnio, but also by the Moriscos and Mudéjares who were now citizens of Algiers, and the Spanish merchants who had licenses to operate their businesses in the port. The sound of Spanish spoken on the streets was an oasis to me. For a moment, I could pretend that Spain was nearer than it was. Sometimes I would stand close to people chattering in Castilian, just to hear the sweet sounds of our mother tongue. The language of Garcilaso and Jorge Manrique never sounded so beautiful to me. I made a practice to approach these people and ask them if they knew where one Rodrigo Cervantes lived. I described the physical appearance of my brother, but no one could help me in my search. Now and then a pícaro hinted that he might know something, but would need a gold coin to unlock his memory.

Each night, before surrendering to the disquieting shadows of my slumbers, my last thought was about discovering Rodrigo's whereabouts; the first thought that entered my mind when my eyes greeted dawn was about him too; and the one thought that colored the hours of each day was wondering when I would see him again. To find Rodrigo, and escape with him from Algiers, became the sole reason for my existence. I was nearly thirty years old, and I had brought nothing except shame on my family. When I returned to Spain—and it was not a question of *if* but of *when*—it would not be as a hero dressed in glory and wealth, as I had hoped years ago, but as a cripple. My redemption would come in the form of liberating my brother and bringing him back safely to my parents. I would do everything in my power not to let them go to their graves knowing that their two sons were still slaves.

Hoping to garner information about Rodrigo, I roamed the dark passageways of the casbah, accosting anyone who looked Spanish or Morisco, stopping at the stalls in the souk where Spanish or Italian was spoken, to make inquiries about my brother. I cared not that my beard was long, my garments filthy, that I was repelled by my own smell, that my feet were permanently swollen and blistered from tireless walking and were often bleeding by the time I returned to the bagnio at sundown.

I needed to find a way out of my indigent state so I could buy ink and paper to write letters to my family and friends to inform them that Rodrigo and I were still alive. I had no way of knowing whether Rodrigo had been in epistolary contact with our family. It tortured me that the lack of news from us must have made our parents suffer a great deal. Making money became an imperative: that was the only way I might find out something about Rodrigo's present situation. One night, as I was getting ready to go to sleep, Sancho said, "Miguel, if you haven't noticed, the nights are getting chilly. In a few weeks your blood will freeze in your veins, and your bones will turn to ice, if you continue to sleep with the sky as your roof. If I may be so disrespectful as to offer my advice to someone so illustrated, to a poet and hidalgo who has seen the world and fought for the glory of Spain, if you don't take care of yourself today, my young friend, you won't live to find your brother tomorrow, let alone escape Algiers with him. My old master the Count of Ordóñez used to say, *Carpe diem.* To which I will add—because two proverbs are better than one—all good things come to those who wait."

I thank God for putting Sancho in my path. Though he couldn't read or write, he taught me many words and expressions of the lingua franca spoken in that Babel. Soon my confidence in my rudimentary knowledge of Algiers's main language grew. I began to accost anyone who looked somewhat prosperous to offer my services as a servant. Necessity made me brazen: I knocked on every door I passed asking for work. But fetching water, scrubbing the court-yards, cleaning latrines, hauling sacks of grain, cutting weeds, digging, picking fruits in the giardini, or harvesting vegetables and other produce, were all impossible tasks to perform with only one good arm. I could grind wheat with a mortar, but I could not move the heavy concave stones after the wheat had been ground into flour. I offered my-self to teach Spanish to the children of wealthy Algerians, but when parents introduced me to the little fiends, they started to shriek as soon as they saw my deformed hand. Occasionally charitable people handed me a piece of old bread or a few figs. Sancho was luckier, finding work carrying food and water to the homes of the well-to-do. My desperation grew. Even thieves needed both arms.

Had it not been for Sancho's industriousness, I might not have survived those first few months in Algiers. For the first time, I knew the fear of those who suffered starvation. The rare days when I earned a few extra aspers selling fish, I treated my stomach to the cheap plates of delicious lamb stew and couscous made by the street cooks. These filling dishes were the staple of the poor of the casbah. Having been my father's reluctant assistant in his barbershop, I thought of offering my services to the local barbers: with my good hand I could empty chamber pots and wash them; I could give medicines to the ill and feed them. But Algerian barbershops were strictly for grooming, shaving, and the procurement of slave boys. The beautiful youths who did not go to sea with the Turkish sailors stayed behind and worked in these places, where they shaved the Turks and satisfied their carnal needs. The loveliest boys were highly valued and sought after, and the Turks wooed them with splendid gifts. It was sad to see Spanish boys become the whores of the sodomites. I could not work in one of those establishments.

I had seen slaves all my life—it was common for wealthy Spanish families to own Africans—but no one knows anything about slavery unless you've lived it in the flesh, unless you've been treated as less than human. We slaves were identified by the iron rings and chain we wore around our ankles. After a while, I became so used to wearing them that most of the time I forgot I had them on. The miserable men who had been in captivity a long time took on the appearance of dangerous beasts emerging from underground caves: their hair was matted, and ragged beards covered their chests. Many of us looked like savages that fed on raw meat. A couple of slaves walking together smelled like

a battlefield of rotten corpses. Before long, I answered to
people who addressed me as "Christian slave."

Slave auctions were held every day, except on religious
feasts, in the section of the souk called the *badestan*. They
provided a source of information: who had been captured;
who was sold; where the new shipments of slaves came
from; who had died; who had been killed by the hook.
I lived on the slim hope that at one of these events conducted by dealers in human flesh, I might get news about
Rodrigo.

I didn't know the name of the man who had bought
my brother, but in piecing together the details I remembered about him from that afternoon when fortune had
dealt us that grave blow, my persistence eventually paid
off: from a renegade who did business with him, I learned
Rodrigo's master was Mohamed Ramdane, a wealthy Moor
who loved music and gave his children a broad education
that included learning European languages and the customs and manners of other cultures. I discovered that he
had journeyed with his family and servants to his villa by
the seashore near Oran, and that every year he returned
to spend the winter in Algiers. Learning this much gave
me the hope I needed to start planning our escape from
Algiers.

I began to take an interest in my appearance, in the
world about me, and to study the layout of the city looking
for possible escape routes. I walked many times along the
wall that encircled the city, which made Algiers impregnable to attacks from the land and sea, and also served as a
deterrent to captives, criminals on the run, and slaves who
tried to escape.

I took mental notes of the wall's nine gates: which ones
were sealed and never opened; which ones opened during
certain hours of the day, but were heavily guarded; which

ones led to the desert; and which ones faced the Mediterranean. I learned about the caves in the hills behind the wall.

Of the nine points of exit and entry, the gate of Bab Azoun, facing the desert, was the most transited. For hours, I would watch the travelers heading to inland settlements in the south; the sand-covered masses that arrived from the desert and dark Africa; the comings and goings of farmers and slaves who worked the fertile green lands that stretched from behind the city to the emerald mountains, behind which the Sahara begins; the farmers who came to the city to sell their produce; a stream of caravans of camels loaded with the treasures of Africa's interior. I stayed in the vicinity of the gate until darkness fell and the door was padlocked. I became aware of the routines and shifts of the guards perched on the turrets on each side of the gate, armed with harquebuses, and on the alert to shoot—without any warning—at people they found suspicious. On the exterior walls of the gate of Bab Azoun dangling from iron hooks were men in various stages of putrefaction.

The desert was like the sea: if you lived near it and spent too much time gazing at it, it called to you and eventually claimed you. It was then I learned about the dangers hidden in the great beauty of that land whose majestic black-maned lions tore elephants apart, the same way that, in better days, I yanked off the legs and wings of a roasted quail to sate my hunger. It took me longer to understand that the extreme beauty of the desert was also an invitation to surrender to death's embrace.

Time crawled in captivity, each day was unendurable, and every day a duplicate of the one before. The snail-paced passage of time was slavery's most pernicious torture instrument. One more day in captivity meant one more day of my life that I would not know freedom. At the end of each day, with no news of Mohamed Ramdane's return to Algiers, I went back to the bagnio fully demoralized. My whole life was about making sure I could find something to eat. How quickly I lost my dignity and became a beggar and scavenger. Yet the will to live is stronger than pride.

By keeping to a strict diet of the fish Sancho and I scavenged, I scraped together a few coins so I could by a good quill, a small bottle of writing ink, and a dozen sheets to write to my parents and friends. Though Luis Lara had never answered my letters from Italy, I wrote to him one more time asking for his help.

Letters from Spain took months to cross the Mediterranean. I was beginning to lose hope I'd ever have any news from home, when a missive arrived from my parents. Nothing made me happier than learning that my parents and my sisters were in good health. My mother added that she prayed to the Holy Virgin that no harm came to me, and that I would soon return to Spain. My parents reassured me they were doing anything and everything to find the money to ransom my brother and me. Unless my father's fortunes had improved—which would have been a great miracle—I was well aware my family could not afford to pay our ransoms. I memorized the letter and placed it inside the pouch under my tunic. There was no answer from Luis.

My parents' letter made me nostalgic for the familiar world I had left behind so long ago; my despondency grew. One day Sancho said to me: "To think all the time about our captivity weakens us, Miguel. Those sons of their whoring Turkish mothers count on that. The more they break us, the less trouble we'll give them. You have to learn to look at our misfortune in a positive light, my young squire. Maybe all these bad things have happened to us for a reason."

"I fail to see how any of my misfortunes could ever be seen in a positive light, friend Sancho," I retorted angrily. Sometimes his relentless optimism was too much for me.

"Well, look," Sancho said, "if my old master the Count of Ordóñez had not died, and his devilish children had not thrown me on the streets, and if I hadn't had the good fortune to meet your saintly father, who treated me out of the goodness of his heart when I was sick and in a pitiable state, I would have never met you and now you would not have me here in Algiers to give you my five reales of wisdom."

He had a point there, but how did it benefit him *his* captivity was a question I did not want to ask. Many years later, I realized that thanks to my imprisonment in Algiers, I had met my second most famous fictional character. It was then plain to see, too, that my miserable experience in that den of monsters had fortified me, and given me the forbearance necessary to withstand all the bad hands Fortune dealt me.

The muse of poetry began to visit me again. It had been years since I had thought of myself as a poet. Since my indigence made it nearly impossible to purchase more ink and paper, I had to compose the poems in my head and then memorize them. I began to exist in a world different than the material one, a place where the Turks could not touch me, a place where I was a free man. This activity became one of the rare consolations afforded me, and prevented me from going mad. Knowing that no one could take away from me writing that only existed in my brain made me feel powerful for the first time since I had been seized by the corsairs. Sancho warned me that spending hours sitting alone and murmuring to myself, while everyone else was out, would attract the unwanted attention of the guards. So I learned to compose poetry wandering in the souk.

It was during these walks that I became intrigued by the Moorish storytellers. All my life I loved listening to the stories perfect strangers told. People of all ages stood enraptured, under the harsh sun, breaking for a moment from their routines, to listen to these men who practiced the ancient art of storytelling. I only knew a few words and phrases in Arabic, so I understood the names of the characters in the stories but not what they were about. When the listeners made approving sounds of "Ehhhh," or laughed, I interpreted their reactions to mean there was a new twist and turn in the tale. Even the women, their hair covered in hijabs and their faces hidden by white almalafas, stopped to listen. Sometimes the same story seemed to go on for days. Merchants, servants who came to buy provisions for their masters, and gaggles of lawless children repaid the storytellers at the end of the day's installment with figs, oranges, eggs, a piece of bread, and occasionally a piaster or other very small coin. The faithful public returned day after day, with their baskets of food and their loads of laundry, hungry for more stories. I was so enthralled by these performers, and the crowd's reaction, that the sounds and meanings of Arabic began to take root in my head. I was reminded of the actors in Andalusia, who performed snippets from their plays in the plazas of towns and cities. The great difference between the Algerian storytellers and our actors was that in the souk one man played all the characters, whether they were people or dragons or creatures out of a nightmarish bestiary.

Could I possibly earn a few coins by telling stories in Spanish? I wondered. The population who spoke Spanish in the souk was large: was it possible I could command the attention of a small audience? The main drawback was that

I was a poet: I thought in verses and rhymes, in syllables and vowels, not in prose. Perhaps I could recite some of the poems by Garcilaso and other poets that I knew by heart?

For three consecutive mornings, when the souk was most ebullient, I stood near a fountain with Sancho as my captive audience: the few passersby who stopped to listen to my recitations for an instant looked at me as if I were speaking in an incomprehensible tongue, guffawed, and then hurried on their way—as if they were running from a leper. Here and there a weary soul stopped to listen to a few poems, but not one of them threw my way even a fleshless bone.

"Don't get so downcast," Sancho finally said to me. "What do you expect? To recite poetry to this crowd is like feeding truffles to pigs. I myself don't understand poetry, if you want to know the truth. I prefer stories. When I've finished listening to one of those poems, I just want to scratch my head. Why are these poets always, always crying over damsels that don't care for them? If you want to eat regularly, my friend, poetry is not the answer. I'm sorry."

"What else can I do to make money, Sancho? My options are limited. My tongue is more useful than my one arm."

"Tell stories like the Arabs do," he said.

The first time I told a story about rival poets, I got the same result. The story of a poet who flees Spain with a band of Gypsies only got a slightly better reception. People listened raptly for a while, and then walked away looking puzzled or bored. One morning, a Spanish washerwoman who had stopped briefly to listen the previous two days, said to me: "Your voice is good, young man. And I understand what you're saying. But you don't know how to tell stories."

"I beg your pardon, señora," I replied. It was the first time a member of the audience had actually addressed me.

"I've been working for ten years as a washwoman in the house of a rich Moor," she said. "I've lost all hope of ever going back to Spain and seeing my family before I die. Every morning, when I wake up, I look forward to the stories I'll hear that day in the souk. Those stories are the only joy in my life." She paused; I could see she wanted to help me. "But you don't know how to entertain a crowd," she went on. "All tales need a love affair and a suffering and beautiful heroine. I don't want to hear a story unless it is about love, and the sadder the better. Look," she pointed to a huge basket filled with dirty laundry that she had set on the ground by her feet, "that's my work every day, if I want to eat and not be lashed. I will shed my tears over young, beautiful, rich lovers who are doomed and die for love. I don't want to weep over my own wretched life. Young man, take me someplace away from here, where I can forget about this shit-hole and these mountains of filthy clothes I see even in my dreams. That's what I want from a story. The Arab storytellers know that." Then she tossed me a piece of bread she had lodged between her breasts, placed her basket atop her head, and marched off.

As my love stories became more elaborate and far-fetched, I gained a loyal following. My listeners did not care about logic. In fact, they preferred stories that made no sense—the more unbelievable the better. Sancho collected whatever people could spare: a few coins and assorted bits of food. He said to me, "Keep those tales coming, Miguel. This is much better than stuffing myself with sea urchins every day."

One morning, as I was spinning a tale about shepherds and unrequited love, among the people in the audience I spotted Rodrigo. My heart stopped beating. Could it really be my brother, not a delusion caused by the Algerian sun? He was in the company of a richly dressed Moor and his servants. This was Mohamed Ramdane, the same man who had purchased Rodrigo at the marina. In Rodrigo's eyes, I read: *Don't say anything. Pretend you haven't seen me. Don't acknowledge or approach me. Continue with your story. Control your emotions!* Rodrigo wore a finely made ankle-length gray cloak with a hood. His master wore the white burnous that identified wealthy Moors. My brother looked well groomed and well fed.

Despite my befuddled state, I continued with my rambling tale. Abruptly, Ramdane walked away and my brother followed, keeping a step behind him. Rodrigo was going to disappear in the casbah, and it might be a long time before I saw him again. I brought my tale to an unexpected halt by having a bolt of lighting strike the hero as he was riding to rescue his beloved princess from the evil vizier. People started booing. I left Sancho to weather the insults, and whatever else the audience was willing to part with.

I followed Rodrigo at a distance, with great discretion, though every part of me wanted to approach my brother and embrace him, kiss his hands, his forehead, and his cheeks. I was dizzy and unsteady on my feet, elated and anxious, but I felt intrepid and invincible.

Mohamed Ramdane eventually arrived at his home— one of the finest palaces in Algiers. Before he went through the front door, Rodrigo turned around, winked his left eye almost imperceptibly, and raised his left eyebrow in the direction of a turret to the right of the main door.

Pine trees and dense bushes made a green refuge below the turret. I hid there and waited, but there was no sign from Rodrigo. Had I misunderstood him? Had something gone wrong? Minutes and seconds had never stretched so long. Hours seemed as long as years. I had trouble breathing. As the day grew hotter, and the sun beat directly above my head, I began to sweat even though I was in the shade. Then, as the sun dawdled west, and the afternoon brought cooling breezes and with them the song of birds, I got chilly and began to shiver. I was determined not to leave yet, even when the evening star appeared in the crimson sky. But when I heard the last call of the mosque before the doors of the bagnio closed for the night, I left my hideout and hurried back.

With the exception of Sancho, I had to keep the momentous news to myself. Information was a currency in Algiers, especially among captives who passed it on to the guards for monetary rewards and to catch the favorable attention of their masters, who might eventually free or adopt them.

The following morning, I did not return to the souk. Day after day, I waited in the little wood under the turret, hoping to at least catch a glimpse of Rodrigo. My meager funds were quickly exhausted, as I had abandoned telling stories in the souk.

Two weeks went by. One afternoon I was dozing, my back resting against a tree, when I was startled by a dull thump on the bed of pine needles that covered the ground. I discovered near my feet an object the size of my fist and wrapped in a piece of fabric. Rodrigo must have thrown it at me while I was asleep. I looked up but saw no sign of my brother. Quickly, I grabbed the object and untied its knot. Inside, there was a balled-up sheet of paper. As I unfolded it, a gold coin fell out. It was more valuable than any coin I had seen in Algiers, but that was nothing compared to the joy I felt when I recognized Rodrigo's handwriting.

Dear brother:
I've prayed every night that in their divine mercifulness,

Jesus Christ and His Holy Mother would intercede with God so that I could see you again. The happiness I felt when I saw you in the souk can compare to no other.

You can't imagine how worried I've been about you with your bad hand. You look thin but in good health. As for me, despite the daily humiliations of the life of a slave, I would be remiss not to mention that my masters don't beat me, and that they treat me with the respect due to a teacher, because Moors value education and respect their teachers. I'm never threatened with being sold to another master, or sent to Turkey, or being branded with a cross on the soles of my feet. I'm fed plenty of couscous, lamb, and dates, and I have two changes of clothes.

My master's children have taken a liking to me. Their innocent souls haven't been poisoned yet by the Muslim faith, so they don't despise me for being a Christian. They are curious about Spain, and Mohamed Ramdane has instructed me to teach them Spanish, along with music. I tell you all this so you won't worry about me, and if you can write to our parents please let them know I am not treated cruelly, and that— God willing—I will make it to freedom someday soon. Every waking moment, I dream of going back to our beloved Spain and joining you and our parents and sisters. Some of the other house slaves have lived here longer than I've been alive. I can bear this life for the present, but not for years and years.

If your circumstances allow it, wait for me hidden in the pines every Tuesday afternoon, when the children go with their father to visit their grandparents. I will be looking for you. I'm not paid wages, but my master is so pleased with the children's education that sometimes he shows his appreciation with a gold coin. Please use the one I've enclosed as you see fit. It would make me very happy to know that you have used it to make your life a little more pleasant.

Your brother who loves you and dreams of going back to Spain
with you,
Rodrigo

To avoid attracting attention to myself, I went back to telling stories in the souk. But I reserved Tuesday afternoons to wait under the turret for a message from my brother.

Hatching an escape plan became my main concern. First, I concluded, I needed to find a few men who were desperate enough not to be afraid of the brutal punishment that befell those who failed in their escape attempts. But other than Sancho, whom could I trust in the bagnio? Sancho had pointed out the unsavory characters, the untrustworthy men, and the Christians who were honorable in their actions. We arrived at a list of a handful of men we could approach without fear of being betrayed.

We had set a date to start approaching the men we'd selected when word got to the bagnio that a mission of Trinitarian priests had arrived in Algiers to conduct negotiations to buy the freedom of Spanish captives and slaves. The Trinitarian monks made these trips at least once a year. The money they brought from Spain was collected from funds provided by the crown, the families of the captives, and the church. The captives who were members of rich families would be the first ones to be liberated. For the rest of us, who relied on the availability of charitable funds, the wait could go on for years, even decades, and in some cases for the rest of our lives.

The morning following their arrival, the Trinitarians were waiting outside for the Spanish captives as the doors of the bagnio opened. Our men rushed toward the monks to inquire whether their names were on the list of captives to be ransomed. I was not in a hurry: it was unlikely my parents could have raised the money. Sancho took me by the hand and dragged me with him. "Come, Miguel," he said. "You never know. Greater miracles have happened."

There was no ransom money for Sancho, as was to be expected. He shook his head, rolled his eyes, and nudged me in the direction of our rescuers.

I took a deep breath, exhaled, and yelled, more to please Sancho than because I believed my name could possibly be on that list, "What news have you for Miguel de Cervantes?"

"Is that you, my son?" one of the brothers asked, as he ran a finger down his list.

My heart beat so hard I could hear no other noise.

"We have good news for you and your brother Rodrigo. We have six hundred ducats to purchase your freedom."

I felt faint, but Sancho's crushing hug kept me on my feet. He kissed my cheeks as tears ran down his face. He seemed so happy that you would think he was the one about to be released. All I could think was: Where could my family have raised such a large sum of money? What sacrifices had they made for us?

"Where's Rodrigo?" the monk asked.

I regained my composure and told them the name of my brother's master.

The following day, my fellow captives who could pay their ransoms and I accompanied the Trinitarians to Arnaut Mamí's palace. All of us belonged to him. When we arrived at the grand chamber where he conducted his business, Rodrigo was already there; Mohamed Ramdane and his two children were with him. We embraced for the first time in almost three years, but before we had an opportunity to say much to each other, Mamí's guards separated us.

Our case came up first because there were two of us. "As for the young one," Mamí said, indicating my brother, "you will have to buy his freedom directly from Mohamed Ramdane."

Ramdane's daughter and son stood by my brother. I judged the girl to be around fifteen, and her brother a few years younger. I disbelieved my ears when I heard the girl say, "Papá, Master Rodrigo has been the best teacher we could have ever hoped for. Sohrab and I would like him to go back to his family without a ransom."

Ramdane seemed as surprised as I was. He was about to respond to his daughter, when she dropped on her knees and kissed her father's hand. "Dear Father, think how painful it would be if we were taken away from you. Master Rodrigo is a good man, Father. Allah will shower you and our family with many blessings for this act of kindness."

"Stop crying, my daughter. Please get up," Ramdane said, taking the girl's hands, pulling her off the floor and embracing her. "You know your father can't deny you anything." He addressed Mamí: "Your Lordship, Rodrigo Cervantes has earned the love of my children and my respect. He's free to go. I will take no money for his freedom because he has given my family gifts that no amount of money can buy. May he go in peace. Blessed be the Prophet."

(I learned later from my brother that Ramdane's children had secretly converted to Christianity and that was the reason why they wanted Rodrigo to go back to Spain.)

"If you want to give away your property, that's your business," Mamí said, making a face of disgust. "In that case," he addressed the Trinitarians, "are you prepared to pay his ransom?" He pointed at me with his bejeweled index finger.

"We can pay for Miguel Cervantes the six hundred gold ducats that we had for the ransom of the two brothers," the Trinitarian who conducted the negotiations said.

Mamí erupted in a high-pitched laugh, which he cut

as abruptly as it had started. "I know how important this cripple is," he blurted out. "He's a protégé of your Don John of Austria and a hero of Lepanto. I also understand he's a poet who has important friends in Rome. I want eight hundred gold ducats for his freedom. And if you're not ready to meet my price, I suggest we move on to other business."

Rodrigo dropped to his knees and addressed Mamí: "Your Excellency, I beg you, if you let my brother go I offer to be your slave. My brother is the eldest, Your Grace, the head of our family. My elderly parents need him. I'm strong and healthy. But my brother cannot continue living in the bagnio and be expected to survive much longer."

Mamí whispered with great animation to a man sitting next to him. I could not let Rodrigo sacrifice himself on my behalf. "Rodrigo," I said, "it's because you are young and healthy, and have many talents, that you should return to Spain first. You can find work and help our parents in their old age. If I return to Spain instead of you, I will only be a burden to them. There is little I can do with one good arm to improve the conditions of their lives." With as much conviction in my voice as I could muster, I added, "As your older brother I order you to go; I order you to accept my wishes for you. Besides, dear brother, your master has been kind and generous to give you the gift of your freedom and you must show your great thanks to him by leaving Algiers, as those are his wishes and the wishes of his children."

"Enough of this," Mamí cried, "the cripple stays. And to you, young man," he pointed at Rodrigo, "be gone before I change my mind and keep you too."

I embraced Rodrigo one last time. "Tell our parents to pray for me and not to despair. I know I will return to Spain, I promise."

Despite my confident words, I knew that once Rodrigo left there was a chance I would never see him, or my parents, or set foot on Spanish soil, again.

As the preparations were being made for the ship carrying Rodrigo and the ransomed men back to freedom, the December rains came. They were a prelude to the arrival of Algerian winter. When the black clouds poured open over Algiers on their way to Africa's interior, they washed the layers of sand and grime off the exteriors of the buildings and the streets; bushes and trees turned a brilliant green; flowers bloomed everywhere; the casbah smelled of honeysuckle at twilight; and the cupolas of the palaces and the minarets of the mosques shimmered gold and turquoise, as if newly minted. Algerians flooded the streets in clean clothes, smiling, after scrubbing themselves for hours in the hammams.

From a solitary, tiny plaza near the high point of the casbah, which had a full view of the port, I saw the vessel carrying Rodrigo to freedom lift anchor, billow its sails, and aim its prow in the direction of Spain. The winter rains made the Mediterranean look fuller, placid, sated.

In the days, weeks, and months following Rodrigo's departure, my despair grew. One single thought occupied me: my freedom. I was determined to die in the attempt, if necessary. What was life worth if I couldn't see my parents before they died?

In all fairness to the Moors and Turks, I have to mention here that they allowed Christian captives to practice and observe our religion and celebrate its rites. In the midst of my misery, our religion was the one solace I could turn to. Only my faith in God comforted me during that time. Priests were allowed to say Mass on Sundays and holy days and to offer Communion. Without the presence of these men of God, hundreds of slaves would have been enticed to become renegades. On many nights, even the most hardened and wicked among us prayed for the souls of the men who had been tortured to death that day. We knew the same fate awaited us at any moment—all we had to do was incur the ire of Arnaut Mamí or Hassan Pasha.

Christians were allowed to own taverns in the bagnio. These establishments kept our men in servitude, as the unfortunates—myself included—spent on spirits every coin for which we had had to sweat blood. But the soul-robbing life of captivity was only bearable if you were drunk. Some Muslims frequented the taverns to drink out of public view. At the end of the day, when the pashas announced the closing of the gate, they dragged the drunken Muslims by their feet and rolled them down the street, to the plaza below Bagnio Beylic.

In one of these taverns, a renegade from Málaga who went by the Arab name of Ahmed, but who was known to everyone as El Dorador, engaged me in conversation. After I had finished telling one of my tales in the souk, he praised my talent for storytelling. My mind and body were warmed by wine, so I bit his hook when he offered to buy me a pint of wine. We chatted about daily life in Algiers, then he asked, "Now that your brother has returned to Spain, you must be desperate to go back home?"

I said nothing. Sancho had warned me, "You cannot be too cautious in this pit of cobras, my friend. Be especially wary of renegades who seek to snare Christians to curry favor with their masters."

El Dorador whispered in my ear: "I can help you and a small party of men escape. I have abjured my conversion to Islam. I want to return to Spain and to our faith, the one true religion. I curse the day I set foot in this land of stinking Mohammedans." Then he showed me a cross he carried under his robe; he kissed it many times, as tears rolled down his face. He wiped his tears with the back of his hand. My desperation to escape Algiers made me blind. Besides, I had imbibed too much wine to be a good judge of the situation: El Dorador had convinced me of his sincerity.

"I want five hundred gold ducats per man to arrange your escape. Your chances of succeeding improve if only a small number of men are involved," the renegade explained. "I won't take more than eight of you."

I knew a few rich Castilians in the bagnio who would be eager to take the risk, who could loan me the money in exchange for arranging their escape. I approached first Don Fernando de Caña, a wine merchant from Castile. He agreed to loan me the five hundred ducats on condition I paid him after I had settled again in Spain and found work. I asked him to finance Sancho's escape too. Don Fernando seemed to balk at this suggestion. "We need a man like him, Your Grace," I said. "Sancho is famous for his resourcefulness, and for his ability to sniff food miles away."

I convinced Don Fernando. It was an exceedingly large debt to assume, but I gave him my word I would repay him. I would worry later about how I would come by so much money. Who could foretell the inscrutable future, anyway? In the meantime, I had to do whatever was necessary to arrange my escape. It fell upon me to organize the flight from Algiers. In addition to Sancho, Don Fernando, and his son Don Fernandito, I decided to enlist the Hinojosa twins, two members of the Spanish nobility, who had been studying painting in Italy; and the young hidalgo Don Diego de Mendiola, son of a wealthy merchant.

From that moment on, anything anybody said to any of us, any look they gave us, was reason enough to become suspicious. If somebody we knew did not greet us when we ran into him, that person immediately became a potential informer. The longer it took for us to leave Algiers, the greater became the possibility of something going wrong. We decided not to have verbal communication in the bagnio amongst ourselves, and never to congregate in the casbah more than two of us at a time. We agreed that all communication had to be verbal; that nothing could be put in writing; that I alone would have dealings with El Dorador.

For the first time in my life I understood what was meant by "sleeping with one eye open." One night, soldiers burst into the sleeping quarters and took away a number of Spaniards. Did the soldiers suspect anything? Did they know there was a conspiracy afoot and they were trying to identify the conspirators? I could not betray my anxiety at such a crucial moment. Whatever misgivings I had, I had to keep them to myself. I could not share my doubts, even with Sancho. It fell on me the responsibility of assuaging everyone's fears. And it turned out the Spaniards were members of a band of thieves.

The holy month of Ramadan fell in January that year. According to El Dorador, this was the most propitious time to attempt our escape. We began our preparations. First, he took me to inspect a secluded grotto in a rocky, steep hill not far from Algiers. I was satisfied with its size and relative inaccessibility. Seven men could hide there and wait for the caravan of Tuareg nomads who, every year at the end of January, camped in the Roman ruins of Tipasa on their journey to the city of Oran, the Spanish colony to the west of Algiers. They traveled there to sell and trade the weapons they made, along with impressive brass and copper ornaments and utensils. This particular sect of Tuaregs practiced their own brand of Islam and did not observe many religious holy days and rites. El Dorador would meet us in the cave with horses and provisions and then lead us as far as Tipasa. At which point we would have to settle on a price with the Tuaregs, to allow us to join their caravan and enjoy their protection. Don Fernando agreed to finance that part of the journey too.

The melancholy mooing of the conch shell, used as a horn, awakened all Algerians hours before dawn on the first day of Ramadan. Somnolent Muslims hurried to eat and drink before four in the morning. The rest of the day, with the exception of the sick, they fasted. But as soon as the sun dropped behind the horizon of the Sahara, people lay on their carpets to consume the delicacies that were specially prepared during the festivities. After the strict fast of the day, Algerians ate until their stomachs were so full they had to take a digestive nap. By ten o'clock, they went out on the streets for the nocturnal revelry. The guards in the bagnio observed this custom too.

During Ramadan, the casbah blazed at night with torches and crowds carrying lamps. Vocal, guitar, flute, and drum music were heard everywhere. Algerians congregated in the plazas to watch the women dancers, whose undulant movements infused the air with their sensuality. The clapping which accompanied the dancers brought memories of the Spanish castanets; the rhythmic sounds swelled up until it seemed to pour out of every interstice of the casbah, and spiral toward the heavens. The snake-charmers' cobras swirled out of their baskets and swayed hypnotically with slithering black tongues to the rhapsodic flute music. Gaggles of children rushed screaming from one act to the next. Even slaves were captivated by the enthralling atmosphere.

As the month wore on, it was apparent the fasting had taken a toll on the Muslims. The late-night eating orgies affected their digestion, and the sleep deprivation showed on their drooping faces and the shadows under their eyes, as they stumbled in a daze through the city during the day. Toward the end of Ramadan, Algiers was a city of disoriented insomniacs with bad breath.

The middle of the fourth week of the festivities, El Dorador received word that the caravan of Tuaregs was just a day's travel from Tipasa. The Tuaregs were famous for the fast pace of their travels through the desert. Once they were ahead of us, it would have been impossible to join them. We decided to escape the next day before the caravan moved on. We would slip out of Algiers during the first evening call to prayer, when the gates of the city were still open and the guards had their heads against the prayer mats. We counted on the severe exhaustion and indigestion of the guards to keep them from noticing our disappearance until the next day.

The night before our escape I could not sleep at all. What if things went wrong? Was I ready to die tortured, unrealized as a man? Other than fighting at Lepanto, I hadn't accomplished any of my great dreams. If Hassan Pasha impaled me, what would have been the meaning of my life? What would I have left behind to be remembered by?

My compatriots and I prayed silently throughout the night, making sure that we did not arouse anyone's suspicions by any erratic behavior. I lay still for hours with my eyes closed, praying to the Virgin to bless our scheme.

During the last call to prayer before the gate of Bab Azoun was closed for the night, we slipped out of Algiers, one at a time. Once we were outside the city walls, covered by the falling darkness, we hurried as fast as our chained feet would permit us for the nearby forest where we crouched in silence in the brush. When the sun finished setting, we scrambled up the hill while the famished guards, weakened and hallucinating from almost a month of daily fasting, gorged themselves. I led the way to the grotto.

We arrived at the cave. El Dorador, who was supposed to be waiting with tools to break the irons around our ankles, provisions for the journey to Tipasa, and horses, was not there to meet us.

"He has betrayed us to ingratiate himself with the beylerbey," Don Fernando de Caña said. "Weren't we warned never to have any dealings with renegades?"

"Cervantes, I thought you said we could trust this man. You told us he wanted to go back to Christianity," said Don Eduardo Hinojosa.

Before the argument made us forget we were friends not foes, I replied, "I take total responsibility for what has happened."

"Not to disrespect you, Miguel, but what good is that to us now?" asked Don Julio Hinojosa.

Sancho broke his silence. "Maybe El Dorador has been detained. In unity there's force, my squires. Fighting among ourselves will only make matters worse. It's quite possible he's on his way here right now. In the meantime, let's wait inside."

Barbary lions roared in the bushes, and that was enough to make us listen to Sancho's counsel. We went into the gaping hole and Sancho lit a torch. The inside of the cave was a rectangular space made of solid rock. We gathered in the front of it; in back, there was a shallow tunnel where a few men could fit in if they crouched.

It was agreed that we needed a lookout. Don Diego de Mendiola offered to climb the rock above the grotto and serve as a watchman. He went to his post armed with two loaded pistols and a dagger.

The night was getting cold and the torch was not

enough to warm us. We started a fire with some pieces of wood and mounds of dry leaves we found inside the grotto, and huddled around it. The warmth of the fire was comforting, but we were hungry and thirsty. Sancho moved to the back of the tunnel and sat with his legs spread apart. With a rock, he began to hammer his chains with concentration and patience. Except for this pounding, we were silent.

We heard someone approaching, and Don Diego burst into the grotto showing great agitation. "They are coming to take us back to Algiers!" he announced.

"Let's fight the temptation to become alarmed," I said. "How do you know it is not El Dorador approaching with the horses?"

"Dozens of lighted torches are coming up the mountain. It looks like a small army, Cervantes. I'm afraid Arnaut Mamí has sent the Janissaries to get us."

Every one of us shuddered. "We will not surrender," Don Fernandito de Caña declared. "We'll fight them."

"Not to be disrespectful," Sancho said, "but if we fight them, we'll be slaughtered like lambs."

"If they take us back, they'll torture and then kill us, anyway," reminded one of the Hinojosa twins.

"If we flee right now we might have the good fortune to find another cave where we can hide," Don Fernando proposed.

I knew it was too late for that. "Let's commend ourselves to Our Lord and pray for His mercy," I said. I remembered my experience on *El Sol* when Arnaut Mamí had captured us. "If we are taken back alive, there's a chance we'll live." I kneeled on the rocky ground.

"There!" Sancho exclaimed, startling me. "I broke the damn chains. I'm free." He crawled to the front of the grotto, shook first one leg then the other. He took a few tentative steps, as if he had forgotten how to walk without chains. "I'm going, Miguel," he said, "come with me. We'll cut your chains as soon as we can get far enough away from here."

"I can't go, my friend," I told him. "I can't abandon our men. I'm responsible for this situation we find ourselves in. I should have listened to you and never trusted a renegade. I have to stay and assume the consequences. It's the only honorable thing to do."

"El Dorador fooled all of us, Miguel, not only you," Sancho countered. "Who will come with me?"

"If you leave by yourself, without a guide or provisions to travel in the desert, you'll die," I said to Sancho. "If we stay together we have a better chance of surviving."

Sancho shook his head. "As my late master the venerable Count of Ordóñez used to say, *Sumus quod sumus*. I'd rather be eaten by the Barbary lions, or die of thirst, or stung by scorpions, or bitten by snakes, or torn to pieces by hyenas, or fill the stomachs of wolves, than to continue this insufferable life of exhaustion, humiliation, sickness, and freezing nights. I've had enough of it. Basta ya!"

I got up and embraced him.

"Our paths will cross again, Miguel," Sancho said. "I'm sure of that. And never forget, *Festina lentil*. You know what I mean, don't you?"

"I do," I said.

I never saw Sancho's stout feet exert such speed as when he ran away from the grotto, up the hill. Soon his shadow blended with the darkness of the North African night. The tar-black sky was studded with countless stars, but moonless. By the time the new day broke, wild beasts would have feasted on Sancho's opulence of flesh and vast reserves of fat, I was sure.

"Let's wait for the Janissaries outside the cave," I suggested. "Lay down your arms. If we offer any resistance, they'll kill us without mercy in this wilderness. Our only chance of survival is to surrender. And may the Lord have mercy on us."

I returned to Algiers with my ankles still chained and my hands tied behind my back. Years later, in *Don Quixote*, I called Arnaut Mamí "an inveterate enemy to the whole human race." Impaling, disemboweling, practicing the infamous torture method called *khazouking*, mutilating arms and legs, severing ears and tongues, gouging eyes, raping, beheading, hanging by the hook, and burning Christians at the stake gave him the pleasures other men found in food or music or making love. Even the Turks were in awe of Mamí's cruelty. Anything could provoke him: a look, a reply, what he thought was a look or a reply, or a lack of one.

The next morning, we were brought to Mamí's presence. He received us lying on a heap of lion skins. El Dorador sat by his feet. There were a large number of captives in the room. Were they there as spectators, to teach them a lesson on what happened to captives who tried to outsmart him?

"Who was the leader of this conspiracy?" Mamí inquired.

Before I had time to speak, El Dorador pointed at me. The traitor met my eyes impassively; I wanted to grab his neck with my good hand and smash his head against the tiles, until his eyes and teeth and brains lay at Mamí's feet.

"Ahmed, you are now my son. I will adopt you," Mamí said to El Dorador.

The leprous rat seemed very pleased to have been rewarded with more than the usual can of lard and gold escudo that renegades received for denouncing Christians.

Though I feared I'd be hanged or lose my ears and nose,

the honorable thing was to assume responsibility. "Your Excellency," I said, "it was I alone who persuaded these men to follow me. Therefore, I alone am responsible."

Arnaut Mamí and El Dorador consulted with each other in whispers. Mamí pointed with his middle finger at Don Diego de Mendiola and Fernandito de Caña. Two guards pushed the prisoners to the corner of the room where I saw a torture device had been set up. Our men had their feet clamped in a wood gadget, and were then elevated by their ankles with a rope.

Don Fernando de Caña dropped to his knees. "Please, sir, take me instead of my son. I beg you, Your Excellency. If the boy is harmed, it will kill his mother."

"Quiet," Mamí said softly. He gave all of us a chilling smile and summoned one of his men. The man tied a scarf around Don Fernando's mouth.

A Turk began to beat the soles of Don Diego's and Don Fernandito's feet with a cudgel. "If any of you opens his mouth, I'll have your tongue cut off," Mamí warned. The torturer flayed our men until the skin on their feet peeled off and their bones showed. Fortunately, they had lost consciousness. Or were they dead?

With a flick of his hand, Mamí put an end to the cudgeling. The blood of Don Diego and Don Fernandito was ebbing through their feet. "When they open their eyes again, burn them at the stake," he said.

Don Fernando fell to the floor. He lay on his side, struggling to free his limbs. Copious tears washed his red face.

It was unbearable to see Don Fernando watch the torture of his young son. I felt guilty: it would have been more dignified to die fighting the Janissaries than to end our lives in this manner. I began to throw up so violently I almost choked on my own vomit.

The captive spectators started to protest and pray in

different languages. Mamí addressed them, his face distorted by rage: "Pay good attention, you miserable rabble. This is what will happen to you if you are foolish enough to try to escape. Take them back to the bagnio."

The captives were herded away, and food was brought in for Mamí and El Dorador. They talked, ate, and drank, oblivious to our presence. Don Fernando still lay on the floor, though he looked so still, his eyes closed, that I thought he was dying. The Hinojosa twins and I remained standing. The brothers seemed to have lost the ability to speak. They trembled, sweating profusely, and terror showed in their eyes.

After Mamí finished eating and washing his hands, he said, pointing at Don Fernando and the Hinojosas: "Take them away and throw them in a dungeon. They will be khazouked in public, as an example. But leave the cripple here."

One of the brothers fainted. My knees were so weak I thought I'd follow him. In one of Algiers's plazas I had once witnessed this torture: a prisoner was tied to a chair, which was then raised off the ground by a chain. A pointed lance was placed under the man's anus, and then pushed in, while the man was still alive. Great pressure was put on the blade until it cracked the prisoner's skull, and the point of the blade, gleaming red, came out of the man's head.

When I was the only remaining captive among El Dorador, Mamí, and his servants, Algiers's infamous torturer said to me, "Cervantes, no man has ever tried to steal my property, and those men were mine." He instructed one of his executioners, "See to it that he gets two thousand lashes." That was practically a death sentence. "When you're done with the beating, circumcise and castrate him." Mamí got up from his divan, walked over to me, and placed the spiky point of his rapier against my Adam's apple. Then, in a change of heart, he instructed his men: "I don't want him killed. Anyone who's willing to risk his own life for the sake of others deserves my respect. I just want this Spaniard's spirit broken."

An imposing Moor pressed the jagged point of his dagger to my spine and took me away. We arrived at a remote part of the palace, an enclosure that consisted of a square of soil surrounded by tall walls. A wooden plank raised by chains indicated the entrance to a cell dug in the ground. "Get inside," the man said. As he lowered the plank, the cell was so shallow I had to crouch on the bare soil with my knees pressed to my chest. The humid hole reeked of urine, shit, and dried blood. A crack on the plank was wide enough to allow a sliver of sunlight to enter. The only comfortable position for me in that dungeon was lying flat on my back.

The following day, my jailer uncovered the plank and handed me a cup of water and a piece of bread. I was terrified that the feeding was just a prelude to a lashing. I chewed and drank, staring at the ground.

"Don't you remember me, Miguel?" The man spoke with a Cordovese accent. I was surprised he had addressed me by my first name. The Moor smiled; he looked vaguely familiar. "It's me, Abu. We were childhood friends in Córdoba."

I spat out the hard piece of bread I had been chewing. The last time we had seen each other we were children. "Abu," I said, as if to make sure I was not dreaming, "I wondered what had happened to you." I was too astonished to move from my spot.

Abu extended his hand and pulled me out of the hole. Then he embraced me.

When we moved away from each other, I said, "I

thought you died in the insurrection in the Alpujarras."

"No, we left Spain when all the Moriscos were expelled. We went to Morocco first. My father died of a broken heart. Spain was his country, the place he loved, where his family had lived for hundreds of years."

"I'm sorry to hear about your father. Is your mother here with you?"

"Soon after my father died, my mother followed him. She had left her heart in Córdoba. After she died, I came here and found employment working for Arnaut Mamí."

I shook my head. My misfortune was nothing compared to what had happened to my friend's family. "And Leyla?" I asked.

"She married a merchant; they live in a village in Tunisia, on the coast." After a pause Abu added, "You'd better get back in the cell. We should not be seen talking to each other. Spain is no longer my homeland. We are supposed to be enemies now. But I will always be your friend, Miguel. Every day I will lash you a few times, and then will lash the ground. You must cry as if I am lashing you, just in case there's anyone nearby listening." He pulled out of his pants pockets a frayed copy of *Lazarillo de Tormes* and handed it to me. "I brought it from Spain. It's the only book I have in Spanish. I know you enjoyed stories. You can borrow it to keep you company while you're a prisoner here."

During the brief hours when a thin shaft of afternoon sunlight pierced the darkness of my dungeon, I read and reread Lazarillo's adventures until I memorized the little book. It was *Lazarillo*—more than the much-appreciated handfuls of food that Abu provided with some regularity—that sustained me and sweetened the hours in that fetid hole and made time move faster. Lazarillo's picaresque adventures took me back to the Spanish soil from which I had been uprooted so long ago, and his tribulations and unbreakable peasant spirit alleviated momentarily the wretched conditions of my existence.

Confined to that damp, shallow grave, I learned to experience the passage of time in a new way. There was light—never more than a thread of it—and then there was monotonous gloom. Sometimes the darkness, and the eerie silence that accompanied it, seemed to last so long that only my bodily functions, and the chilling screams of the tortured in the dungeons of Arnaut Mamí, reminded me that I was still alive. I learned that I could illuminate the innumerable hours of soul-killing darkness with my glowing memories of Córdoba. So I revisited in my memory that city whose name was synonymous with pícaro; the city where alluring women sat knitting while facing each other on their window seats and pretended never to lift their dark eyes off their needlework—but when one of them met your gaze, great passions were awakened and men could lose their minds; that city of fabled leather artisans where the making of wool and silk was a great talent; that city that always resounded with tapping tambourines, shaking cymbals, and the piercing wails of the Moorish flutes imploring to the heavens. In my torture cell in Algiers, where water was more precious than gold, I remembered the city of my childhood whose cool streams flowed down from the springs in the Sierra Morena, making song as they splashed out of Córdoba's fountains and then rushed down mosaic-lined channels in the Alcázar, filling the ponds that teemed with fat orange fish, and irrigated the flower beds in their gardens and the fruit trees in their orchards. The waters of the sierra brought with them cool breezes that felt like the caresses of hands oiled with balsams imported from the New World.

During those times when I began to lose hope—the only thing I possessed—I remembered too, with gladness in my heart, that city in whose gardens countless doves sang in unison all morning long, their music rising with the heat of the day, until your head was so swollen with it that you felt lost in the crescendo created by their feverish chorus; that city where flocks of swallows swelled at sunset, flying in such great numbers and so tightly together that they resembled airborne carpets sweeping the cross-topped towers of the churches and the needlelike tips of the minarets of the mosques. But foremost, I remembered that Córdoba was the birthplace of Seneca, whose philosophy of stoicism became important to me as I grew older, helping me on many occasions to take the blows of adversity with equanimity and forbearance.

In the darkness of the hole in the ground where I spent my days and nights, I found a measure of solace remembering my favorite place in Córdoba, the magnificent former mosque. Córdobeses did not care to notice that the spirit of the place was not Christian. My mother took the whole brood there to Sunday Mass. But I enjoyed much more visiting it with Abu, whose family had converted to Christianity. I was transported by Abu's stories about the learned Arab rulers who had built the mosque, men whose exotic names—Abd Ar-Rahman, Al-Hakim II, Al-Mansour— seemed more fitting for mythological creatures than for human beings. As we walked around admiring the arches laminated in gold leaf and lapis lazuli hugging the columns of cool and smooth pink granite, dazzled by the imbricate designs of the panels of mosaics, and the patterns that the sunlight made on the tiled floors as it filtered through the circular stained-glass windows, the building became an enchanted place created not by mortal men for other mortals, but by magicians for a people who worshipped color and elegant design as elevated manifestations of the divine.

Abu also told me about the treasures hidden in the ruins of Medinat Alzahara, the fabled city not far from Córdoba that had virtually disappeared five centuries before, leaving few traces. During school holidays we searched the region, hoping to unearth a treasure that was said to be as great as that of El Dorado. It would take us hours to walk from Córdoba to the slopes of the Sierra Morena, where Medinat Alzahara once stood. For all our zeal, we uncovered only fragments of ancient glazed ceramics. I would carry these pieces in my pocket, fingering them often and dreaming of a city that Abu said had been the most beautiful and civilized in Europe.

The Moriscos were forbidden to use Arabic in public, but Abu's family spoke it at home. He had one sister, Leyla, older than us by a few years. She had blond hair and golden eyes, like many Moorish women in Algeria. Sometimes the women of the household got together to dance for each other, and Abu and I spied on them. Leyla moved with the grace of a feral cat. Her eyes were like almonds dipped in honey, and her arched eyebrows and eyelashes were as black as the hairs of a panther. Swathed in transparent veils, shaking her tambourine, she transported me to the gold-colored desert dunes of Arabia, and to lush oases that could have rivaled the Garden of Paradise.

Abu's parents were as poor as mine. To help out his family, after school he worked in the hammam where the old men paid boys a few maravedíes for scrubbing and massaging them. I started frequenting the bathhouse with him. I was entranced by the world of the Arab baths, centuries old, built by the Romans, where men exposed their nakedness without shame. In Algiers, in the rare occasions when I had a few extra coins, I had visited its hammam, which reminded me of those early and happy times. In Córdoba's bathhouse there were three pools—one icy; one warm, like the waters of the Guadalquivir in August; and one hot, like boiling soup. My favorite corner of the building was the steam room, where people seemed to vanish and flit about like naked ghosts.

But not all my memories of Córdoba were pleasant. In Mamí's torture cell, where all my fears multiplied like maggots feeding on carrion, I also began to relive the terrors of my childhood. My great-grandfather, Ruy Díaz Cervantes, was the first member of our clan to settle in Córdoba. For generations, the Cervantes family was known as makers of wool and cloth, an industry normally reserved for Jews. My grandfather Juan Cervantes had inherited a handsome fortune, which had dwindled over the years. His round, black eyes regarded the world and its creatures through the lenses of scorn and bitterness. I remembered my mother saying that he had the face of an old vulture that had "feasted on poisonous snakes all his life." Even as a child, how I pitied my grandmother who had to share a bed with a man who excreted hatred through his pores. My father was the special target of his bile. It's true that Father was impractical and reckless, but he was also kind and brimmed with gaiety. Grandfather Cervantes showed publicly his disappointment in his son, who was a failure as a doctor, and even as a barber. Frequently the cupboards in our kitchen were bare. Ham bones were saved for weeks, and boiled with cabbage and onions in salted water until they were as white as pebbles in the river. Many days that was our entire sustenance. Often, my mother had to ask for my grandmother's charity and suffer the ridicule of my grandfather. One day my grandfather came by our house at suppertime and said to Father in front of all of us, "Look at your miserable children. They are as uncouth as a herd of wild pigs. And the girls, wearing those wretched rags, look like washerwomen. They will never get married."

I was getting physically weaker, and my spirit was as shattered as it had ever been, when one day Abu said to me: "I have good news for you, Miguel: I heard from a man close to my master that you will soon be released from this cell. Arnaut Mamí will probably ask to see you before you are sent back to the bagnio, so I will have to increase your lashings—it's better for both of us if you look like you've been receiving your punishment. But don't worry, I'll soften the strokes so you are not killed."

As the lashings increased, it was no use trying to hold back my screams. I could not block out the excruciating pain inflicted on my flesh. My back became swollen and the skin began to tear. The lashes would have hurt more if I hadn't known they were coming to an end soon. As I bled, I lay with my face resting on the ground, breathing in the stench of the blood-soaked earth.

One morning soon thereafter Abu informed me, "My master left Algiers a few days ago. I have orders to release you from the cell today. I will walk you back to Bagnio Beylic." Then he handed me a little blue bottle. "Apply this balm to your skin, Miguel. It will prevent the wounds from getting infected with maggots and will make them heal soon."

Abu gently helped me to get up, but my legs would not hold my skinny frame. With my friend's help I took a few steps. The chains around my feet had never felt heavier. I dropped on my knees to the ground. After a while, the fresh air began to revive me. While I sat still on the ground, Abu left the enclosure and returned with a large bucket of water and a bar of soap. As he helped me to remove my rotten garments, I handed him back his copy of *Lazarillo*.

"I heard you laugh in there many times," he said. "I knew that if you could laugh, you'd survive."

Abu poured water over my naked body while I soaped myself. The pain in my wounds made me moan and contort. I tried to soap my head, but my hair was so matted that water would not penetrate the thick shell. When I finished washing, Yessid handed me the two pieces of clothing given to all prisoners when they were released.

On the way back to Bagnio Beylic, I was so weak I leaned on Yessid's arm. The outside world seemed unreal. At that moment I thought I understood what Lazarus must have felt like when he returned from death. Before I passed through the doors of the bagnio, Abu said, "Take good care of yourself, Miguel. Despite the circumstances, I thank Allah that we met again. But remember, we cannot be friends in Algiers. If we ever run into each other in the casbah, you must not talk to me. If my master finds out that we are friendly with each other, I will lose my employment and be punished. Who knows," he added, "we might meet again someday, away from this country, in a place where Moors and Christians can live side by side in peace." He turned around and walked away so fast I did not have a chance to speak.

Weeks went by before I was strong enough to wander into the casbah. How I missed Sancho; I had no idea how much I had come to depend on the fat man. I survived this period after my release thanks to the generosity of my fellow inmates, to whom I became a symbol of our resistance. They gave me any bits of food they could spare. One man gave me several sheets of paper and an inkpot. "Write about this place," he said. "Make sure the suffering of our martyrs has not been in vain."

At that moment when my future was still so bleak, a

human angel entered my life. I will preface her story with some verses by Ibn Hazn of Córdoba:

> Were I to conquer your heart
> The entire earth and the human race
> Would be to me but motes of dust
> And the citizens of this country, insects.

Her name was Zoraida; I called her Lela Zahara in the plays I later wrote about my years of captivity, and Zorayda in the story "The Captive's Tale" in *Don Quixote*. There is no letter as rich or elegant as the last letter of the Spanish alphabet: it contains a 7, an L, and a sideways N. It is as much a portal as it is a letter, an initiation to a mystery. The first letter of her name contained the key to Zoraida, who was many things at once: Muslim by blood, a Christian in her soul, the most beautiful woman my eyes had ever seen, and the noblest Algerian.

Agi Morato, a Moor of high rank, was the alcaide of Bagnio Beylic. His residence shared a wall with our courtyard. It was a tall wall with two oval windows near the top; the shutters were always closed. The windows were too high up for any captive to try to escape through; they might as well have been sealed.

Following my failed escape attempt, I had acquired in Algiers a reputation as a valiant and fearless poet. Sancho had been right when he told me the night we met that poets and madmen were revered by the Moors as holy men. Nobody bothered me when I chose to stay alone in the bagnio writing my poems. It was at this time that I began to write down ideas for possible plays. One day my works would be performed, and from beyond the grave my writings would inform the world about what our men suffered in captivity. My works would incite the Christian nations to attack and destroy the Algerian pirates. These thoughts were my only consolation.

One morning in the courtyard, leaning my back against the wall of Agi Morato's house, I was engrossed writing a letter to my parents when I heard little pebbles pelting the floor near me. I glanced around and saw no one nearby. I continued writing, and another pebble hit the floor. I looked up at the wall behind me: a rod emerged from one of the windows that was always shut; a thin rope dropped from the tip of it. It resembled a toy fishing device made by a boy. At the end of the rope was a tiny white bundle attached with a white ribbon. The guards were at their usual posts, but distracted by the life of the casbah. I placed my writing instruments on the floor and went to inspect the strange object. The bundle turned out to be a white handkerchief tied in a knot. I undid the knot, then the rope went back up immediately and the rod disappeared behind the window.

I returned to my writing place, sat down with my back against the wall, and drew up my knees, sheltering the handkerchief in the space between my legs and my chest. Inside were ten small pieces of gold. Was this a dream? Was my mind playing tricks on me? I bit one of the coins—it was solid gold. From the window a woman's hand waved at me and then was pulled back inside. The window closed again. It was as if the shutters had never opened.

What was the meaning of this? Should I move away from that spot and never come close to it again? Was Arnaut Mamí testing me? Was this a trick to draw me into conspiracy again? My achy bones, my scarred skin, and my despondent mind had not yet recovered from the months I had spent holed up. Who was this woman? Had Mamí asked her to lure me into a trap? It was best to resist the flights of my wild imagination. In case she was still watching me, I crossed my arms over my chest in the Moorish style, to show my gratitude.

I tied the gold coins in the handkerchief, which was made of the softest cloth and was delicately scented with a perfume of lotuses, and left the bagnio in a hurry. I hoped walking until I was exhausted would drain the intense emotions pent up in my body. In Sancho's absence, there was no one with whom I could share the strange happening. Even the usual bustling life of the casbah could not dispel the woman's hand from my mind. Was she an angel or a devil? And why had she selected me? Could she be an abducted Christian who had been forced to become a renegade and marry Agi Morato? It was known that his harem was filled with Christian women.

Not wanting to arouse the slightest suspicion, I refrained from asking questions about the woman. In Algiers I had learned not to trust even my thoughts. Superstitious captives feared that the agents of the beylerbey could read their dreams while they slept.

I waited for another sign from the house, and for many days I did not leave the bagnio. But there was always a sick captive who stayed behind, or a person of rank in Spain who could borrow from moneylenders in Algiers: they could stay all day in the bagnio sleeping or playing cards. For weeks nothing happened; I began to think that my benefactress would never try to contact me again.

One morning when I found myself momentarily alone, the rope dropped again near to me with another small bundle tied at the end of it. I grabbed it quickly. Wrapped in a perfumed handkerchief, I found a balled-up sheet of fancy paper. Again the rope was quickly removed and the shutter closed. I held in my hand—I counted twice to make sure I was not hallucinating—forty crowns of Spanish gold. The letter was signed with the drawing of a cross. The calligraphy of the writer was exquisite:

> *Christian,*
>
> *I have to be brief, but I swear by the holy name of Lela Marien—the blessed Virgin—that I am your friend. Tomorrow midmorning, in the section of the souk where herbal medicines are sold, an old woman will approach you. Her name is Loubna. Do not speak to her. She will show you the palm of her hand, on which you will see a cross drawn in ashes.*
>
> *Follow her, but make sure that no one is following you. Walk behind her at a distance. She will lead you to a remote part of the casbah where you will meet a young Moorish gentleman.*
>
> *Do not ask him any questions, but follow him.*

Was fate playing another cruel trick with me? Regardless of the dangers, I had to find out what was behind all this. If necessary, I would risk torture all over again if it meant there was a glimmer of hope that I could escape from Algiers. After my thwarted first escape attempt, I was more determined than ever to taste again the sweetness of freedom. Freedom is a slave's Holy Grail; without it, his life has no meaning.

I couldn't sleep that night. I wished Sancho had been around so that I could share my disquiet with him. How admirable of my noble friend to risk a terrifying death knowing his chances of survival were infinitesimal. At least Sancho was at peace now. Death had restored to him what every slave was robbed of—his dignity.

The next morning, I followed the instructions of my mysterious benefactress and met Loubna in the casbah. I trailed her at a distance, until the crowds thinned out and we reached the edge of a forest of pines behind one of the great houses of Algiers. She entered it and I walked behind her. In a sheltered spot we met a young Moor dressed in splendid clothes. "Follow me," he said. The old maid turned around and began retracing our steps. The young man walked fast, deeper into a thicker, darker part of the woods. I was too excited to feel any fear. I noted the youth's gentle voice, his lithe steps, his long neck, his pink lips, and his soft manner. Stopping under a tall rock, he faced me and removed his turban—whereupon long black hair cascaded to his shoulders. I was flabbergasted: my eyes had never beheld such a beautiful woman.

"I'm the one who dropped the money from the window," she said. "I've been watching you for a while, and have seen you telling stories to the other captives. I have come to the conclusion that you're unlike any of the other men in the bagnio, and that you're the only one I can trust."

"Who are you?" I asked. "Why have you blessed me with your trust?"

"My parents gave me the Moorish name of Zoraida, but my Christian name is María," she said. "I'm Agi Morato's daughter; that's all I can tell you now. Later I will answer your questions. I have prepared this billet which will explain many things." She pulled out a small envelope from her sleeve and handed it to me. "Read it later. Now you must listen to me carefully because I don't know when we will get another chance to speak to each other face-to-face. Don't worry about being discovered here: my maid will start singing if there's anybody coming this way. I'm in a desperate situation and the passage of time is my enemy. I've had many suitors from all along the Barbary Coast and from as far away as Arabia, but to the dismay of my father, who is entering an advanced age, I've turned down all of them. Father has informed me that Muley Maluco, king of Fez, has asked for my hand in marriage. My father is planning for a wedding at the end of October. The king is a good man, cultivated and kind, which pleases me." She paused to stare at me briefly, as if to make sure I followed her story. "But I don't love him. My father, as you may have heard, is very wealthy and I have access to a great deal of his fortune in gold escudos and jewels. I will provide you with funds in gold so you can purchase a well-built vessel to carry me to Spain, where I hope to enter a convent. I know you will not betray me. Your gallantry and bravery are well-known in Algiers—you are admired even by your enemies."

Her words made me dizzy. I felt as if God had sent an angel to carry me back to Spain.

"I know you are good and honest," she went on. "My people are deceitful, and there's no one I can trust, except my loyal maid, who also wants to go to Spain with me. She's an old Christian woman bought by my father many years ago, when she was a girl. She wants to return to Spain before she dies, to die in the bosom of the only true church. Await my instructions, sir. Tomorrow in the market, in the same place where you met Loubna today, she will hand you the funds you will need to start preparing for this enterprise. I have to go now. We must step with the caution of cheetahs."

I dropped to my knees. "I vow to serve you with all my strength," I said. "I pledge to defend you against any harm."

She extended her hand, in which she held a handkerchief, which she surrendered to me. Then she turned around and disappeared among the trees, leaving me inebriated with the heavenly scent of her body. I lay on my back on the pine needles and moss that carpeted the ground, with her handkerchief spread across my nose and lips. I closed my eyes and stayed in that position oblivious to the passage of time. I wanted that moment of perfect happiness never to end. If this was a dream, I did not want to awaken from it.

When I began to get cold, I found my way out of the woods and directed my steps to the little plaza in front of the ruins of the ancient Christian church. There were no people around. I squatted on a large rock from which I could see the harbor. For the first time since my arrival in Algiers, the Mediterranean looked conquerable. Zoraida's billet read:

Señor Poet:

I've been told your name is Miguel Cervantes. When you have read this letter you will perhaps take compassion on me. I never knew my mother, for she died at my birth. My father, grief-stricken, swore never to marry again. But he had high hopes for me from my earliest days. He said I was destined to be a princess, and he would prepare me to marry a man from a noble house. He made it a priority that I would receive a good education that would fit my later station in life.

One day, when I was still a child, he came home with a young Spanish lady he had bought at auction. Azucena had been a lady-in-waiting to the Countess of Paredes. My father purchased her to teach me Spanish and everything a lady needs to know. Azucena was a devout Christian. Although my father had surrounded me with servants who fed me, washed and dressed me, played games with me, and made sure that no harm came to me, Azucena, despite her despair at finding herself deprived of her freedom, took pity on me: a lone child growing up without a mother. Azucena would be the only mother I ever knew. Instead of hating me for being the daughter of her captor, Azucena devoted herself to my happiness and to teaching me everything she knew. She slept in my chamber; I could not bear to be separated from her for a minute. My father was pleased with Azucena because she had taught me beautiful manners, to play the guitar and sing, and to speak Spanish, the language in which she and I communicated so that nobody in my father's house could understand what we were saying to each other.

The following year, Azucena's mistress, the countess, sent Spanish priests to Algiers to buy her freedom, but my father said he would not sell her back for any amount of money because he needed her for me. Azucena cried whenever the two of us were alone. She stopped eating and became frail and pale. I was afraid she was going to die. "When I grow up and get married," I would say to her, "I will give you back your freedom." Azucena would take me in her arms and kiss my face. She said the Rosary on her knees every night. My people taught me that Allah was the only God. But when I saw the consolation Azucena received from her prayers, the forbearance her faith gave her, her complete belief that Lela Marien would relieve her sorrows, I too wanted to know that peace of soul and mind. Among the few possessions Azucena still had from her old life was a little statue of Lela Marien.

"When you pray to the Mother of our Redeemer with true faith and a pure heart, she will hear you," Azucena would say. I asked Azucena to let me pray with her, but she said my father would not approve and would send her away if we were discovered. I could not bear the idea of losing her. It was then that Lela Marien began to appear in my dreams, wearing a crown of stars.

At first I was afraid to mention my dreams to Azucena. When I did, she said this was proof the Holy Virgin wanted me to convert to Christianity. Azucena said she would be burned or impaled if anyone found out, but I swore it would be our secret, that I would never break my word if it meant I would harm the person I loved the most in the world—after my father.

The letter described Azucena's death years later. She began to appear in Zoraida's dreams and instructed her to go to Spain and live as a Christian. Though Azucena did not say anything on the subject, Zoraida was sure she was destined to become a nun and a bride of Christ. *Not if I can help it*, I told myself. Almost ten years had gone by since I had fallen in love with Mercedes. But she was now no more than a beautiful memory of my youth. During my captivity in Algiers, the idea of my falling in love again seemed preposterous. I could never hope any woman would reciprocate my love. What woman would fall in love with a cripple and a slave? I felt a pure, enveloping happiness that day—knowing that the beautiful and uncorrupted Zoraida trusted completely in me, and had put her life in my hands. So many years had gone by since I had known joy that I had forgotten it was also a part of life. In my years in the bagnio, my heart had atrophied, until I met her. I had forgotten that even in the most awful circumstances the world can remind us that beauty exists, that people are capable of kindness, that Satan's offspring are no more numerous on earth than the children of God. *She has seen my soul*, I murmured to myself. *This is love because I feel generous not selfish about it*, I repeated to myself that night before I went to sleep.

From that night on, Zoraida suffused my every waking minute, and became the bright light that burned in my dreams and made them happy. I knew hope once again.

The plans for my second escape attempt were begun in earnest but with much prudence. This time I had to succeed; I could not fail Zoraida. An abundance of money would make things go easier: her father's coffers were bottomless, as long as his suspicions were not aroused. After my experience with El Dorador, I had learned that betrayal was the favored currency in Algiers. I was suspicious even of the flies. Under no circumstances would I deal with renegades. Once these men had abjured Christianity, their souls were corrupted, as if they no longer cared whether they were on the side of God or the devil. Money became their true God.

One morning in the souk, Loubna made a sign indicating I should follow her. She was accompanied by a tall, older, well-dressed Moor I had seen walking about in the casbah. His name was Abdul and he informed me he had secretly converted to Christianity. He had worked for Zoraida's father all his life, and was in charge of many of Agi Morato's business dealings in the city.

As we ambled up a sparsely populated section of the casbah, Abdul began to speak in the lingua franca in which by that time I had become proficient enough. His voice was sonorous and mournful: "The Lady Zoraida, who I held in my arms when she was an infant, has handed me funds with instructions to buy a frigate that will take her in safety to Spain. She has asked me to go with her, as that is my desire—to live as a Christian. Besides, a lady of her station must not travel to a foreign land unaccompanied." He paused, and interrogated me with his eyes. I nodded to indicate that I understood everything he had said. "Her desire is to depart as soon as possible, in view of the proximity of her betrothal to King Muley Maluco. I've already purchased for the purpose of our trip a frigate in excellent conditions, which I inspected myself. It has twelve banks: one oarsman per bank. Men whom I trust completely, and who wish this venture to succeed, will row it as far as a safe harbor, since they cannot leave their families behind in Algiers. The most propitious time to escape will be during the summer. Christian," he continued, slowing down his speech, as if to make sure I understood him perfectly, "in August, as you may know already, in search of healthy breezes, rich Algerian families retire to the sierra bordering the sea. The Lady Zoraida will accompany her father to his villa by the seashore. My master's house is many leagues from Algiers, which is an ideal place from which to sail to Spain. Parallel to my master's garden runs a stream that empties into a hidden harbor where our vessel will await us."

I was speechless. Everything had happened so quickly, so unexpectedly, it still seemed like a dream—a perfect dream.

"Here," Abdul said, waking me from my reverie, "the Lady Zoraida asked me to give you this." He handed me a billet.

I had to find out immediately the content of the letter. The sheet scented with her familiar perfume read:

Miguel,

If I may be so bold as to call you by your first name. The days I will be waiting for you in my father's orchard to take me to Spain will be the longest of my life. I will pray with all my faith to the Virgin and her Divine Son to keep you safe, to quiet the rough and dangerous seas, and to give speed to the wind that will blow the sails of your vessel coming to free me so that I can live as a Christian woman. I know I do not need to remind you that I've put my life in your hands.

"Tell my lady that with God's help we will come to take her to Spain," I said to Abdul. "Tell her to wait for me in tranquility in her father's garden where my constancy to her will be revealed, and where she will have proof that I am a man who keeps his word."

All that was left for me to do was find, without delay, a dozen strong and trustworthy men who could row with vigor to freedom. Fortune seemed to have given us her blessing when a shipment of Spanish captives arrived at the bagnio. It included two young Dominican priests and nine Castilian noblemen, who had been on a mission at the Vatican on behalf of our king. It was a dangerous gamble to approach them, but experience had taught me it was better to deal with recent arrivals before, as was so often the case, they were broken in body and spirit by the vicissitudes of life in the bagnio, or became corrupted by the sodomitic pleasures readily available in that land of heathens. I approached my compatriots with considerable trepidation.

To establish my bona fides I introduced myself as a soldier in the Battle of Lepanto. The scars on my chest and my useless hand corroborated my story and established me as a true patriot and a Christian. When the Dominican priests found out I had worked for Cardinal Acquaviva in Rome, they embraced me as someone they could trust. The men were unanimous in their desire to join me in my plan. I prayed there were no potential Judases in the group.

Zoraida, her father, and his servants and slaves left Algiers for his summer residence in a caravan. From the gate of the bagnio, I saw her go by, high up on a chair atop a camel. Despite the veils that covered the chair, and the veil that covered her face, I recognized her features. For a moment I thought our eyes met and she nodded at me ever so slightly. Happiness made me light-headed. My former vitality was restored and I felt young again.

Word spread through Algiers that Hassan Pasha, commanding a large fleet of corsairs, was leaving to attack Malta. It might be a long time before conditions were so well aligned in our favor.

Late one afternoon, after we'd had the chains around our ankles removed by a friendly blacksmith, we walked undetected out of Algiers through the gate of Bab Azoun.

Walking without chains for the first time in five years, I could almost taste freedom. We were dressed as farmers returning home at the end of the day after selling goods in the souk. We blended in with the stream of farmers carrying empty fruit baskets, or riding in their burro-drawn carts to reach their homes before night fell. Our men were instructed to travel alone and not to acknowledge or speak to each other. Under no circumstances were we to utter a single word in Spanish. Even if addressed in our language, we should pretend not to speak it. When I passed through the gate of Bab Azoun in the middle of a group of Algerian farmers, my lungs constricted as if they had been put in a vise. Arnaut Mamí's punishment for my first escape attempt was still vivid, and I bore the scars on my back as a reminder.

My fellow conspirators and I walked for about half a league before we reached the trident in the road where Abdul had instructed me to go left. It was dusk. All our men had walked this far without being discovered; we marched in a group entirely formed by Spanish captives. I began to think that we would reach Agi Morato's giardini without any incident. We came upon another fork in the road and turned right on a narrow path of pebbles that ran between leafy trees.

Wolves called each other: their howls echoed with eerie clarity across the nocturnal desert sky. A pride of hungry Barbary lions, not wolves, was our concern. We marched through the wilderness in silence. A few of our men carried pistols; in case of an ambush we had a chance.

It was a clear night, like most nights in the desert, and a moon shaped like a golden grapefruit poured so much light there was no need of torches. We trekked for hours in open country, on the narrow pebbled road until we reached the place in the woods where Abdul and his men were waiting for us with horses.

Led by Abdul, we headed through hilly dense forests in the direction of the sea. With the wind of the Mediterranean on my face, I rode under the jeweled Algerian sky feeling the old excitement that had gripped me the night before the Battle of Lepanto. Back then, my heart was aflame with love of God and country; now it was the desire to be free once more, abetted by my love for a woman, that made me fearless. It was ten years since I had felt so close to Spain, to my family, to my old dreams. Why not dare dream again? Perhaps Zoraida would fall in love with me for my courage. If she had seen my soul, she must have seen that there was greatness in me.

We arrived at the walled-in house. The heavy door was unlocked. Abdul's men rode away with the horses. I had made this decision in advance so we were not tempted to try to go back, if things did not go according to plan. Abdul went in first. Stealthily, one man at a time, we entered Agi Morato's orchard.

The night birds started tweeting when they became aware of our intrusion. Little frightened animals scurried about. Suddenly, a flapping of wings startled us as a large white owl swept over our heads. Its wings extended so far that they created a ripple of warm air over our heads. Abdul shushed us and led us to a drinking well in a grove of date palms. It was here that Zoraida, accompanied by Loubna, was supposed to wait for us. Only Abdul and I knew about this. "She's been delayed," I whispered to him.

"No, something is not going according to plan," he responded in a calm voice.

One of the Spanish gentlemen overheard us. "We've fallen into a trap," he said to the others.

I had complete confidence in Abdul: Zoraida would not have put our fates in the hands of a man she didn't trust. To appease the men, I said, "There's no reason for alarm yet. Something must have detained the Lady Zoraida. Let's proceed on our toes to the house and find out what has prevented her from meeting us." *Please, God,* I prayed silently, *let Zoraida be unharmed. If anything has happened to her, it will be a blow I don't think I can withstand.*

I was overcome with joy when I saw Zoraida in the silvery moonlight, standing by the open door. Loubna accompanied her. "I couldn't meet you at the appointed place because my father didn't go to bed until a short while ago. I think he suspects something," she explained softly. Rows of pearls roped her neck; bracelets of gold, encrusted with diamonds, adorned her arms and her ankles. "Follow me this way."

Our men were amazed to hear a Moorish woman speaking like a Castilian. She instructed the men, "Make sure not to make any noise. My father has a light sleep."

I said to my compatriots, "Let no harm fall to anyone living in this house. I want no blood spilled."

We followed Zoraida down a dark corridor, which led to her chamber. She pointed to a row of mother-of-pearl coffers on a table. I opened one of them: it was filled with gold coins. Another one overflowed with jewels. We picked up the coffers and left the room. We were close to the front door when, in our rush to get away, a man slipped on the mosaics and knocked a metal ornament off the wall. It hit the bare floor, clattering like a cymbal. We froze on our feet momentarily.

Holding a burning candle, Agi Morato stepped out of his apartment in his sleeping garments. "Lights, lights!" he shouted. "Christian thieves! Christian thieves!"

One of our men rushed toward Agi Morato and thumped him on the forehead with the handle of his dagger. He dropped to the floor, unconscious. How could I have been prepared for this? Zoraida ran to her father's side, kneeled on the floor, and gently cradled his head. "Please, wake up, dearest," she implored. "Forgive me, Father." To us, she said, " I beg you, gentlemen, do not harm him."

The commotion had awakened the rest of the servants. Two Moors, wielding pistols and carrying torches, ran toward our stunned party. When the servants saw themselves outnumbered, they surrendered their arms.

"I don't want any bloodshed," I repeated. "Disarm these men, tie their hands and feet, and cover their mouths." The subdued servants were dragged to Agi Morato's apartment and left there.

Servant women huddled together trembling in the corridor and watched us with terror shining in their eyes.

I had to take Zoraida away from the house before more servants came forward to defend their master. But Zoraida made no effort to get up from the floor; her father's head rested on her lap.

Agi Morato began to come to his senses. When he saw Zoraida he said, weakly, "Daughter, go to your chamber and lock your door. Do not open it until I tell you."

Zoraida lowered her eyes and began to shed copious tears.

Agi Morato realized his daughter's complicity. "The betrayal of one's child is the most painful of all punishments," he said to her. "How could you do this to me, who gave you life, who nurtured you and protected you, who thought of your well-being every day of your life? May Allah strike me dead!" he wailed.

We were all transfixed by this scene, until Abdul spoke: "We've lost too much time. Let's bring my master with us. Any minute we delay here we're putting our escape at risk."

Two of our men helped Agi Morato get back on his feet. He stepped out of the house without further protestations, as if the betrayal of his daughter and his most trusted servant was too much for him to bear. Zoraida walked behind him but Agi Morato refused to acknowledge her. Abdul led the way down a path in the orchard that would end at the sea. We were crossing a stream when Agi Morato fell in a faint.

"Go ahead," Abdul said to us. "I cannot leave my master behind. Prepare to man the oars. We will be there as soon as he's revived."

"I'll stay with Abdul to help him," I offered.

"I can't leave my father behind in this condition," Zoraida said to her maid. "Go with the Christians. We will join you as soon as my father is conscious again." Loubna protested but Zoraida was firm: "This is an order. Go; there's no time to waste."

Don Manuel Ulacia, one of the Castilian noblemen, said, "You are endangering all of us, Cervantes. Leave the old man behind. We can't take him to Spain with us."

"I'm in charge here," I reminded him. "Do as I say or I'll consider your words an act of insubordination."

If the Dominicans had not intervened, I probably would have been killed then and there. Finally, one of the Castilians said, "If you are not there when we are ready to sail, we will leave you behind."

"I'll take that risk," I said.

The men left, accompanied by a reluctant Loubna.

Abdul had propped Agi Morato's limp body against the trunk of a willow that grew at the water's edge. Zoraida cupped some water in her hands to wet her father's forehead and cheeks. He opened his eyes. Overcome with joy, Zoraida embraced him.

"What have you done, my daughter?" Agi Morato murmured with such sorrow in his voice that I was moved to compassion for him.

"I won't lie to you, dear Father," Zoraida said. "It was I who financed this enterprise with your coffers. May God forgive me, but after you brought Azucena to live with us, I secretly became a Christian. Once I saw the light of the true God, I could not return to the old darkness. I've been reborn, Father."

"Don't you know, blood of my blood, that you have offended Mohammed? You're no longer my daughter," Agi Morato rasped with difficulty. "You have offended the Prophet so you could become a whore like the Christian women. I curse the hour you were born of my seed and your mother's womb. By the name of Allah, the only true God, I disown you. From this moment forward, you're nothing to me."

"Father, Mohammed is not my Lord. I only answer to the Christian God."

"I curse you! I curse you forever!" Agi Morato screamed, his entire body shaking. Then he pulled a dagger from under his robe and, before anyone could react, plunged it between Zoraida's breasts. Her back hit the mossy ground; her quivering hands, like broken wings, fluttered in my direction. Agi Morato drew the bloody dagger from his daughter's body and with ferocity stabbed himself once, twice, in the vicinity of his heart. Staring at me, holding the dagger in his chest with both hands, he mumbled, "I swear by Allah that if I had any strength left, I would remove your heart with my own hands and feed it to the jackals of the desert. May Allah punish you with His mighty wrath and His divine righteousness." Then he fell forward and his face hit the rushing stream. His hair floated, spreading like dark algae tendrils on the water's surface.

I took Zoraida in my arms. She was still alive, and my tears washed her face. "Don't cry for me, Miguel. It's not wise to mourn for those who die and go to heaven," she whispered. "To die in this manner is but to begin a new and better life. In this world I was far richer in pain than in gold ducats. Now, for the first time, I'm the richest woman in the world because no one else can welcome death so willingly. I die so happily in your arms, Miguel, that death herself must envy me."

"Sun of my darkest days," I said, weeping, "when I dragged my chained feet up and down the harsh streets of Algiers, I dreamed of the day when my fevered forehead would be cooled by the touch of your beautiful hands."

"May Lela Marien protect and bless you," she said. "Kiss me . . . on my lips."

As I placed my lips on hers, Zoraida's last breath slipped out of her body.

Two of our men returned to look for me. When they saw Agi Morato was dead and the lifeless body of Zoraida cradled in my arms, they dropped to their knees and said the Lord's Prayer aloud.

"It's time to go," Don Eduardo Ospina said, getting up and making the sign of the cross. "We have to leave now, if we want to have a chance to reach Spain."

"Go without me," I said. "If I returned with you, freedom to me would taste like hemlock. Go with a tranquil heart, my friends. Take advantage of the cover of night to put as much distance as you can between yourselves and Hassan Pasha's ships. Do not delay. Freedom is waiting for you. I only ask that one of you goes to see my parents. Don't tell them about this tragedy; but tell them I will return soon."

The men gave me their word, we embraced, and they left. "I must bury my master as soon as possible," Abdul said, lifting Agi Morato's corpse in his arms. I knew Muslims are buried without delay. He walked up the stream and soon disappeared, leaving me alone with Zoraida. I took her in my arms and walked toward the seashore to find a place to bury her. I found a small cave on a hill facing the sea. I deposited her body inside, but not before all my tears had been shed. In death, Zoraida would be looking in the direction of Spain and the life she had wanted so much for herself.

To protect her human form from being desecrated by the beasts of the desert, I sealed the entrance to the cave with rocks. I worked without interruption. Using just one hand, it took many hours. By the time I finished my fingers were raw and bleeding profusely. The rising sun had tinged the horizon rose. I looked in the direction of Spain: the vessel carrying my friends could not be seen. The serene sea would deliver them on Spanish soil by the next morning.

The morning star glittering in the dawn sky was the only witness to my misery. I let my feet decide my fate. I could have walked south toward the Sahara to die; instead I headed for Algiers, for the bagnio, where I could at least die surrounded by other slaves. I would give myself up. I hoped I would be killed, because life without Zoraida— God forgive me!—meant nothing to me.

I walked for days in the wilderness, disoriented, sleeping during the day and resuming my journey at night. I took no precautions, ready to let the beasts of the desert feed on my wretched flesh. As I approached Algiers, I noticed in the distance a dark cloud advancing toward it from beyond the Sahara. What was it? This was not a rain cloud. It shifted shape as it advanced, making a deafening droning din. As the swirling obsidian cloud got closer, its furious monotonous whirring grew louder and louder.

It was not the sound of thunder, or the howling produced by the dusty siroccos, but a chattering in a language that could be spoken only in the netherworld. I hurried so that I could get back inside the bagnio before the ominous cloud arrived.

I entered through the gates of Bagnio Beylic and approached the pashas on duty to turn myself in. They were not interested in apprehending me: they were too concerned about their own lives.

The cloud stopped advancing and stationed itself above the nearby hills, waiting. A searing wind blew from the desert for several days and nights but brought no sand with it. By then everyone knew the cloud was the voracious African locusts against which there was no human defense. Everyone had heard of the plagues of the locusts in the past, but it had been many years since they had last descended upon Algiers that only Talal, the old madman who prayed naked in the plazas all day and all night, had any memory of them.

Talal ranted on the steps of the holiest mosque: "The locusts have returned, they will eat anything green until the land is bare and you have nothing but your own feces to feed on. Fog will shroud your faces, and globules of fire will fall from the sky and burn your skin and bore holes in your bones and skulls. All sinful cities on earth have their time of reckoning and yours has come. Allah will punish you, Algerians, for all your offenses against Him. Allah has sent the locusts to you as a reminder of His righteousness and to punish the abomination of your ways. Beware of those who disbelieve the signs of Allah. Only the strict believers will be saved. The sinners will serve as kindling to stoke the fires of hell. Allah's punishment will be severe. The offenders will wander forever in a labyrinth of fire. Ask for Allah's forgiveness, pray to Mohammed to intercede for you. Blessed be the name of Allah, the all powerful, the Avenging One."

The devout and the fearful flocked the mosques. Rich people began feeding the poor. Everywhere in the city, Algerians prayed in the direction of Mecca, promising to make their journey as soon as the cloud of death passed. In the public squares, Algerians begged Allah for clemency, promising to change their sinful ways, to observe fasting during Ramadan, to stop drinking alcohol, to stop eating pork, to stop practicing sodomy, to stop stealing and cheating in their business deals.

One morning, after the mosques had called for dawn prayers, there was no sign of the sun in the sky. A quivering ebony tent covered the entire city, and it hissed like a swarm of demons. By midday locusts rained like a raging tempest on Algiers. They fell so thickly that people couldn't see farther than an arm's length. The pests invaded the houses, filled the drinking wells, hid in the cooking pots, found their way inside locked coffers, sealed peoples' throats and choked them to death. Even in the privacy of their sleeping chambers, people had to shout in order to hear one another. Sometimes the locusts gathered so thickly in one spot that people died for lack of air. I staggered around with my nose, mouth, and ears covered by a scarf.

The mosques now overflowed with penitents who recited the Qu'ran until their voices gave out. An imam preached, "Allah has compassion for His people. Allah forgives. Allah is all compassionate." The verses of the Qu'ran were recited in the plazas, in the mosques, in the houses of the wealthy and the dwellings of the poor. But the recitation of these verses did nothing to placate the locusts.

Their hissing only got louder. No matter how many you squashed with brooms, or any other object you could slam them with against the floors or the walls or the cobblestoned streets, the locusts just seemed to multiply. I gave up trying to sleep and wandered around dazed, praying to

God to take mercy on me so that I could join Zoraida soon. No one could sleep, no one could rest; there was no place to hide from the plague.

The people of Algiers had reached the end of their desperation and had become resigned to dying when, late that night, a raging wind blowing from Africa's bowels swept over the city for hours. By daylight it looked as if every single locust had been buried in the sea. Algerians prayed on their knees in front of their homes, thanking Allah for ending their torment.

The world we woke up to was colorless: the green hills behind the city were as bare as the desert, as naked as rocks, and the leaves of every tree, every little shrub, as well as the flowers in the gardens, the fruit in the orchards, the herbs that grew wild or in pots in the courtyards, had been consumed.

Everyone rejoiced to be alive. For a few days a spirit of brotherhood blossomed in Algiers. People shook hands with their enemies; strangers embraced and wept on each other's shoulders, commiserating on their losses; all hatred was set aside, replaced by displays of kindness and charity. Those fortunate enough to have a piece of bread broke it in half to share it with a hungry person.

But there was no drinking water left in the city. Large crowds left in the direction of the mountains to collect water from the icy springs that fed the valley. Those too old or too sick to go in search of water drank from the sea and died bloated, contorted, and screaming. People drank olive oil, turned a jade color, and died sweating green oil. I survived by drinking my own urine.

There was nothing left in the city to eat. The granaries of the rich overflowed with weevils and rodents and rotten wheat. Wild-eyed mothers staggered on the streets, offering their skeletal babies to the sky, begging Allah to take pity and deliver the innocents from the evil that had settled upon the land. Algerians survived by gobbling down the undigested grain in the still steaming mounds of camel and donkey dung. They followed these animals to drink their piss. Then they killed, quartered, and ate them. Cats disappeared from the city. I saw mothers selling their infants to people who bought them for consumption. Cannibalism became common. I witnessed people being decapitated so that the thirsty could drink. People lost their human forms; their eye sockets seemed the size of chicken eggs. Hyenas and jackals roamed the casbah to feed on the dead and dying. The wild beasts lost their fear of people; the sated lions no longer bothered to kill.

Hassan Pasha's ships had still not returned from the attack on Malta. A rumor that the beylerbey's fleet had been defeated and he had been taken prisoner by the Italians spread like flames over dry firewood. Fear spread that the European nations would invade the weakened city, and conquer it without the least resistance.

One morning, guards went about the bagnio announcing to the surviving slaves that Arnaut Mamí was preparing his ships to leave for Constantinople. The slaves taken to Turkey never made it back to Christian soil and were not heard from again. There was no more fight left in me; I resigned myself to my fate.

On October 10, 1580, shortly before the ship carrying me away from that city where I had known the greatest depths of misery sailed off for Constantinople, a group of Dominican monks, who had arrived just as the locusts moved on, came aboard with my ransom. Mamí was eager to let me go: I had the body of a decrepit of old man, was useless as a worker, and had caused him too much trouble. Mamí grabbed the ransom money, and my days as a captive came to an end.

"There is no happiness on earth equal to that of liberty regained," I wrote upon my return to Spain. But the happiness I had yearned for over five years was puny compared to my infinite sorrow. My grief-filled heart had no room left in it for the balm of joy.

In the erosion caused by time and memory loss, the colors of those years have shed some of their hues, the faces of many of the main characters have blurred down to a single expression, a tone in which they spoke, a hardness or softness in their eyes, the shapes of their noses or the lack of noses and ears and sometimes even lips. The pain and the anguish of those years have lost much of their sting; the few happy moments I experienced in Algiers seem happier now than they were in reality.

Many years later, in Spain, I could hardly believe that part of my past had really happened, because it seemed like a fantastical chapter in a chivalric novel written by a capricious historian with no regard for the truth. Former captives lucky enough to return from Algiers tell me that the ignominious Bagnio Beylic, filled with an ever changing fresh supply of unfortunates, stands in the same place; that captives still go there to suffer, and many to die; that the oval window where I saw Zoraida's hand for the first time is still there, though its shutters have remained closed since her death; that the tale of the tragic love affair between the Moorish woman and the Christian has endured. I've been told, too, that some leagues to the west of the city, on the rocky, hilly coast bordering the azure-green Mediterranean, her father's house still stands; and in the orchard, that sacred stage of the final act of our love, visitors can find the weeping willow under which Zoraida's father killed what was most precious to us both. What nobody tells is that when Agi Morato took the life of my beloved, he also robbed me of half of mine. It is said, too, that the stream by which Zoraida died is now a bed of sand, of the same color as blood that has dried in the desert and turned to rock. But what does not remain in that land across the sea, only in my dimming memory, is the feel of her warm, smooth skin, and the taste of her scarlet lips, as sweet as currant juice, fleshy and delicate and unlike any lips that ever touched mine again.

BOOK TWO

People are the way God made them, and often they are much worse.
—Cervantes

CHAPTER 6
A FAIR AND GENTLE WIFE
1580-1586

~*LUIS*~

My experience with Miguel de Cervantes taught me that hatred of an ex-friend who has betrayed our trust—or a woman who has deceived us—outlasts love. Once in a while, I imagined revenge scenarios in which I would hire somebody to travel to Algiers to cause him grave harm. These thoughts frightened me, but I also drew comfort from them. As the years passed, and it began to look as if Miguel would end his days in captivity, my hatred lessened. By the time the news of his liberation from the bagnio reached Madrid, he was a blurry figure of my youth.

But the reports of the red-carpet treatment the city of Valencia lavished upon Miguel and the other liberated prisoners reawakened my odium with an intensity that surprised me. What was so heroic about being ransomed? My aggravation swelled when I learned that the good-hearted Valencianos created a fund to provide the ex-prisoners, whose families had few resources, with the means to return to their hometowns.

In the ten years since Miguel had fled Madrid, I had not answered a single one of his letters. Even somebody as shameless as Miguel de Cervantes must have realized I was no longer his friend. If he ever approached me again, I would discourage—forcefully, if necessary—any attempt to reestablish our old friendship. The chances we would meet again were few, since I had withdrawn from the world of Madrid's would-be versifiers. I decided to continue living exactly as I had before, as if Miguel were still across the Mediterranean, held captive in a Moorish prison.

Not long after Miguel arrived in Spain, I was relieved to hear that he had been sent on a diplomatic mission to the city of Oran in North Africa. Then, a year later, a letter from my old friend Antonio de Eraso arrived from Lisbon, with the news that Miguel was at the Spanish court in the Portuguese capital looking to get a position in the Indies.

Antonio was a high-ranking official in charge of important business in the Royal Council of the Indies, an agency that made judicial decisions regarding the king's territories in the New World. As a reward for my loyal service to the crown in the Department of Collections of the Guardas of Castile, I, too, had become an official in the Royal Council, and I had resolved to work indefatigably so that I would make myself indispensable to my king. Corruption was widespread in all the offices of the council. Nepotism was the norm; many officials enriched themselves with the crown's funds. Influence could make a man wealthy. But the men who worked under my supervision were expected to behave ethically and to remain above reproach.

Miguel had informed Antonio that we had been school friends at the Estudio de la Villa. Since I worked in the headquarters of the council in Madrid, Antonio asked if I would recommend Miguel for a post in the Indies as compensation for his heroism at Lepanto. There was nothing unusual in Antonio's request: in Spain, only the well connected were awarded government positions. For men without prospects of employment in the service of the crown, and for all sorts of adventurers and rogues, the New World was the Promised Land.

Along with his letter, Antonio also enclosed Miguel's letter to him. The calligraphy was beautiful and elegant. His years at the Estudio de la Villa had not been a complete waste. The document was a lamentation about waiting for many years to receive his wounded soldier's pension or employment in the court. Besides his service as a soldier, he stressed his diplomatic mission to Oran. The letter concluded with Miguel's boast that he was working on a novel called *La Galatea*. Was this a hint to Antonio de Eraso that he would be acknowledged as one of his patrons if he helped Miguel to get employment? Miguel obviously had not forgotten how to ingratiate himself with important people who could help him.

Although Miguel had failed at everything he'd attempted in life, I could not take the chance that he might prosper in the New World. I was not yet ready to return his evil with good. But if I was going to thwart his plan to start a new life, I would have to use impeccable logic to ensure that Antonio did not suspect that personal motives had influenced my decision not to endorse Miguel's request. In my answer to Antonio's letter I pointed out that although I was aware of my old friend's diplomatic mission to Oran, as far as I knew it had been a minor assignment that Miguel had inflated to make himself appear more important than he was. Yet the main reason I could not endorse his petition, I wrote, was that there were still questions about the purity of blood of the Cervantes family. As long as that was the case, granting him a government position would risk the displeasure of the church and, potentially, might embroil the crown in controversy. I concluded my letter: "Let Miguel de Cervantes look for employment here in Spain."

It did not occur to me that by denying his petition I would force Miguel to return to Madrid. The following winter he was back in our city. His mere proximity was enough to reawaken the beast of jealousy. I was tormented by the thought that Mercedes would cuckold me with Miguel once more, and make me the laughing stock of Madrid. It was imperative that I sever at the root whatever connection they had. Though Mercedes and I had continued to live in the same house after I discovered her betrayal, we maintained very separate lives, and there was no one I could ask to spy on her for me. If my suspicions proved correct, I would have to catch the two of them in the act myself. So I would leave for work at the usual time in the morning and then return to the house a few hours later, making sure to tell one of the servants that I had forgotten an important document in my chamber, or that I needed to consult a law book in my library. This strategy, however, revealed nothing in the behavior of the servants, or in their eyes, to indicate anything was amiss.

My son was too small and fragile for his twelve years, so he was tutored at home. Little Diego already knew Latin and Greek, and had finished his studies of the trivium: grammar, rhetoric, and logic. His tutor, Father Jerónimo, and I were both aware that my son was a prodigy. But Father Jerónimo was against Diego embarking too early on his studies of arithmetic, geometry, music, and astronomy, the quadrivium necessary as preparation for attending the university.

I decided to mention to Diego that I was leaving Madrid for several days to journey to Toledo on business. I returned with an excuse two or three days before expected, but the unchangeable routines of our home did not reveal any disturbances. I thought of intercepting Mercedes's mail, yet this meant I would have to make an accomplice of one of the domestics, and I could not bear to let a domestic know what was perturbing me. I could not even confide in the faithful Juan, who had been my personal servant since I was a child.

At night, after I had supped, I would ask Diego about the events of the day, hoping that in his innocence he would tell me whether Miguel had visited the house. I hoped, too, that he would inform me if Mercedes had left the house unaccompanied, or accompanied by Leonela, and stayed away for hours.

No matter how much time I devoted to my duties at the council, my jealous feelings toward Miguel threatened to devour me like a voracious leprosy.

One day I returned home at noontime and asked Isadora, a young domestic who did the cleaning, if her mistress was at home.

"Doña Mercedes left the house with Señorita Leonela, Your Grace," she said.

"How long ago was that?" It was a simple question, but the girl seemed perturbed and did not reply. "Well, was it more than an hour?"

She lowered her head and mumbled, "I don't know, Your Grace."

"Don't you know how to read the clocks? Be gone," I said. The girl curtsied, and I was left alone in the hall.

I summoned Juan to my chamber and asked that I not be disturbed. I paced with increasing agitation; it felt as if an incubus were trapped inside my chest, banging with closed fists to be let out. I considered leaving the house to look for Mercedes. But where would I start? Despite my impatience, I would have to wait for her to return home. The clock on the wall of my chamber ticked, and each minute was an interminable agony. What if she took hours to return? I felt like a prisoner in my own chamber. I did not want to disturb Diego's lessons, or let him see my agitation.

I left for the council, hoping to lose myself in work. Once I was settled behind my desk, I gave word to my assistant not to disturb me for the rest of the day. I forced myself to read obtuse reports and take notes, until my head pulsated, my neck felt as rigid as marble, and my vision blurred. I closed my eyes and sat immobile at my desk; I pretended I was dead so I would not have to move or to think. I lost all sense of where I was. When I opened my eyes, late-afternoon light poured through the windows.

I exited the council building and dismissed my carriers, thinking that a brisk walk in the cool spring air might help quell my agitation and rage. The building that housed the Council of the Indies was in the vicinity of the Plaza Mayor. Beginning in late March, when the first daffodils broke the ground and the weeping willows turned from gold to light green, large crowds took up residence on the public benches. The women sat on the sunny spots of the plaza and picked lice from each other's hair. The splendidly attired gentlemen who rode their prize horses, and the ladies who passed by in their carriages in their showiest finery, their heads covered in black lace mantillas, were the targets of sarcastic comments from the unsavory crowd. Gone were the days when the common people showed respect to their superiors. I was convinced that this deterioration of our society had begun with the discovery of the Indies. It had given the poor and ignorant the belief that if they just went to the New World, and encountered a bit of good luck, they might return as rich as the wealthiest marquis. Money had become the true new sovereign. Lineage did not count half as much as the weight of the gold coins in your pockets.

As I walked, I told myself that if Mercedes and Miguel were meeting surreptitiously, it was my right to defend my honor and kill him, even though this would mean my eternal damnation. If Mercedes and Miguel were lovers, she and I could no longer live in the same house. But Diego loved his mother and I would not do anything to hurt my son. Miguel was a different matter: the thought of thrusting the tip of my sword through his throat excited me. I had walked as far as the bridge over the Manzanares River. The balmy sun dawdled in the sky. Then I spotted the scandalous women who, on warm afternoons, bathed nude in the Manzanares. A number of them were sunning themselves on the rocks, their long hair loose, their legs spread apart. One of them saw me staring and yelled, "You, the one who looks like a Jesuit!" I stood still, paralyzed by her brazenness. The woman cupped her breasts in her hands, squeezed them, and said, "Come and taste these juicy melons. Have a taste of life. Your wife can't give you this sweetness." I fled; the women's laughter and their jeers trailed after me.

The bells of the Church of San Nicolás de los Servitas were tolling nine times when I arrived at my front door. I could no longer remember where I had been or what I had seen after I left the bridge. I was in a cold sweat; my mind was racing; my hands shook; my mouth and throat were parched.

Once inside my chamber, I locked the door. Candles were lighted and the coals in the brazier blazed. My usual supper was laid out on the dining table: a smoked trout, a small loaf of bread, a square of Manchegan cheese, olive oil, salt, an orange cut in half, and an ewer filled with red wine from my grandparents' vineyards in Toledo. I poured myself a cup of wine, drank it in one gulp, and sat on the chair next to the brazier to warm my hands and feet. But the proximity to the live coals made me feel feverish, and the lack of air in the chamber was oppressive.

I opened the glass panes that faced the patio and sat on the windowsill. It was a moonless starry night; the frosty breeze stung my face. The dark-leafed fig trees, swathed in black shadows, encircled the drinking well in the center of the patio; the bed of white roses was heavy with dew. An eerie quiet gave a funereal air to the scene: the patio reminded me of a secluded portion of a cemetery, a spot that even night owls shunned. A chill raced down my spine. The longer I sat on the windowsill, the more agitated I became. It was imperative that I speak with Mercedes; it was a discussion that could not be postponed. I would not have any peace until I heard from her own lips what had transpired between her and Miguel.

I knocked on Mercedes's door and entered her chamber without waiting for an answer. She was kneeling at her pew, praying to a figure of Christ on the wall. When she saw me, Mercedes made the sign of the cross and got up. She stood, dressed in a black chemise; a Rosary dangled from her hands. She didn't seem surprised by my unannounced visit—it was as if she had been expecting me. As she removed the black mantilla that covered her head I almost gasped: she had shorn her beautiful golden mane almost to the roots. It looked as if she had used garden shears.

I closed the door behind me and approached her. Candleholders illuminated the shrine to the wood crucifix that had been in the family for generations. The rest of the room was bathed in darkness. The Christ figure was rachitic, the body and face distorted with extreme pain. I hadn't been to Mercedes's living quarters in . . . could it be years? The walls were bare; she had removed all mirrors; the drapes that covered the canopy of the bed were the color of a funeral shroud. It looked as if a mystic lived in the chamber; it would not have surprised me to see blood marks splattered over the walls. Yet the serene expression in Mercedes's eyes, and her peaceful demeanor, were disconcerting. Had I made a dreadful mistake?

"Luis, to what do I owe the pleasure of your visit?" Her tone was detached, as if she were speaking to a distant acquaintance.

"I came home early from the council and was informed you were out. I waited for you for hours. What could have kept you away from your home so long?"

"I went out to do some errands," she said softly.

"What kind of errands can take you away from your home for hours? It pains me to say that I don't believe you. Stop lying to me, Mercedes." Then the words came out of my mouth: "You went to rendezvous with Miguel de Cervantes, didn't you?"

Mercedes smiled. "Is that the reason you've barged into my chamber like this? Are you mad, Luis? I haven't seen Miguel de Cervantes since he left Spain many years ago."

"I'm sorry you think this is an amusing matter. Do not mock my gentleman's honor. Why would I believe you? You spent my trust in you when you betrayed me with Miguel. You robbed me of the right every man has to trust his wife."

"I haven't forgotten how I deceived you when we were young, Luis. But you forget we were not yet married. It's true that our families intended you and me for each other, but we had never discussed matrimony among ourselves. What Miguel and I did was a thoughtless and unforgivable indiscretion of youth." She paused. When she started speaking again it was with gravity in her voice. "Your false accusation forces me to inform you about a decision I have made. I went to see my Father confessor today, and we talked for hours."

As Mercedes took several steps in my direction, the lights of the tapers caught the tears that streamed down her cheeks. She stood so close to me that I could smell her hair, her skin, her breath.

"For some time Father Dioniso and I have been discussing an important matter. Today I made a final decision. I had hoped to prepare little Diego first, but you leave me no choice. Your hurtful words force me to defend my honor. I've been inspired by the example of the Reverend Mother Teresa of Ávila to renounce the world and live the rest of my life as a discalced woman. I will beg for alms for the poor, and devote myself to helping them. Mother Teresa believed that true equality exists only in the vow of poverty. By following her example I'll discover the road that will lead me to my true self. From now on, my actions will speak louder than your hateful words; and I will wear my heart, for all to see, on the fabrics that cover my chest."

Mercedes paused again, as if to give me time to respond. No married woman in Spain left her husband and home without incurring the punishment of society and the church. Adulterous women were often brought before the Inquisition. Besides, among the noble families of Castile there was no precedent for what she proposed to do.

"I realize that to move to Ávila to be near the community the Reverend Mother founded would be too much of a scandal. And I don't wish to bring more shame to you, our son, or the name of our family. So I will move to Toledo, live in our grandparents' home, and accompany Mamá Azucena during her final days on earth. Father Dionisio has given his blessing to my plans. I hope that by living in our ancestral home my conduct will be above reproach and I will placate the vicious wagging tongues of those who have nothing better to do than to point a finger at other Christians. Nothing society says will harm my heart and my soul, as I am guilty of nothing more than dedicating my life to help others, as Jesus Christ bids us to do."

"Who do you think you are, a saint? That takes more than praying, all dressed in black in a morbid room. I don't care about the damage your selfish action will do to my name," I remonstrated, "but what kind of mother abandons her son? Only animals that are an aberration of nature do that. No true Christian woman behaves in this manner."

"Heaven will be my judge, Luis. I don't believe God will condemn me for leaving little Diego with you. Our Lord Jesus Himself left the side of His parents when the time came to do the work He had been called to do. As for me, only service to God and doing good works will bring me the peace I seek. I will leave the matter of the salvation of my soul entirely in God's hands. In my prayers I feel God has revealed Himself to me and asked me to be one of His soldiers for Our Redeemer Jesus Christ, in the battle against the deeds of the devil. I believe the Almighty has ordered me to bear my cross. I must accept with gratitude all the blows I receive. Since Our Lord has drawn me to His service, I have faith He will pardon me for my sins."

"How do you know it is God you are listening to—and not the devil?"

"Your anger has afflicted your thinking, Luis. Your heart is so full of jealousy that you are in grave danger of letting your rage blind you. I cannot go on living in the same house with you; your unjustified and irrational jealousy has deprived me of all my joys, large and small."

Nothing she said would convince me that she had not seen Miguel de Cervantes since his return; or that she was, as she claimed, beyond reproach. Listening to her was the same as listening to the Angel of Darkness.

"Good night," I said and left her chamber. Back in mine, I sat on the open windowsill and wept until the dawn sky absorbed the stars in the heavens.

Mercedes's move to our ancestral home in Toledo was all the proof I needed that she was still in love with Miguel.

She had chosen a life devoted to good works and penitence merely to avoid temptation. In the months after she left, my fantasies of revenge were like rapacious maggots eating me from the inside out. The disturbing thoughts I had by day continued to haunt my dreams by night. I considered denouncing Miguel to the Inquisition regarding the accusations that the Dominican Juan Blanco de Paz had made about his immoral conduct in Algiers. It would not have surprised me if he had indulged in the depraved pleasures of the flesh for which the Turks were infamous.

Even more damaging were the insinuations that, during his captivity, Miguel had become a renegade. An investigation was started, but the charges were dismissed when supposedly respected Christians attested to Miguel's irreproachable conduct. Then Father Juan left for New Spain. Without his presence in Madrid, it would fall upon me to start on my own inquiry; it would cost a fortune and consume me for years to come. On what grounds could I justify my interest in having Miguel de Cervantes investigated by the Holy Office? People in the church might question my motives.

In my heart, I knew I would not be free of Miguel and Mercedes until I forgave them. I would have to pray, pray, and pray until God took pity on me and released me from my misery.

Although Mercedes and I had led separate lives for a long time, it was only after she left that I realized how quiet and sepulchral our home had become over the years. Now Leonela became mistress of the house, and her hand left an impression everywhere: lovely flower arrangements brightened the rooms, their delicate aromas dispelling the musty odor that had settled like a moth-eaten shroud over everything. I had forgotten what the sound of laughter in a house was like. Now I could hear the servant girls' giggles, and the saucy airs they hummed distractedly as they went about the house doing their chores.

I didn't trust Leonela, whose allegiances, I knew, would always be to Mercedes. But she was like a godmother to Diego and, in the absence of his mother, she provided the maternal care the boy needed. I was sure my son missed his mother a great deal. She had doted on him, and they had spent a good deal of time together when he was not occupied by his studies. It was impossible to explain to him why his mother had left us without revealing many sordid details. I didn't want Diego to grow up hating his mother. I would keep Leonela in my service until he went away to university.

The first indication of Diego's upset frame of mind came from a conversation I had with his tutor. Father Jerónimo and I were in the habit of meeting for a libation at least once a month to discuss the progress of my son's education.

"Up until now, Don Luis," he said, "Diego has been a model pupil. He has always been studious, wise beyond his years, the model of obedience. The fact that there's never been any reason to complain about his conduct makes his recent behavior all the more troubling."

"Has he been disrespectful to you, Father? If that's the case, I will not tolerate it. I will make sure he apologizes to you and he never disrespects you again."

Father Jerónimo sipped from his foaming cup of chocolate, his favorite libation. With the tip of his handkerchief he dabbed at his lips. "Don Luis, I'm afraid what has been happening lately is worse than that. Diego has disobeyed my instructions not to read the Holy Scripture by himself. Despite his great intelligence—and he is the brightest pupil I've ever had—he is obsessed with theological discussions about God's intentions, which no boy of his age should be having." The look of curiosity on my face must have been great. "I'll give you an example, Your Grace. Lately, he is obsessed—yes, obsessed—with Original Sin." Father Jerónimo rested his cup of chocolate on the table. Then he clasped his hands on his lap, as if in prayer. "One day, not too long ago, Diego asked me: *Father, isn't it true that if Adam and Eve had not eaten the forbidden fruit, then there would be no human race?* I explained to him, Don Luis, that we have to assume that God's plan was to allow Adam and Eve to become man and wife when they were mature enough. Their sin had been one of disobedience, I added. I thought that was a satisfying enough answer."

"An excellent answer," I said.

"I wish that had settled the matter, Your Grace. But Diego had other questions. *Then why did God expel Adam and Eve from Paradise, if Satan had been allowed to tempt them and seduce them before they had full understanding? Wasn't Satan then the guilty one?* As a way to put an end to a futile discussion that could have gone on for a long time, to the detriment of his studies, I told him that many wise men have pondered these questions for centuries; that when he was mature enough, if he was still interested, he could read the theological arguments made by the Fathers of the Church. He seemed satisfied with that suggestion."

I let out a breath of relief. "Then it's all resolved, Father."

"On the contrary, Don Luis. Lately Diego has been troubled with the story of Judas Iscariot."

"Does this mean that my son will be a philosopher of the church? That like you, Father, he will grow up to become a priest?"

"I don't know. When I was his age, Your Grace, despite my great love for Our Redeemer Jesus Christ, I did not trouble myself with questions of this nature."

Despite his calm manner, I could detect a current of disapproval in Father Jerónimo's words. This was more serious than I thought.

"I do not wish to abuse your gracious hospitality, but I will give you one last example, Your Grace. The other day he asked me: *If it was written in the Scriptures that Christ would be betrayed, wasn't Judas Iscariot then predestined to betray Him? Isn't it actually unfair to Judas that he was chosen to betray Our Lord? If it was written that one of Christ's apostles would betray Him, why punish Judas then?* I wonder," Father Jerónimo continued, "if so much questioning, at such an early age, will disorder his brain, and lead to arrogance and lack of humility. Worse, it might end up distancing him from the blind faith we must have. Faith, as you know, Don Luis, needs no proof. Otherwise, it would not be faith."

The matter was cause for concern. I worried that Dieguito, so precociously wise, would end up becoming a hermit living in a cave and praying all the time. Might his conduct be a natural reaction to Mercedes's devoutness? My hope was that like his nighttime sobbing, which ended suddenly, he would outgrow this phase of his life too.

"I agree that Diego should not be troubled with these morbid questions. Please tell me what to do, Father."

"I suggest you don't do anything for the time being, Don Luis," he said, "unless the situation worsens. He's at that age when some inquisitive children, blessed with intelligence and wisdom beyond their years, wrestle with these questions. Let's wait and see. He may just outgrow this phase without harming himself. In the meantime, though, it's better to be aware that his mind could become the devil's playground. We both must watch him vigilantly."

Shortly after I had this conversation with his tutor,

Diego asked me for a lens to study the night sky. Maybe this was the distraction he needed from his melancholic theological questioning. Before long, I was delighted to see him on clear nights studying the constellations from his bedroom window. There could be no harm in that.

The muse of poetry seemed to have turned against me. My duties as a servant of the crown prevented me from dedicating my life to poetry, and the occasional poem I composed was stillborn, as if the muse had taken delight in stripping me of my gift. I continued to show my undying love to her by reading avidly the new volumes of poems that were sold in Madrid's shops.

Diego was like all our Lara ancestors: he loved poetry. After Mercedes left, we fell into the habit of reading to each other after supper. The time we spent together was an oasis from the affairs of daily life. Those hours were an offering to the Goddess, to placate her anger. I had given up all hope of being a poet, but perhaps my son would grow up to be one of Spain's great bards.

Though Diego appreciated Garcilaso, the beloved poet of my youth did not speak to him the way he had to poetry lovers of my generation. Since my son preferred poets who were still breathing, we read some of them in manuscript form. San Juan de la Cruz was our favorite. Diego memorized many verses from his scant—but sublime—body of work, reciting them with such feeling that he often moved me to tears. We also delighted in the poems of Hernando de Acuña, who had distinguished himself as a soldier in Africa and in European battles. Our favorite poem of his was "Sonnet in Response to the Past." We read and reread the two tercets of this sonnet without ever tiring of them:

And if there are humans blessed by excessive fortune

let no one despair with envy of them
since everything human undergoes alteration;

better to be wary of any medicine for it;
we suffer, My Lord, what is meted out to us,
trusting blindly Your strength and discretion.

We were admirers, too, of the Sevillian poet Baltasar del Alcázar—whose verses were heavily influenced by Petrarch. And we rejoiced in the poems of Lope Félix de Vega Carpio, which circulated in Madrid in manuscript. Fray Luis de León's poems were also only known in manuscript form. Diego and I reread Fray Luis the way in my youth I had never tired of rereading Garcilaso. We loved his subversive use of Horatian versification, and delighted in his disdain for court life and city pleasures. Not since the days when Miguel and I had shared our great passion for the immortal bard of Toledo had I found another person with whom I could share the love of poetry. That I shared this bond with my son, a mere boy, made it all the sweeter.

Diego and I indulged ourselves in musing about the not-too-distant future, when one day we would live a pure and simple life in a pastoral setting. One night, I read to Diego some of my favorite verses by Fray Luis:

I want to be awakened
by the birds' natural
untutored singing;
not by the din made by the grave
concerns which always
shadow one who marches to the tune
of the affairs of men.

What a peaceful life

is lived by one who has
fled the world's clamor
to trek on the hidden
path traveled by the few
wise men who have
graced the Earth.

I felt a sudden tightening in my throat and placed the manuscript on the table at which we sat.

"Why have you stopped, Papá?"

"I'm sorry, Diego, but these verses by Fray Luis bring to mind the happy days of my early youth, when I spent the summer with my grandparents in Toledo and accompanied Papá Carlos on visits to his farms."

Dieguito's eyes clouded.

"What is it, my son?"

He shook his head, wiping off his tears with his wrist, then said, "Please go on reading, Papá."

It had been years since, to my great relief, Diego stopped sobbing in his sleep. As if to compensate for that behavior, he seemed never to have shed a tear since.

His sudden weeping alarmed me. "If something troubles you, remember there are no secrets between us."

"I don't wish to upset you, Papá. But Fray Luis's verses remind me of Mother. She, too, fled the din of the world, like the poet says. Didn't she?"

This was the first time he had mentioned his mother to me since she'd left us.

"Yes, she did," I said.

I always kept a book of poems at one corner of my desk, and I would read from it daily, as a respite from spending so much of my time on the dry affairs of the council. One afternoon, when I was engrossed in *The Works of Garcilaso de la Vega with Annotations* by Fernando de Herrera, there was a knock on my door. I looked up from my book and said, "Come in." My assistant, Pascual Paredes, entered. This time of the day was sacred to me. He knew that.

"I would not trouble you, Your Grace, but some documents have arrived that require your immediate attention."

"You may leave them on the desk." I wanted to go back to reading de Herrera's book.

Pascual did not move. I was about to scold him when he pointed at the book with longing and observed, "What a beautiful jacket."

He was referring to the fawn-colored soft cover of the book, which depicted two muses standing on pedestals on the sides of a marble doorway above which a view of the city of Sevilla was framed by two cherubs. It was a bit too Andalusian for my taste.

"I see Don Luis is reading the controversial new book by Fernando de Herrera. Poetry lovers talk about nothing else."

This was interesting. I closed the book. "I just started reading it. I was not aware there was a controversy surrounding the work. Are you a poet, Pascual? Do you frequent the poetry tertulias in Madrid?"

"I don't aspire to Parnassus, Your Grace. But I admit I've scribbled verses since I was a boy."

For an instant I was afraid Pascual would ask me to read his poems.

"I'm not myself a learned person, Don Luis. I haven't gone to university, though not for lack of desire, but because of the penurious circumstances which have in recent years affected the finances of my family." He sighed. "But that's neither here nor there . . . Anyway, I've heard that some Castilian poets believe that the book aims to tarnish the glory of our Garcilaso de la Vega. As I said, I haven't read it; my budget won't permit me to purchase such an item, much as I would love to own it. I do attend the poetry tertulias, and I pay attention to what others more learned than I have to say on subjects which I don't have the necessary preparation to fully understand."

I moved de Herrera's *Annotations* to one side of my desk. For the first time since he had been working for me, I took a good look at Pascual: he was just past youth's first bloom. He wore a black cap, a short pointy beard, and a waxed mustache that curved at the tips into a semicircle. His velvet vest at some point had been lilac but was now an indiscriminate color. His white shirt was spotless, the collar starched and neatly pressed, and the cuffs slightly frayed. His black leather boots gleamed, but it was apparent they had made many trips to the shoemaker for repairs. He looked like a young man who wore stylish hand-me-downs from rich relatives.

I decided to test him. "Even though you admit to not having read the book, do you believe that the criticism has merit?"

Pascual's lower lip quivered. "My ignorant opinion is not of the slightest importance, Don Luis. It would be disrespectful of me to presume to have opinions about subjects on which wise men have already deliberated with admirable reasoning and great erudition."

His command of Castilian was precise, even fastidious, in the manner of intelligent but not highly educated people. He had the fine manners of a man from a good family that had come down in the world. My curiosity had been awakened. "I'm interested in your opinion," I said.

"Since Don Luis insists," he paused, as if to measure his words, "I will say I believe, with all my heart, that Garcilaso de la Vega is our greatest poet; a shining treasure of *la madre patria*."

"That goes without saying, Pascual. It's not a topic worth discussing. It's as obvious as the fact that the sun warms the earth."

"I also love the poetry of Fernando de Herrera," he went on. "He's a magnificent bard. I disagree with those who consider him aloof and criticize him because he does not attend the poets' tertulias."

I, too, was a great admirer of de Herrera. I felt my lips stretch in an involuntary smile. "Then, Pascual, that's the answer to your question. A pious man of high moral standards such as Fernando de Herrera, a soldier who has fought in important battles against our enemies, is above petty criticism. Spain would not be the great nation it is without men like de Herrera, who has no use for the effeminate posturing of our new poets. Besides, as a lover of Italian poetry, and a devoted and serious student of the classics, Fernando de Herrera would have nothing but the greatest admiration for our beloved Garcilaso, wouldn't you agree?"

"I do, Your Grace. I entirely approve of the title 'The Divine One' bestowed on de Herrera by Miguel de Cervantes."

"Miguel de Cervantes Saavedra? Is he a friend of yours?" The high-pitched tone of my own voice startled me. I had grimaced involuntarily; I was mortified.

"Not a friend, no. I only see him from afar. But his opinions are admired by many young poets, so some of the things he says reach the ears of poetry lovers."

It was plain to see that Pascual was a gossip, a bureaucratic underling dazzled by the world of the famous and important to which he had no access, and which he could only contemplate with longing and, very likely, envy. "No doubt Cervantes admires Herrera because of his fine poems celebrating the triumphs of the Spanish armada under the command of Don John of Austria," I said. "Though we are no longer friends, I knew Cervantes many years ago. I've heard of his return to Madrid. I do not wish to renew our old acquaintance, but I've wondered how he fares these days."

"If Your Grace is interested, I could give you the little information I've garnered about him—from a distance, as I said earlier."

With a wave of my hand, I invited Pascual to take a seat. Then I struck a match and lit a candle on my desk. "Would you accompany me in a glass of sherry?"

This was such a departure from protocol that Pascual blushed deeply. "It would be an honor, Your Grace."

I went to my liquor cabinet and took out two glasses and a bottle of Jeréz. I poured two drinks. "Salud," I toasted. "Miguel de Cervantes," I then said, to remind Pascual of the business at hand.

"As I mentioned, Don Luis, I don't know Miguel de Cervantes personally. Our young poets are enthralled with his adventurous life: his heroism at Lepanto; his captivity in Algiers; the rumors about his past and about his colorful family."

I frowned. His roundabout way of telling a story was irritating.

Pascual promptly continued: "It is said that in Algiers he fell deeply in love with a Moorish woman who wished to convert to Christianity. Though it is hard to believe, there are those who say that the Moorish beauty was killed by her own father when she tried to escape with Cervantes." Pascual shuddered. "All his misfortunes have driven him to drink inordinately. He's always starting brawls."

Pascual paused in his narrative, as if to invite me to comment. I remained silent.

"Your Grace said you haven't seen Cervantes in a long time? Well, if you saw him now, I wonder whether you'd recognize him: he wears dirty mended clothes; the soles of his boots have holes; and his bushy facial hair looks as if it hasn't been touched by a barber's scissors in years. When he's not drunk you can find him in the square in Calle de León, where he will entertain anyone with his foreign tales in exchange for a bowl of that disgusting olla podrida our common people are so fond of." Pascual paused again. "Is this what you want to know about Cervantes, Don Luis?"

I sipped my sherry slowly and then said, "Please, go on."

"Apparently he has incurred large debts since he returned from Algiers. Recently he tried to pawn, to people in his circle of acquaintances, a large bolt of taffeta that he said came from India. Spiteful tongues say that the fabric was part of the dowry an Italian named Locadelo gave Cervantes's sister Andrea for defiling her name." Pascual smirked. "I've also heard that Cervantes brags about the large inheritance he'll receive when his old teacher, the famed and esteemed man of letters López de Hoyos dies. This seems incredibly cruel to me, to talk that way about his professor who is still alive. I'm afraid that's all I know, Your Grace."

Later, as he was about to leave the room, I said, "Here, take de Herrera's book and return it to me when you've finished reading it. I'm too busy at the moment to give it the attention it deserves."

Pascual seemed overwhelmed. "How can I ever repay you? What can I do for Your Grace?"

"If you read the book and give me your impressions when you've finished it, that will be payment enough."

After he left I told myself that I would have to be careful about sharing confidences with Pascual; his manner of dispensing gossip about Miguel—almost gleefully—could one day be turned against me. In the meantime, though, he would be useful in satisfying my curiosity about Miguel, without my having to come in contact with his sordid world.

A week passed. One evening, as I was getting ready to go home, Pascual entered my office to return de Herrera's book. I crossed my hands on the desk and waited for him to tell me what he thought. "You read it very quickly," I said, to prod him into conversation.

"I'm a fast reader, Your Grace."

When it looked as if he had nothing else to add, I asked, "Well, what did you think of it?"

"It is a well-argued book, Your Excellency. And a tribute to Garcilaso, as you said it would be."

I realized that Pascual was one of those people who read a lot but did not have the education to discuss a book in an intelligent manner, or to make an informed commentary. He seemed uncomfortable being asked to express his opinion, perhaps for fear of saying something inappropriate.

I was about to dismiss him when he said, "I have a tidbit of news about Miguel de Cervantes. Your Grace said you were . . ."

"Yes, yes," I said.

"A young poet close to Cervantes told me he is busy gathering the paperwork he needs to receive a pension for his service as a soldier. He's desperately poor. Apparently his father is in bad health and can no longer attend to his patients, so the entire family—with the exception of his younger brother Rodrigo, who is away on a military campaign—has moved into his sister Andrea's house, whose husband has been in the Indies for some years."

The mention of the temptress made me shiver. I hadn't seen Andrea since the afternoon she tried to enlist me in her scheme to declare Don Rodrigo dead. I prayed fervently to be rid of the desire to visit her again—or to take any steps to ruin her family.

Pascual continued: "The other sister, I believe her name is Magdalena, who is married to Don Juan Pérez de Alcega, has also moved into Andrea's house."

"It seems that the entire Cervantes family has fallen on hard times."

"One might conclude that, Don Luis. I venture to say that Cervantes lives off the handouts he receives from his young rich poet friends, to whom he is a kind of hero. As you probably know, every writer in Madrid feels the need to ask Cervantes for a laudatory poem to preface his book."

"Yes, I see his unfortunate sonnets everywhere." I immediately regretted showing to Pascual so much of my true feelings about Miguel.

Pascual chuckled. "He has become a protégé of the young aristocrat poet Luis de Vargas Manrique."

To hear that Vargas Manrique, who descended from one of our noblest families, had befriended Miguel felt like a stab in my heart. He must have seduced Manrique the way he had beguiled me many years earlier. It hurt me that my name meant nothing to the new generation of poets, except as an officer of the crown, whereas they venerated Miguel. Not that I wanted veneration from the rabble of drunken poetasters who filled the most disgusting taverns of Madrid.

"Thank you for returning the book so promptly, Pascual. I'm glad to see you take good care of books. If there's ever one in my library that you would like to read, it would give me great pleasure to loan it to you, to contribute to your education and the improvement of your mind."

Months went by without any news about Miguel. I was

flattered that Pascual, as foolish as he was, considered me a mentor in his humanistic education. In turn, he amused me with tales about the backstabbing world of poets. We fell into the habit of taking walks after work, conversing about books and poetry. On one of these walks Pascual mentioned that Miguel was trying to get his plays produced in Madrid. "He keeps company almost exclusively with theater people."

"I had no idea he was interested in the world of the stage," I said. "There was a time, not too long ago, when actors were considered the equals of free Africans. Decent people might patronize the theater, but never kept company with that crowd. I remember my parents saying that beggars were more honest than thespians."

"What's more, Your Grace, he drinks with the kind of actors who are only paid a few reales for a performance."

"You're probably too young to remember the days when actors were held by Madrileños of good breeding in the same esteem as men who deliver water from door to door." Once again I regretted having expressed my distaste for Miguel so openly. "We'll have to see what kind of plays he produces," I said, hoping to diffuse the impact of my careless tongue. "The great Greek dramaturges are incomparable artists, but most plays written in Spain are very primitive. I would give anything to see in Spain the birth of the equivalent of a Sophocles, an Aeschylus. Our great Lope de Vega is our only hope. Have you read the Greek tragedians?"

"I have seen some of the plays of Lope de Vega. He is all that Don Luis says of him. But I don't read Greek, Your Grace. And their plays are not staged in the Corral del Príncipe."

"Of course, why did I think they would be? I have in my library some translations that almost do justice to the originals. If you are interested, I will lend them to you."

We arrived at the door of my house, shook hands, and said good night to each other. I had resisted inviting Pascual in. I did not want to encourage him to think we were anything more than friendly acquaintances. I still smarted from the high price I had paid for introducing Miguel de Cervantes, a plebeian, into my home. Besides, Pascual made me uncomfortable when, in ever so circuitous a manner, he inquired about court life. Was this how he wanted to be repaid for the news he brought me about Miguel? I determined to be careful about dispensing information about the royal family and the great families of Castile, which he might turn into gossip and spread in his circle. It would have to suffice for him that I loaned him books and filled the lacunae in his deficient education. I didn't mind it so much if he bragged about knowing me.

For a while it seemed that a new play by Miguel de Cervantes was advertised every week on the broadsheets glued to the walls of public buildings. Pascual must have spent a good deal of his meager wages going to the theater. I could count on his review of each new play. Miguel's numerous plays failed commercially. Every single one, I heard, met with public hostility. I knew Miguel would fail as a playwright: what little talent he may have had was untrained. Nobody could be a good playwright without having studied the ancient Greeks, and to a lesser extent the Romans. I doubted Miguel knew anything about the nobility of sentiment that great characters must possess. But he continued staging his plays undeterred, no doubt harboring the hope that they would bring him the wealth and fame he had craved all his life. I pitied the gullible people who produced his works, and wondered how long it would take before his credit ran out with them.

When the opening of a play called *The Bagnio of Algiers* was announced, the temptation was too great. I was curious to see how Miguel had treated the fascinating material, and what the play would reveal about his captivity in the bagnio.

On one of those autumn afternoons when the breezes that swept down from the sierra blew in the direction of the Manzanares River the excremental foulness of the city, I directed my steps toward the Corral del Principe. The cool air was invigorating and yet balmy enough to allow one to stand outside comfortably for the duration of a play. I paid the fee for standing room on the clay floor in the back of the Corral, where I was surrounded by a rowdy crowd of students, pickpockets, and others who could not afford seats near the stage. I did not want to be recognized, or to give Miguel the satisfaction of hearing that I had been seen in the audience, so I hid myself under an old cloak covering my nose and mouth with a scarf, and avoided eye contact with my fellow theatergoers. All around me, students and their friends emptied their wineskins and made crude comments about the actors and the playwright. When I was not looking at the stage, I rested my chin on my chest. There seemed to be a competition among this rabble about who could fart the loudest and the smelliest. Each loud fart was met with cheers.

From the first scene, it was clear to me that Miguel had not read the dramatic works of Sophocles, Euripides, and Aeschylus. Still, the actors sporadically spoke some lovely verses, and I had to admit he had breathed life into his characters: they seemed drawn from experience, and their emotions were as recognizable as the emotions of people I knew. But it takes more than one jewel to make a king's crown. His characters talked in garrulous speeches, which were out of place on the stage. I doubted he would ever understand that in the theater, silence can be more suggestive than long soliloquies. Miguel was no Lope de Vega. I wondered how long it would take him to recognize his own mediocrity and admit he could not compete with the great master. My curiosity satisfied, I would not be tempted again to attend a performance of one of his wretched plays.

On fine evenings, I dismissed the carriers of my sedan chair and walked home. How the Madrid of my youth had changed: now Moors, black slaves, Italians, Flemish, and French hawked their wares everywhere. Prosperous merchants paraded about dressed in luxurious silks and expensive woolen garments, making it hard to distinguish them from the true hidalgos. I remembered the time, not long ago, when only members of the nobility were allowed to carry a sword.

The most dangerous part of my walk was through La Puerta del Sol, where an ever-growing population of beggars, both of the legal and the illegal kinds, milled about. Given the slightest opening, they assaulted the passersby, reciting couplets and prayers—for which they demanded a maravedí or two—or peddling almanacs, twine, and fans. Cripples and mad people aroused the compassion of Madrileños more than mutilated soldiers, so there was an abundance of men and women pretending to be mad. Pickpockets, burglars, and assassins for hire blended in with the swarm.

On this particular evening, on the sidewalls of the churches I passed, I noticed funeral notices announcing a grand Mass to be said at the cathedral for the soul of Professor López de Hoyos. Though many years had gone by, I still could not forgive my old professor for discarding me in favor of Miguel. Had his favorite—as was expected—inherited the bulk of his considerable fortune?

A few weeks after the public funeral of the professor, Pascual came into my office to deliver documents that demanded my attention. I recognized the gleam in his eyes that preceded interesting gossip. I invited him to take a seat.

"All Madrid is talking about the last will and testament of Professor López de Hoyos, Don Luis," he commenced. "Everyone is astounded that the professor bypassed his former favorite student and left his entire fortune to Luis Gálvez de Montalvo who, as we all know, has become prosperous from the proceeds of *The Shepherd of Fílida* and certainly doesn't need the money. Not as much as Cervantes, who is completely destitute. As you can imagine," Pascual added, without bothering to disguise his delight, "Cervantes staggers around drunk all the time, lamenting his rotten luck and pulling his hairs for all too see."

I pursed my lips to avoid laughing. "Somehow I'm not surprised, Pascual," I said. "I understand the professor's reasoning: he chose to reward achievement, not need. As it should be."

Afterward, it was as if the earth had swallowed Miguel: months went by without any news of him. Was he so crushed that he had finally left Madrid? One thing I didn't envy him was his luck. I had become accustomed to seeing Miguel overcome his misfortunes. Still, I was surprised when Pascual, in a flurry of excitement, informed me that Miguel had been seen at his mistress's tavern. "It's situated on the infamous Calle de los Tudescos, so Don Luis can imagine the sort of place it is: every other house on that street is a brothel. Anyway, he's been announcing to the four winds in his mistress's tavern the completion of his pastoral novel. He kept the secret very much to himself. No one knew he had ambitions as a writer of pastoral novels."

"I heard about this project some time ago," I said, "in a letter he sent to a good friend of mine who serves His Majesty in the court in Lisbon."

Pascual remained quiet, as if he were waiting for me to mention the name of my friend in the Portuguese court. He relished learning the names of important people, and anything he could glean about their private lives.

"Since when does he have a mistress?"

Pascual did a good job of masking his disappointment that I would not reveal the identity of my friend at court, but that was not sufficient reason to prevent him from gossiping. "Her name is Ana Franca, also known as Ana de Villafranca. She is a Jewess born in Madrid. I've seen her at her tavern; she's a young, pretty wench, half Cervantes's age. Her parents married her off to a man named Alonso Rodríguez, an Asturian merchant who is away from the city on business for long periods of time. It seems everyone knows about her and Cervantes, except her husband."

It appeared Miguel had lost none of his charm with the ladies. He must have seduced the young innkeeper with tales about battles, captivity, and his sallies into the world of the stage. How convenient for Miguel that he had found a lover who could offer him, besides a place in her bed, free food and drink. Of course he would choose a Jewess—one of his own people.

Pascual continued: "People have heard him say, in a state of inebriation, that his novel, *La Galatea*, will put to shame all the pastoral novels written to this day. Considering that he's a close friend of Luis Gálvez de Montalvo, whose *The Shepherd from Fílida* is considered the best pastoral novel yet written in Spain, I think it is the height of insensitivity. I haven't read it myself, though not for lack of interest."

"I have a copy that I'll loan to you. As for Cervantes,

I wish him all the best with his novel." Then I turned the conversation to some documents that had arrived on my desk the day before. "Could you read them and give me a report? I need it immediately," I said and dismissed him.

The imminent publication of La Galatea dominated my thoughts. I awaited its appearance in the store windows, as impatiently as if it were my own novel. *Of course it will be dreadful; of course it will fail*, I repeated to myself. The fear that it might be good tormented me. The mere idea made me lose sleep. What if Miguel became a celebrated author and a man of property? Then the "de" his father had inserted before Cervantes would no longer look ridiculous.

But before the publication of La Galatea, Miguel had another surprise in store for us. While sharing a glass of sherry (to which I had discovered he was very partial) with Pascual, I found out that Miguel had moved to a town in La Mancha called Esquivias. "I am proud of my knowledge of Spanish geography, which was expanded during the time I was employed in the Guardas of Castile, but I have to admit I haven't had the pleasure of visiting the place," I said.

"It seems, Your Grace, that even Esquivianos themselves try to forget that they were born there."

"I thought his novel was due any day. Do you know why he went there?"

"I heard that Doña Juana Gaitán, the widow of the poet Pedro Laínez, invited him to visit her. It seems that Laínez left hundreds of poems in manuscript form and the widow has asked Cervantes, who was a good friend of the late poet, to edit them for publication in a cancionero. The widow Laínez lives in Esquivias, where the manuscripts are deposited in her husband's library. Has Don Luis read the poetry of the late Don Pedro? May he rest in peace."

"I understand he has admirers, but I'm not one of them.

Perhaps I just need to read more of his work. In any case, we can assume Cervantes will return to Madrid as soon as he's done with that business. Don't you think?"

"I haven't seen much of the world, though not for lack of interest," Pascual said. "But Esquivias in not on the list of places I'd like to see. Much less live in."

Not long after this conversation, Pascual delivered the extraordinary news of Miguel's marriage to a woman from Esquivias. Her name was Catalina Salázar, a member of a good, but impoverished Esquivian family.

"I have it from a reliable source that his entire dowry consisted of five vines, an orchard, some tables and chairs and cushions, four beehives, a few dozen chickens, one cock, and a brazier. Not even a burro or an olive tree," Pascual gloated. "I guess that's the most a lame and penniless groom, and a failed playwright at that, can fetch in the provinces. In any event, if nothing else, he will have plenty of eggs, honey, grapes, and some of the famous Esquivian wine. Is it true, Your Grace, that this is the only wine our great king drinks?"

"I wouldn't presume to know what kind of wine our king drinks, Pascual."

"Anyway, as long as there isn't a chicken plague or a bad drought, Cervantes will not go hungry."

Barely three months had passed since the wedding when I was informed that Miguel's mistress in Madrid had given birth to a girl named Isabel. Apparently everyone in Madrid's demimonde knew that Miguel was the child's father. That explained why he had married Catalina in such a hurry. It was not an auspicious beginning to his marriage. How would his new wife react to the news of the birth of this bastard child? It was just a matter of time before a charitable soul told Señora de Cervantes about it and Miguel's villainous nature was revealed. As for the unfortunate bastard child, would she ever even find out who her real father was?

La Galatea finally arrived in the bookshops. I must have been one of the first Madrileños to read it. It was a true abomination: an undigested concoction of bad Latin, feigned erudition, and appalling verse. Pastoral novels were aimed at idiotic men and sentimental women. The characters in the stories were llorónes who, every other sentence, singly (and often in a chorus) wept about everything on earth. Sheep, goats, and calves did not bleat, they lamented. It was a wonder that the rocks on which the shepherds sat, and the trees that sheltered them and their animals, did not cry too.

Why people were enthralled to read about dim, unhygienic, flea-ridden shepherds who smelled worse than the flocks they tended was beyond my understanding. And what could anyone say in defense of the stories? I dare any rational person to make sense of their absurd convolutions. The writers of pastoral novels were vulgar, mercenary traffickers in words. Where were the writers of the great and noble Spanish epics? Weren't these books a sign of the corruption of our national values?

With his characteristic brashness, Miguel must have believed that a man lacking a classical education could somehow trick others into believing he was a qualified writer. The same weaknesses I had noticed in the one play of his I'd seen glared at the reader from the first sentence of *La Galatea*. It was apparent to me that one of the main characters, Elicio, the wellborn, represented me, and Erastro, the humble one, represented Miguel. They are both shepherds, in love with the beautiful shepherdess Nírida, who is an idealization of Mercedes. She is described as a woman so beautiful that it seems as if "Nature had assembled in her the extremes of her perfection." Nírida, in turn, is in love with neither man, and rejects them. And that, as unbelievable as it may sound, is the entire story! Toward the end of the novel there's an endless list of all the living Spanish poets whose work Miguel supposedly admired. It was a way of currying favor with anyone who had ever scribbled a verse, no matter how rotten. That section was further proof that Miguel's brain had been curdled by the raging sun of the Barbary Coast.

There were the usual fools and immoral clowns who applauded *La Galatea*, and wrote sonnets praising it. Even the great Lope de Vega, who should have seen the book for the mediocre thing it was, disgraced his quill. Obviously these writers praised the unfortunate cripple, the survivor, the charlatan, not the dreadful writing. Yet I myself could not refrain from visiting the shops in Madrid where books were sold, and inquiring about the novel's success with the public. To my relief, despite the efforts of Miguel's cronies to pass off shiny beads for jewels, readers of the pastoral novel did not embrace Miguel's *opera prima*.

Miguel had failed as a soldier, a poet, a playwright, and a novelist. Might shame keep him from showing his face again in Madrid's literary enclaves? Esquivias sounded like the perfect backwater where he could disappear for the rest of his days. There—far from the civilized world—he could live the miserable life of an indigent hidalgo, and spend his idle hours amusing the ignorant old men of the village, gathered in the town's malodorous taverns, with his fanciful tales about his days as a soldier and slave. These country bumpkins would no doubt be impressed with the exotic tales he would regale them with for a pint of wine. If the Algerians had failed to finish Miguel off, the boredom of life in that godforsaken place would do it.

With Miguel gone from Madrid, I lived for my work and my son, making sure he received an education fit for the scion of a family of our rank. Father Jerónimo and I were relieved that Diego had lost all interest in Byzantine theological arguments. Under Father Jerónimo's supervision he completed his studies for the quadrivium. In a year's time he would be ready to enter my alma mater, the Universidad Cisneriana at Alcalá de Henares, where he would stand out as one of the youngest—if not *the* youngest—student. Diego had always been a solitary boy, uninterested in the company of other boys his age. The world beyond the confines of our house held no attraction for him. I wondered how he would react once he had to engage with his peers in the larger world.

It was a source of disappointment to me that my son gradually lost interest in reading poetry with me at night. Instead, he had fallen under the spell of the night sky and the stars; his habits became nocturnal. Except on overcast or rainy nights, Dieguito sat by his window with his long lens, where he remained absorbed with the activity in the heavens until dawn.

Something rankled me. Despite the abysmal failure of *La Galatea*, for better or worse, I could no longer refer to Miguel as a would-be writer. I, on the other hand, was a mere high-ranking bureaucrat of the crown.

Perhaps to fill the void created by the loss of the cherished hours Diego and I had once spent together, for the first time in almost twenty years the idea of starting a novel began to interest me. I would not write a pastoral novel, despite their great popularity. I was not an admirer of the novels of chivalry, either. And the world inhabited by the characters of the picaresque novels was unknown to me; I had no desire to explore the lower depths of our society and write about people I found repugnant. During my days as a student at the Estudio de La Villa, after I met Miguel de Cervantes and his family, I had briefly entertained the idea of writing a story concerning an improvident dreamer who ruins his family with his fantastical schemes. The inspiration for this character was Miguel's father, Don Rodrigo, who, with his chimerical aspirations, epitomized a certain type of Spanish man. Since my fount of poetry had apparently dried up for good, perhaps I should try to make a reality of my old idea. I had no experience with prose, so I started by writing a list of the main characters I would depict: the irresponsible Don Rodrigo; his suffering wife, Doña Leonor, a descendant of a good family who tries unsuccessfully to bring her husband, and her male children, back to reality; and Andrea, the daughter whose indiscretion becomes a source of great shame to her family.

All these years later, I could see with clarity that Miguel and his father were different sides of the same coin: dreamers who failed at everything they attempted; ruined men who could not stop dreaming.

Months of quiet went by until the winter of 1586, when an envelope was delivered to me with the seal of the cardinal of Toledo. It was a letter from His Eminence—written in beautiful Gothic script, on thick, smooth, golden paper—appointing me as a prosecuting attorney of the Inquisition, in recognition of my "outstanding love of the church." In the pyramid of officers of the Inquisition, the cardinal reminded me, the prosecuting attorney was ranked fourth in order of importance. My main duty, His Eminence added, would be to conduct investigations of the heretics accused of grave offenses against our religion, and to report my findings directly to the Grand Inquisitor. *Is this what God wants me to do to atone for my sins?* I thought. *Is this the best way to*

serve Him—to defend and protect our faith, to wage war against her-
etics and Jews and the devil's disciples? Was I was put on this earth to
be a soldier in His Divine Army? Another thought entered my
mind: the day might come when, if Miguel de Cervantes
threatened my well-being again, I would have the power to
send him straight to hell, where he belonged.

CHAPTER 7
IN A REMOTE CORNER
OF LA MANCHA
1584

On a road leading to Toledo from the heart of La Mancha, a traveler will come upon Santa Barbara, a mount crowned by a church in ruins, which dates from the time when Moors and Christians fought over who would rule Castile. Santa Barbara is renowned for the white oak trees growing on its slopes, which produce acorns prized for their nutty flavor. On cloudless days, the traveler who reaches the top of the mount will be rewarded with the indigo-blue outlines of the Sierra of Guadarrama on the horizon, and with a view of the vineyards and grain fields of the village of Esquivias and its surrounding countryside, the Sagra Alta where the Goddess Ceres was worshipped in antiquity. The Visigoths who founded Esquivias also gave it its name, which in Old German means an extreme and remote place.

My friend in the Algerian bagnio, Sancho Panza, had been the first person to mention Esquivias to me. Sancho had praised the quality of its red wine, above all others produced in La Mancha, and he never tired of reminding me it was consumed only by the lucky Esquivians and King Philip II. Over the years, I wondered whether Sancho had died of thirst in the desert, or had been bitten by a viper, or devoured by lions or wolves, or kidnapped and enslaved by Berber raiders. If his family still lived in Esquivias, I would pay them a visit to show my respect for my Guardian Angel during my first years in Algiers.

I directed my mule onto the unassuming path that breaks off the main road at the foot of Santa Barbara, and entered the village late one afternoon at harvest time. The mule passed chattering and cackling country girls in open wagons, and girls on foot leading donkeys loaded with baskets of green and purple grapes. The breasts, hands, lips, cheeks, clothes, and especially the feet of the Manchegan wenches were dyed purple with the juices of the harvest. A strong smell of must trailed in their wake.

I entered Esquivias with a weary body but a hopeful heart. I was relieved to have left Madrid behind me, after reaching the conclusion that to continue frequenting Ana de Villafranca's bed would lead to great tribulations. She was a good mistress who satisfied my manly needs and desires and did not ask for much in return, except that I appease her amorous appetites. But tavern life, with its clientele of ex-convicts and other shady and dangerous characters, where brawls often ended in the spilling of blood and sometimes in death, was not conducive to writing. It was just a matter of time before Ana's husband, goaded by a drunkard's comment, challenged me to a duel—and I was tired of running.

Another good effect of leaving Madrid was to distance myself from its cutthroat literary world. I had good reason to be hopeful for the first time in years: after many delays *La Galatea* was scheduled for publication in the spring. The dream that my novel would bring me fame and respect, and improve the material circumstances of my life, was fed by my optimistic nature.

I had been invited to Esquivias by Doña Juana Gaitán, widow of my good friend, the estimable poet Pedro Laínez, whom I considered my literary master. Pedro had died suddenly early in the year, and Doña Juana was concerned that unless my late friend's poems were compiled and published, he would be forgotten. My admiration for Pedro's poetry was sincere and well known. Doña Juana (God bless her!) decided I would be the appropriate person to sort through the handwritten poems Pedro had left on loose sheets and scraps of paper and prepare them for publication. Pedro, a true Castilian hidalgo, had befriended me when I arrived in Madrid from Algiers, at a time when I had few remaining friends in the city from my student days, and he had introduced me to some of the most talented poets then living in the royal city. To this select group of bards Pedro had praised with vehemence the few poems I had managed to jot down during my years in the bagnio. With his endorsement I was accepted into Madrid's exciting, though querulous, literary life.

"You can stay in my house in Esquivias for as long as you need, to get Pedro's poems ready," Doña Juana said in her drawing room in Madrid, where she had summoned me. "I promise to leave you alone, so you can work in peace. Our home is one of those big La Mancha houses where people can live under the same roof and see each other only when they want company. I don't know what's a proper remuneration for this kind of work, but I can offer you twenty escudos for your labors, if that seems fair to you."

My astonishment must have shown on my face because Doña Juana paused to give me a quizzical look. Her offer came at a moment when, except for Ana's charity, I was practically destitute. Not only were my pockets empty, but just a few days earlier, in a haze of wine, Ana had accused me of having relations with one of the serving girls in the tavern; I was getting ready to go to sleep in our chamber when she attacked me with a pair of scissors. I was lucky she did not harm my good hand.

"Does your silence mean the offer is agreeable to you?"

Doña Juana asked. As she smiled, her black eyes sparkled. "Esquivias is a tiny village of no more than three hundred people." In an effort to make the place more enticing she added, "Thirty-seven of our good families descend from hidalgos. Besides, Señora Petra, my cook, makes the best rabbit and partridge stews, heavenly lentils, and carcamuzas that are praised to the skies by anyone who has had the good fortune to taste them. As a poet who has seen the world, I'm sure I need not tell you about the unsurpassed excellence of our red wine. My wine cellar, if I may be so immodest, is one of the best in La Mancha."

I hadn't had such a tempting offer since Cardinal Acquaviva's invitation to work for him, when I arrived in Rome as a young man.

The widow's words were ringing in my ears as I entered the town. Old men dressed in faded hidalgo finery strolled about with skinny white hounds on leashes. I passed Esquivias's handsome church, built on a hillock. Its tall Mozarab tower dominated the town. Mournful and elegant cypresses, shaped like inverted exclamation points, grew in a small park next to the church.

Every other house I rode by displayed a dusty, faded coat of arms. On the grand houses a stone cross was carved above every window. The intricate designs on the imposing doors announced the pedigree of the family within. They reminded me of the doors of the dwellings in the casbah, except that these were more austere, in accordance with the sober Manchegan landscape. I felt I had entered a place lost in time. As I followed the directions to the widow's house, I rode with great anticipation in the golden and languid Esquivian twilight.

On my first night in the splendid old house the widow and I supped alone in an intimate dining room, where she must have taken her meals with Pedro in happier days. We sat at a red oak table, on high-backed armchairs whose seats were draped in burgundy velvet. Two large old paintings of saints decorated the room; I could barely make them out in the feeble light that emanated from the candles on the sideboard and the table. The window behind Doña Juana's chair was open, revealing the starry Manchegan night; a balmy breeze blew in from the dark plain.

"I divide my time between Esquivias and Madrid," Doña Juana said, as the food arrived. "There's the matter of the vineyards that have been in our family for generations, and I have to make sure my tenants pay their rent." A sad expression came over her face. "Pedro and I had three children, but only one—named after his late father—survived childhood diseases. My son lives in New Spain, where he is an important official in the court of the Viceroy." She made a sweeping motion with her hand. "That's where all the silver adorning this table comes from. I'm happy for him, because it is what he wishes. But it means I'm the only one here to attend to the family properties. I'd rather have my son in Spain than own all this fancy cutlery," she sighed.

Although she wore a widow's clothes, her lustrous silk dress framed to good effect her considerable bosom, on which she had pinned a brooch made of two large emeralds—one square, one hexagonal—set on a thick gold frame carved with fauna from the New World. Her gleaming black hair was held in a chignon and secured by a black shell comb adorned with tiny pearls. The darkness of night complimented her bewitching eyes. No wonder my good friend Pedro had been devoted to her. I had to remind myself I was there strictly on business.

"People in Esquivias are very curious to make your acquaintance. I want you to meet the best people here," Doña

Juana said. She took another bite, savoring the succulent stew of rabbit, carrots, and chickpeas. "Otherwise you'll die of boredom."

I partook of the aromatic and silky wine; its rich flavor traveled up my nostrils to my brain. The intoxicating elixir surpassed its reputation. In the future it was going to prove a great disappointment to drink any other red wine. "Doña Juana, you exaggerate, I'm sure," I said.

"Miguel de Cervantes, you seem to forget that you are a war hero, a man who has seen the world, a celebrated poet, and the author of a forthcoming pastoral novel. Believe me when I say that all these achievements put you in the upper echelons of Esquivian society. To enumerate your duties, my young friend: You will have the whole day to organize Pedro's work. You may come and go as you please. But your evenings belong to me. When I come to Esquivias my neighbors expect me to liven up our provincial life. They are always eager to know the news from Madrid. I will endeavor to make sure that we have many tertulias in my house, which I want you to think of as your own. And I plan to accept every single invitation I receive from my friends." With a conspiratorial air, punctuated with a wink, she added, "My esteemed friend, this would be a good place for you to settle and put down some roots. There are a few young women, descended from noble Esquivian families, who would make a worthy wife to a man of your standing. Let's face it, my friend, sooner or later you'll have to put an end to your peripatetic bachelorhood."

A wolf howled in the distance. Then another wolf echoed the howling of the first.

"Yes, we have wolves here," Doña Juana said. "As long as you don't go walking by yourself at night in the countryside, you have nothing to fear."

I inquired whether she knew Sancho Panza's family.

"How do you know the Panzas?"

I explained how.

"Oh, we all know each other in our village. Poor Teresa was left with a child after those wicked corsairs abducted Sancho many years ago; he was never heard from again. She will be happy to learn that you met her husband in that dreadful land of idol worshippers. Teresa has worked for our family all her life. And now her daughter, Sanchica, also works for me."

After we said good night, I went out in the courtyard to smoke my pipe: Venus shone brightly and golden; it reminded me of my first night in Algiers. What would life bring me in this town during the next months? In the meantime, before the future unfolded itself, this was as good a place as any to fill my empty coffers, to mend my mangled body, and to stop striving.

My first morning in Doña Juana's house I awoke to the songs of birds; their cheerful notes seemed to come from everywhere in the village. After a cup of chocolate and a slice of buttered, freshly baked bread, I went out on an exploratory walk. Flocks of sparrows, swallows, and doves fluttered in the cool Manchegan morning. I hadn't felt so happy since I had set foot again on Spanish soil almost five years earlier. The village seemed like a kind of pastoral Paradise, far away from wars and destruction, where man and nature lived in harmony. Gentle streams coursed down the middle of the cobblestone streets; their pure water smelled as if they had sprung in a grove of orange blossoms. Perhaps this was the place where I could finally heal from the years in Algiers. Perhaps I could hide in Esquivias until I broke the chains that bound me to Ana de Villafranca and to Madrid's underbelly, where death or incarceration seemed my likeliest end.

I settled into my pleasant but melancholy work. Although some of Pedro's poems were written in notebooks, most were scribbled on loose sheets. There were approximately two hundred unpublished poems, almost all undated. Many of them were signed *Damon*, Pedro's pseudonym for his pastoral compositions. In the trove of poems, some of them known to me, I found the usual imitations of Petrarch and of the cancioneros. It was the echo of the music of Garcilaso that had drawn me to Pedro's poetry. But Pedro was no mere imitator of the immortal bard: he had used the usual conventions to create works of originality and sincerity. His baroque love poems were explorations of the brevity of our passage through the world. It would take much patience to decipher his knotted calligraphy, but it would be a pleasurable task to catalogue the poems. It was almost a way of continuing the conversation with my friend beyond the grave. This was the most gratifying job I had ever had. Might my luck be about to take a turn for the better? I wondered.

Doña Juana was happy to preside over frequent supper parties at which the Esquivian red wine flowed freely. Her cook's meals were invariably outstanding: white beans with rabbit or partridge; carcamusa, made with the choicest veal and large quantities of onions, celery, and the freshest legumes; and the Manchegan migas, prepared with spicy chorizos, plenty of garlic, generous portions of bacon, and red peppers topped with the ripest and juiciest grapes of the harvest. In Doña Petra's hands, a simple dish like lentil pottage was earthy, fragrant, and succulent, as satisfying as any delicacy. Her mistress's appetite for good food insured that the fire in the kitchen was always lit, that there was always a pot simmering, and that all day long the most enticing aromas penetrated every room of the house.

The widow loved village gossip as much as she loved to

eat. At the first supper party, which she gave in my honor, I met the town's elderly priest, Juan de Palacios. His hair and beard were white, and his face had been furrowed by the merciless sun of La Mancha. But his small eyes sparkled with curiosity.

"Doña Juana sings the praises of your poetry. She also says that your plays have been much performed in the Corral del Principe, and that you are a soon-to-be-published novelist. I am a lover of chivalry novels, Don Miguel. I own the four volumes of *Amadis de Gaul*, which in my opinion, though I'm a simple country priest and not a man of letters by any means, are the best books of their kind ever written. However, I do not care for any of the imitations." He paused, waiting for me to respond.

"Doña Juana is far too kind in her praise of my talent. As for the ersatz *Amadises*, I couldn't agree more: I find those imitations odious."

Father Palacios smiled and went on, "I also own a much-leafed copy of *Tirant lo Blanc*, which I treasure as one of the most amusing books I've ever read. And I must confess to a weakness for the *Diana* of Jorge de Montemayor—though, here again, I do not care for any of the imitations. I have many other books, of course, but those are the jewels of my library. As for books of poetry, I'm ashamed to admit, Don Miguel, I have none, as all the poetry I need I find in the Song of Songs. At the risk of offending you, my most excellent new friend," he continued, "for I understand your forthcoming novel is of the pastoral genre, I will admit that I don't care for them at all. Only writers who have never plucked an onion from the ground, or milked a goat, could write such nonsense."

"I don't care for most of them myself, either," I said.

"I can see we will be friends. We have much in common. You are welcome to stop by the sacristy for a visit anytime. I assume that as a good Christian you must go to Mass and confess with some frequency—for one never knows when the good Lord may summon us to His side, and it's best to be prepared. You may borrow any books you haven't read or wish to reread. It will give me great pleasure to lend them to you. We can talk about them over a glass of our never-too-highly-praised wine. I believe there's much truth in the saying *In vino veritas*. You can't imagine how starved for literary conversation I am when Doña Juana is in Madrid. The only other person of literary taste in these parts was my excellent friend, the illustrious hidalgo Don Alonso Quijano, a man of refined knowledge in books, who loved chivalry novels, and who, in his later years, became a monk. It's hard to believe, but he has been dead for a good forty years. Ah, how time passes; so my advice to you is *Carpe diem*."

We had consumed the first course, a delicious carca-musa ladled onto our plates with such largesse I feared I would have no room left in my stomach for the second course. But from the kitchen there wafted the gamy fra-grance of roasted quails.

"Don Alonso died before I was born," interjected Doña Juana, who was wiping her plate with a chunk of bread. "In fact, Don Alonso's great-grandniece and Father de Pa-lacios's grandniece, Doña Catalina de Palacio, the mother of the delicious Catalina, our greatest beauty, will join us for supper next week. I would have invited them tonight, as I am anxious for you to meet the beautiful and virtu-ous Catalina, but her mother is in Toledo with her, where they went to collect the rents owed to my friend by her tenants."

"She does not exaggerate, Don Miguel, when Doña Juana says my grandniece Catalina is Esquivias's greatest beauty," said Father Palacios.

My interest was aroused, but before I could ask a question about the beautiful Catalina, a mound of the honeyed quails was set on the middle of the table.

Later in the evening, after we had retired to the drawing room and reclined on comfortable cushions, Doña Juana announced: "In your honor, Miguel, to show my appreciation for having you in my house as a guest, I have committed one of my greatest sins of vanity: I've written a sonnet."

Many years have passed since that remarkable evening, but I still remember some of Doña Juana's verses:

> Oh hero of Lepanto, that dreadful place
> Where as proof of your hidalgo's honor
> You left behind your valorous left digits
> In defense of our Magnificent Sun King Philip,
>
> Our Holy Roman Catholic Church—
> The only true church—and of our Motherland;
> You noble son of Alcalá, captured
> By the infamous Barbarosa brothers and abducted
>
> To the hellish dungeons of Algiers . . .

By the time she recited the third stanza, I had drunk too much wine to appreciate the rest of the lofty verses inspired by my "heroism." The end of the recitation was met with thunderous applause.

"Unfortunately, Don Miguel," the priest lamented, "Doña Juana writes only one poem per year because she only sings of the most momentous events that take place in our village. If only she were as prolific as Lope, I tell you, Spain could boast of being the birthplace of the Tenth Muse."

His words were followed by more toasts to me, to poetry, and to Doña Juana.

After I had been in Esquivias for a few days, I asked
my hostess for directions to the home of Sancho Panza's
family and set out one afternoon to meet his wife and
daughter.

"Pass the chapel at the end of town and stay on the
path that runs alongside it until you come to a drop in the
road," said Doña Juana. "You'll see a big rock on your right.
Make a sharp turn and follow the narrow trail for a short
distance. You can't miss their home; there are no others
around."

The chapel to which Doña Juana had directed me was a
simple rectangular structure made of limestone, with a low
bell tower atop. A naked cross was carved on the door of
the chapel. The austere building was as striking and eerie
as the dry landscape on which it was set.

I followed her directions and walked under the warm
sun on a pebbly, dusty path that led to a rombo made of
stones. In its front yard grew a few grapevines, which had
already been harvested. Noisy chickens pecked the red
dirt of the yard. A hutch on stilts housed fat rabbits. "Good
afternoon!" I shouted.

A plump older woman, with loose, uncombed hair and
pendulous teats, covered—but not disguised—by a blouse
of indeterminate color, appeared at the door. Her face was
sweaty and red, as if she spent a great deal of time near
live coals.

"Doña Teresa Panza?" I said.

"At your service, Your Grace." She stared at me with
suspicious eyes, as if she was not used to having visitors
come to her house.

I told her my name. "I'm a guest at Doña Juana Gaitán's house, and I've come to pay my respects. I met your husband Sancho in Algiers, where we were both captives in the bagnio."

Doña Teresa's facial expression changed from one of puzzlement to one of radiant joy. She wiped her hands on her untidy skirt, rushed in my direction, and then dropped to her knees.

"Allow this humble woman to kiss your hands, Your Lordship," she said as she grabbed my good hand and washed it in tears.

"My good Doña Teresa," I responded, "please get up. It is *my* honor to meet the wife of my dear friend."

"It's been many years since I had news of my good and honest husband," she said, getting up. Through her tears she added, "I curse the day my Sancho went to Málaga to work for His Excellency, the count. It was near that city that he was kidnapped by those godless African corsairs. Please excuse my appearance. I was ironing. But just don't stand there. Come inside our humble abode, which is also yours. Mi casa es su casa."

The inside of the rombo was almost dark, except for a fire next to which was set a table used for ironing. On the dirt floor there was a large basket heaped with laundered clothes. Doña Teresa looked around and found a wooden chair, which she offered me.

"May I bring you a cup of our wine? It's very refreshing at this time of day."

I sat on the rickety chair and accepted her offer. She filled two pewter cups, then pulled out a stool from the ironing table and rested her considerable buttocks on it.

"Pray tell me, Don Miguel. What news do you have of my Sancho?"

I told her about the last time I had seen him; and how I still remembered him with affection and gratitude. "Without your husband," I concluded, "I would not have survived my first years in Algiers."

"That's my Sancho," Teresa Panza sighed, her eyes becoming teary once more. "He's a simple laborer but he's made of gold, like the king's crown."

There was a commotion outside. I heard grunting pigs and a young woman's voice calling out, "Come here, you devil! Where do you think you are going, fatso? Get inside the corral before I slap your ass."

"My daughter Sanchica is here. She's the greatest blessing of my life; the biggest fortune my husband left me." Without getting up, Doña Teresa yelled, "Pray come in, my daughter! And be hasty about it, we have a visitor!"

A barefoot girl came in. Even from the door she smelled of dung. Her cheeks were powdered red by the dust of the road; her clothes looked as is if she had been rolling in the mud; her feet were dark in color. On top of her upper lip she had a black mole that looked like a dead beetle stuck on her face. "I just brought in the pigs and was going to feed them their slops. The big sow is ready to expel her piglets. Who is this gentleman, Mother?" Sanchica inquired, studying me.

Teresa told her who I was, and then explained to me: "Sanchica takes care of Doña Juana's pigs. All of us worked for her family. These hands"—they were big and scarlet, almost raw—"have washed the clothes of Doña Juana's family since I was a young girl. And before me, my mother. Our whole family have been humble servants of the Gaitáns since anyone can remember. Before he went to work for the count, and was so cruelly taken from me, my good Sancho tended their herd of goats."

"Signor, I was a little baby when I lost my father to those Turkish demons," Sanchica chimed in. "But I remember him like I saw him this morning. People say, *Long absent, soon forgotten*, but not in our house."

"Your Grace," Doña Teresa cut in, "we Panzas are firm believers that absence makes the heart grow fonder."

Speaking in proverbs seemed to be a family trait.

"What news have you of my father, signor? Tell me about the last time you saw him." Sanchica sat at my feet, crossed her legs, and covered her knees with her ragged skirt. She was not older than fifteen and exuded the strength of a young mare. She would have been pleasant-looking if she brushed the nettles and bits of hay out of her matted black hair, washed her face, removed the dirt from under her fingernails, wore a proper petticoat, and cut her long black toenails.

I gave her an abbreviated account of what I had already told her mother.

When I finished, Teresa Panza said, "Tell me, Don Miguel, does my husband still laugh as much as he used to?"

I told her he had made me laugh on many occasions and that he was always cheerful and optimistic.

"So long as he still has his good sense of humor, he'll survive his misfortunes. Because it's true that laughter is the best medicine. Laughter can light up the darkest tunnel, and it can make a stale chunk of bread taste as good as a roasted partridge."

Teresa proceeded to tell me about the last time she'd had any news about my friend. A monk headed to Toledo had stopped by to give her a message from Sancho. "On his way to Spain, he met my husband in some dreadful desert across the sea. Sancho sent him to me with the necklace you see around my neck. I showed it to people in the village who know about such things and was told they are chunks of salt. And they do taste salty, if you care to lick them. Here." She began to remove her necklace.

"It's not necessary," I said. They did look like chunks of salt.

"Whether they be rocks of salt or something else, I don't take them off even to go to sleep. And so, my Sancho is never far away from me. Fray Nepomuceno, that was the monk's name, said that Sancho had wanted to remind me not to forget that God may take a long time but He goes by His time, not ours, and that one of these days we will see Sancho again."

This was astonishing news: Sancho had survived the desert! "Did the monk say anything else about where he last saw Sancho? How long ago was this?"

"I descend from a long line of onion eaters, Don Miguel. I don't know of years and dates or countries. Fray Nepomuceno told me he bid adieu to my husband as he set off on a camel on the way to the kingdom of King Micomicón, where he hoped to become rich and then return to us to make me a lady. When I received the necklace," she went on, "Sanchica was too small to take care of Doña Juana's pigs, for I feared they might eat her. Still, God is great: He took my Sancho, but not before I had Sanchica. It's true what they say, Your Grace: two people in distress make sorrow less. In the meantime," she sighed, "I believe no news is good news. People like to say that hope is a good breakfast but a bad supper. For people like us who sometimes must do with a cup of water for supper, hope is plenty."

We exchanged pleasantries for a while longer. As it was getting dark, I got up to say my goodbyes.

"I can't let you go, signor, without sending my lady Juana some eggs my chickens just laid today; they are so fresh they are still warm. Tell my lady that I kiss her hands. She's not like all the other stuck-up ladies of Esquivias who forget we are all equal in the eyes of Our Lord; that when we die He won't judge us by the quality of the dress we are wearing or the money we leave behind. Doña Juana judges people by the quality of the work they do. Since words don't butter a piece of bread, if you don't mind, I would like you to bring her a few acorns. I know how much she loves them; tell my lady that they are the first of the season. Sanchica and I know a secret spot in the forest on the slopes of Santa Barbara that faces Toledo and produces the best acorns, which we pluck before they fall to the ground and the wild boars gobble them down. I don't believe in the wild boars eating better than we do, even though nothing makes them taste better than a good harvest of acorns. Mind you, Don Miguel, don't go there to collect the acorns yourself. The wild boars visit the forest in the afternoons and the wolves at night."

"But we are not afraid of them," said Sanchica. "I always go armed with a pointy log and dare any wild boar to attack us. When they see me raise my arm they run away in terror." Sanchica punctuated her words by spitting on the ground. Then she flexed her right arm to show me her musculature.

Teresa Panza laughed. "It's true, Don Miguel. I believe my Sanchica could scare a lion."

As I stepped out of the rombo, evening had begun to fall. Teresa Panza handed me a small basket filled with acorns. "If you haven't already, you must visit our Blessed Lady of Milk in the church. She is the patroness of the town and most miraculous. I always bring her a mugful of milk when I visit her, although I know the curate drinks it. But she's very happy to receive cheese, and butter too. Pray to her, Don Miguel, and she will grant your wishes. Sanchica and I always pray that Our Blessed Lady of Milk will bring my husband back to us." Then she added, "I rejoice in your visit, Your Grace. Anyone who is a friend of my Sancho is our good friend too. To show you my appreciation, let me wash and iron your clothes, and Don Miguel can pay me whenever you can."

I thanked her for her generous offer and then walked back to Doña Juana's house, carrying a basket filled with the famous Esquivian acorns. I was glad she had forgotten to pack the eggs.

Doña Catalina Salázar and Doña Juana both descended from old Esquivian families. Like Doña Juana, Doña Catalina was a widow, and Catalina was her only daughter. The widow was also the mother of two younger boys, I was informed by my hostess. On the evening Doña Catalina and her daughter came to supper there were no other guests. Once more I was introduced as a war hero, a captive who had suffered unspeakable tortures at the hands of the Turks, a successful playwright, a well-known poet, and the author of a much-awaited pastoral novel.

At the dinner table the two older women fell into a conversation about crops and tenants and village gossip, which excluded Catalina and me.

Doña Juana's praise of the young Catalina had not been an exaggeration: she was a Castilian beauty, of medium height with black hair and eyes, and a fair complexion darkened along the way with a drop of Jewish blood. Her lovely hands looked strong, as if they were used to working in the house. In contrast to the older women, she was dressed simply. Her velvet dress was of a faded burgundy color, and she wore a plain gold ring and earrings. A black shawl draped her shoulders, making a stark contrast with her ivory-colored neck, around which she wore no jewelry. Catalina's beauty rendered me silent.

Doña Juana interrupted her animated heart-to-heart with Catalina's mother and said to me, "Miguel, don't be shy. Tell Catalina about the glorious Battle of Lepanto, and the time you spent in Rome, and slavery in Algiers. She will find all of it fascinating."

I was getting tired of repeating my story for the benefit of Doña Juana's guests.

Seeing me demur, Catalina remarked: "I'm afraid you'll find me very dull, Don Miguel. I have seen little of the world. I've been to Toledo, and went with my mother once to Madrid on business, after my father died. I accompanied her only because my two brothers are too young to be good traveling companions for her. A gentleman who has seen the world like yourself must find it so unexciting to talk to a provincial like me. What's more," she blushed, "I confess I don't read much poetry and have never seen a play. But I do like pastoral novels. So you can count on me to read yours."

She held my gaze and spoke with a directness that was unusual among Spanish ladies.

The following afternoon, I took advantage of Doña Catalina's invitation to stop by her house. During my first visit, she sat with Catalina and me in their parlor, the furniture of which was of good quality, but from another century. Afterward, in what became daily visits, Catalina's little brother, Francisco, chaperoned us.

As the late-September afternoons had become cooler, I proposed going for walks. We would head not to the church or the town's fountain, as most couples did in Esquivias, but away from the town, into the countryside, accompanied by Francisco, who always ran ahead of us chasing lizards or aiming at birds with his sling. Catalina was devoted to her little brothers. After her father died, her mother had come to rely on her help in managing the housekeeping as well as the family's finances. Despite her beauty and her pleasant disposition, she did not seem to have any suitors. When I remarked on this, she said abruptly: "I don't care for the good-for-nothing men of Esquivias, Miguel. I'd rather become a spinster than marry one of our irresponsible men."

Catalina asked me many questions about the adventurous life I had led. I was flattered that this beautiful young woman relished my company; and the direct way in which her burning eyes looked at me, a penniless man with a bad arm, made me feel hopeful about the future. When she peered at me, I saw admiration and respect in her eyes. Not since Zoraida had a woman gazed at me in that way.

I had sworn off love after coming to understand that both Mercedes and Zoraida were unattainable ideals. The only women I had known in a carnal way were whores, or women like Ana de Villafranca, whose bed had been shared by more men than bedbugs. Catalina's gentle manner made me want to be around her constantly. During the day, as I sat at the desk of my late friend Pedro, I felt more inclined to write love poetry than to work on deciphering his manuscripts. Or, when I managed to do a little work, I would come upon one of Pedro's love poems that expressed so well the feelings I had for my Esquivian beauty.

Maybe Doña Juana was right, after all. Perhaps the time had come for me to marry and grow roots in one place. All I needed to settle down to write was an understanding wife who had the means to support us while I did my great work, which I was convinced lay ahead of me. But what were the chances that a fine young woman of noble lineage, and with properties, would become interested in me?

One afternoon in October, Francisco was unable to accompany us on our walk due to a cold. But the weather was so balmy that Doña Catalina insisted we take advantage of the perfect conditions. Catalina and I reached one of our favorite places, a secluded hill to the south of town rarely visited by the locals. Up to that point, Catalina and I had held hands furtively, whenever Francisco was distracted, looking for bugs under rocks. To rest our limbs after the climb, we sat on a patch of grass beneath an oak tree. The moment we were alone, and our hands brushed, the first kiss followed and every feeling that had been held in abeyance flared up in abundance. The skin of Catalina's face, and her hair, smelled of ripe grapes. Her warm and soft lips lacked experience kissing but searched mine with eagerness, as if they had been waiting for this moment for a long time. When we lay on the grass pressed against each other, and I buried my nose in her dewy breasts, I knew that what had been started could not be stopped. Afterward, as we lay panting and sweating, I suddenly remembered the saying that a pickle cannot be turned back into a cucumber. After what had happened that afternoon, the only honorable thing to do was to marry Catalina.

That I was twice her age, with only one good arm, could bring no dowry to the marriage, and was a member of a notorious family whose purity of blood was in dispute, were no longer obstacles under the circumstances. In a village like Esquivias, a dishonored daughter was the worst of all stains on the name of a family of good stock.

On December 12, 1584, barely three months from the moment we first met, Catalina de Palacios and I were united as husband and wife by her uncle, Juan de Palacios, at the Church of Our Blessed Lady of Milk. The wedding happened with so little preamble that no member of my family was able to make the journey from Madrid to attend it. Besides Doña Juana and Catalina's mother and brothers, the only other people in attendance were Rodrigo Mejía, Diego Escribano, and Francisco Marcos, Doña Catalina's Esquivian neighbors who served as witnesses.

Several days before the wedding, I presented Doña Juana

a clean and corrected manuscript of Pedro's poetry. In addition to the twenty escudos we had agreed upon as my fee, Doña Juana gave us another twenty escudos as our wedding present. Forty escudos was a handsome sum with which to begin our married life.

The idea of returning to Madrid became unappetizing. For the time being, I was content to stay in Esquivias with my beautiful young wife. I wanted to rent a house where we could settle down to a life of domestic happiness that would be conducive to writing, but Catalina was reluctant to move away from her family. "My mother and my little brothers need me too much, Miguel," she said. "Our house is large enough so that we can still have privacy as husband and wife."

We installed ourselves on the second floor of the Palacios's ancestral home, which was shaped like an L. Three large rooms with high ceilings offered views in every direction of the village and the Manchegan countryside. It was a tranquil place where I could have devoted myself to writing, except that now that I had finished cataloguing Pedro's poetry, and the impending publication of *La Galatea* became all too real, I was apprehensive about beginning a new project. It took great determination to scribble a few inert lines of verse.

Catalina was eager to learn every trick I had mastered in bed from countless whores of many nationalities. I had also picked up a few new tricks from Ana de Villafranca's vast repertoire; but Catalina's youthful and virginal body, her desire to please me and please herself, were a delicacy of which I could never tire. Late at night, when Esquivians were immersed in their deep slumber, Catalina and I made love with such abandon that the dogs in the town, and the wolves in the countryside, answered my groans and her ecstatic yelps with excited barking and howling. In the mornings, when I went to the kitchen for my breakfast, Doña Catalina couldn't look at me, or talk to me, without blushing. As I walked around town children would follow me, agog at anything I did. When women alone, or accompanied by other females, saw me going up the street, they would hurriedly cross to the other side and walk by quickly, their eyes on the ground. And the old men who sat outside their front doors, smoking a pipe and saying hello to the passersby, would blurt out: "Hostias! Hombre! Joder!" and blow plumes of smoke as I greeted them.

Many Spanish women covered their faces with a veil while their husbands made love to them; Catalina, on the other hand, lit all the tapers in our chamber so that we could admire and explore each other's bodies from head to toe. While most Spanish women made love in the horizontal fashion, Catalina, after I had shown her a few variations, wanted to ride me, bobbing up and down my crotch as if she were riding a camel; or she made me sit on a straight-backed chair and, pressing her breasts to my chest, impaled herself on my organ, until I felt I was deeper in her than I had been in any other woman. Whereas the whores I'd made love to performed in every position known to man, their pleasure felt feigned and they never asked for more; with those women lovemaking ended when I climaxed, but Catalina was not satisfied until she had pleasured herself. Whereas all the whores I had known had allowed me to penetrate them, Catalina was eager to penetrate me as well—with pickles and cucumbers and carrots; with the whores, affection ended when I had sated myself, but Catalina loved to stay awake, whispering the parts of her story I didn't know, and now and then pausing to nick my nipples, slap my ass, or give my manhood a moist suck. We cuddled until exhaustion made us close our eyes and they opened again only to greet the new day. All the lovemaking

I had known before expired by the end of the night. With Catalina I had found a woman whose love did not vanish in the daylight. I was never again as happy as that winter of my honeymoon in Esquivias, when our lovemaking made the chilly nights of La Mancha as warm and embracing and supple as the sands of the Sahara just after sunset.

If Catalina had been an orphan, we might have found lasting happiness as man and wife. But she had a mother, and not just any mother. Soon after our wedding, I realized that Doña Catalina was desperate for a man to take charge of the properties and precarious finances of the family. At his death, three years earlier, Catalina's father, the late Fernando de Salazar Vozmediano, an improvident man and a gambler, had left large debts, and the family's financial affairs were in disarray. Fortunately, Catalina's properties were inherited, and Don Fernando's many creditors could not claim a piece of them. But my mother-in-law expected me to collect the rents from the houses in Toledo and other villages of La Mancha, and to oversee the planting, harvesting, and selling of the produce from the orchards and vineyards.

My newly acquired duties as the head of the family kept me away from the writing desk. My dream of a bucolic life in which I could devote myself to writing began to seem like another chimera. At first, I went along with my new responsibilities without complaining. I hoped the publication of La Galatea would make me financially prosperous so that I could hire a man to oversee the family business. I failed miserably at collecting the rents owed by Doña Catalina's tenants in Toledo and nearby villages. Extracting money from these families was like trying to squeeze milk from a rock. These were people who barely managed to survive. In the best cases, most of them paid their rent in the form of chickens, eggs, a few bottles of wine or olive oil, and—this was indeed a miracle—a piglet, or a kid goat.

Upon my return to Esquivias with a menagerie in place of money, Doña Catalina showed her displeasure at my lack of experience in dealing with her tenants. "If these people can't pay their rent, you must put them out on the street, Miguel. By force, if necessary. If I were a man I'd do it myself with my own hands. I'm not made of gold. I, too, must feed my family, and now you!"

But how could I evict old people from their homes when they could have been my own parents?

"Miguel, try to understand my mother," Catalina told me one Sunday on our way to Mass. "My father couldn't tell a maravedí from an escudo. To him money was there to be spent. When it comes to finances, my little brothers have more sense than he did. Mamá is no longer young, she's tired, and she feels overwhelmed. She needs a man who can relieve her of her duties. I know you are a poet, and you have a compassionate heart, but you must make an effort, Miguel. Our livelihood depends on collecting the rents owed to us. If *La Galatea*, as we all hope and pray, turns out to be a success, we can hire a man to take care of business, as you want, so you can devote yourself to writing without annoying interruptions."

I didn't want to disappoint my lovely wife, who was a lady in the parlor and a whore in bed, and who treated me with tenderness and respect.

My blissful marital life was in imminent danger of deteriorating if Catalina and I continued to live with her mother. The house of the late hidalgo Don Alonso Quijano de Salazar had been recently put up for rent. Many years ago it had been regarded as the grandest house in the village and one of the finest in the environs of Toledo, but it was now dilapidated. Its walls were crumbling, and it was too large and expensive for most Esquivians. At the risk of displeasing my wife, I decided to use the money Doña Juana had paid me, and I rented it. The house's main appeal for me was that it was on the other side of town, as far away as possible from my mother-in-law.

Father Palacios had told me about the bachelor Alonso Quijano at Doña Juana's first supper party. He had been a rich landowner and a distant relative of Doña Catalina who went mad, Esquivians said, from reading too many chivalry novels, and in his old age he regained his sanity, ending his life as a friar. The room that Don Alonso had used as his library became my writing room. It was the first time in my life that I'd had a room that was mine to use exclusively for writing. On the library shelves there were a handful of dusty novels of chivalry. Marianita, an old, half-blind servant who still lived in the house, had saved them when Don Alonso's niece, in an effort to restore her uncle's sanity, had thrown all his books out the window and planned to burn them in the street. With the squire's sturdy desk in front of the same window, all I needed was a chair, a quill, a pot of ink, writing paper, and the muse to shower me with inspiration.

From the desk there was a view of endless tawny fields where lentils and chickpeas were cultivated. Sitting there every day, staring at the ochre and treeless Manchegan landscape, I indulged the fantasy that I was a well-off country squire who wrote good, but popular novels that made me prosperous. In view of my financial success, my mother-in-law had finally shut her mouth and left Catalina and me in peace. In my fantasy, my aged parents lived with us in comfort, and my wife and I were blessed with many children who were my parents' joy in their old age.

As I wandered through the empty, disordered rooms, I felt the presence of Alonso Quijano. The house had a large courtyard paved with smooth square stones. Huge vats for wine and olive oil were stored in a warehouse on the property that was cold even in the hottest days of summer. The vats were empty; I dreamed of a day in the near future when they would be full again. The granary, too, would be filled with wheat and barley. To the right of the warehouse there was an arched entrance to a tunnel that had been built around the time when the Moors regularly attacked Esquivias. The tunnel, which was decorated with Arab motifs and Gothic arches, led to the belly of Mount Santa Barbara. At one time, all the houses in Esquivias were connected by these tunnels. During the attacks from the Moors the families used them to make their way to the top of Santa Barbara, where they could better defend themselves.

When Father Palacios came by to visit, he would regale me with stories about Alonso Quijano. During the cold winter nights, when we gathered around a brazier in the room on the second floor where the women did their knitting, I would read novels aloud, but sometimes Marianita, who had worked for Don Alonso from the time she was a young girl, would entertain us with stories about her eccentric master. The more I heard about Don Alonso, the more he seemed like the hero of a tale that had yet to be told.

With the arrival of spring, *La Galatea*, my first child, made its appearance in Madrid's bookshops. I had so many expectations for my novel, hoping it would make me famous and relieve me of financial worries once and for all. I was sure my genius would finally be recognized. I knew I had penned a pastoral novel unlike the ones written by my contemporaries. No one before me, I was sure, had the audacity to write a novel that was both in prose and in verse.

Despite some favorable notices written by my friends, who praised the book for its innovations, agonizing weeks and then months went by before it became apparent that *La Galatea* had failed to find a receptive audience among the readers of pastoral novels. Copies of my book languished on the shelves of Madrid's bookshops. Each unsold volume was an accusation, a bleeding wound that threatened to shorten my life. On my rare visits to Madrid I was ashamed to walk into bookshops, for fear of being recognized as the author of a novel nobody was interested in.

I had given up the idea of earning my livelihood by writing for the stage. If I couldn't support my wife by writing novels, what was left for me to do? My dream of rescuing my parents from a poor and undignified old age was shattered. I began to think that it would have been better for me to die at the hands of the Turks, than to have returned to Spain and failed in such a public manner.

In the midst of my despondency, I received the news of my father's death. Although he had been in poor health in recent years, I expected him to live much longer, harboring the hope that, before he died, my father would see me become a success. I neglected my parents for a long time in order to pursue my dream of becoming a writer, and I failed them. It had begun to look as if I would never succeed at anything I did. As the eldest son, I should have entered my father's profession to relieve my unwed sisters of the burden of supporting our parents. Mother's worst fear had become a reality: I had become an irresponsible dreamer. My grief was bottomless. I thought it would be better to die so that Catalina could begin a new life. She was young, beautiful, and a woman of property. It would not be long before a more deserving man asked for her hand in marriage. What right did I have to ruin her life too?

I abandoned myself to the ways of Bacchus. I took to drinking at the tavern of Don Diego Ramírez, and ignored all obligations to my wife. Hoping I would at least have luck at the card tables, I became a gambler, like my father; I practically lived in the disreputable taverns where the working women had long blond hair and green eyes, and were pure descendants of the Visigoths.

One morning I woke up with a hangover that felt like nails being hammered into my temples, only to hear my mother-in-law screaming in the yard: "Are you awake yet, Don Miguel de Cervantes? I want our neighbors to know how you spend your days drinking and gambling what's not yours to gamble away, and telling tall tales to the old men of Esquivias! I want everyone to know that you return home drunk every night, expecting to find supper ready for you; and if your wife tries to talk to you, you reply, *Don't distract me. I can't be interrupted; I'm writing a sonnet in my head for my friend Don so-and-so's new pastoral novel.*

"Listen to me, my good neighbors! You all know me; you know I didn't raise my daughter to take care of a cripple. Her dowry may not have been magnificent, but this moth-eaten log should be grateful that such a beautiful girl, from an old Christian family, married him. Just a few months ago, before she married this worthless scribbler, her skin was smooth as a mirror and her eyes sparkled with gaiety. She was like a rose in May, whose every petal is perfection. You deceived all of us with your Luciferian tongue, Don Miguel! All that talk about how *La Galatea*, the most abominable pastoral novel ever penned, was going to be so popular; how it was going to sell more books than eggs are fried every day in our kingdom; how your fame was going be so great that our magnificent King Philip himself would come to visit our home. Well, I'll become a duchess before you earn a maravedí writing anything. Next time try writing a novel with your left hand, maybe you'll do better that way!"

Thinking she had stopped, I got up from bed and reached for my chamber pot to relieve my bladder. I was in the middle of this when my mother-in-law started up again: "I'm not through with you yet, you miserable cripple! Look how I have aged in less than a year since you married my treasure. I walk about as if I carry a loaded camel on my back. Know this, in case you have any illusions of the kind in your diseased head: if I were to die today, I would not leave you even a rotten egg!"

When I again thought she had run out of insults, she continued: "Mark my words, Catalina. And you too, my good neighbors. This crippled scribbler will end up like my great-granduncle Alonso Quijano who, as we all know, went mad from reading all those chivalry novels."

I waited for a while after she stopped her harangue before I went to the kitchen for a cold drink of water to soothe my parched throat. Catalina was kneading dough for bread. She lowered her eyes and said, "Miguel, I'm so embarrassed. Now all our neighbors know about our problems." She left the kitchen rubbing her hands and crying.

The old days in the Algerian bagnio began to look like an oasis of tranquility to me. And just when I thought my life could not get worse, I returned home one afternoon in an inebriated state and found Catalina in the front parlor, cradling an infant. An older woman I did not recognize, and who looked like a domestic, sat in the parlor.

With humid eyes, Catalina raised the child and offered it to me. "Miguel, this is Isabel, your daughter," she said. "Ana de Villafranca has sent Isabel so that you can meet her."

I was astounded. I had no idea Ana had been pregnant

with my child when I left Madrid. Had she known all along and kept it a secret? I felt brutally awakened, as if I had been drenched with a bucket of icy water.

Catalina got up from her chair and placed the infant against my chest; I secured her with my good hand. I stared at the tiny girl in disbelief. She smelled like a mug of fresh milk scented with rose water. Her head was uncovered: I recognized Ana's raven hair. But her agate eyes were unmistakable: they were large and brilliant and danced with excitement like the eyes of the Cervantes. Her clothes were new, and she wore knitted boots. With her chubby little hands, Isabel grabbed my beard, pulled it, and smiled. "My daughter," I murmured, fighting tears.

"Señora María," Catalina said, nodding in the direction of the woman sitting in the parlor, "is Isabel's wet nurse. Ana sent word that we could keep the child for a few days, if we want to. Without waiting for your permission, I've taken the liberty and I've asked Señora María to stay here while Isabel is visiting us." Catalina held out her arms so that I would return my daughter to her.

During Isabel's stay in our house, not once did Catalina have words of reproach for me. I stayed home, resisting the temptation to go out to get drunk. Catalina embraced Isabel as if she were her own child. Her maternal instincts should not have surprised me: Catalina had helped her mother rear her two brothers. She bathed Isabel with great tenderness, fed her porridge, and sang her to sleep. While the child slept, Catalina knitted bonnets, boots, gloves, and scarves for my daughter.

After Isabel went back to Ana, an uncanny hush settled on our home. For a few days, her crying and guttural sounds had brought happiness to the house and made it feel full of life.

Catalina moved out of our chamber. From then on,

anything I said to her was met with silence. Once more, the taverns beckoned to me, as places where I could forget my circumstances. One night, as I staggered into our parlor, I found Catalina sitting near the brazier. Other than the glow of the brazier, one taper on a table provided the only illumination. I was too drunk to talk, so I began to totter in the darkness in the direction of my chamber. Catalina called my name with an anger that chilled my entire body. I turned around and saw her, taper in hand, following me. I entered my chamber and Catalina followed me. I threw myself on the bed and closed my eyes.

"You can pretend to go to sleep, Miguel. But drunkenness has not made you deaf. Listen to what I have to say because this will be the last time I will utter these words. I'm your wife by the law of the church, and in the eyes of our Lord, but I will never again be a wife in the conjugal bed. I could not bear to lie with a man who abandons a woman with his child; a man who seduces another woman and marries her when he knows that another woman carries his child."

I turned around. "Please, Catalina, I beg you to stop. When I married you I did not know Ana was pregnant with my child. I swear it on my father's grave. May our Lord Jesus Christ strike me dead this instant if I'm lying to you."

"That may be true, Miguel. Regardless, you have destroyed my trust in you. May God forgive me for what I'm about to say to you: I will never bear you a child. You already have a beautiful daughter and you must devote yourself to being a good father. I will treat Isabel and love her as if she were a child of my own flesh. But I could not bring a child of mine to this world, a child who would have for a father a drunk without scruples; a weak man who cannot take care of his family because wine and gambling are his true masters. I will live with you until the day I die, Miguel, and I will be by your side in illness and misfortune, and while to the rest of the world we'll continue to be a married couple, as a bond created by God cannot be dissolved by man, from now on—and I'm a woman who keeps her word—you have no claims on me."

Through my tears I saw her walk out of the chamber and close the door, leaving the room in complete darkness. Catalina and I never slept together in the same bed again.

All I had left were my dreams, which no one could strip me of. I would be like Christopher Columbus: no matter how crushing my failures, I would not, I could not, stop dreaming. It was at this time that I began to conceive of a novel, not a pastoral or chivalric or picaresque novel, but a new kind of novel, about a man who in many ways was like Alonso Quijano, like my father, like myself; a man who personified the age in which I lived; someone like Columbus, a man of humble origins, who dared to be an individual at a time when men like him were only allowed to have small aspirations. My hero would be a man who believed he was as deserving of human dignity as any nobleman; a man who would break away from all the others who had come before him, just as Columbus had, as all dreamers had from the beginning of history; a man who dared to be different; who, like Alonso Quijano, lived his life outside the imprisoning conventions created by society; who would not be afraid to be considered mad; a man who embodied the qualities of a new kind of gentleman; who was as much a soldier as a man of letters; who understood that the ancient relationship between the common man and the prince was obsolete; a man, a true gentleman, who could relate to the suffering of other human beings; who would help create new ideals to aspire to; who knew that good deeds and admirable actions, a kind heart and fairness for all, were more important than privilege and birth.

My new hero would exemplify Castiglioni's ideal of the courtier: a man who believed he was capable of dominating the world and forging his own destiny. In many ways, Alonso Quijano had been that kind of man. From the moment I set foot in his library, and took a look at the empty shelves that had once been filled with novels, and I sat at his desk and looked out the window at the endless plains of La Mancha, I knew I could not escape the pull of Alonso and of that inhospitable, waterless place, where the fields were made not of sand dunes, like the Algerian desert, but of pebbles and rocks; a place that seemed to have been formed to shatter the dreams of dreamers like Alonso, like me.

As I sat at his desk, for hours that turned into days, for days that ended with nights that felt like the very light of life was being extinguished, I understood the desperation with which Alonso Quijano must have longed to escape from a place where nothing ever happened, where people were afraid to grow wings and fly away. It was as if I started metamorphosing into Alonso Quijano, becoming his double, just as I was sure that I, too, had my double someplace on earth, at this very moment, and would have one—no, not one, but legions of them, in the future, for centuries to come—who thought and felt and dreamed as I did.

Three years of marriage were enough for me. I never stopped loving Catalina, but perhaps, like Alonso Quijano, I was meant to be a bachelor, after all. For three years I'd felt as if I had been sentenced to the gallows. I prayed to escape from my marriage as desperately as I'd prayed to be liberated from the Algerian bagnio. It was as if the creativity that had flowed in my veins all my life had dried up after I'd arrived in Esquivias.

From a friend who passed through town on his way to Sevilla, I heard there were openings in my beloved city for tax collectors of the crown. My friend said he knew someone who would help him secure a position. "Why don't you come along?" he asked. Then he added, "I will intercede with my friend to help you find work too."

I didn't need any other argument to convince me to leave for Sevilla: I was ready to go. I did not care that tax collection was one of the few official jobs open to Jews at the time, that taking such a job would be an acceptance on my part of the impurity of my blood. I was certain that if I did not leave Esquivias, without the slightest delay, it would not be long before I, like Alonso Quijano, went mad.

Once again, I would begin a new life. Middle-aged, weary, disillusioned, a complete failure, I nonetheless remained ever the dreamer: I could not help but hope that better times were ahead. So I fled Esquivias, abandoning my good Catalina—not an unreachable or imaginary love, but my flesh-and-blood wife—and I left the only house I had ever been able to call mine.

I will let future historians tell what happened to me in the next twenty years, the continuation of disappointments in a life filled with an endless list of them. Suffice it to say that I had to go on the road so that I could see the rest of the characters that Spain—and by extension the world—contained. I had to go on the road to learn what remained for me to know about man's nature, about life, and about my growing disillusionment with the brutal age in which I had been condemned to live.

Often during those years, I felt as if I were back in a place that was as cruel and as hope-crushing as Algiers, but upside down: in Spain the Muslims were treated as poorly as the Christians on the Barbary Coast, and the Christians were as oblivious to their suffering as the Turks were in the lands over which they ruled. The cruelty I saw was as great, as soul-killing, as that which I had experienced in Bagnio Beylic. That was the place Spain had become in the last years of the sixteenth century A.D., a country that shackled, bound, and destroyed the weak, and those who were different in race, religion, or ideas.

It might seem paradoxical how so much devastation can be a liberation, but eventually I came to understand that everything that had befallen me, the highest and lowest points, had forged in me the desire to write not just one more novel, one more book to add to the library shelves of the world, but a book that contained—and truthfully—all of life as I had known it.

Many years later, when I was an old man, when the usurper, Avellaneda, had published his cursory and insincere *Don Quixote de la Mancha Part II*, that aberration of a novel, that undigested regurgitation of the adventures of my knight and his squire, that offensive imitation written for the basest of motives: to hurt another person, its author, the man who had opened his veins to birth his characters—at that moment when I despaired to see the child of my invention stolen from me, and turned into a ludicrous parody of itself—a remarkable occurrence took place. One autumn morning, before the first decade of the new century came to an end, as I was leaving Esquivias for Toledo on business, I saw a fat man at the town's outskirts ambling toward me on an Andalusian horse, the kind that was ridden by ambassadors and the nobility. The horse's palomino coat was so shiny that it seemed to be powdered with gold dust. Its long neck and wide chest projected themselves like the prow of a ship with the wind behind its sails. A thick, beautifully groomed mane draped the sides of its neck and fell on its long and narrow face in two blond strands. Behind the horse trotted a donkey loaded with small trunks; on its sheepskin-covered saddle rode the rich man's servant. The man on the horse wore pants tied above the knees, black Córdoban boots that shone like onyx, a long-sleeved velvet coat the color of the ripest grapes, and a brown cap with a visor, the kind favored by traveling gentlemen. A long, thin sword with a wooden haft hung on the left side of his sizable belly.

The noses of our horses were about to meet when I heard: "Don Miguel. Don Miguel de Cervantes. Blessed be my eyes!" The fat man leaped off his horse with astonishing speed and ran in my direction. I stopped my horse. The extravagant traveler took my hand and, without my permission, as if he knew me intimately, covered it with kisses. "Your Grace, it's me, your friend Sancho Panza," he said.

More than twenty-five years had passed since the night we said goodbye at the cave in the hills, outside the walls of Algiers. Many tears of joy were shed as we embraced each other anew. Despite his apparent wealth Sancho was the same salt-of-the-earth man, just a quarter of a century older and twice as bulky. We directed our horses to a grassy patch off the side of the road and sought the shade of an oak. Sancho's servant opened one of the trunks carried by the donkey and spread on the ground a luxurious carpet with Arab designs. Then he produced silver cups, which he filled with wine. Next appeared cheese, bread, olives, and a leg of ham. We toasted Fortune for crossing our paths once more. I was dying to ask Sancho how he had survived the desert, and how he had come by his obvious prosperity. As if to prepare himself for the story he was about to tell me, Sancho bit off a chunk of bread from the brown loaf and chewed it quickly. Then he washed it down with the wine.

"Thank you, thank you, my illustrious master, most celebrated son of Alcalá de Henares," he began, taking my right hand, which once again he kissed and washed with many tears. "Thank you for making me famous, Your Mercy. Wherever I go in Spain, as soon as I say my name, I'm recognized as Sancho Panza, the immortal and sublime creature, the faithful and loving companion of the magnificent, noble, and wise knight, Don Quixote, that creation of yours that will live as long as the sun rises over *la madre patria*."

He had more to say on the subject of *Don Quixote*: "You know I'm no learned man, Your Grace, and they may say that old dogs don't learn new tricks, yet it is my firm intention to hire a local scholar to teach me how to read now that I'm back on Spanish soil, in my old beloved town of Esquivias, where I hope to retire from my wanderings and spend the rest of the time enjoying my family, and Teresa's delicious cooking, in particular her rabbit stew. So I beg you to please forgive my immodesty, except that what I'm about to say, I say with all the respect due to the greatest living Spaniard, Your Magnificence Don Miguel de Cervantes Saavedra."

He paused to bite on another chunk of bread and finish his cup of wine, which his servant immediately refilled. "Without delay, my old and dear friend, I urge you to continue the adventures of Don Quixote. Put him on the road to Zaragoza atop Rocinante, that noblest horse of all. And I almost don't care whether you do it with or without me as his squire. I say this, Don Miguel, not because I hunger for more fame, but because the grave injustice and offense committed against you by that infamous thief, the accursed Fernández Avellaneda, must be set right. The world must be instructed once and for all about who the real characters are, so that the counterfeit creatures created by the devilish Avellaneda, who is a disgrace to the mother who brought him into the world, can be exposed for the pallid, malnourished inventions that they are, and his work can be ridiculed and then forgotten, as it deserves to be."

I was about to say that I was at work on *my* Part II and hoped to finish it soon despite my poor health, but Sancho had one more piece of advice: "I respect and worship every word your incommensurable pen has set down on paper, yet I must confess that I find the tales that keep interrupting the story a bit distracting. I, for one, want to know only about Don Quixote and his squire. And now you will never again hear another word of criticism from me about your sublime book."

I reassured him that I would consider his advice, and that other readers, too, had complained about the tales within the novel. Now it was time for me to ask questions. "Friend Sancho," I said, "I see that fortune has smiled on you; you are the very picture of prosperity. Please tell me of your whereabouts since last I saw you."

Sancho leaned back on the trunk of the oak, and placed both his hands on his contented belly. As I sipped the cool wine and nibbled on slices of cheese and ham, which Sancho's servant kept cutting and feeding us, my friend regaled me with his curious story, full of twists and turns, each more fantastic than the one before.

Sancho spoke long enough for the sun to cross the line of midday into the west, so I will summarize his tale: A few days after he went off into the desert by himself, lost in the Sahara, thinking the burning sands of the North African desert would be his final resting place, he was discovered by a caravan of Berbers on camels, who abducted him. With this group of bandits, who pillaged other caravans as well as small villages, Sancho roamed the desert for a long time. Then, on a journey to a kingdom in the heart of Africa where the people were as black as midnight, he was sold to the king; in that land, where everyone was tall and lean, with long, giraffelike necks, fat white people were worshipped as harbingers of abundance. Nothing was required of Sancho but to sit in his luxurious palace made of mud and straw, where he was attended by virgins of the nobility, and received the pilgrims from all over the kingdom who came to touch him and pray to him, hoping he would grant them abundance in the form of children, cattle, or rain. During droughts, when the crops failed and starvation took a toll of infants, old people, and cows, Sancho was carried on a golden chair from village to village, until the rains came. The king's doctors visited my friend on a daily basis to measure his girth and make sure he was not getting thinner. Over the years, Sancho filled many trunks with the gold and jewels that people brought as offerings. The old king became his best friend, and finally, when he was about to die, Sancho requested a favor of him. "I asked His Majesty for permission to return to my country because I knew that my own journey on earth must be nearing its end, and I wanted to see my wife, my dear Teresa—who I had never betrayed, despite ample opportunities to do so with the most beautiful virgins of the kingdom—if she was still alive, and my daughter, who I remembered as a toddler taking her first steps, and the good neighbors of my hometown, where I opened my peepers to the world for the first time. And that, Your Magnificence, you greatest bard of our land and our national glory, is how I chanced to run upon you again. Now, pray tell me, why were you coming from Esquivias? What is your business there?"

I told him about my marriage; how Esquivias had been, off and on, my home for over twenty years; that the best news I had for him was that both Teresa and Sanchica were in good health; that I saw them with some frequency and that he was now a grandfather because Sanchica was married and produced a large family composed only of boys: Sancho I, Sancho II, Sancho III, and so on. At this news, Sancho once more took my hand, kissed and moistened it. Then, to my utter surprise, he and his servant embraced and cried in a most disconsolate manner on each other's shoulders. This was indeed a rare scene and I wondered what story lay behind it. When both of their eyes were dry and red, Sancho said: "This man, Don Miguel, is not my servant. He's my former neighbor, Mohanad Morricote, a citizen of Esquivias, who left our country shortly before I was cruelly abducted and taken to the bagnio where I had the great fortune of meeting you who has made me rich, and given me immortality."

Morricote, who had remained silent until that moment, spoke: "Don Miguel, in 1570, when I was a married young man and the proud father of Amina and Afid, my family and I were expelled from Spain by order of King Philip II, may his soul rest in peace—even though our ancestors had been on Spanish soil long before Castile and Aragon were united and this became one country—unless we converted publicly and renounced our faith and customs, which I couldn't do, Don Miguel, as it was an offense to my ancestors. Someone as learned as Your Eminence surely knows that after the fall of Granada, when the last of the Muslim rulers were exiled, my ancestors converted to Catholicism, yet we managed to keep many of our customs, and some of us taught Arabic to our children, not because we did not love Spain, and not because we had dreams of reconquering it, as we have been accused of, but because the history of our people is written in Arabic."

Sancho interrupted Morricote's narration with, "My dear friend, Don Miguel must have business to attend, and we must not abuse the kindness of a man of his importance, so please do not linger upon what happened centuries ago."

"Thank you, my friend Sancho, for your wise words of advice," Morricote said. "So, to proceed with the history of my misfortunes: We were ordered to leave Spain with just the clothes on our back. We were forbidden to take any gold, silver, or precious stones with us. I was not a rich man, Don Miguel. But through hard toil, good fortune in commerce, and the habit of saving for unforeseen circumstances, I had become a man of property. So I did the only thing I could do: I buried two earthen jars filled with gold and other valuables behind the house of my good friend Sancho Panza. Thus we left Spanish soil without a coin to our name, and with just enough money to buy our passage to the Barbary Coast. As you well know, because I've heard from Sancho about your time together in Algiers, in that capital of disgrace we were not well-received. The Turks thought of us as Spaniards; and because we had converted to Christianity, we were not trusted as Arabs. After many years of suffering insults and unjust treatment, we saved enough money to move to the kingdom of Morocco, where we've lived ever since. It was there that I ran into my friend, Sancho, one day in the market, when he stopped at my stall in the bazaar to admire the carpets I sold. I hadn't been so happy since the birth of my first grandchild. Though Fortune has been kinder to us in that land, my children and grandchildren and I dream of going to the New World, where, we understand, Arab people are welcome. But God has blessed me with a fertile family, and it is expensive to buy passage for fifteen people. All these years I've dreamed of the gold I left behind in my friend's backyard, which could buy our passage to the Indies and allow us to settle there. When I shared this sentiment with my good friend Sancho, he convinced me that, despite the high risk, I might be able to enter Spain disguised as the Christian servant of a man of great wealth, as my friend Sancho now is. If caught, I know I will not live to see my family again. But I made up my mind to try this scheme when Sancho said: *Victory favors the bold.* But just as we set foot on our beloved Spanish soil, where my ancestors are buried, a new decree was promulgated, as you must have heard: converted or not, all Arabs must leave Spain—all Moriscos and their descendants are to be banished forever. My friend Sancho convinced me not to go back to Morocco right away, but to return to Esquivias and move forward with my plan, so that I have a chance to begin a new life, in a land where Christians and Muslims live in peace."

As Morricote seemed to have concluded his tale, Sancho joined the conversation once more: "I don't need to remind Don Miguel I'm a true patriot, a respectful and obedient subject of our great king. But I had to defy his decree because Morricote and his family were the best neighbors the Panzas ever had, and since I do not have the great honor and pleasure of knowing our glorious king, nor have I ever been his neighbor, or think it's likely I'll ever be, and powerful bonds of decency and kindness unite me to my friend, I have journeyed with him this far and plan not to abandon him until he has recovered his gold and other valuables and can reunite with his family."

I had seen countless Moriscos mutilated, burned, stripped of their possessions, ejected from the land they had cultivated for generations, the only country they had ever known, where their ancestors had lived for centuries and where their parents had become dust, indistinguishable from the Spanish soil. "Your secret is safe with me, my friends," I reassured them.

We embraced. I wished both of them well and made plans with Sancho to see him on my next visit to Esquivias.

And, though I was dizzy, both from the excellent wine and from Sancho's fantastical story and the great joy of encountering him so unexpectedly, so many years later, I climbed back on my horse and continued on my way to Toledo.

Months later, when I returned to Esquivias, I inquired about Sancho and was told he had bought the finest house in town for Teresa and Sanchica, but that his daughter had refused to give up her business of raising pigs. Sancho had left town once more, with his loyal servant Diego. Though he was old, and his health was not good, he announced that he had been too long on the road to remain in any one place. Teresa told me Sancho had said, "My incomparably virtuous, good, and faithful wife, my beloved daughter and grandchildren, my hunger for adventure is not sated; the open road calls me again, and I still have a great desire to see many places I haven't yet seen, and I would like to do it before God calls me to His side and I have to give an account of my doings on this earth. The grass may not be greener on the other side," he had concluded, "but at least it is new and grows on different ground."

I do not know what became of him, or of Morricote, though I hope he journeyed to the New World, the place I had so desperately tried to reach in my youth, and was never fortunate to visit because that was not my destiny; Fate had decided for me that I would never again leave Spain, that I would travel its roads and meet its people, so that I could write about Don Quixote and Sancho.

The earth seemed to have swallowed up Sancho once more. I wished that, wherever he landed, he found out that his adventures continued in my own *Don Quixote Part II*, where the encounter narrated in this chapter appears, though disguised as fiction.

CHAPTER 8
THE FALSE DON QUIXOTE
1587-1616

~ *PASCUAL PAREDES* ~

I blame the way my life turned out on my youthful love of poetry, which, if my memory serves me, Don Quixote—rightly so—calls an incurable vice. It was the innocent remark I made to Don Luis Lara, shortly after I began to work at the Council of the Indies, about the copy on his desk of *The Works of Garcilaso de la Vega with Annotations* by Fernando de Herrera, that made him notice me for the first time. Had I at that moment held my tongue (the one appendage of mine I've never been able to control), who knows what would have become of me? That first conversation was the seed that grew into a long association that trapped me in the web of enmity Don Luis had for Miguel de Cervantes Saavedra and made me a participant in a story of revenge that cast an ominous shadow on much of my adult life.

By enlisting me as a kind of spy, Don Luis singled me out among all the other dull, unimaginative men who worked in our branch of the council. After Miguel de Cervantes left Esquivias and moved to Sevilla in 1587, my principal duty became to remain informed of Cervantes's every move, and to pass on this information to Don Luis.

It was thus I escaped the dreary nature of my odious job, my entombment in those stuffy, penumbral, poorly ventilated rooms that smelled of rank ink and dusty documents, where my coworkers hunched over their desks for long hours every day, whispering so as not to call attention to themselves, scratching reams of paper with their quills, entering numbers on waxy parchments and moving them from one column to the other, drafting reports that no one ever read, which were destined for archives visited only by roaches and rats. These pathetic souls paused only to cough, or to scratch themselves, or to blow their noses, or to go relieve themselves, and struggled to stay awake in the afternoons, after they returned to work from dinner and their siestas. I despised their shallow lives, the tedium and sterility of the way they spent their existence, because I knew that, if chance hadn't intervened, this would have been my own destiny in Spain.

On one of my monthly trips to Esquivias, presumably to supervise the accounts of the local government, I learned that Cervantes had left his wife behind and traveled to Sevilla, where he hoped to get a job working as a collector of grain for the soldiers of the armada, which had begun the ill-fated hostilities against England that helped to precipitate the decline of our empire. This was my opportunity to visit Sevilla, a city I longed to see, so rich in history and famed for its beauty, its Alcázar, its poets and painters. Upon arrival I learned that Miguel de Cervantes had managed to secure one of those positions. He was now an employee of the government, as Don Luis and I were.

"His job title is itinerant collector for the armada," I informed Don Luis when I returned to Madrid.

He gave me one of his rare happy smiles. I had come to understand that his greatest joy consisted of learning about the bad luck of Cervantes, though securing a position as collector for the crown seemed hardly a misfortune.

"You've done an excellent job, Pascual," Don Luis said.

I could count with the digits of one hand the occasions

on which he had praised me for anything I did for him, as if it were his absolute right to expect nothing but perfect service from those who worked under him. I was sitting across from him, sipping a Jeréz. It was late afternoon; his large office was almost dark. Twilight was the favorite time of day for Don Luis, as if the deepening shadows reassured him.

"As someone whose purity of blood has not been established," he continued, after sipping his glass, and pointing his almost fleshless pinky at me, "this is the perfect occupation for him. I don't need to remind you that when it comes to extracting money from people, Jews are leeches with an insatiable appetite."

I chuckled, but immediately straightened my back and assumed a serious expression. The look Don Luis gave me was not of disapproval.

"There is rampant corruption in that world of people who collect taxes for the king, Pascual. Even the most honest man—which, let's face it, Miguel is not—sooner or later will join the thieves and lowlifes who work with him. He will have to do as they do, if he wants to keep his job. Then he'll get what he deserves."

He sipped his sherry slowly, staring at a point behind me. His lips were stretched in the faintest of smiles, but there was something almost frightful in the dreamy eyes. With a wave of his hand, not bothering to make eye contact with me, he bid me to leave the room.

I became a bloodhound tracking Cervantes's footsteps in the godforsaken villages he visited in Andalusia. I thanked my lucky stars: it was a much better existence than being glued to a desk. Additionally, I had escaped the sepulchral building of the council, and daily coexistence with my co-workers, who made me think of solitary souls doing penance in purgatory. Also, and this was no small advantage, I got to see more of Spain, which had always been a dream of mine.

One day, after I had finished giving him a report of Miguel's travels, Don Luis confessed to me: "You don't know what comfort I derive when, before I close my eyes to go to sleep, I imagine Miguel—dusty, hungry, worn-out, holding the staff of justice in his good hand—entering on an old mule one of those desolate towns in the Andalusian countryside where, as tax collector of the crown, he must be met with hostility and hatred."

I was glad I would never be important enough in his eyes to become a target of his hatred.

For three years there was little new to report, though Don Luis demanded to know the names of every insignificant village Cervantes visited and how he had been received by the peasants whose grain he had to extract in the name of the armada. Then I learned through one of my contacts in Sevilla that Cervantes had applied for permission to travel to the Indies. I asked my informant for a copy of the document and left for Madrid, riding as fast as I could, barely stopping to eat or relieve myself or sleep. In his petition to the court, Cervantes was specific about the four posts he wanted to be considered for: the comptrollership of the viceroyalty of New Granada, the governorship of the province of Soconusco in Guatemala, the post of auditor of the galleys in Cartagena de Indias, or that of magistrate of the city of La Paz. All of these were important positions, usually given as rewards to those who had distinguished themselves in the service of the king; but often they were secured by the influential families of good-for-nothing señoritos, who were an embarrassment to their kin in Spain. To me it showed that despite the setbacks of his life, Cervantes had a very high notion of his importance. But he didn't seem to have considered that, at forty-three years of age, he was asking for employment that required the energy of a much younger man.

Don Luis had never shown so much delight to see me as he did on the day I delivered, at his office in the Council of the Indies, the copy of Cervantes's petition. He extended me an invitation to sup with him that night, at the finest inn in Madrid, the Mesón de los Reyes, where many of the personages who came to the court on business stayed. Though we had taken many walks in public places over the years, and I had often walked with him to his home, he had neither invited me inside for a libation nor suggested a drink at a tavern where we could be seen socializing as equals.

While we waited for our first dish to arrive, Don Luis said to me, "Pascual, I want to show you my appreciation for the work you're doing for me. As of next month, your salary will be raised by one hundred maravedíes."

"Thank you, thank you, Your Grace," I said, shocked. "I kiss your generous hands a thousand times." My salary was already higher than those of my pitiful coworkers.

"I want to make clear to you, Pascual, that this compensation will not be coming out of the treasury of the council. That would be embezzlement."

I hurried to say, "I would never have thought such a thing, Don Luis. I—"

"Let me finish. I'm not done yet. I know perfectly well my conduct is above all reproach. I just want you to know that the extra maravedíes will be taken out of my own coffers. I will continue to fight assiduously against corruption in our public employees."

As the soup arrived, I couldn't help but wonder if it had ever occurred to him that paying me more than my coworkers, and keeping me busy tracking down Cervantes's every move, was itself an abuse of his power. But I already understood that Don Luis Lara was the sort of man who would never see flaws in himself. Like all Spanish aristocrats, he thought his excrescencies smelled better than those of his inferiors in rank.

The rest of the evening we talked about the new volumes of poetry that had arrived at the city's bookshops. Thanks to Don Luis, I could now purchase any new book that interested me, or copies of the classics I hadn't read. I still kept up with the output of new poets, but I did it to please him, and to continue to have access to the world of writers—not because I drew the same pleasure I had experienced from poetry before I started working for Don Luis and learned how ruthless these sensitive men who wrote beautiful poems and novels could be.

Cervantes's petition was denied, and soon after he was again on the road collecting grain. I didn't find out what role Don Luis played in this scheme, and the truth was I didn't want to know: that way it was easier for me to continue working as his spy. But after Cervantes experienced what must have come as a crushing failure, Don Luis seemed to have lost all interest in his activities. Regularly, I continued giving him my brief reports, which he listened to with a bored expression—making me feel as if I cared more about Cervantes than he did.

"What a sad creature the cripple of Lepanto has become," Don Luis once said to me. "To think that at one time he was considered the great hope of Spanish letters. To think we were good friends! That miserable life he's living will kill him before too long, you'll see."

As there was less cause for me to travel to Andalusia to keep abreast of Cervantes's peregrinations, I became Don Luis's factotum at the council. Yet he did not ask me to stop spying on the man I secretly began to call the Commissioner of Sorrows.

Then, while retaining his position at the council, Don Luis was appointed as prosecuting attorney for the Holy Office. With a zeal that struck me as fanatical even for such a religious man, he became immersed in his work for the church. His responsibilities kept him in Toledo a great deal of the time; it must have been painful for him to spend so much time in the city where his wife lived in the Lara's ancestral home, which she had converted into a hospice. Later, though he did not mention this to me, I learned through an acquaintance that young Diego Lara had abandoned his studies in theology at the Universidad Cisneriana in Alcalá de Henares to join an order of the Carmelites in Toledo. I learned, too, that a maid named Leonela, who had been in Don Luis's service since the days of his marriage, had left his home to join Doña Mercedes. Was I now spying on Don Luis?

It was around this time that I became his confidant, which speaks volumes about his loneliness. He did not seem to have close friends, but like all of us he had a need to share his intimate thoughts with other human beings. In that regard we were similar: my position with Don Luis was the closest I came to intimacy with another person.

One day he said to me: "Pascual, I'm not sure I am the right person to act as prosecuting attorney for the Holy Office." He explained: "Do you know that my main duty is to go before the tribunal of the Holy Office with the evidence I've gathered about the accused, and then to make a case for an auto-da-fé? It troubles me that the accused are not informed of the charges against them. Years can go by before these unfortunates are informed of the reasons they're imprisoned."

About the workings of the Holy Office I knew only

what people whispered. No one dared to openly try to find out how the trials worked. I said nothing; I waited for him to unburden himself of the thoughts that pained him.

"I thought I was going to help the church purge Spain, and the Christian world, of the infidels who seek to undermine our religion with their heretical views." Don Luis paused, his face locked in a scowl. "But from what I can tell, the only crime of some of these people is to be wealthy."

So it was true what people whispered about the Holy Office: they burned so that they could eat.

"The worst part of it," he continued, "is that I have to be present at the torture of these people and then their burning." What he said next surprised me: "Pascual, I wonder, how long can I continue working for the Holy Office and exposing myself to so much suffering?"

That day I felt sympathy for him. Behind the cold façade he projected, and the nature of his hatred for Miguel de Cervantes—which seemed to be the motivating force of his life—he was not untouched by the suffering of others.

Like thousands of Madrileños, I had attended the autos-da-fé in the Plaza Mayor. They were one of the few free distractions for the people. There was a public procession of those found guilty, and when one was formally charged and his sentence was read, the mob jeered at the accused, threw garbage, and hurled insults. At the autos-da-fé the pestilential rabble released the anger they bottled up over their own wretched lives. These ceremonies lasted for hours, and many people brought food and drink to while away the time. At the end a Mass was said, followed by prayers for the souls of the damned. The condemned were executed later, out of public view, which incensed the masses, who felt cheated that they could not see the condemned being burned to death in public.

I have no sentimental notions about the human race; I

believe we are God's most flawed creations, that He was extremely tired and distracted the day He created Adam and Eve, and used His cheapest and most damaged fabric to fashion us.

I was once again trapped in my office, which felt like a kind of death. During those years, whenever Don Luis came to Madrid from Toledo, he invited me to dine at the Mesón de los Reyes. He counted on me to give him a detailed account of how the department worked in his absence. I reported on my coworkers, who were too broken by life, and lacking in imagination, to create any trouble. These creatures' major source of happiness was to sit at their desks all day long, shuffling papers and wasting ink. At the council, everyone knew of my friendship with Don Luis and treated me as a superior.

At one of our dinners, I noticed that Don Luis looked more downcast than usual. All I could do was wait, and hope he would tell me what was troubling him. That night, he barely touched his food but drank more wine than I had ever seen him drink. This surprised me because he was not a man of excesses. We were still in the tavern well after midnight, and I became concerned that he was visibly inebriated, beginning to slur his words. I was reassured that his carriers were waiting for him outside. I tried to cheer him up by offering bits of gossip about my coworkers and the poetry world, spicing them up a bit to distract him from his gloomy mood. Though he was sitting across from me, it was as if he were so far away my voice could not reach him.

He stared at me with heavy eyes; his silence made me feel ill at ease. Then he said: "You never met my son." Why had he referred to him in the past tense? I knew Friar Diego Lara lived in Toledo. This was most unusual: Don Luis never talked about his private life. Tears fell from his eyes. "Well," he said, "Dieguito, my beloved son, the only joy I have in this world, left for the New World to convert the Indians. He sailed from Sevilla two weeks ago. Had I found out about his plan," he continued, his words slowed by all the wine, "I would've stopped him. Oh, yes," he exclaimed, shaking his fists, "I would've moved heaven and earth to keep him here in Spain!"

He broke down and started to weep, uncontrollably. It was so late that we were the only diners left in the Mesón de los Reyes. The young woman who had served us approached our table; with a flick of my hand I waved her away.

"Pascual," he grabbed my hand and went on, "as long as Diego was in Spain, and I could see him, there was a spark of happiness in my life. Now, now," he raised his voice and shook his head, "I probably won't see him again. Oh Pascual, maybe God has punished me for the way I've lived my life."

I said, "Don Luis, it's very late. You should go home."

With the help of one of the workers at the inn, I carried him outside to his chair. When I placed my hand on his rib cage to steady him, his bones protruded through his skin. The man we put in his chair, a grandee of Spain, had as much life left in him as a broken marionette.

Don Luis's prediction about Miguel de Cervantes came true: late in 1592, I learned through one of my contacts that in the month of September Cervantes had briefly been thrown in jail in the village of Castro del Río. I barely understood the nature of the accusation, and getting the details secondhand did not help to clarify what had happened. But Cervantes had been accused of mishandling the royal accounts and taking some funds for his personal use.

That was all I cared to know. I kept the news to myself since Don Luis hardly ever mentioned him anymore.

Two years after young Diego Lara sailed for the New World, the news reached Spain that he was killed and eaten by cannibals in the viceroyalty of New Granada. His shrunken head was found in a Motilón Indian village and sent to the governor of Cartagena, who forwarded it to Luis. All of Madrid was horrified.

Don Luis never returned to work. It was announced that Don Carlos Calatrava, a scion of a noble Spanish family, had been appointed to replace him. I feared for my future. If I were fired, how would I support my ancient mother and aunt? Would this man replace all of us (as was customary) with his own people and his friends' friends? Would I ever see Don Luis again? Now that he had no use for me, would he still be interested in cultivating our acquaintanceship? I knew perfectly well that I could not approach him. I did, however, send a letter of condolence.

Long weeks went by. Then, for the first time in the years we had known each other, I received a note from Don Luis thanking me for my letter and, to my utter disbelief, inviting me to stop by his house on Sunday afternoon. After years of waiting to be invited inside the august Lara house, legendary for its elegance, the important paintings and magnificent tapestries hanging on its walls, I barely paid attention to the furnishings of the mansion as the major-domo led me to the library, a vast rectangular space, with shelves that went all the way to the ceiling and were accessible by a ladder leading to a metal corridor that wrapped itself around the room.

Don Luis sat by an open window facing the courtyard. As I approached, he greeted me. "Pascual, how good of you to come see me. Please sit down."

I took my seat and noticed a horrible object encased in

glass on the table beside Don Luis. I could not tear my eyes away from it. He noticed my interest.

"It's little Diego's head," he said softly. "This is how the savages he was trying to bring into the fold of God repaid him."

His voice was feeble, yet filled with anger. I felt nauseated, and fixed my gaze on Don Luis. I could not bear to look at the monstrous head again. It had been just a few months since the last time I had seen Don Luis, but if I had run into him on the street I might not have recognized him.

"Two days ago, I sent a letter to the cardinal resigning from my position as procuring attorney for the Holy Office," he began. "You know, Pascual, at first I thought work would be a distraction. But it's become apparent I can't think about anything except the fate of my son. I'm not fit for this world anymore." He sighed. "I spend my days praying in the family chapel, but praying cannot bring relief from my pain. It just helps me to pass the hours. I've lost my appetite; I cannot sleep; even to talk is often excruciating. I cannot bear the presence of most people. Unless they have gone through the tragedy of losing their only son, they will never know the depths of my sorrow. The only person I talk to with any regularity is Father Jerónimo, who was Dieguito's teacher. He's the only person who understands how I feel. He knows what I've lost."

Don Luis fell silent and stared out the window at a parched garden. I tried to distract him with my usual gossip, but he remained unresponsive. Now and then he nodded to indicate he was listening. I felt sorry for him. Life's tragedies make equals of us all.

As I got up to leave, the hand that shook mine was cold and clammy. *It's like shaking hands with a dead man*, I thought.

"I'm glad to see you, Pascual," he whispered, becoming a little more animated. "I'm afraid I'm not good company these days. But if you can bear to be around me, do come to visit again. It will comfort me to see you, even if I talk little."

My beloved mother died, after a short illness that took her in a matter of days. My father had passed when I was still a child, and I had lived the rest of my life spared by tragedy. If there was any purpose to my life, it was to support my mother and her sister. My mother was barely in the ground when Aunt María announced she was packed and ready to go to Jaén, to spend her last days close to another of her sisters. I was relieved the morning I put her in a carriage going south, but when I returned to the empty house it was as inhospitable as a mausoleum.

My grief drew me closer to Don Luis. It comforted me to visit him after I left work at night. He seemed to tolerate my visits. He still walked and ate and talked, like any other man, but he was in another world most of the time. I no longer went to see him out of morbid curiosity; it had been a long time since I had extracted from him any news about the important people he knew. It was hard to admit, but he was the only person I was close to.

Don Luis began to talk about a novel he was planning to write. I was surprised because he had never shown any interest in writing novels. During one of my visits, he said: "Pascual, I need to keep occupied. There are those who enjoy doing nothing, but I'm not that kind of person. As you know, I'm devoted to poetry, but nowadays after I've read a few verses I don't know what I'm reading. I've been dreaming about writing a novel since I was a student. Perhaps the time has come to attempt it."

"What wonderful news," I said. "May I ask, if it's not too much of an impertinence, what it is about?"

"Oh, I only have sketches for a few characters." He

paused. "My main character is based on Rodrigo Cervantes. Yes, Miguel's progenitor."

He had not mentioned Cervantes's name in a long time. In 1596, I'd heard that Miguel Cervantes had left his occupation as a tax collector. By my calculations, he had been working in that capacity for almost ten years. When I heard the news I thought: *That's the end of him. May God help this pitiful man who carries a cloud of misery over his head, wherever he goes.* The following year I was astonished to hear he was incarcerated again because more serious discrepancies had been discovered in the books he had kept during his years of service to the crown. I had kept all this to myself. It seemed that for Don Luis it was as if Cervantes had already died and turned to dust.

"Pascual," he said, breaking my recollection, "how would you like to work for me as an amanuensis? I'm looking for someone who will live in the house."

"It would be the greatest honor of my life, Don Luis," I was quick to respond. When he began to talk about monetary compensation for my duties, I could no longer hear what he was saying. Even in my wildest dreams, it had never occurred to me that one day I would be living in one of the great houses of Spain. How I wished my mother were alive so that she could rejoice in my great good fortune.

Working at the Council of the Indies, after Don Luis left, had become insupportable. Without him as my superior, I had returned to the bleak life he'd rescued me from when he put me in charge of spying on Cervantes. I did not have the connections to advance myself in my career as a civil servant. Any position I could obtain as a government bureaucrat would be as deadening as the one I had served in for many years at the council; it would have meant moving to another gloomy building, working with dismal people, and shuffling different stacks of dusty documents. But

I needed to work. Don Luis could choose not to work, but I needed a salaried position in order to survive.

There was something else: I had turned thirty-five years old and was still a bachelor. I had become acquainted with a group of hidalgos who frequented the gambling houses, where sex of both kinds could be procured for money. The king's secretary, Antonio Pérez, was a prominent member of that coterie.

I couldn't tear myself away from the life I had discovered, anymore than I could stop hair from growing on my face. I rejoiced in the exquisite pleasures of the body, despite the church's condemnation of any kind of sensory pleasure as immoral. The king's secretary was shielded by his association and closeness to our monarch; but it was only a matter of time before insinuations would be made about me, and I was in danger of being apprehended and accused of having abandoned my interest in women and lusting after men. I was in grave danger of being burned at the stake, or assassinated in a dark alley like the notorious poet Álvaro de Luna. Early in the reign of Philip II he had begun publicly executing sodomites. Although these executions were infrequent, not a year went by that a well-known sodomite wasn't burned in a pyre. And the men who met this fate were not members of the nobility, but men like me. Marriage was the best way to avoid any accusations, but for me, getting married would entail another kind of death. Don Luis's offer was providential; working for an important man of irreproachable character, and being part of his household, might be what would save my life.

I closed the house in which I had lived with my mother most of my life. We possessed almost nothing worth saving: I kept a few mementos and gave the rest away to charity. At

Don Luis's house, I was given the lugubrious chambers that had formerly belonged to Doña Mercedes. I brightened the walls, replacing the morbid statues of tortured saints and bleeding figures of Christ on the cross with colorful carpets, curtains, and tapestries, which had decorated guest rooms nobody used.

Don Luis began to talk in earnest about the composition of his novel. He showed me drawings he had made of the characters, and read intricate outlines to me, explaining how they would be developed. But time passed and he did no actual writing. I was expected to meet with him in the library during the morning hours and to dine with him every day, but the rest of the time I had no responsibilities. It took me awhile to become accustomed to the fact that I lived in one of Madrid's great houses, and could for the first time wear clothes designed especially for me, clothes that made me look like a member of the nobility. I became a regular at the most exclusive gambling establishments. Perhaps for the first time, I was happy.

Then, in 1603, Miguel de Cervantes moved to Madrid with his sisters and his daughter Isabel. It was curious to see the extinguished flame of hatred light up again in Don Luis's heart.

One morning, when we were in the library discussing the order of the notes for his novel, Don Luis said, abruptly: "You've heard that he's here, haven't you? I understand why you didn't mention it to me: you're trying to protect me. But I won't have any peace until I find out how he occupies his time here."

I offered to resume my old spying duties.

"No, I won't hear of it, Pascual. You have risen in your station: you are my personal secretary. To spy for me would be beneath your new rank. However, I authorize you to hire a man to follow Miguel's every movement and to report back to you. I won't rest until I've found out why he has returned to Madrid after all these years. I'm convinced he must have something up his sleeve."

The Cervantes brood had rented a house in a neighborhood of artisans. The women supported the family by sewing garments. It was rumored that Andrea still received monetary reparations from an old lover. Of Cervantes himself, little was said. He seldom went out and no longer frequented the infamous taverns he had patronized in his youth. Every night he was seen seated at a table by the window on the second floor, with a lit candle, writing until just before dawn. One of the sisters had mentioned to a neighbor that her brother was writing a novel.

When I mentioned this to Don Luis, he said, "Miguel *was* a writer. Since that appalling *Galatea* appeared, he hasn't published anything. And that was almost twenty years ago. No, I don't believe he will write another novel again. Or at least one of any literary merit."

Even as he was saying this, I sensed Don Luis doubted his own words. The thought of Cervantes never publishing again pleased him in the extreme.

Then, as mysteriously as the family had arrived in Madrid, they packed their possessions and moved to Valladolid. I informed Don Luis of this new development immediately. It was at least something to talk about, other than his would-be novel.

"Why all this moving around, Pascual? It's costly to move to another city. They are getting too old to continue their constant peregrinations. No, I'm convinced he's hiding something, don't you agree? It has to be more than just writing a novel. But what could it be?"

It was around this time that it dawned on me I was working for a man whose brains were disordered. I was troubled: madness is contagious; being around a person who has lost his reason, one begins to see the world through his distorted imagination.

The news reached Madrid that a man had been murdered on the doorstep of the Cervantes's residency in Valladolid, and the family had been briefly incarcerated.

"How sordid! How sordid!" Don Luis exclaimed. "I'm sure he killed that man, Pascual. It had something to do with those whoring sisters of his. It's too bad the Cervanteses were cleared of the charges. Miguel should have been exiled from the kingdom for good a long time ago. He's been a criminal since his student days."

Then, in December of 1604, *Don Quixote* was published in Valladolid by Francisco de Robles. Without delay, Don Luis asked me to order the book from one of the most reputable booksellers, for fear it would sell out before he could get his hands on a copy. There was already a long list of names of customers waiting for copies to arrive in Madrid. *Don Quixote* had been out only a matter of weeks when it was instantly embraced by the Spanish public with a passion I had not seen in all my days. Overnight, Miguel de Cervantes Saavedra became famous. Wherever I went, people were talking about the novel. Even people who hadn't read it knew at least one funny incident from it.

When I placed a copy of the book in his hands, Don Luis went into the library, where he secluded himself for two days. During that time, when I walked past the library door, I heard him cursing Cervantes's name, or groaning as if the Holy Office were torturing him.

The death of Don Luis's son had been a devastating blow. On his good days, he looked like a corpse just risen from the grave. But the success of *Don Quixote* and Cervantes's celebrity were almost like an affront to his honor. One day, while we were dining, he suddenly said: "I heard that even the king has been seen reading it and laughing heartily. That means all the courtiers have read it too, to ingratiate themselves with His Majesty." His voice quivering with controlled rage, he continued: "What you don't know, Pascual, is that many years ago, when Miguel and I were young friends, on a night in which I had imbibed too much wine, I told him of my plan to write a history of a dreamer who ruins his family with his fantastic schemes." Don Luis paused, as if to let me absorb what he was saying. "I tell you this so that you don't think I'm merely a jealous man. He stole his celebrated Don Quixote from me!"

That day I understood that envy and hatred were the forces that kept Don Luis rooted to this world, and the hope that one day he'd get his revenge. I pitied him. "If it is any consolation, Your Grace," I told him, "I've heard he sold his rights to his publisher for a bowl of lentils. Despite his fame, Miguel de Cervantes Saavedra is as poor as ever."

"Ha!" Don Luis exclaimed. He smiled, his face glowing with satisfaction.

Some months after the publication of *Don Quixote*, Cervantes and his entourage of female relatives returned to Madrid.

It was our habit to meet in the library every morning, except on Sundays. Don Luis would sit in his comfortable chair by the window, I at the long table in front of a stack of writing paper and an inkwell, my quill ready to take dictation. Most of the time, he would talk about the book he wanted to write. "I will write something important," he would say. "I'm going to produce a great work. Nothing else will do."

I was beginning to think he would never write anything— important or not. Many mornings we sat there for hours, in total silence. Then one day, shortly after he had found out that Cervantes was settled again in Madrid, Don Luis said: "Pascual, I cannot let him have all the glory."

I picked up my pen as if to start writing; it was a reflex.

"What are you doing, you imbecile! I'm not dictating my book."

It was the first time he had insulted me. Despite his condescending manner, he had never mistreated me. I swallowed hard and tried to hide my humiliation.

"I've concluded, after much thought and prayers, that I will write the second part of *Don Quixote*. If other people can write second, third, and fourth *Dianas* and *Amadises*, who's to say I don't have the right to pen *Don Quixote Part II*? It's an old and honored tradition." He stared at me and waited for my response.

"Of course, it's your right, Don Luis," I rushed to say. "Besides, your second part will be better than Cervantes's first."

"Thank you, Pascual. Of course it will be much better. I'm an educated man, I know the classics, I went to university where I learned Latin and ancient Greek. I'm convinced I can write a better novel than Miguel's, not just because of my superior education, but also because I am a *moral* person. His *Don Quixote* is a sacrilegious book. Yes, sacrilegious. I'm choosing my words carefully, Pascual, fully aware of their exact meaning. If our king had not endorsed it, that novel would have come under the scrutiny of the Holy Office." He paused to catch his breath. "My novel, on the other hand, will mirror the state of immorality I see everywhere in Spanish society, of which Miguel's *Don Quixote* is patent proof. You know how at the end of his novel Miguel hints at the knight's future sallies? Well, I'll just pick up the story where he left off." Having concluded his tirade, Don Luis fell silent. He looked spent.

I thought we were done for the day; I was about to replace the cork on the inkwell when I heard him say: "But I'll write it under a pseudonym, as my motives are selfless and I am not interested in glory for myself. What do you think my nom de plume should be?"

I wanted to run away from that room and his presence. His voice, dripping with more bile than usual, nauseated me. *He's a repugnant man*, I thought. "I can't think of any fitting names, Your Grace. If you give me some time to mull it over, tomorrow I'll present you with a list."

"You may go now," he said.

The next morning, before I had a chance to read him the pseudonyms I had jotted down as possibilities, Don Luis said, as I took my usual chair at the table: "Alonso Fernández de Avellaneda—what do you think, Pascual?" Before I had time to say anything, he went on: "Alonso, because I want a name that starts with the first letter of the alphabet; Fernández, because every other plebeian in Spain has the surname of Gutiérrez or Fernández; and Avellaneda, because of the fruit of the avellano tree, the filbert which poor people pick from the public parks to supplement their diet. Of course," he added with relish, "to people like *us*, avellanas are just food for pigs."

He smiled to himself, deeply amused by the pseudonym he had chosen. *This man is deranged!* I thought. "I knew Your Grace would find the perfect nom de plume," I said. "It's for the ages."

Finally, after weeks of struggle, Don Luis dictated the opening lines of *Don Quixote Part II*:

The sage Alisolán, a modern yet truthful historian, writes that after the expulsion of the Mohammedan Moors from Aragón (the nation where he was born), he found among certain historical records written in Arabic a narration of the third sally

of the indestructible hidalgo Don Quixote de la Mancha, who
journeyed to the renowned city of Zaragoza to participate in
some tourneys being held there.

Even I, who was no literary critic but merely someone who read chivalry novels, could tell that this beginning compared poorly to Cervantes's: "In a certain corner of La Mancha, whose name I prefer to forget . . ."

This is not an auspicious beginning, I thought. But Don Luis employed me to write down the words that passed through his lips, not to judge their merit—certainly not to his face.

Instead of continuing to dictate the rest of the narrative, Don Luis began to draw maps of the possible routes Don Quixote would follow. "In order to be truthful, Pascual," he told me, "I need you to travel all the way to Zaragoza and bring back a report on the conditions of the roads on which *my* knight will travel, the different inns where he'll stay, the quality of the food and the sleeping accommodations, and the names of the trees in the forests where Don Quixote and Sancho will sleep on occasion."

I was all too happy to get away from him and visit the best inns on the road to Zaragoza, where I requested accommodations that were reserved for aristocrats and important travelers.

A year after he had dictated the first paragraph of his novel, Don Luis had not written another word. Perhaps to excuse his dawdling, one day he said to me: "My research must be impeccable, Pascual. I'm sure my readers will appreciate the veracity of what I write. When it comes to the creation of literature, I believe the tortoise is always superior to the hare, don't you agree? I want my readers to know that when I set down a period, it is meant as a philosophical statement."

Our sessions in the library were made bearable only by his madness, which now amused me. Besides, my salary allowed me to frequent the gambling houses, where many noblemen had befriended me, since my pockets were always full of escudos, reales, and maravedíes. Even so, my bad luck at the gambling tables, in addition to other costly pleasures to be purchased at these establishments, kept me in debt. But I was not inclined to give up my new life.

Don Luis kept coffers in his chambers that he filled with the revenues from the family's vineyards and orchards near Toledo. While he prayed in the family chapel every day, I began to remove gold coins from the largest coffers. The fortune he kept in his chambers was so large he would never notice the few escudos I removed to make my life more enjoyable. I would never see the world, so the gambling houses would be my recompense.

He might have thought that, like so many novels that were the talk of each new season, *Don Quixote* would be forgotten. That might be one of the reasons his writing of Chapter One had not progressed beyond the opening paragraph. But when it was announced that *Don Quixote* had been published in translation in Brussels in 1607, and that it had become a sensation there and in France, and that translations into English and other languages were being undertaken, Don Luis rushed to dictate a second paragraph and then a third and so on, until he had completed the first chapter.

Instead of continuing the composition of his narrative, my employer announced to me that he would now write the prologue of his *Don Quixote Part II*, which he subsequently rewrote endless times over the years. In essence, his prologue stated that his novel would be "less boastful and offensive to its readers" than the original; that Cervantes had no right to complain about "the profit I take away from his second part," or be angry at Avellaneda for writing a second part because "there is nothing new about different persons pursuing the same story." He cited in his defense the many *Amadices* that had been written; that he could never please Cervantes because it was well-known he was "as old as the Castle of Cervantes . . . and because of his advanced age . . . he had annoyed everybody and everything"; and that he excused the errors of Cervantes's *Part I* because "it was written among people in prison" and everybody knows that prisoners are "gossipy, impatient, and short-tempered"; and finally, that his *Don Quixote Part II*, unlike Cervantes's *Part I*, did "not teach lewdness but rather not to be crazy."

I realized this spiteful man was not my superior, except in wealth. I never again used, at least not in my head, the honorary *Don*. It was understandable that he had become obsessed with the friend who betrayed him in his youth, but to write a book to destroy another man's economic future, a man who was old, crippled, and poor, was something only a heartless Spanish aristocrat would do. It was an unpardonable sin.

He must have sensed that I was drawing away from him, because shortly after he had penned his prologue, at the end of one of our working days, he said: "Pascual, for a long time now you have proven to be a faithful friend, and I'm extremely grateful to you for your steadfastness during these years when so much tragedy has befallen me. You have given me every reason to trust you. But I must ask you never to mention the book I'm writing to anyone. Do I have your promise?"

"If it is any reassurance to Your Grace," I quickly replied, "I swear on my mother's memory that the secret will die with me."

Soon after this exchange, Luis announced to me he had

drafted a new last will and testament. "You are remembered most handsomely," he told me. I had no reason to doubt the veracity of his words: he was immensely wealthy and had no close relatives or friends: his wife, Doña Mercedes, had died shortly after word got to Madrid of Friar Diego's death. I understood this was his way of buying my unconditional allegiance, making sure I kept silent about his secret and remained his loyal accomplice. *I have sold my soul to the devil*, I thought.

Luis Lara was almost twenty years my senior. After the death of his son, he had lost interest in his appearance. Other than attending Sunday Mass, he rarely went out for a walk; left most of his food on his plate; spent hours praying on his knees in the chapel; slept but little; and had grown so thin his body would not have withstood a serious fall or illness. I couldn't ask him about the nature of his bequest to me, but sometimes I would let my imagination carry me away, and I believed that, at his death, I would inherit his house with all its furnishings, in addition to the revenue of at least one of his vineyards. Also, there were those coffers in his chamber filled with gold escudos. Besides his valet Juan, no one knew about them. But Juan was so old and feeble-minded that I had no reason to fear anything from him. Until the moment of his death came, all I had to do was to please Luis, and wait with patience to become a wealthy gentleman, restored to the station of my ancestors. The day would come when the shield of the Paredes family replaced that of the Laras on the front door.

Luis continued working on his novel at his unhurried pace. When a new edition of *Don Quixote* appeared in 1608, he seemed unperturbed. His leisurely method of composition suited me fine. As long as I continued visiting the gambling houses, and tasting their exotic and forbidden African and Moorish delights, I was content.

* * *

As the years went by, and the popularity of *Don Quixote* grew, Luis's obsession with Cervantes swelled. In 1609, when he heard that Cervantes had become a member of the Congregation of the Slaves of the Very Holy Sacrament, and that his wife and sisters had entered the Third Franciscan Order as novices, he scoffed: "If they think they are going to be less Jewish by becoming devout, it won't work."

The following year it was announced that Cervantes had traveled to Barcelona in the retinue of the count of Lemos, who had been appointed as viceroy of Naples. "If only the count knew!" Luis screamed as I delivered the news. "It is my fault, Pascual, because I should long ago have let the world know the kind of scoundrel Miguel de Cervantes is!"

His anger was placated when he heard that Cervantes had not joined the count in Naples and had instead returned to Madrid.

Don Luis at last finished his *Don Quixote Part II*. As he did not want anyone, even the eventual publisher, to know he was the creator, he authorized me to arrange for its publication. I was in the process of doing so when Cervantes announced that his *Exemplary Novels* would appear in 1613.

"Stop all negotiations regarding the publication of my *Don Quixote*. We will wait until next year," he ordered me. "If I've waited this long, I can wait another year to show the world my superiority as a writer. Besides, when my novel appears, I don't want another Spanish work to compete with it!"

By then, Cervantes was so famous that the public consumed the first edition of *The Exemplary Novels* in just a few weeks. Like everyone else, Luis read them. His verdict was: "They are not novels, Pascual. They read like plays. In any case, they are satirical, rather than exemplary. I would be wrong not to admit they are ingenious," he conceded. "The one about the talking dogs is quite clever, though it rambles, like everything he writes. And his lack of knowledge of Latin is evident; his erudition a sham. He will always be an ignoramus!"

I had begun to think Luis would die before the publication of his novel. When it finally appeared in 1614, he was an old man. To my surprise, though his novel was vastly inferior to his rival's—it lacked what Cervantes possessed in excess: genius!—the false *Don Quixote* became a success. Many readers were amused by it, and the first edition quickly sold out.

"Its success does not surprise me," Luis boasted. "People can see I'm an artist of the highest order, not a vulgar one. Just to give you an example, instead of saying, *I took a shit*, as Miguel does in so many places in his crude novel, as if taking a shit were a worthy subject, I wrote: *The beehive that nature installed in my posterior distills wax*. You see the great difference, don't you? What's more, the adventures of my heroes are more noteworthy than those gathered and published by the writer of the first part." Usually he could not bear to mention Cervantes's name. "In addition, 'The Desperate Rich Man' and 'The Happy Lovers,' the tales within my *Don Quixote*, are wholly original and better written than the meandering, boring tales by the writer of *Part I*. Don't you agree?"

I concurred, "It is as you say, Your Grace."

Luis de Lara's moment of glory was short-lived. The following year, after a ten-year hiatus, Cervantes published his own *Part II*. Like everyone else, I agreed (though I never mentioned this to Luis) that Cervantes had surpassed himself. What's more, his novel exposed the shallowness of Luis's, and dealt it a mortal blow. If Cervantes had not written *Part II*, I'm of the opinion that Luis's novel might have survived as an oddity. Its lean style allowed the action to move faster than in Cervantes's novel; though when it came to the depiction of Don Quixote and Sancho, Luis's lack of empathy for other human beings exposed his true nature. Worse, he had not expected—I had not expected, no one had—that in Cervantes's *Part II*, the crippled soldier of Lepanto would borrow the adventures and the characters created by Luis.

When he finished reading Cervantes's *Part II*, Luis had an apoplectic fit. I found him in the library, collapsed on his chair, unconscious, a copy of Cervantes's novel at his feet. The doctor was called. Though Luis was by then mostly skin and bones, he was bled until he turned the color of wax. But the will to live was strong in him, and after a few weeks he regained his strength and was able to speak. The first thing he whispered to me was: "Pascual, he wrote *Part I* without my help—although he stole the idea from me—but he could not have written his *Part II* without me. And he has the gall to steal my character Álvaro Tartuffe, and to mock my novel! My characters helped him to develop his own feeble creations."

He looked so pathetic, so diminished, like an ancient child, that I wished he had died. Was it pity or revulsion I felt?

"Don Luis," I said, "you shouldn't try to speak too much. The doctor's orders are that you must rest and eat nourishing meals. We can talk about everything when you've regained your strength."

He attempted a smile that came across as a grimace. Then he grabbed me by the lapels of my vest. "I made him a great writer, Pascual," he whispered in my ear. "I *compelled* him to write *Part II*."

I thought: *What is unbearable for you to contemplate is that*

you were outsmarted; that Cervantes stole from the thief. When
Cervantes made references to Avellaneda's *Quixote*, and inserted Avellaneda's characters into his own story, he had
linked his Quixote to Luis's. Now the two characters (the
real and the fake one) were Siamese twins. Cervantes had
written a novel that joined the two of them forever.

Before long, the *Apocryphal Don Quixote* (as it became
known) was reviled and then forgotten. Luis spent his days
praying, or in silence. He was a ghost in life. At night, he
wandered down the halls of the great house in his night-
shirt, barefoot, holding a burning taper and praying. One
night I heard him imploring: "Help me to forgive, My Lord.
Please help me to forgive him before I die."

I had remained loyal because I knew his death was approaching, and I assumed I would come into my inheritance
and would not have to work again for any man, aristocrat or
not. Then, finally, it occurred to me to search his archives
for his last will and testament. I was desperate to know
exactly how rich I would be at his death. Luis, it turned
out, had lied to me to buy my constancy: he had left all his
money to his alma mater, to establish a chair in his name
in perpetuity.

But I was not about to give up my nights in the gambling house, and the company of the children of the gran-
dees of Spain whom I could address with the familiar *tú*,
as if I were their equal. In less than a year, I practically
emptied the coffers in Luis's chambers. And I started to
strip the grand mansion of everything of value: the paintings by the Italian and Flemish masters, the monumental
medieval tapestries, the silverware, the gold plates, the
furniture, the linen, the carpets, the old shields and lances
and swords displayed on the walls. I sold everything to
finance my nights of bliss. By then I was fifty years old, and
I lived as a rich man.

The negative feelings I had harbored for Luis during all the years of my servitude had festered, until it poisoned every aspect of my life. If you've hated a person more than you have loved anyone else, the hate becomes a kind of love. Perhaps my hatred of Luis was the closest to love I had ever come. My need to destroy him was becoming as severe as his need to destroy Cervantes. I wanted to crush the man who had corrupted my soul; I wanted to twist his head and tear it from his neck. It would have given me great happiness to see him tortured by the Holy Office and then burned in a pyre. That he had been born rich and aristocratic was an accident; he could also have been born a mangy canine.

The formerly great house of the Laras was denuded of its splendors and overrun with rats. Luis's old servant Juan was blind, but still tried to dress his master and serve him his meals. Juan was like an ancient dog that could barely crawl and yet refused to die out of loyalty to his master. And there was Maria Elena, the cook, who prepared the meals Luis didn't touch. Her insalubrious children, who worked as servants and laborers and God knows what else, came by on an almost daily basis to be fed by her. They ate and drank and sang and danced in the kitchen, and stole whatever was left to sell or pawn.

At the beginning of 1616, I informed Luis that Cervantes had entered the Third Order of St. Francis. I expected him to say, "That will not make him any less a Jew!" But he said nothing; it was as if he had finally conceded defeat and was completely, irremediably annihilated. He had lost the feud. Cervantes was the undisputed victor.

One April morning, the news spread through Madrid that Miguel de Cervantes Saavedra, the beloved and celebrated author of *Don Quixote de la Mancha*, was dying, and would be buried in the Convent of the Discalced Trinitarians. After all the many years I had deferred to Luis Lara—"Yes, Don Luis," "Of course, Your Grace," "As you say, Your Eminence," "Kiss your ass? Lick your feet? Eat your shit? Of course, of course, of course, Your Worship"; the years when I obeyed his every command, was at his beck and call, the years of my humiliating servitude—the moment I had been waiting for had finally arrived.

I mentioned to Luis the approaching demise of his archenemy, and the news put him in a good mood. It was a sunny spring afternoon. I asked him if he would like to go out for a stroll. The body that just a few hours earlier had been as stiff as a mummy's was now filled with energy. At the end of his block on Lara Street, I stopped and pretended to see the new sign for the first time.

"Why have you stopped, Pascual?"

I raised my arm in the direction of the new tiles adorning the corner. Fate works in mysterious ways. Lara Street, for centuries the name of the street where the Lara house stood, had been renamed Cervantes Street.

Later that night, I found Luis dead in his library, a copy of Cervantes's *Don Quixote Part II* on his lap.

I lived on.

THE END
APRIL 22, 1616

My own farts—detonating like small revolvers—startle me awake. For days, these sulfurous explosions my body makes, as if to remind me my final rotting has already begun, are the only messages I send the living.

Outside my bedroom I can hear chirruping sparrows in the courtyard, splashing in the birdbath and beating their wings, as if to chase away the chilly days and cold nights of winter; as if they are celebrating the impending return of a season of abundance and light. Today, their merry chirps sadden my last hours on earth, as they are a reminder I will not live to see another summer dress in green the red plains of Castile. If the chirruping of the sparrows is a prelude to my final departure from this life, I'm ready.

So, my story, the story of a man with a long, lean face, brown hair, smooth and high forehead, merry eyes, hooked yet well-proportioned nose, silver beard (which just twenty years ago was gold), wide mustache, small mouth, teeth neither small nor big, of which he has only six diseased and badly matched ones placed randomly in his gums, a body neither large nor undersized, a vivid complexion more white than brown, somewhat hunched and slow on his feet—the story of that man, my story, comes to an end, the way all earthly things must.

As the priest gives me the Last Rites, and I hear crying—my wife? my sisters?—growing fainter, as the darkness gathers around me, dimming the shapes of the world, as my skin begins to cool, anticipating the coolness of the ground, I glimpse a moment in the future (it must be the future because everything is brighter, and faster) when a man will outdo Avellaneda's *Don Quixote Part II* and accomplish the impossible feat of writing the exact same *Don Quixote* I wrote, word by word, in just a few pages; this masterpiece, in turn, will be followed by an explosion of *Don Quixotes* (which people in that future time will be able to read in the air, and every page they read will disappear as soon as they are done reading it); and in that distant time, in all the known languages—and even the languages that died long ago, leaving no trace of them—people will also read Alonso Fernández de Avellaneda's false and monstrous *Don Quixote Part II* and not care that it is a heinous theft, a vulgar distortion, an abomination of man's intelligence, until, after a while, as the texts flow toward each other in the air, finally blending into one, no one will know anymore the real from the false characters, nor who I, Miguel de Cervantes Saavedra, its true creator, was. And the people of that future time will think that *Don Quixote* is an ancient tune; nothing but a song about a man and his dream.

My Thanks

I owe a great debt of gratitude to many people who generously gave of their time to help with the multiple facets of the research that went into *Cervantes Street*: in Spain, to the poet Dioniso Cañas for an eye-opening tour of the places in La Mancha where many of *Don Quixote*'s most famous scenes are set; to my good friend Eduardo Lostao, my guide in Madrid and Alcalá de Henares; and to José Luis Lara, my Virgil in Esquivias. A very special thanks to Ghassan Zeineddine, who accompanied me during a memorable trip to Algeria, Rome, and Greece; to Robert Parks of CEMA, whose invitation to lecture in Oran made it possible for us to obtain a visa to travel to Algeria, who arranged a memorable tour of the casbah, and who introduced me to his Cervantista friends in that country.

I'm also deeply grateful to Pilar Reyes, who acquired the Spanish rights to the novel when I was beginning to write it; and to my agents Tom and Elaine Colchie, for accompanying me in the life-changing adventure that became the creation of this book.

Finally, my thanks once more to my dear friends Jessica Hagedorn, Maggie Paley, and Robert Ward, for their encouragement and steadfast support.